A REVERIE TALE

BOOK ONE

BORDERLANDS AND TRANSIENCE

ANNA M. TUSK

CRANTHORPE
MILLNER
PUBLISHERS

First published by Cranthorpe Millner Publishers (2023)

ISBN 978-1-80378-161-7 (Paperback)

www.cranthorpemillner.com

Cranthorpe Millner Publishers

A STORY NARRATED BY:

Lilly-Anne Skyrose

Dianne Globesglory

Orle Giggly Lobbster

Beatrice Goldtear

Persephone Butterbless

Damsel Goldtear

Jacob Globesglory

Iona Jake

and Nin

°LA'DORE-ONO
THE EMPYREAN FEDERATION
KAH-A'MISS
°VIAK'MUL
FONSLA
THE EARTH ISLANDS

NTINENT
BRIGHTWOOD
LOONS CITY
SPACETIME SEA
E
WN
DS
THE CARCERY

PROLOGUE
NIN

I closed my eyes as one of the servants dipped her fingers in ochre paste and traced them down my forehead to my chest. It was a reflex – to close my eyes – back when I had reflexes. They dressed me in fineries too; robes so intricately woven they took three moons to weave; jewelled ornaments from my father's prized collection, nose rings, belts, and armbands. Tonight, we prepared to give a precious gift, and this gift, it was my death.

My father was a great warlord. There were no equals to his rule among neighbouring polities, whom we pillaged and terrorised whenever resources ran dry. Yet lack of food or drought were not our biggest concern. All of that was trivial when faced with our most salient threat: the demon gods. Deiform creatures, more powerful than any human, faster than the eye could trace, unpredictable. We told little children they had scales like fish, and horns, fangs, and tails of land animals otherwise familiar, but really we did not know. Nobody lived to tell once they got a closer look. When demon gods descended on our settlements, little was left except a stubble of bloodless, drained bodies following their human harvest. To the demon gods, we were food.

So we started offering them scheduled meals. And this worked, for a while, until their demands intensified in appetite and interval.

The servant pinned the last broach to my costume; a final touch that I doubted my hosts would even care for.

Finally, they paraded me out and across the courtyard. Large crowds had gathered, celebrating, a racket of cries, applause, and trumpets. Smoke from bonfires and torches that lit up the twilight sky stung my eyes. A group of dancers crossed my path. A feast was already underway, my blood the final course. They followed me down to the settlement gates, already heaved open by the warriors. There, they pushed me out.

I didn't resist. There was no point.

The gates shut behind me, drowning out noise from within. A cool breeze accompanied the silence, and all of a sudden, fear set in. I hadn't allowed myself to feel frightened before, nor had I expected to have time for panic once outside the gates. Such were the tales told about the demon gods that I expected to be killed almost instantly. Yet this is not what happened.

Clueless in my newfound situation and still breathing, I marched towards the forest. Twilight turned to night, astral beings waking in the realms above and shining down on me. I looked up at them – the stars – my only comfort. Sometimes, I thought these astral beings spoke to me, whispered of things past and future. I never admitted to this publicly. A few others claimed to hear them too – mad preachers, we called them. Tonight, those lights in the night sky reassured me to go on: find shelter, they whispered, find food.

As time passed into the night and I gathered suitable firewood, I only grew more furious. The last childless daughter of a great ruler, I was chosen as the sacrifice to appease the demon gods for a good while. A precious gift, I was assured, that they were bound to covet. Now they didn't even seem to want me, not instantly at least, unlike my imagination had me believe.

I tried to spark a fire. What if I was still to live another several nights, unknowing and unsuspecting of my end, abandoned by my people and destined to starve? What if the demon gods cared not for fancy offerings, gold regalia only sticking like fish bones in their teeth? What if I was drained of blood tonight, but the demon gods marauded our settlement tomorrow regardless? Our world was a precarious one, and for the first time I admitted to myself what the astral beings intimated to me in their whispers. No sacrifice, myself or a thousand more, would appease the demon gods. We were destined to die out. Such was our fate.

I felt the astral beings' proclamations deep inside my core, their energy inside my veins. Like the mad preachers who spoke of blinding lights and fires, an energy that predetermined our course, I felt it inside me, and I allowed myself to listen now. Intuitively, I listened to them. I sparked a fire. Perhaps, the astral beings whispered, I would live to see another day.

Suddenly I heard a branch snap in the bush behind me. There was a stillness in the air. Another snap of branches, a crunching of leaves underfoot, light step and erratic. An animal, perhaps. Grabbing a lit branch off the fire, I waved my humble weapon, hoping to scare off the intruder. Yet it was still there, hidden in the undergrowth, watching me. Then it pounced.

*

I awoke from a dreamless slumber that seemed to last a lifetime. I expected to feel fear, bewilderment, aches and pains from whatever wounds my last memories resulted in.

Instead, I felt nothing. I wasn't even sure if I was still alive.

Putting hand to chest, I felt my ribcage expand and shrink. I noticed my skin had turned ghastly pale, almost white, my body covered in scars and a layer of dust that had accumulated untouched for an apparently long time. I repeated deep breaths just to make sure. Then I noticed: my breathing did not disperse the dust. With each breath, my lungs pushed out no air. My ribcage moved out of habit, it seemed.

Looking around, I sat up. I was in a cave with sharp, roughly carved stone walls and a domed ceiling, a hole in which permitted a shy beam of light. We rarely reached this type of stone when building tombs. I was far underground, in the netherworld perhaps. *So it was true*, I thought, *there was an afterlife.*

"Welcome." A voice broke the silence.

I scrambled to my feet, trying to locate its origin. Standing and grasping at my torn-up robes, I took stock. I had just moved, but moved all too fast. Faster than I had ever done before. The movement sent waves of dust through the air. My eyes focused on each speckle shining in the light, seeing the individual shape of every particle too clearly. My mind was racing, analysing every minute detail of my surroundings, my body, my existence – *all* existence.

It was as if my mind had been switched off, restarted and hijacked to comprehend all things to an infinite depth, much beyond what I had ever personally experienced. Images formed inside my head that never were my own. My mind was not my own. My body was detached from any conscious thought, and yet more consciously comprehensive than I had ever known it to be.

"Who are you?" I addressed a hooded figure stood across the cave. "What is this place?"

"I am Rachthaw." She pulled back her hood. "I have waited many years for your awakening, chosen one."

"I remember you." I studied the aged, yet familiar face briefly. "You are one of the mad preachers." Her features were still recognisable, though I remembered her as a young woman of a similar age to myself.

"This world is mad," she spat at the accusation, "but we have been given a chance to change this. You see, child, a lot has changed while you slept," she continued, moving closer, into the light. "But you already know that, don't you?"

I shook my head, although I did know. It was in there, inside my mind, though the memories were not my own.

"There are few of us left now, us humans. We hide underground like mice, hoping that the demons will not smell us. But she wants us to live, to thrive. And she has given us a chance! She will teach us how, give us weapons. We will return above ground, fight back, and carve our way to greatness. You, child," she said, "she has chosen to oversee this."

"Who?"

"The light, the energy, the fire! She who transcends all life and shines in the realms above. You have felt her, you have listened, and she has chosen you. Fate, I call her. She is everything that has ever been, is, and will be; across space, across time. She is the energy that surrounds us, guides us, maps out our lives like puppets on a string. She is what is within us – our blood, our life-force. She keeps us alive until she decides our time is up. Fate is the master of us all. Now she reveals herself to us, giving us the chance to defeat the demon kind – *if* we listen. Fate is throwing us a lifeline, child. *Us* – the dying kind! She will teach us to materialise her Force, to channel it." Rachthaw raised her palms, and they engulfed in beautiful, white flames. "Only if we comply with whatever Fate has prepared for us."

I gasped at the sight, staring, mesmerised by the flames dancing across her palms. Yet Rachthaw didn't seem frightened, nor in pain.

"This is the energy of Fate, the Force she is willing to gift us." Rachthaw raised her flaming hands. "You, child, Fate has chosen as her vessel. She saved you from the demon, tasked me to bring you here, to turn you into her eternal companion, our weapon. I have waited many years for you to wake; now you are ready. With Fate's Force flowing through your veins, your body filled with her fire, you are her eyes, our witness to it all. You are the most powerful creature to ever exist, chosen one. You will defeat the demon kind and free us. You will exist forever, child. Like Fate herself, you are invincible."

*

For over six thousand years now I have witnessed the worlds take shape. I never grew old; unchanging and frozen in time, neither dead nor alive. I wasn't human anymore, my body merely a receptacle of Fate's pure energy materialised. White flames filled my veins, guided me, and granted me unbeatable strength. Fate was immortal, and so was I with her.

I hunted demons. They were not gods, it turned out; perfectly mortal when faced with an opponent they could not outrun. One by one, I rid our heartland of them until humans regained their strength, their numbers. Settlements began re-growing.

Thereafter, for hundreds of years, with Rachthaw's female descendants, we spread the message. We educated the masses about Fate, recruited Fate's servants, persuaded, preached, proved, and prayed. Demon after demon, I freed the realm for human opportunity, though human survival was already contingent on, and tied to, symbiosis with Fate. Such was the bargain that we struck.

I watched our message grow, civilisations sprout and thrive. I saw the worlds take shape, those we know about and those that Fate still keeps to herself. I observed the Rachthawnian line establish their privileged position as unchallengeable, gaining the status of royalty. I stood by as they subjugated the reluctant clans of the Empyrean – a world with ancient roots, its own traditions, and ties to Fate. I watched as one of the worlds, the Continent, emerged as a seat of power. I saw the interworld Authority be established and banish those who did not comply to the harsh lands of the Carcery. I witnessed the Earth Islands lose their intuition and detach themselves from Fate, switching their allegiance to beliefs in atoms and electric signals. I watched the last Rachthaw sacrifice herself, as Fate commanded, for a complete rebirth of the symbiotic tie.

All their struggles and hopes, I watched, all the while Fate toyed with humans as she pleased.

CHAPTER I
LILLY-ANNE SKYROSE

I'm a pretty down-to-earth person, when I need to be: pragmatic, non-confrontational (mostly) – outwardly boring, you could say. Perhaps that's a trait that I've inherited, but it's hard to tell (and you'll find out why in just a minute). Lynne said I was a mishap magnet, an oddity, a bit of a freak. The latter she never said *aloud,* but she thought so, I could tell. She wasn't the only one either. After all, I had a lot of strange things happen to me. Despite that, I tend to let things be, to unfold, since most things are beyond my ability to change; the big things, anyway. The little things – if someone crossed a line – they could unleash my temper sometimes. I won't be sorry for that.

Do you ever feel like you don't belong? And don't shrug it off as a typical teenager feeling that we all somehow magically outgrow because I don't just mean among your peers, or in your times and place. It's not the case that I like 70s music or big city lights but we live in twenty-first century English countryside. I mean more generally, *fundamentally,* in this world.

When I was little, I'd make up stories and daydream to compensate for my lack of belonging anywhere. I still do, to a degree. My actual dreams – those that weave together when I sleep – are wild enough. Yet sometimes I still get so drawn into my daytime reveries that when I'm eventually forced to snap out of it, I still go on pretending that the mundane is not *really* how things are.

Though that's just pretending, of course, and that's why I accept my life as it is. It's hardly the case that life could suddenly change into a fairy tale.

No knights in shining armour were coming to rescue me. And in so far as being a freak went, the best strategy was trying not to stand out from the crowd.

"Be careful what yer wish fer," Lynne would say when I used to whine about being bored. "'Cos I'll find yer somethin' to do," she would then add, meaning mopping the floors or cleaning out the chicken hutch.

I didn't whine much about boredom anymore – it gets a bit embarrassing when you're sixteen. By this age there's a sort of untold expectation that you're somehow supposed to entertain yourself. Most kids did, sure enough; they got in trouble for most of it. But living outside a daydream is easier said than done when you don't really have friends and you don't like TV. Nowadays, I'd just pick up the mop or bucket and get the job done. But as I got on with it, I'd let the reveries suck me in.

Right now was one of those moments. Except I wasn't getting on with anything, I was just waiting. Yet it was on this very day that a reverie so grand began to unfold that everything I knew so far did, in fact, fundamentally change. Or at least I still haven't snapped out of it.

Sat in a stained plastic chair in the dingy doctors' surgery waiting room, I watched names ping up across the noticeboard. My appointment was already twenty minutes behind. I sat alone. Uncle Bill insisted on waiting in the car. Not that I needed him to go in with me. These appointments were routine by now; I had a pretty good idea of what the doctor would say.

Skyrose – Consultant Room 6 floated across the noticeboard, then flashed a couple of times, like some outdated Powerpoint effect they'd encourage in IT. I made my way through the corridors, their décor straining to give the impression of hygiene and propriety – light colours, leaflets, wood-effect fire doors. Safe. Sanitary.

"Come in, please," was the answer to my light knock on the door marked number six. "Ah, Miss Skyrose, sorry about the wait today. Please, take a seat."

I did as instructed. My doctor this time was a man in his mid-thirties; I saw someone different each time. I wondered what he'd have to say. Had he been briefed? Was he going to be concerned, try to find a solution to my peculiar case?

"I've just had a look at your blood test results. There are a few things that seem a bit off. Nothing to worry about, however. They seem to be quite consistent with your previous tests."

He had been briefed. That, or he had no clue what further tests to offer, so he was trying to get my case off his pile of work.

When I was about eight years old, I fell ill with an infection. Nothing major, but the doctor ordered blood tests. That's when they discovered it: there was something wrong with my parameters. Nothing to indicate a major illness. Nothing to indicate *anything* in particular, in fact. The composition of my blood was skewed in every direction. An array of follow-up tests was initially done. Doctors followed each skewing but could not put them together. One indicated illness X, but contradicted another, which indicated illness Y. Eventually they gave up, and my condition never worsened. Doctors ordered a self-serving blood test every six months since, having given up seeking a solution. I felt fine physically, after all (though I'll admit to playing this card to get out of PE, once or twice).

"It will be good to monitor it, so we will see you again in February. Please make an appointment," he concluded with a smile, which begged that no further questions be asked.

I smiled too, said my thanks, and left. He didn't have the answers; I wasn't going to be difficult.

Uncle Bill's old Defender was parked in the same spot I'd left it. I climbed in, pointlessly trying not to touch against the muddy frame. Inside was dirty too, it was his farm truck.

"How'd it go?" he asked, battling with the engine to spark.

"Same old. I'm back in six months."

The engine revved, disturbing pensioners' lives across a small market town. The Defender rolled down the road, gears stiff to change, eventually reaching narrow country lanes. We sat in comfortable silence. Uncle Bill wasn't exactly what you'd call a people person, never straining to make small talk when it wasn't absolutely necessary. I looked across the dashboard.

"You're low on fuel again," I commented.

Uncle Bill had offered to drive me to the surgery. Our farmhouse was surrounded by fields and scanty woodlands. The nearest amenities – other than a post box that wasn't even emptied regularly – were in a small market town about five miles away. It was summer, and I wouldn't have minded the walk as it would have passed more time. Yet I couldn't decline when Uncle Bill tried to act a parent. His efforts usually resolved to a silent, protective gaze from the sideline. He rarely intervened.

"Fuel's fine, the gauge is broken."

"How do you know when fuel's running low, then?"

"Intuition," Uncle Bill laughed.

We made it back home for dinner. Lynne, on the other hand, *loved* to intervene. Not to offer solutions or solace, however. She wasn't brains, or a shoulder to cry on. Lynne was all talk, especially if it wasn't her business. They should do more tests, she said, offer treatment, it was unacceptable. It wasn't my health that concerned her; Lynne just liked to complain.

I set the table and we sat down to eat.

"They should really look at the *parental* medical records, if yer ask me. Maybe there's somethin' there," Lynne said between a potato and a brussels sprout. She was fishing for a fight, and the mention of my parents was a sharp hook.

"I doubt they'd be able to dig those up," Bill said without looking up.

Uncle Bill was an outstandingly calm person. I can't recall ever seeing him mad, even in the face of Lynne's most determined goading. He didn't seem too concerned about the precise nature of my illness; naming it was pointless, in his opinion, as long as I felt fine.

My biological parents died of carbon monoxide poisoning, a gas leak, when I was a baby less than a year old. We hardly mentioned them, and any mention resulted in a tension of sorts. Their presence always hung in the air however, at least in my dealings with Lynne. Understandably, I suppose. The older I got, the more reasonable her grudge seemed. What would I have done, if my newlywed husband turned up one night, not even a year into our marriage, with a stranger's baby, refusing to explain himself? She was kind enough to keep me, though she never pretended to accept me, let alone like me throughout the last sixteen years.

"Such things could be inherited ye'neh," she pushed.

The bait was ignored; Bill chewed on.

A few potatoes in, Uncle Bill cleared his throat, apparently about to announce something uncomfortable. For a second, I thought he'd decided to pursue the subject after all, that a corner of the mystery of my past – usually so neatly swept under the rug – might be lifted in the end.

"Dianne would like to visit," he eventually said.

"*Di-anne!* When?" Lynne straightened herself up as much as her posture allowed, already defensive.

Auntie Dianne, Bill's sister, was a blacklisted topic in Lynne's books too.

"Tomorrow. Just her and the boys. Jacob's busy. Nothing fancy, just a quick visit. They'll only stop by, being on their way to—"

"Tomorrow? Does that *woman* think we're a roadside motel? There's no food left in the house at all. What do yer think I'm go'en offer them ter eat? Such short notice – that just ain't right, now, is it?" Lynne shook her head. "Not'er single Christmas card ov'r the years either, and I thought that woman could write!"

Dianne was a journalist.

"She always sends me a birthday card," I offered in Dianne's defence. The cards she sent me were really fancy too, although usually a few weeks late.

I left them then, to argue about it. Having washed up, I headed upstairs to my room. It was the smallest bedroom, modest, with only a few bits of furniture. Despite the rarity of visitors, Lynne insisted that the nicest bedrooms be kept as guestrooms.

"I'll need yer to do'er grocery run tomorrow, Lilly, first thing in the mornin'!" I heard Lynne call after me as I climbed the creaky stairs.

I couldn't help smiling to myself. Dianne's visit was the best news all summer, which was now drawing to an end – hers and *the boys*: Vincent and Gilbert, my makeshift cousins, twins. We weren't really related, but it didn't matter. I called Bill an uncle, but the address had no blood ties. I looked forward to the human company, and the twins' rare visits were always fun. I'd spent the summer alone; outdoors, yes, but alone, looking after the sheep and chickens on the farm.

I changed into pyjamas and got ready for bed. Teeth brushed, I detangled my hair. This was a bit of a job because it was long and had a tendency to curl. One of the comb teeth caught and pulled my necklace. Immediately, I stopped. The necklace was my most prized possession, my only connection to my parents: an eight-pointed star, each arm uneven to the rest, with a ruby centre. It belonged to my mother, or so Uncle Bill said. I'd worn it for as long as I could remember. It never left my neck; each PE lesson a battle over taking it off.

Frustrated, I yanked the bathroom light cord. It sprung back and nearly pulled out of its socket. As if doing that would somehow redeem my carelessness, transfer the pain I'd inflicted on my necklace to another object. As if objects could feel, or cared. Aren't you silly, Lilly-Anne?

They were still arguing downstairs when I pulled my duvet over, ready to get into bed. That's when I spotted it: an envelope on my pillow. It was stained brown, with my name and address on it in neat calligraphy. I picked it up to get a closer look. Above the address, there was a drawing – a logo or crest of some kind: a blue and black dragon perched atop a building, its tail wrapped around a tower, hand-drawn in shiny ink. What *was* this?

Without hesitating, I opened it. Inside was a sheet of similarly brown paper, disappointingly blank; blank, except for a single straight line with the words 'I hereby confirm receipt of this correspondence' written by it.

It made no sense. A crafty joke? But who? How? I ran through the possible culprits in my head. The list was long, though I doubted any of the kids were smart (determined, or even psychopathic) enough to leave this under the covers on my bed. I ventured downstairs with the envelope in hand.

"Found it in the mailbox this mornin'," Lynne rumbled before I could ask.

Of course she had. Then she had intruded into my personal space, placing it right over my pillow, so that I'd know she knew all about whatever I was up to. All this effort she routinely wasted, seeing that I never gave her any reason to suspect me.

"You better not 'ave been orderin' crap online, young lady, or joining any cults! Bill, hide yer credit card."

They were sitting by the fireplace. Uncle Bill directed a pleading glare in her direction.

"What?" she retracted, taking a big sip of tea. "Oo knows what kids get up to online these days."

"I have no idea what this is." I held up the envelope, though I knew well enough she wouldn't trust in my defence. "I was hoping you would know where it came from."

Lynne shook her head. Uncle Bill prodded the fire, indifferent as he always was towards mine and Lynne's squabbles. Casting a quick glance at the envelope, something seemed to catch his eye. He stared, turned pale, and let a log fall out of the fireplace.

*

As soon as I closed my eyes, I was there. It all looked very real. I was *there*, I swear, physically present in the familiar dream's surroundings. Synapses fired, muscles clenched, and I felt my body take flight. I stood on top of a hill, with a beautiful view stretching beneath. I knew it very well; every few months, and more frequently as of recent, when my blood slowed and my limbs numbed, but with my mind still crisply awake, I drifted off to this dreamy realm. Once I'd drifted off, I was in the borderland: not quite asleep, not quite awake. Not quite sure what was real, in fact.

Any moment now, my feet would carry me forward into the pine forest blanketing the valley beyond. I started to run, crossing the boundary of the forest's darkness, its trees double the height of trees back home. Giants, regal and majestic, they were kings of this land; I, the invader. Yet they seemed to let me past willingly, sometimes even leaning out of my way.

I ran further, never getting out of breath.

Breathing wasn't a part of this dream. Neither was time apparently, for this place was timeless, strange, and magical, existing out of time. As always, I reached the meadow and made my way across a sea of tall, dry grass until I reached a gate.

Beyond the gate was a neatly kept garden, heavily landscaped and engineered. All sorts of colours beamed across the flowerbeds among small trees with twisted branches, tied and cut to shape by generations of groundskeepers. Towering over the garden were high walls marking out the back of a castle. My feet carried on down the path, into the fortress.

Most rooms I never got to see, since the way I'd always enter was the same, starting in the hall. It was an empty, spacious tower, with stairs circling the walls so high up that the eventual ceiling was obscured. As far up as the eye could see, walls were lined with huge green tiles, each a good five feet tall, depicting strange scenes in relief: battles, crowds, coronations. A separate set of stairs, crooked and narrower, led below ground level too. I never went downstairs. Instead, I always hurried up.

After several flights, I reached a door leading to a terrace. There were no clues as to how to orientate myself in this dream; nobody had taught me how to navigate this world. It was intuitive, it seemed, and I'd lived it enough times to foresee the steps. Silent thus far, sounds slowly began returning: cheering, clatter, applause. I walked across to the stone balustrade lining the terrace edge and raised my arms. Below, at the front of the fortress, was a vast crowd spreading all the way to the horizon. They cheered louder at my appearance.

It all happened very quickly then. Cheers were replaced by screams. A commotion of panic spreading through the crowd. But before anyone could help, before anyone could run, all of it was gone – everyone was gone – swallowed up by a blinding, white light. It appeared in the sky above the horizon line, spreading rapidly and engulfing everything on its way. It reached me in the end, crushing my body, as if trying to compress me from the inside out, trying to shrink me to fit the confines of its nonexistence.

I woke up at that moment, jerking upright. Covered in sweat and terrified as always, I assured myself that it was only a bad recurring dream, though I could swear I still felt a tightness in my chest, as if something continued to press on it. *Deep breaths*. I lay back down and tried to relax. *Deep breaths, focus on the moment.*

"Go down ter the shops, will yeh. List and money on the table," Lynne's screechy voice drifted past my bedroom door.

*

I wrangled my pushbike out of the shed and pedalled down the narrow road towards the market town. It was a relatively quiet road, although not wide enough for vehicles to overtake me at speed, let alone for two cars to freely pass each other. I made it to the passing places twice, being forced into the hedge only once by a hurried driver. Welcome to the Norfolk countryside.

I picked up everything on Lynne's list, including chocolates, which I bet she wasn't even going to put out while our guests were here, hiding them for herself instead.

"Oi, Skyrise!"

I made the mistake of turning around, alerted by the pun. Why, oh why, did I have to have an odd name? *Thanks, Uncle Bill*, I thought because I took his surname. Thanks for the double-barrelled first name, too.

"You ain't very tall for a skyscraper, are yeh?" Some boys I recognised from school were sniggering and prodding at each other, clearly satisfied with their bad joke.

"Very funny," I said dryly, loading the shopping into an over-handlebar basket.

"What's that jacket for, ey? Cold, are we? Thought you're usually feeling a bit too hot!"

I ignored this and set off, straining to keep my balance on an overloaded bike. Wow, two unrelated insults at once; they'd clearly upped their game. The latter referred to a biology lesson we'd had just before summer. Learning about human thermoregulation, the teacher had a 'fun' practical in store. We measured our temperature in class. He called on me in front of everyone to demonstrate, and each reading showed that I had a fever. The thermometer worked just fine, it turned out – everyone else had normal readings. They sent me home early that day. After that, old jokes were resurrected.

I thought about the folded envelope in my pocket; perhaps it was their doing. I'd been nicknamed *dragon* before, despite the fact that my character resembled more of a shy mouse who bottled up emotions. Restrained emotions tended to fester and explode, however, once someone crossed the line. It started in primary school, when a boy who chased and tried to kiss me in the playground ended up with burn marks down his arms. I'd barely shoved him away with my bare hands. It then resurfaced in secondary school, when, determined to do well in a science practical, I managed to light a Bunsen burner with the gas supply still shut off. They pestered me after that, a favourite running joke being leaving matches hidden in my backpack. *Will Skyrose burn the building down today?* I thought about lighting them sometimes, just before handing them back to my bullies. But of course I never did, and in any case, I couldn't explain these incidents either.

*

Animated voices inside the kitchen indicated that our guests were already here. I hurried in, dropping shopping bags by the front door.

"Lilly!" Dianne exclaimed as soon as she spotted me. "Aw, come here, you. Look at you, big girl!" She gave me an enthusiastic hug. "Are you excited to start the new school?"

"Very," I smiled. Thankfully, the horrors of secondary school were now past. In September, just days from now, I'll be starting sixth form. It was a much larger school, quite far away too, but that didn't matter. I pleaded with Lynne and Uncle Bill to let me pick this one, promised I'd sort out the transport and get a petty job to cover the bus pass. It was a place where I could be anonymous, somewhere where I'd come across as completely normal and average. No backstory, no taunting. A fresh start.

Dianne and company had apparently only just arrived.

"Coulda let us know earlier that you intend on comin' over, yer know, given me a chance to clean this mess, cook up somethin' nice. Now you'll just have to excuse the state of this place." Lynne bustled around, pretending to tidy a perfectly clean house.

"Oh, it's okay, we—" Dianne started.

"Forgotten how ter write, have you? Or do too much of it fer work that you couldn't be bothered to write ter us?" Lynne cut her off. "What's that paper of yours called again?"

Dianne took a deep breath, then slowly answered, "*The Interworld Seer.*"

Uncle Bill glared at her.

"Haven't 'eard of it."

"Don't read much, Lynne?" Dianne retorted, smug.

"A do."

That was a lie.

"But clearly not that kindef tabloid press," Lynne continued.

"Hm, clearly just not your niche. Anyway, we won't be trouble, we'll be off shortly. Just wanted to see how Lilly's doing." Dianne turned to me with kindness in her eyes. "To check you've got everything you need for the new school."

"She's doin' just fine, thank yew," Lynne answered for me.

"Morning, Lilly!" came a duo of voices from behind me.

I started at the sound.

Vincent and Gilbert laughed. "No need to jump, only us," said one of them. "Look what we found." The other had fished out Lynne's chocolates from the shopping bags.

"All right, no more mayhem. Give me those, boy. Now, get you out. Lunch won't make itself now, will it?" Lynne shooed everyone out, confiscating the box.

"Can we go and see the sheeps?" Gilbert (or Bertie, for those who knew him well) was already on his way.

Vince and I followed. They were a couple of years older than me, taller and less lanky with each visit, with mops of thick, dark hair that had a certain vibrancy about it, as did their character.

"Sure, the *sheep*. Don't see many of those down in Brightwood?" I asked. I wasn't entirely sure where they lived, as we'd never visited. In fact, we never travelled. An internet search suggested Brightwood was a town somewhere in the USA.

"None at all," Vince smiled, as we walked around the back of the house. Bertie was already bleating at the sheep.

"How was your journey? How many hours was the flight?"

"Many. Very long, yes, but not too bad," said Vince.

"My legs hurt from walking all that way," Bertie added.

"Walking?" I laughed. Their sense of humour confused me sometimes.

Bertie looked to his twin, unsure. "United States are far away from the Joint Kingdom, aren't they?"

"*United* Kingdom, you mean," I corrected.

"Yes, they are, Bertie, but we took the *aeroplane*, remember," Vince scolded his brother. "He means he was walking up and down the aeroplane. Couldn't sit still, could you, Bertie?"

"That's right, there weren't enough seats left. Had to stand, got bored, walked about to pass the time," Bertie said without the slightest flicker of mockery.

I was about to protest. *How could there not be enough seats on a plane?* But Bertie carried on.

"We're off to see the pyramids next," he said excitedly.

"The pyramids? There are no pyramids around here."

"Oh." He thought for a second. "In Egypt?"

"So," I thought through it, "you came all the way out to Norfolk from London after some dozen hours on the plane, to spend only a minute here, and then head back to London and fly to Egypt?" It made no sense, and they'd played too many tricks on me in the past. I wasn't gullibly giving up this time.

They looked at each other, brows crossed. "Y-yes."

"Mum's on a work trip, and we're only tagging along. Don't know the full details I'm afraid," Vince offered.

We reached the fence enclosure.

"Ay, yes, didn't want to leave us to our own devices home alone, so here we are." Bertie hopped up and sat on the top plank. He called out to the sheep, and they bleated back. He was grinning, clearly fascinated.

On previous visits, rare as they were, they were also fascinated by our microwave, overhead telephone wires, and Irn-Bru.

"And your dad?" I leaned on the fence next to them. I hadn't seen Dianne's husband, Jacob, in many years.

"Busy at the Senate."

"The Senate? Blimey, didn't realise he's a senator!"

"Oh, he's not, he's an advisor," Vince clarified.

"Look what I got. Wanna share it?" Bertie fished out what looked like a crumpled cigarette from his pocket.

"Did you take that off Mum? She'll find out, you know." Vince was disapproving.

"Nah, she's got plenty." Bertie put it between his lips.

"They're bad for your health, too," I offered, hoping Lynne wasn't by the kitchen window to see. That seemed to throw him off.

"Not if you light them yourself, then it's meant to help you focus, concentrate your thoughts," said Bertie, hand hovering by his mouth, as if to snap his fingers. He didn't have a lighter.

"Don't do that, not here, Bertie," Vince said, even more disapprovingly.

"Oh yeah." Bertie put the roll-up away.

I looked from one to the other, generally confused by the whole exchange. Only then did I notice what Vince was wearing.

"Where did you get your jumper from?" I asked, recognising the logo.

"Oh, this?" Vince noticed me staring at the shiny black and bright blue stiches set against a navy background. The shape was familiar: a dragon perched atop a building, wrapping its tail around a tower, flames on the end of its tail. "It's just school merch."

"He likes to represent, thinks it'll swoon the ladies if they see a Sapphy's boy," Bertie laughed.

Vince rolled his eyes, then turned to me. "Why'd you ask?"

"Oh, it's nothing. I thought I recognised it." It was definitely the same logo as on the mysterious letter I received. As soon as I said this, Bertie jumped off the fence, and they both moved closer.

"You recognise it?" They were intrigued, vividly enthusiastic.

"Yeah… I got a letter the other day, strange story really…"

"I *knew* it!" Bertie punched the air. "Told you she's not one of the unknowing! You owe me three heads, brother, three heads! Let's see it then, Lills – the letter. Have you opened it?"

I produced the folded envelope from my pocket. "Yes, but it's blank inside." I showed them.

"That's not blank, you poddlywonk!"

"It's just encrypted," Vince explained. "You'll need to sign it. It needs to make sure that it's in the rightful hands before revealing the contents, and what better way to do that than by signing it with—"

"Here, take my signing quill." Bertie rummaged the inner pockets of his jacket, taking out a nibbed, tousled feather. "Sorry, chewed the end a bit, but works just fine." He gave it to me.

I took the feather between my thumb and index finger and immediately felt a sting.

"… blood," Vince finished his sentence.

"Ouch!" I yelped, dropping the instrument. "What was that about?"

Bertie was quick to hand it back. "Quickly now, sign away, don't want to have to pierce the fingers twice. We'll patch you up right after."

I rested the envelope against the fence. Pressing nib to paper, a blob of red ink was released. Was this really my blood? I slowly wrote my name on the line.

"Aren't you a scarletan," Bertie commented, as they hovered over my shoulder, grinning. "What's it say now? What affiliation did they give you?"

"Blue on the crest, that's an indication," Vince was quick to point out.

The paper soaked up my bloody signature, vanishing it from the line. Then slowly, writing began to materialise across the page. I stared in disbelief.

'Dear Miss Skyrose', it read.

'With Fate's blessing, we are pleased to invite you to commence studies at Sapphire Dragon's Respected School of Force Control and Lawful Magic. Room has been reserved for you in Ranger Bastion. Please may we draw your attention to the timetable and list of required equipment attached. We look forward to welcoming you in Loon's City by the twenty-fifth rise of the eighth Thotun turn for induction, or no later than the Korasort's full moon for the start of the semester. Please reply by pixie post if you wish to arrange a carriage. May intuition guide you truly. Witness my hand this second rise of Thotun's eighth turn,

Prof. Timothy Fellblue,

On behalf of Chancellor Martina Arden'.

I looked from Vincent to Gilbert, their faces beaming with excitement. "What on earth is this?"

"Oh, it's not on Earth," Bertie said casually. "A bit beyond."

CHAPTER 2
DIANNE GLOBESGLORY

I stepped out of the kitchen and into the yard, shaking my head. What a welcome. The kids headed off to see the animals. Bill slipped out after me, heading for the garage. I followed him. My dear brother. I was usually good at getting to the bottom of things, but him, I couldn't figure out. Why he'd made this choice.

"Charming as always, your wife," I said.

Bill smiled, but it quickly faded. He wasn't happy here – how could he be, so far removed from everything we knew?

"Did you use a safe portal opening? I can't have anyone tracing you back here," he asked, concerned.

I sighed. "Yes, I used a pen name to request it."

"Pen name? Really, that's the best you could do? That's easily linked back to you, then me, then…" he trailed off.

Then Lilly. I didn't know her parents, I had no idea how my brother was connected to them, or why he was so paranoid. The child apparently appeared out of nowhere. But my brother's paranoia sure rubbed off on me. Regardless, now she was of age, Lilly deserved the best of what the worlds had to offer.

"Honestly, William, even if so, who do you think will come after you?" I erupted. "It's getting a bit ridiculous, don't you think? It's been sixteen years. Things have been quiet for you here, haven't they? Unless you can give me a good reason now, I think you should consider retur—"

"I won't," he cut me off.

I patted my pockets for a packet of Focus; one was missing. Bloody Bertie. I snapped my fingers for a small spark, lit the stick, and took a drag.

"You shouldn't be doing that here," Bill put on his big brother voice.

"And who's going to see me, in this…" I made a point of looking around, "middle of nowhere?"

Bill began rummaging around the shelves.

"Things have changed. It's a lot safer now, there are hardly any incursions. They've shipped the lot of them to Carcery, so it's not spreading," I tried.

"Wouldn't know, I don't really keep up with the news here, as you can imagine." He was tinkering with some metal cogs and chains, trying to ignore me.

"Why do I have a bad feeling, Bill?" The words escaped my mouth.

"About what?"

"About you," I said quietly. "That this is the last time I'll be seeing you. I've had some worrying dreams lately."

He looked up at me with a sorry expression; he'd dreamt it too.

"Don't worry about me, Dianne. What's meant to be will be."

Bill had always been calm, controlled – a trait much needed in his former profession. Yet ever since the events of sixteen years ago, it was even harder to get a word out of him. If only he'd come back home, leave the coy wife behind (though I suspected he cared more for the animals) and spend the rest of his days with us.

"Is that for the telephone?" I asked, changing the subject.

"What, these?" He held up the cogs, laughing. "Bicycle gears."

"Oh. I'm doing an article on telephones for the *Seer*, investigating how they work. I'll need to buy one while I'm out here, too. Rumour has it that the Senate is debating accepting the Technology Pass, so we want to be ready for when they do."

"So I hear." Bill fitted two cogs together.

"Thought you didn't keep up with the news."

He stared at me. "Why are you really here, Dianne? Technology Pass has been on the table for years now."

"Just wanted to check in." I took a long drag; the subject would have to be breached sooner or later. "Lilly's sixteen now, isn't she? I guess I just wanted to make sure you'll be sending her to school."

I braced myself, rehearsing the list of arguments in my head. *It's unfair, William, for you to keep her here. She belongs to the worlds, she has intuition. You've been away so long that you're probably getting sick, and do what you want with your health, but for goodness' sake, spare the child. Stars, I'll pay her school tuition fees myself!*

"I won't be," he said, but before I could start my litany of reasoning, Bill added, "but it seems that Fate wants her back. She received an invitation letter yesterday."

A wave of relief washed over me. "Sapphy's?" I asked.

Bill nodded.

I thought back to our own school days there. "The boys are going to be thrilled, they're still there for another couple of years. They can help Lilly settle in."

"Muuum!" I heard from a distance. "Mum, you'll never believe!"

"I guess they already are," Bill said wryly.

CHAPTER 3
LILLY-ANNE SKYROSE

Weary, I sat in one of the armchairs by the fireplace. Our visitors left by afternoon. Uncle Bill was out, giving them a lift back to the airport, or whatever it was they'd used to get here. I wasn't so sure anymore. In fact, I wasn't sure of anything. I studied the letter over and over again. Was this another vivid dream? Or was Lynne selling me to the circus, like she'd always threatened? Given her expression during lunch, however, it appeared that Lynne was just as clueless about the situation as myself.

The front door creaked as Uncle Bill returned.

"How you doin', Lills?" He sat in the chair opposite me.

He'd never been particularly conversational. If we were in for a heart-to-heart, I didn't quite know where to begin.

"This letter I received the other day…" I showed it to him, now filled with writing.

"Oh good, you managed to open it, then," he said casually.

I was taken aback.

"From Sapphire Dragon's Respected School of Force Control and Lawful Magic, I take it. Doesn't exactly roll off the tongue, that. Most people just call it Sapphire Dragon's, or Sapphy's."

"How do you know?" I managed eventually.

"Because I went there myself, of course."

"You know about—" I started the question, though I wasn't sure exactly what it was he knew. Something he'd clearly been keeping from me. Where was this school? What was force control? Magic? Lawful magic? Dragons?

A joke? Some kind of trivia society? "What?" I frowned.

Uncle Bill smiled, apparently humoured, as if he'd read my mind. "Uhh, what's the best way to say this? And I'm sorry, there's a lot to explain. I'm not great at explaining things; the teachers at Sapphy's, they'll tell you all about everything. Professor Fellblue, I think he's still there – tremendous teacher. But for now, hmmm… I know, I'll show you." He got up and headed to his desk. "Come here, look at this."

From his bundle of keys, he chose one, golden with three wards. Uncle Bill's desk was an old, worn piece of furniture. He never used it; the top was covered with unwanted takeaway leaflets, an unwashed mug, and a pretty glass paperweight that he never let me play with as a child. He moved those aside, inserted the key, and turned it. *Clank, clank, clank.* The top slid apart in jolts to reveal a secret drawer underneath. From there he took out a folded piece of paper and a feather.

"You'll recognise what this is by now." He held up the feather quill, much nicer than the one Bertie had given me earlier that day.

Oh no.

"It's very clever, this identification mechanism. Everyone's blood is unique, so it's a way to make sure documents are read only by those intended to do so." He signed a bloody Skyrose onto the page.

I breathed out with relief – not my fingers this time.

"Kind of like password protecting your PDFs, I suppose," Uncle Bill added.

"I thought fingerprints were unique; blood has types," I muttered, as if that even weighed in on the surreal events of today.

"Well, that's what they say over here," he said, then caught himself to clarify. "Here on Earth."

The paper soaked up his blood. Uncle Bill unfolded it, and inside, shapes started to materialise. Not only that, some shapes – clouds, perhaps – were moving across the page. One side was lighter, brighter, the other shadowy.

"We are here." Uncle Bill pointed to a recognisably familiar shape in the shadowy bottom left-hand corner, where a small golden dot was glowing.

A map, I realised. "I don't understand, why are all the continents so small? What are the other places?" Maybe I couldn't tell the difference between the Lake and Peak Districts, but I sure knew the world didn't look like this.

"The other worlds."

I wasn't ready to say anything, so Uncle Bill continued.

"Europe, Asia, Africa, etcetera, these are referred to as the Earth Islands. They're fairly small in relation to the other worlds. This here," he pointed to the top left, where the shadow ended, "is the Empyrean Federation; the suns rise and set there. And this, directly across, is the Continent. Down here, below the Continent, is the Carcery – you don't want to go there. And this," he pointed in the middle, where the map was slightly burnt. "Well… this was Fonsland – not much of that left now."

"But… is this in space? Are these other planets? Surely we'd have flown past them on the way to the moon?" I said quietly, as the flames crackled gently in the fireplace behind us.

Uncle Bill laughed. "Not planets, not exactly. Worlds, we call them. They exist in… hmmm… spacetime, by virtue of a sort of energy that keeps us alive, surrounds everything, is in everything, knows everything," he mused. "We call her Fate, this energy. The idea of the cosmos is an Earthly invention, a barrier, if you like, which covers this area," he placed his hand over the Earth Islands, "where the energy doesn't reach. She was abandoned, after the Middle Ages – you know, the witch hunts and everything. That's why you wouldn't have felt her very strongly here."

I stared at the clouds drifting across the page. The shadow too, was slowly moving, as if night was drawing in across the worlds.

"This here," he pointed to a spot on the Continent. "Brightwood, where

I grew up. Biggest city, richest, capital. Dianne still lives there. And this one," he traced his finger across, still on the Continent, "Loon's City. This is where we are heading tomorrow."

I perked up. "What?"

"Need to get you some books and things, plus I think it'll be good if you see it before you start school. You'll have missed induction by now. I hope you're not too upset about that, but truth be told I don't remember much of mine, so let's just say you won't be missing much. Now," he spread his fingers across the map, then drew them upwards together, as if picking something up, "get some sleep, early start tomorrow." The contours disappeared off the map as he did so.

I stared at the blank page.

"Six a.m. downstairs," Uncle Bill said in a voice that tried to contain excitement, then snapped his fingers, and thus extinguished the fireplace.

*

I don't think I slept that night; tossing and turning, mind racing, a million and one questions to be answered. I couldn't decide if I slept or not because I wasn't sure if yesterday's events weren't all a dream. Jumping out of bed at five forty-five a.m., I was dressed before I even knew it, flying down the stairs. I expected to find Uncle Bill sat on the front porch, preparing chicken feed as he did each morning. I expected him to raise a brow and ask what on earth I was doing up so early. And then I'd go back to bed, embarrassed at my own gullibility that something exciting was finally happening in my life.

Uncle Bill sat on the porch all right, but bounced up when he heard me coming. "Ready, kid?" he asked.

I froze. It was really happening. Or I was still dreaming.

He looked odd.

"What are you wearing?" I studied him.

He held out his arm to show it off, the long sleeve draping behind. "Thought I'd make a bit of an effort for the occasion, haven't been back in a long time." Instead of a coat, Uncle Bill wore a hooded robe. It wrapped around the same old safety boots he wore around the farm. "Let's be off, then."

I stepped outside, locking the door and making my way over to the Defender.

"Won't be taking the car, come this way," I heard behind me.

We walked around the house to the back of the barn.

"Now, I haven't done this in a long time, so just bear with me a moment. Stand aside," Uncle Bill warned.

He clasped his hands together gently, as if holding something delicate inside, muttered something to himself, and eventually drew them apart vertically through the air. As he did so, the air blurred where his hands had passed, like a heat haze refracting distant images in the desert sun. He then gripped this blurry, airy line, and drew it apart as if it were a jammed lift door. Little sparks, like live electric, sprung off the haze.

"There we are. Careful, it's a bit rugged at the edges. A spacetime portal – much faster to get around than cars and planes. After you," he indicated with his arm.

I stepped forward, looking through the portal. In the middle of the wet, muddy field behind our barn was an extensive sandy shoal with a rocky outcrop in the distance, framed within the portal haze like a landscape painting. Warm, sunny beams slipped through the portal into our muggy, English day.

"Go on, Lills, can't have this open for too long."

Before I knew it, Uncle Bill pushed me through. My stomach flipped and guts churned. I don't know how long it took – a second or three years, I couldn't tell. Inside was timeless. I stumbled through, and the next thing I was aware of was being hunched on all fours on dry, sandy ground, trying not to throw up.

"First time's always grim, don't worry." Uncle Bill emerged gracefully behind me. He closed the portal in a similar manner to how he opened it. "Are you all right to carry on?"

I nodded, slowly getting up. We stood at the end of a long footbridge, connecting two sides of a forested valley. Not too far below, gentle whirring indicated a river, into which a distant waterfall gushed. The other end of the bridge connected to a rocky landmass, an outcrop from the other verge of the valley, rising from the sandy shoal. The rocky landmass was encircled by concentric rampart walls, each marking off a level higher than the last. Crowds of roofs were packed inside. Crowning the city was a huge stone complex, clearly much older than the rest. Marked off by the highest ramparts and a deathly vertical drop, it boasted great edifices, column rows, parapets, ribs of flying buttresses, and a warped alignment of five towers. Atop the tallest tower, with its tail wrapped around the stonework and its wings stretched out, sat a dragon. Blue scales glistened in the sunlight, the tail's end burning like a beacon underneath the fifth tower roof.

"Is it real?" I asked, taking in the magical view.

"Oh no, that's just a statue," said Uncle Bill. "Come on, then."

He started off along the bridge, and I hurried after him before I managed to rephrase. I didn't just mean the dragon; I meant this place.

"Now, you know I like to set a good example, but I must say that you shouldn't just go around opening portals here and there," he said, slightly embarrassed.

As if I could.

"It's kind of against the law, er, ever since the... incidents... sixteen years ago. Used to be able to open 'em up freely – portals, I mean. They taught you how in school. Was very handy to get around. It's more controlled now, proper terminals, corridors, tickets. The Authority monitors every opening in spacetime. That's why we had to be quick."

At the bridge's end, we reached the outer gates and gradually sunk into a deepening sea of people. They hurried past, bustled, cloaks and gowns fluttering behind them. Others walked more slowly, blocking the dashers' way, pointing things out to one another and window shopping. Not only the human crowd was busy; tight congregations of houses, shops, cafes, pubs, alleyways, terraces, towers, and stairs (some apparently leading nowhere) filled the city's every nook and cranny. Filled to the brim, the city was a cup of life.

"Welcome to Loon's City, Lilly-Anne," Uncle Bill beamed. "Also the Continental tourist spot, as you can see."

We pushed our way through the crowded boulevards, gradually ascending the landmass, sometimes escaping the winding streets through narrow staircases and passageways when Uncle Bill remembered, like a real-life game of snakes and ladders.

I followed him, gazing, awe-struck. Suddenly I bumped into an obstacle at my hip. "Sorry," I blurted automatically. Looking down, I nearly screamed. Already walking away was a dwarfish creature, big-eared and glaring with its tiny, hollow-set eyes. It muttered something that sounded like a curse and waved a clenched fist terminating a freakishly long arm.

"Gremlins – always grumpy, don't worry about it," Uncle Bill commented and beckoned me into a shop.

Inside, the shop was crammed with rails of clothes: jumpers, blazers, robes like Uncle Bill's, hats, ties – you name it. A special section, in dark navy blue and black, housed garments decorated with the school crest. Variations of the dragon's scales included blue, red, and gold. I recognised Vincent's jumper on the rail.

"It's Sapphire Dragon's so shouldn't it all be blue?" I asked.

"Colours correspond to affiliations. You'll want the blue, for Rangers. It's a single institution, though you're given an affiliation – kind of like a house group, I suppose. It's where you live, whom you share lessons with," Uncle Bill explained.

A group of short, plump ladies with hands full of shopping bags glided past us effortlessly. Only when they passed, did I notice little wings flutter at their backs.

"Fairies."

I tried on cloaks – one lighter, another a heavier, winter version – and a couple of school uniform pieces.

"Oh, and you'll need one of these, too," Uncle Bill remembered, handing me something that resembled a dog harness with pen loops.

"What's this?"

"Wand holster. You want an arm or leg version?" He held up an alternative.

Next, we ventured to purchase a wand, which turned out nothing compared to what childhood books and my imagination had me believe it would be like. It was a simple instrument, sleek, tapering off towards one end, the transaction business-like and involving merely a choice of colour. It was possible to buy wands in multipacks, in fact, the range spanning from cheap Biro-equivalents to fancy fountain pen-like lines. For a small extra fee, my wand was personalised with a lily flower engraving at Uncle Bill's insistence. A signing quill was purchased too, also at his insistence. There was no way to bypass the sting of piercing fingers, apparently.

From there, it was a short walk to Sinnerstroke's Texts and Tales, where Uncle Bill left me to find the books listed on my reading list. "Just popping out, hopefully I can catch an old teacher of mine. Won't be long, I'll meet you back here. Shout for assistance if you need anything." He nodded towards a girl sat reading behind the counter.

I wandered among the bookcases, unable to figure out their classification order. Through pure luck I located a few items on my list, and after an embarrassingly long while, gave up on the rest. The girl behind the counter, round-faced and apparently not much older than myself, shot quick glances in my direction as I turned the same corner yet again. She finally put her book down when I started on yet another lap around the front row.

"Need any help?" She slid off her stool, revealing she was even shorter than myself.

"Yes please, I'm looking for all of these." I held up the list.

"Oh – first-year standard. One tick, I'll get these for you." She took a quick glance at the list. "We're out of Meagles's *Understanding Islanders*, unless of course you want to buy a signed copy – much more expensive, but I got plenty of those."

I thought about how much Uncle Bill had spent on me today already – not that I had any idea of the equivalent costs in pound sterling, but everything we'd bought seemed high quality, sturdy, handmade. "I'll probably just skip that one then, thanks."

"Sure, lots of people are. Nobody cares about the Islands, right?" she joked. "Have you ever visited? I heard they're strange people. Never met one though, and I'd like to make that judgement myself."

Something clicked in my brain then: the Islands – the *Earth* Islands. She meant me. "Uhh… yeah I've been… there." Unsure, I quickly added, "Once or twice."

"Wow, really? I doubt I'll ever get the chance, being stuck here every summer." She was nearly done gathering my books, an uneven pile towering on the counter. "This is my grandad's store. I help out so I can afford tuition. I'm Charlotte Sinnerstroke, Theorist, starting this year."

She reached out, and I shook her hand.

"Lilly-Anne Skyrose."

An awkward pause followed. "Are you Theorist, Ranger, Champion…?" she finally prompted.

"Oh! Sorry, Ranger," I blushed.

"Might see you around then," she smiled and started adding up my bill on a notepad. "That'll be two wholes, ten heads, and seven fingers please."

I stared at her, my bafflement only cut off by the doorbell when Uncle Bill stepped in.

"All done?" he asked. "How much do we owe?" He fished out a sack of coins from a robe pocket.

We wandered further upwards through the boulevards, passing through gates lined with stone gargoyles at each new rampart level. I noticed Uncle Bill subtly put up his hood at each of these entry points. The crowds were sparser here; with each higher level, fewer of the touristy type were present. Uncle Bill entrusted me with the sack of silver coins. I walked along examining these in the sunlight. They were fairly literal, it turned out. A 'whole' depicted a splayed body, different quantities of 'fingers' were pressed on others – a sideways, crooked hand pointing out between one and four digits, thumb tucked in. The 'head' was a woman's profile.

"Whose face is this?" I asked, showing him the coin.

"The queen's," he answered without looking, then staggered as if catching himself make a mental error. "*Was* the queen's."

Of course, I thought, *every fairy tale of might and magic in lands far, far away had to have a queen.* "Was?" I mused, holding the coin up to the sun and squinting. "What happened to her?"

Uncle Bill didn't, or chose not to, hear.

"Now, if you don't mind, I've arranged to see an old friend of mine," he said after a while. "He's come a long way too – him and his son, actually, little Gabe, helping poor, old Harry along."

We turned a corner to a dead-end street, where two figures sat waiting in a viewpoint turret on the rampart. One sprung to his feet as we approached, the other rose more slowly, supporting himself with a cane.

"Don't get up, you fool!" Uncle Bill greeted the latter with a hug that almost knocked the man off his feet. "Glad to see you made it, Harry."

"Made it?" Harry waved his cane, jokingly. "It's not *me* who seems to have a problem with spacetime travel! Where have *you* been hiding? All these years, Bill – nice to see that ugly face of yours again."

"That's your boy? Blimey, Gabriel, you're a young man now, ain't you! How are you getting on?"

"Very well, thank you, sir," replied the young man stood with Harry.

So much for *little Gabe*. He was tall and tanned, with broad shoulders and tousled, dark hair pulled back into a short ponytail. I looked at the ground, so not to look at him.

"And this must be Lilly. Pleased to meet you." Harry turned to me with a nod, and I returned a shy smile. "Well, whatever your reasons for leaving, Bill, I can see you've done a fine job of bringing this one up!" he teased.

"Lilly, Gabriel – Gabriel, Lilly," they introduced us.

I gave a nod and muttered a hello, still not looking directly at him.

"Now, why don't you kids go off and explore the city for a while, while Harry and I catch up?" Uncle Bill offered.

I was about to protest, embarrassed by the thought of being baby-sat by this stranger, when Gabriel accepted with an enthusiastic 'sure!' and a sincere grin. He set off, turning halfway up the alley to see if I was following, and so I had no choice: I followed.

Gabriel and I wandered through the little streets of the busier, lower levels, pushing past the never-subsiding crowds. I nearly lost him a few times. We looked in shop windows, commented on this and that, the weather, I *hmm*'ed and *err*'ed mostly in response, still shy, unsure how old he was. Judging by his height, the age-gulf separating us seemed disproportionately big to my sixteen-year-old self.

"Crazy this place, isn't it?" Gabriel thought aloud. "I've never visited before, always wanted to, though. Have you ever been before?"

I shook my head, so he continued.

"Dad doesn't really get around much, so we never travel far. So when he said he was finally seeing Bill, in Loon's City of all places, I just had to come!" He paused. "You live on Earth, don't you?"

I nodded.

"What's it like there?" he prompted, forcing me to give a verbal answer.

"Uhh… I guess it depends *where* on Earth you are. It's a diverse place."

"Really? Surely it's too small to be *that* diverse," he teased, seemingly eager to make conversation. "Come on, give me a description. What's it like compared to here?"

"Dull, I guess." Wanting to sound more mature, I thought through my answer. "It's almost like there's a dimension that is missing there, I don't know… Like everything on Earth is lacking some kind of focus or internal depth – things here seem so much more… alive, sharper." I searched through my vocabulary. "Dainty."

"You mean they're lacking Fate?" he laughed.

"What?" We got caught in a swarm of bugs fluttering through the street. I was later told these were, in fact, domestic pixies.

"I said, you mean it's Fate things lack – on Earth?"

"No, I heard what you said. What do you mean they're lacking fate?"

"You don't… know… Fate?" Gabriel stopped and scrutinised me, alarmed. "Stars, you're not one of the unknowing, are you?"

"No, I know what *fate* means – destiny, things turning out the way they're meant to and outside of your control."

"Yeah, exactly." He seemed satisfied. "Outside of our control indeed. She has everything planned, she controls us – sometimes I think we're just Fate's playthings," he smiled. "But! In return she gives us gifts – Force – and she keeps us alive, of course. Though if your gifts are like the ones I've been given, then I'd say it's a pretty crappy deal," he joked.

I had a feeling we weren't quite on the same page, but left it there. We walked in silence for a while. A group of lads in fancy, crested gowns ran past us then, laughing and shouting. I swear I saw one of them carrying a naked, white flame – a torch perhaps, but why in the daylight?

"You're starting Sapphy's then?" asked Gabriel, prompted by their presence.

"Yes. Are you? I mean, do you go there?" I blurted automatically, my mind still processing the white flames and totally forgetting that he said he'd never even been to Loon's City before.

"No, I don't." He ignored my slip-up. "I was meant to, actually. When I was a kid, my parents had a place reserved for me. I was kinda bright, too. Let's just say it all went downhill from there." He forced a smile, covering a palpable hint of sadness. "Are you ready for the entrance exam, then?" Gabriel suddenly perked up.

"Entrance exam?" I echoed, horrified. I didn't even know what half the subjects on my timetable *meant*, let alone how to pass an entrance exam.

"Yeah – you have to fight a dragon to pass." Gabriel looked me straight in the eyes, his tone earnest.

My guts churned and I think my jaw also dropped because he started laughing.

"I'm just kidding – but honestly, you should see your face. It was priceless."

"Thanks for that." I laughed along with him. Gabriel, it turned out, was the sort of person it was impossible to be angry with.

"No but, on a serious note, I heard they used to do that, hundreds of years ago. Hence the name and everything: Sapphire *Dragon's*. That's why dragons went extinct."

"Oh really? How long ago did they go extinct?"

He stared at me, forcing back a howl. "I'm still kidding! Stars, you really are gullible, you'd buy anything, wouldn't you?" he grinned.

We had stopped at a viewing terrace, momentarily sheltered from the city's traffic.

"I guess that's a good thing, otherwise I'd never believe any of this is real," I said, taking in the view across the shoal, river, footbridge, and forested valley beyond.

Gabriel stood next to me, seemingly just as awestruck with the magic of Loon's City as myself. "I can't believe you'd lived on Earth all your life, though. And you didn't know about the worlds?" he asked carefully, as if the question was insulting. I shook my head. "Wow. I can't imagine…"

"And vice-versa." I was starting to like him.

"And Fate – did you know about Fate?" His eyes narrowed in that same scrutinizing way, as if he'd just caught on to us not being on the same page. "Never mind. I'm sure you're intuitive, she's in you. Fate's in all of us," he smiled warmly at me.

Us. *Us.* I was one of *them*, welcomed and accepted.

"Shall we go for a drink?" he suddenly asked, taking me by surprise. Though *surprise* was an understatement; I was not used to going out, never mind being asked out by boys.

"Uh, okay then, sure."

Not far from where we stood was a pub; all sorts of creatures, human and otherwise, poured from the doorway. Others stood outside, waiting for a space to free up, enjoying their drinks on the window ledge. A gilded sign above the doorway read The Lair. How fitting for a city watched over by a dragon.

"This is the most famous place. If you tell someone you've been to Loon's City, they'll ask: did you go to The Lair? Look at them all crowd inside." Gabriel shook his head disapprovingly. "But! I've heard this is not where the locals go. Oh no sir, not at all. There's another place." He burrowed his dark eyes into mine, the suspense almost theatrical. "The Nest."

I burst out laughing.

"What?" he laughed too, unsure of what I found so funny.

"This is another one of your *I'm just kidding* moments, isn't it?"

"No!" he protested. "No, come, you'll see. I think it's probably somewhere in the upper levels, nearer to the school." He was already on his way.

I swiftly followed. The worst case scenario? Getting lost in this mad city with my newfound friend, and I was game for that.

*

We sat across a table from each other, sipping our drinks. Gabriel had asked for a willow juice, spiced, and I ordered the same because I had no clue what any of the other drinks were worth. It was nice though, warming thanks to hints of ginger, slightly fizzed. The Nest – a real place indeed – was much less busy than The Lair, though sparse, excited groups of students loitered here and there. This was induction week, I guessed. One such group stood out in particular, a mix of seniors and wide-eyed first-years ecstatic to be off the leash, all huddled around a sheepish-looking boy with limp blond hair and glasses. They cheered and joked, girls giggling at his every uneasy word, showering him with attention he seemed to all but want.

"Hey, Gabriel, I was wondering: how do your dad and Uncle Bill know each other?" I quickly shoved the question in when a pause in conversation allowed.

He looked surprised. "Has Bill never mentioned?"

I shook my head.

"Ever?" he pressed.

I shook my head again.

"Well, if only Dad heard this, stars – he'd rip Bill's head off!" Gabriel laughed. "They're best friends, always have been, since school I believe. We used to all hang out as kids – me, my sister Billie and our parents, Bill, his sister, and her kids."

"You know Vince and Bertie?"

"Yeah! That's the ones. Haven't seen them since we moved to the

Empyrean. They all worked together then, our parents – my mum, Dad, Bill, and Jacob Globesglory.”

“That’s Dianne’s husband.”

Gabriel nodded.

Suddenly two more drinks were plonked down on our table. I looked across and downwards below the table-top, from where a set of abnormally long hands released the glasses. A gremlin waiter stared back.

“Oh, we didn’t order—” I began explaining.

“On the house, on account of Mr Spells Junior visiting, says housemaster,” the gremlin said as he stomped away.

I wondered who this Mr Spells was, and Gabriel too raised his brow at the name, scanning the room quickly. Too preoccupied with our conversation, Mr Spells was soon forgotten.

“And where did they work together?” I said, sipping the willow juice.

“*Really?* Bill *never* mentioned it?”

I rolled my eyes.

“At the Authority, of course. My dad was one of the queen’s chief advisors; my mum too, because of her gifts. Then after Rachthawnian rule ended and the Senate was established, Dad stuck around a bit as a justiceman, until…” he trailed off and took a sip, dropping the thought. “Jacob Globesglory, though, he’s still the high judge’s consultant, I believe. And Bill – well, Bill was in the queensguard.”

“The queen’s guard!”

“Yes, but, *shush*, keep it down.” Gabriel looked around. “The queensguard didn’t exactly walk around with their titles printed on their hats. Anyway, after the Rachthawnian Murders – and for my dad, after the bombing – they both pissed off as far away from it all as they possibly could have, it seems. And that’s how,” he took a sip, “you and I ended up living in the middle of bloody nowhere at opposite corners of spacetime. Stars, had they not done that, we could have been friends since a long time ago!”

He hesitated at the word *friends*, but, although we had just met, there was already an unspoken understanding between us: a comfort, an ease, emanating from a shared past that wasn't even mine to share.

"We used to live in Brightwood, that's where the Authority is based. After the bombing, that's when we moved to the Empyrean. Dad remarried – not for love, I highly doubt, and he'll never admit it, but I think it was all strategic. He couldn't take care of us no more, you see, being a cripple – not to mention being devastated – and we were only kids, Billie and me. So he found someone who'd look after us, and somewhere we could be far removed from it all, secluded, *sheltered*." Gabriel rolled his eyes at the last word. "Now we're pretty much stuck on the lands. The clan lands. That's why I'm so excited to travel out. I'm still a Continental bloke at heart, you know." Gabriel grinned at the thought of his homeland reunion; the enticing, unreserved grin that made him such an easy-going companion.

"And you think Bill removed himself as far away as possible too?" I asked, meaning Earth.

"Yes – well, I don't know. I'm only guessing because he and Dad lost touch. But I suspect that after the Murders, when the queen was killed, he shunned himself away completely. What would you have done, if you failed your life's purpose?"

"The murders?" I bit my lip, trying to get at a piece of dry skin nervously.

"Stars, Lilly! Yes, the Rachthawnian Murders, sixteen years ago. And you must understand the scale of these – it's not just a one-off. It's not the case that the queen was killed and that's it. No sir, not at all. Nearly the whole Authority was wiped out, the whole system, hundreds of people died – perished. Fonsland, where the Rachthawnian palace was – the whole world was pretty much destroyed."

I chewed my lip mindlessly, trying to process everything I'd just heard. We sat in silence for a while.

"D'you want a healing spell for that?" Gabriel asked, studying my lips. "I only know a petty one, but I promise that it works."

*

We walked along a rampart, late afternoon by now, gazing down on the odd sea of rooftops below: gabled, dormer, spire, all apparently constructed without a predetermined plan in mind.

"I'm glad I finally met you. Dad talks about you all the time – I mean, not *all the time*, but when he mentions Bill, he always mentions you," Gabriel smiled.

"Oh yeah? And what does he say?" I asked, for nothing better to say. I was glad to have met him too, but somehow the words got stuck in my throat.

Gabriel gave a nervous laugh. "Well, he's fond of you both. But – and please don't take offence," he cast a quick sideways glance at me, "he always wonders where you came from."

"None taken. I wonder that too."

"Can I ask you a favour?" He seemed embarrassed.

"Sure," I said automatically. I expected he'd ask me to keep quiet about the details of our conversation. There were reasons for which Uncle Bill never talked about his past, I guessed, and although I was relieved to be entrusted with these snippets today, I would have to respect said reasons still until he opened up.

"Will you write to me?"

"What?"

"Letters. Will you write to me? So I can read, and reply. I want to practice writing." Gabriel plucked a leaf off a shrub we passed, as if to divert attention from the question.

"Sure, no problem." I gave him a reassuring smile. I wondered why someone his age would need to *practice* writing. Was he illiterate?

"I can read, you know, and write. Mum taught us how when we were little. And I go to school, all right. It's not a fancy place like this – nowhere near, just a comprehensive on the lands. But they don't exactly value writing there. Empyreans are superstitious that way, say it's all Continental tricks, and – well, I'm worried I'll forget how to," he said, answering my thoughts. "I don't have anyone else to ask, and I noticed you reading the drinks menu."

"Sure, I will. I'll write to you," I reassured.

*

We found Uncle Bill and Gabriel's dad, Harry Hale, sitting in the same spot we'd left them, engrossed in lively conversation. We walked together to a portal terminal, signs by the doorway reminding passengers that authorised spacetime travel is permitted only.

"Do one last thing for me, Harry, will you? Request us a portal back to Cley next the Sea," Uncle Bill implored.

After that it was final jokes and quick goodbyes before we parted. Authorised portals were scheduled like trains or buses, and the Empyrean ones 'departed' earlier than ours. Uncle Bill and I sat in the waiting room, shopping bags at our feet. Gabriel gave a final enthusiastic goodbye wave as they neared towards the front of the Empyrean queue.

"Good chap, Gabriel, well-mannered," Uncle Bill commented. "Did you have a nice afternoon?"

"We did, thank you. Went to The Nest," I said, swinging my legs from the chair.

"Oh! Not The Lair, then? Gabe must know his stuff."

"I suppose he does."

"I think he'd be a good choice for you, you know, if you ever—"

"Woah – please, no, just stop that thought there." The conversation suddenly took a painfully awkward turn.

"I'm just putting it out there," Uncle Bill laughed. "At least I'd rest in peace knowing you're in good hands. They're a righteous, good family."

"That's enough, thank you." I burned red in the face.

"Ha, okay. Now then," he straightened up. "When we get home, Lynne is going to ask about where we were. We'll tell her that we were shopping for school supplies, and we'll tell her that you'll be going to a boarding school. But," he made sure he had my full attention before continuing, "there are certain things that Lynne won't, and cannot, know."

"You mean she is unknowing?" I'd picked up that much.

"That's right. Lynne is *one* of the unknowing, as are all the other Earth Islanders."

"It's a bit unfair, don't you think? That nobody on Earth knows about this magic."

"Well, it might seem that way, but they abandoned it. Fate was fervent on Earth, at one point. People were very intuitive, devoted, and Fate rewarded them. Civilisations didn't just spring from mere human ingenuity, after all. But, with time, Earthens turned to a different devotion. They burned Fate's servants on stakes – witches, they called them. They pushed Fate out, replacing her with a different kind of energy: electrical currents. They invented the idea of the universe – stars and moons in faraway galaxies – when in fact they are just very high in the sky. They can see them, but don't understand their true nature."

"So they can't see the other worlds?"

"No. All the worlds exist in spacetime, including Earth, though the Islands have become sealed in on themselves. The idea of a round planet which you can circumnavigate… ridiculous. Though I guess the idea of the universe itself has ancient roots. It's like spacetime: infinite. And the suns, the stars: they're all burning bundles of Force – that is, Fate materialised. Fate's energy can be concentrated, channelled into a flame, you see."

He snapped his fingers. Out of nowhere, a playful, white flame encompassed them.

"Force, we call that." He explained the flame. "I hear Earthens are now arguing whether there's life on other *planets* – as if they didn't shut themselves in on their own little world in the first place. Still, Fate seems to have gone along with all of this."

"Why would Fate go along with being rejected?"

"Well, because she allowed it to happen. There's nothing outside of Fate's control, Lilly. Stars! Perhaps she even planned this all along, for Earthens to forget."

"Am I one of the unknowing?"

"No," Uncle Bill answered too quickly. "No, you must not think that way – you living on Earth all this time, that's my doing. But it's not where you belong, it seems. Fate wants you back." He gave a short, forced laugh.

"What do you mean, back?"

"Well… here is where you came from: the other worlds. It's where your mother lived, where—"

He was interrupted when the terminal conductor called out, "Special request, Hale! Portal for…" He looked at his list with a flummoxed squint, "Clay in the sea."

*

Perhaps I had been asleep and dreaming all that time. Perhaps I only just woke up. Perhaps I'd lost my mind. I wasn't sure which was correct.

Lynne wasn't pleased, that was real enough. She demanded to know where we'd been all day, how exactly the boarding school would be paid for, and why she wasn't involved in the decision-making. By the next day, as I scurried about the house picking up all of my few belongings to pack, she refused to say a word to me. In a way, silent treatment made it easier not to lie.

Uncle Bill had asked Dianne to arrange school transport for me. By five o'clock in the afternoon, we stood in a field among local castle ruins, suitcase in tow, waiting. Uncle Bill insisted I wear my new cloak 'to fit in'. I checked my watch every thirty seconds. By 5.13 p.m. I was still hopeful; a quarter of an hour late wasn't damning, after all, and there were still two positive minutes left until then anyway.

As the hands neared to 5.16 p.m. I sank a little inside. Eighteen, nineteen, twenty-one. With each minute, I only grew angrier with myself for having ever believed in any of this. *Here's your fresh start, Lilly-Anne.*

"That's it, they're not coming. Where's the *You've Been Framed* crew?" I tried to shrug my cloak off, furious I'd even dressed the part to play the fool.

"Relax, kid, they're probably just lost. This is a slight detour, after all." Uncle Bill leaned on his Defender, unbothered.

A growl of thunder reverberated through the clouds, and suddenly a portal opened in mid-air. From its midst flew out a lopsided carriage pulled by winged creatures, half-lion, half-eagle.

"Embark! Embark! Late already!" yelled the gremlin driver, pulling the griffins to a halt, a pair of long arms struggling with the reins.

"Go on, Lills, show them what you're made of," said Uncle Bill, handing me the suitcase in a hurry.

"Will you visit?" I lingered on the step, but before he could answer, the gremlin slammed shut the door.

Thus off I went, by myself, into the greatest unknown that I'd hardly tasted yesterday. I think that's what happened anyway. Perhaps my mind had finally closed itself off, fortified itself against the boring, outside world and created its own within. Perhaps I was finally stuck inside a daydream.

The carriage started with a jolt, sending my suitcase flying across the floor. I realised then, that the inside was much larger than its outside contours possibly allowed.

A group of students sat at the end furthest to the door, gawking at me. "Where even are we?" I heard one hiss.

I quickly retrieved my suitcase, shoving it under the nearest available seat, and sat down.

Bound for Brightwood, the carriage rolled swiftly along, jumping a portal here and there, sometimes taking off in flight thanks to the griffins, picking up more students along the way. Pulling back the curtains, I gazed out of the window, mesmerised and enlivened by every detail.

The ride was smooth until we reached the cobbled streets of Brightwood's Metalsmiths District. There, the carriage halted to pick up its final passengers.

"Let go, Mum, you're pulling my plait." I heard a whiny voice before the door flew open, revealing two students, their mother fussing to arrange the younger's hood.

"There, now you look presentable. Tina, you look after your sister. Anything goes wrong, you go to Ross. Write to me, promise, every rise!" She gave her daughters a smothering cuddle each. "Have you both got your wands? Invitation letters? Good. Look, there's some free seats," she nodded in my direction. "Quickly now, they're running late."

The two sisters scrambled in, and we were off again, wheels lifting off the ground.

The girls sat opposite me.

"First year? Welcome to Ranger Bastion," the older smiled, indicating the blue crest on my cloak. Both their cloaks were similarly embroidered. "I'm Tina, and this is my sister—"

"Ruby Jones." The younger reached out to shake my hand.

"Lilly-Anne."

"I'm just starting, too. Are you excited?" Though before I could answer, she continued. "I'm *super* excited. I've waited for this moment for *years*.

I've memorised all the first-year spells, some of the second-year ones too, but I don't want to get *too* ahead of myself, you know. How about you, what do you want to specialise in?"

"Uhh… I don't know yet."

"Well, that's okay, I suppose, we still have several years to decide. But I *know* I want to focus on magic, or alchemy; laws, only if all else fails – I don't really have the disposition for mindreading, you see. And Force, well, that's not really my thing at all. What need is there for it nowadays anyway? Duels, if anything, and I'm not interested in duelling."

Tina left to join her friends at the back of the carriage, while Ruby chatted, and I tried my best to appear knowledgeable about whatever question she threw at me.

"So, where are you from?"

The dreaded question was finally asked. Despite Gabriel's agreeable tone towards my Earthly upbringing, my fellow passengers' reaction was rather one of suspicion and demur. And that was based solely on where they'd seen me embark from. A quick mental calculation, and I suspected that if they knew I'd actually lived on Earth my whole life, clueless of the other worlds until yesterday, their unease would only intensify to my detriment. In other words, I feared being shunned.

"Umm…" I gulped. The only otherworldly places that I knew were Brightwood and Loon's City, and while I could potentially get away with stating the former given its large size, if Ruby decided to bond over our shared hometown, I'd be ratted out over a lie before we even reached the school. "Cley next the Sea." I figured she wouldn't know where that was.

"Is that in the Empyrean? Sorry, I only know that Empyrean place names are lengthy."

Dammit. "No, actually…" Unable to think of a solution, I braced myself. "It's in Norfolk, England." She looked puzzled. "It's on Earth." I was defeated.

"On *Earth*? Are your parents diplomats?"

I sighed and, without intending to, spilled my life story's guts to Ruby. She listened intently, surprised at my Earthly upbringing, but not suspect, like I'd feared. Rather, she seemed amazed and probed me with questions like some scientific specimen.

"I'm glad, you know… Well, I mean it's awful that you've lived away from Fate for so long, but I thought that you're just one of them spoiled, posh ones – no offence. When you didn't recognise basic elixirs, or said you hadn't read any introductory texts, I thought you just didn't *care* because you're made of money and bought your way in – like most of them over there." Ruby leaned in from her seat, lowering her voice. "I'm on a scholarship. Wouldn't be here if my essay on revised spell categories wasn't selected." She looked so proud.

Relieved that she cared more about hard work than having an ex-unknowing in her midst, I reassured her that I cared very much about good grades and kept the mysterious trust fund, which apparently paid for my tuition, out of the conversation. Uncle Bill said my parents must have reserved a place for me at Sapphire Dragon's before I was even born. It reassured me, knowing I belonged here.

*

The carriage dropped us off in the uppermost levels of Loon's City. As twilight fell and air filled with a playful whizz of fireflies, the hubbub of the city dimmed to only a faint buzz up here. We queued at the gates leading into the school grounds.

Ruby, who'd clutched her invitation letter tightly throughout the entire journey, stepped forward to the checkpoint and handed it over. Snatching the letter, a gremlin guard scanned and sniffed it, held it up to a flame, apparently looking for fraud, and finally, satisfied, ticked a position off his list, opening the gate. I followed suit and the procedure was repeated, only that instead of opening the gate, the gremlin handed me my letter back.

"Not on list, no entry."

"But—" I began to protest.

"Not on list, no entry," he repeated. Sitting high inside the checkpoint, he looked down on me, no longer the benign, puny creature I'd bumped into just yesterday.

"I'm sure we can sort this out," Ruby called from inside the gate, looking around for Tina, who loitered only long enough to ensure her sister made it through.

We were alone.

"Not on list, no—"

"That's all right, Sesame, thank you – you're doing a splendid job, but it looks like there's been a clerical error." An elderly man approached us, his blue, excessively patterned robe dragging behind him. "Good evening," he greeted us, briefly lifting his matching round hat, and pointed his wand at Sesame's list. "There, that's sorted. In you come, young Ranger. Hurry now – assembly is about to start."

CHAPTER 4
ORLE GIGGLY LOBBSTER

In the great hall, there were three long tables running the length of the room. Along each table, on either side, ran very long benches. They didn't really run – they just kind of stood there, as much as furniture can stand. Anyway, on one of these benches, and in one spot only – let me be precise – sat my arse. The whole of me sat, actually. But it was my arse that touched down on the bench. How did they manage to make such long benches? How did they get them through the door?

My leg had a mind of its own. It twitched under the table, and I tried my best to stop it, but it had a mind of its own. Next to me, next to my arse, sat about a hundred other arses on the benches running along the tables. One hundred people sat, actually, or a few more, but it was their arses that sat on the benches. It was loud because everyone was chatting. Their mouths were chatting, their minds making up the words. Perhaps my leg was chatting to me, twitching because it had a mind of its own.

I won't last any longer. It's all a bit much. I bent forward and buried my face in the sleeve of my elbow, my elbow lying on the table-top. I muttered an invigorating spell to myself. And suddenly… oh, what bliss.

"What did you say?" I heard. The arse that sat next to mine was connected to a body. The body leaned in – the head, actually – and said, 'What did you say?'

"I didn't say anything," I said to my elbow.

"*Shush*, she's about to start."

My ears picked up a different voice, a voice coming from a different mouth, a mouth connected to a body which sat – on its arse, naturally – across the table on the bench running down the other side.

"Geez, Mel. She says the same thing every year anyway," said the mouth – the body, the arse – next to mine.

"Good evening, everyone," said yet another voice, disconnected to a body because it came from all the way across the hall, and about whose arse I didn't want to think about because it belonged to Chancellor Martina Arden. Old woman, wrinkled, dry prune.

I sat up and rubbed my eyes. That only made them sting worse. Chancellor Arden was stood – not sat – at the lectern, the lectern that stood before the high table; the high table that crowned the head of the hall, where stood the head of the school. We the body, the student body, sat on the hall's bench body.

"Welcome to another year at Sapphire Dragon's school. Please put your hands together and welcome our new first-year students."

The hall erupted in applause. Hand to hand, hand to hand, both hands coming from the same bodies, hinged on different arms, together in applause.

"Please, will each respective house affiliation make our new students feel at home – the home our walls truly offer. Those of you who have joined during induction will already be familiar with the grounds and buildings. Can I remind you that the hard work starts now. For those of you who have only just arrived today, you will be allocated the remaining dormitories and shown around the grounds by senior students. I hope some of our seniors will volunteer for this role."

Tickety-boo, the clapping hands were now only two.

"Oi, that's enough. Stop clapping, idiot. Honestly, what is with you today?" whispered the voice belonging to the mouth, the head, the body next to mine. The head so identical to mine, the mind so different.

My hands still clapped, palm to palm, palm to palm, my hands had a mind of their own. I trapped them together to make them stop. Clenched. Wrapped. One hand hugging the other, I trapped them. That stopped them clapping.

"In terms of announcements, this year we will be trialling a raffle system for winter ball tickets. Aside from the usual purchasing system, a number of tickets will be raffled for the benefit of those students who are discouraged by the price from going to the ball. Raffle entries will be significantly cheaper."

One for me, one for you, a ball ticket each for the whole crew.

"Try-outs for sport duel teams will take place in the new year, with the games themselves beginning in early spring semester. Existing teams are welcome to practice and work on their strategy until then, though may I remind you not to be excessively competitive about the matter."

Gather, aim, strike through, run, our team dressed in blue.

"Though introduction is hardly necessary, as most of you will recognise him from his days here as a student, allow me to present to you Ross Jones in his new role as school counsellor!"

Jones loved it so much, he stayed – who knew?

"And finally, it has come to my attention that a certain individual, who goes by the name of…" There was a pause as Arden checked her notes. "Orle Giggly Lobbster…"

A wave of giggles spread through the crowd, each of them infected with the giggles of the Giggly Lobbster. *Oh sweet stars, the whole school at my fingertips.*

"… has been dealing in unauthorised spells, experimental potions, and cheating charm formulae within the school grounds. Can I remind you that such behaviour is *not* permitted and is in fact unlawful. Anyone found utilising the Giggly Lobbster's services will be punished or expelled."

My eyes looked around the room; behind my eyes I looked around the room, taking their reaction in: an array of muggins, students arranged in rows. Not all of them ready, though many willing to try, curious, in need of my recipes to add a little flavour to their lives. Yet not one of them who'd *really* understand – who'd see, see like I see, behind my eyes I see, and feel, feel like I feel, alive and fed on their curiosity.

I was an unofficial spellsmith, you see, Orle's name already somewhat famous. His name but not his form; they had no clue which body Orle might be hiding in. They looked at my body, and that person to them was known as someone else. To those looking at my eyes, I wasn't Orle. As Orle, I looked at them from behind that someone else's eyes.

"Any information about this individual's identity will also be rewarded."

Catch me if you can, I'm like the flu.

The door at the back of the hall opened, the rear end of the hall's body. Professor Fellblue glided through, dressed like blue diarrhoea. Behind him were two frightened students.

"Oh stars, that's my sister. This is so embarrassing," my ears heard nearby.

"And look who else – I thought she'd never make it," replied the voice next to me.

"Ah, there's always one or two. Thank you, Professor. Welcome, please – take your seats," said the chancellor.

Sirloin and beef stew, a late greeting for two.

"Now, let the feast begin, and may Fate treat us kindly."

CHAPTER 5
LILLY-ANNE SKYROSE

After the assembly, which Ruby and I pretty much missed, and the lavish meal that followed, Tina showed us around the grounds. I tried to make a mental map of key locations: the great hall (for formal events), the library, the buttery (for informal meals and snacks), the various classrooms and lecture theatres, the chantry (inaccessible), the cloisters and courtyards, the infirmary ('let's hope you'll never need it'), and finally, Ranger Bastion.

A separate building, with a gremlin porter keeping close surveillance on the door, Ranger Bastion was situated across the grounds from Champion Hall and Theorist Keep. Tina showed us to our dormitory. The last two free beds in the bastion were thankfully in the same room, so at least I had the comfort of sharing with someone I already vaguely knew. Ruby pushed open the door, visibly stiffening as she did so. I peeked in. The place looked like a bomb had dropped, scattering belongings everywhere.

"Welcome, friends!" We were greeted instantly by the current occupier, who quickly introduced herself as Sephy, giving us a hug and kiss on the cheek each. "I'm so pleased to meet you. I've made the room feel homely just in time for your arrival!" she said.

"Homely..." Ruby repeated in disbelief. "Which bed is yours, sorry?"

Sephy's things were splayed across all three beds, the floor, cabinets, and chairs.

"I've slept in this one." Sephy pranced to the back of the dorm, jumping up on the nicest bed located in a raised part of the room, a couple of steps leading up to it. Surrounded by windows, it was a small turret.

"Well, do you mind moving your things off the other beds so we can unpack?"

"Oh, but they're in *aura*," Sephy pouted. "I arranged them specifically to create a homely atmosphere for you, so we can feel like family."

"That's very kind of you, thanks – we feel at home. Can we move them now that they've done their job?" I tried.

"Okay, lovely! I'm glad you feel at home, friends," Sephy beamed.

She had no intention, however, of clearing her belongings, and in the end we moved them to the side ourselves. I took the bed tucked in a nook behind the door, and Ruby the one opposite, both perpendicular to Sephy's stately turret. Sephy helped us to unpack (much to Ruby's annoyance), and as she arranged our clothes in the wardrobe, it became apparent that Sephy had only the faintest notion of personal space.

They were polar opposites, not only in appearance, but in character too. Ruby – controlled in her tone, behind which a thousand thoughts a second were weighed up before she came to a decision, and Sephy, whose carefree and light-hearted attitude seemed to indicate consequences was not a word she understood. Unpredictable and wild, like her bushy brows and golden ringlets on her head, Sephy was very slight and impish. And yet her character was huge; it filled the entire room, painting us in the dullest light in a comparison that Sephy herself apparently didn't notice. Vibrant and bubbly, her style and belongings (not to mention their arrangement) often clashed with Ruby's passion for precision, neat appearance, and remarkable foresight, while I found myself tiptoeing the fine line that kept both appeased.

Her name was Persephone, it later turned out – Sephy for short. Her parents had a travelling show, acting out myths and stories from across the worlds. The Greek name was a nod to home for me, though nobody else seemed to know the connotation. I asked Sephy once if she knew the myth.

"Of course, I love that one!"

"So you know what happens to Persephone?"

"She goes away from home for some time every year," she said, no Hades or pomegranates or the Underworld. "That's why my parents sent me to school."

Her name was so much more fitting though, I soon realised, than separation for half the year: Sephy was springtime, personified.

"Has anyone seen a plug socket?" I searched around the walls, phone and charger in hand.

"A slug pocket?" Sephy perked up.

"Is that a remote control?" Ruby's eyes widened at the sight of my outdated smartphone. "I heard they're like Island versions of wands! You can command things at a distance."

Of course, I remembered, *there is no electricity here.* In fact, I quickly learned the word itself was suspect, associated with the false god who replaced Fate on Earth. It followed that there were no telephones, no internet, plug sockets, or the like. I wasn't going to charge my phone, and soon enough I'd lost the obsolete device to Sephy, who sat examining her reflection in the screen, mesmerised.

*

My first few weeks passed in a blur. I felt like a baby: clueless, helpless, having to learn to walk. Thanks to Ruby, however, I was beginning to take my first steps. Sephy helped too, though often it seemed like she was even more out of touch with reality than me.

Despite her many pedantic quirks, Ruby's presence was a blessing. Firstly, she put up with my silly mistakes unquestionably, when others were starting to catch on that something was odd about me. Secondly, she answered all my many questions patiently, often pre-empting them and taking on a teacher role, which suited her well. And thirdly, she willingly spent time with me, which indicated that I'd finally found a real friend. Vince and Bertie were around too, though their third-year timetable meant I'd often catch up with them in the Ranger common room.

"Ready to fight the dragon, Lills?" Bertie said to me one evening.

"Sorry, too late, someone tried that one on me already."

Our first ever class was laws, and it started off badly. We funnelled into the lecture theatre. Ruby always sat in the front row and, unwillingly, I sat with her. Chatter filled the room, falling silent suddenly as a side door swung open.

Professor Asset Artsback marched in. "Welcome to laws," he said in a harsh, dry voice, lips pulled into a tight grimace as if he hated us already. "In this class, you will learn about the foundations on which our worlds are built. We will start with how our end of the bargain with Fate is upheld: the three Unbreakable Laws."

Artsback waved his wand. Writing appeared on the blackboard as he spoke.

"One: you will not cheat Fate."

I quickly opened my notebook and copied off the board.

"Two: you will not take the life of another – that is for Fate only to decide."

Yikes, grim, but understandable and at least easy to adhere to.

"Three: you will not covet the plans Fate has spun for others."

I wrote in my neatest handwriting. There was a pause. I looked up to see why class wasn't continuing.

Everyone stared at me.

"Are these laws not ingrained in you, Miss…?"

"Skyrose," I gulped.

"Miss Skyrose. So much so you feel the need to write them down?"

I felt twenty pairs of eyes piercing into my back. Artsback raised a brow, and I hoped that meant I was dismissed as a compulsive note-taker.

"Next, we will study the multitude of secondary laws that keep our worlds in order, ensuring that in four years' time – providing that you make it until then – you will leave here as law-abiding citizens." He scanned the room. "That, I'll consider a great success. If any of you were capable even in the slightest of appreciating the intricacies of politics, you'd be sat here with red crests on your attire."

Artsback was Head of the Champions. Affiliations were randomly assigned, officially. Rumour had it, however, that they were handed out based on disposition. Champions, it was said, were natural-born winners; ruthless and ready to gamble risks, they went on to successful careers and highly-paid positions (or so their track record and ease of securing internships would suggest). Rangers – well, we were the good guys, Bertie told me; fair, loyal, with intuition unmatched by the other affiliations. Theorists, according to Bertie, were good at thinking about everything *in theory*, though incapable of action (unless you were a Theorist yourself, of course, then the house prized itself on wisdom and pioneering magic). Each affiliation had a colour assigned: blue for Rangers and red for Champions, while Theorists sported gold. Rangers were the best, Bertie said, because it was *Sapphire* Dragon's after all.

"In any case, we'll work to ensure that you have at least a *ru-di-men-tary* understanding of laws, *priming* your young minds to be strong enough not to succumb to the poison that we call Hate," Artsback sounded out his t's with a *tut*, "which our Senate and Authority have worked so *tirelessly* to eradicate over the last decade. Isn't that right, Mr Spells?"

Attention of the class turned to someone else then, but I didn't dare look up, still embarrassed.

"It's a great shame, you ended up in blue." Artsback crossed his arms, addressing Mr Spells. "I want an essay from each of you, on the three Unbreakables. I need to be sure that we are all… familiar… with the basics." He looked at me as he said so. "On my desk in two rises' time."

And that is how, by our first ever class, I managed to land everyone extra homework.

In history, I learned that the human 'bargain with Fate' was initiated by someone called Rachthaw thousands of years ago. Humans were powerless, apparently, before Fate offered them a helping hand. It was a *symbiotic* relationship – I underlined that word three times. In exchange for doing as Fate pleased, humans were given superpowers – at least in my understanding. Fate had always existed; it was the substance of space and time, an all-present energy. Only Rachthaw was willing to listen to Fate however, at a time when no one else did. Fate taught Rachthaw how to channel its energy – Force, the white fire. That made Rachthaw powerful, and over time and generations, her descendants came to rule the worlds. The Rachthaws, as each subsequent female ruler was called, represented the human race in dealings with Fate. They orchestrated, enforced the laws, and judged those who disobeyed, for eventually many grew jealous and suspicious of their privileged position. *Poisoned*, was the word. And although Professor Meagles did not say this directly, it sounded like the Rachthaws' iron grip had weakened by the end. They raised the worlds to power, and in the end the worlds' bureaucratic systems overpowered them, relegating the Rachthaw – the queen – to a puppet. As bureaucracy and industry grew, so did the gap between those whom Fate (or more likely, business) found favourable, and those who were deprived.

That's when it happened: the Rachthawnian Murders, sixteen years ago. Dissent had previously simmered; this time it over-boiled. The puppet-queen and members of her council – the Authority – were nearly wiped out by an army stemming from the depths of the dissatisfied populace; a revolt by the aptly-named lawbreakers. Those were dangerous criminals, Professor Meagles said, poisoned by the mysterious substance, Hate, which turned them against Fate and the Unbreakable Laws. Thankfully, the Senate was quickly formed from what remained of the Authority, restoring order.

Unable to execute lawbreakers under the second Unbreakable Law, the Senate banished them to the Carcery – an uninhabitable world far away in spacetime.

"Thanks to the efforts of our beloved lawkeeper, high judge, justicemen and justicedames, our worlds are much safer than just a decade ago!" concluded Professor Philip Meagles. "But we must remain vigilant of lawbreakers, of course. Hate strikes when we least expect it."

"What about demons, professor?" someone asked.

"Ah, this takes us back to the beginning of the story. It's true, ancient texts do talk about such creatures, but we cannot ever be sure if they existed. They were said to be unnaturally fast and strong, all thanks to their diet: human blood. It's no surprise, really, when you consider that our blood is the conduit of Fate inside our bodies – feeding on blood is analogous to feeding on Fate herself. But," Meagles straightened up with a smile, "the last alleged demon sighting was over three hundred years ago, and the source is questionable, so you can sleep soundly tonight. Any more questions?"

"What about demon involvement in the Murders?" The attention of the class was tangible.

"Silly rumours. As I said, even if they ever did exist, demons aren't around anymore – especially demons who meddle in political affairs," Meagles dismissed, and I joined in with the rest of the class laughing at the idea.

The message about blood was confirmed in alchemy. The most basic magical element, blood was the substance of these worlds. Blood was where Fate flowed within bodies, reaching every muscle, every cell, every thought and feeling. One's awareness of this – one's ability to feel or listen to Fate – was measured as a level of *intuition*. Blood was reactive too. Breaking the laws, thus breaking the contract with Fate, caused blood to turn whiter and whiter, until – as was said of the most committed lawbreakers – it turned translucent.

"Don't worry, I won't make you show your true colours," said Professor Gregoria Sprause, our alchemy teacher. She adjusted her goggles and stained lab coat before disappearing in the supply cupboard for a while.

"Go on then, let's see if there are any whitebloods here," one of the boys egged the others on.

Unlike core classes (magic, laws, and Force control), for secondary subjects, year groups were divided in half, and each half joined with another affiliation. Alchemy, we shared with the Champions.

"Bet some of you here aren't scarletans." The boy reached for his signing quill, ready to pierce his fingers.

"That the best you can do?" Another pressed his wand into his wrist. "Go on, I'll do it if you do it!"

"Only if Spells does it – I wanna see what the benchmark is."

They turned to the same sheepish boy with glasses I recognised from The Nest. He put down his pen, too aware of the attention, swallowed, and looked around, searching for someone to rescue him.

"*Kindegory* doesn't have to prove you anything. Anyway, there are no whitebloods here, I'm sure, because *my daddy* makes sure they all get sent over to the Carcery straight away," a Champion girl with sleek black hair butted in. "Damsel Goldtear, I'm *sure* you remember me." She reached over to the sheepish boy, offering her hand out for a kiss.

He took it awkwardly, turning her palm over to shake her hand instead of planting the expected peck. "Hi," he said.

"As I'm sure someone of your standing is well aware, Kindegory, blood doesn't just have *colours*; it has flavours. Those of us made of finer substance should stick together, lest we be… polluted… by those of a fouler taste."

"Thanks, I'll bear that in mind," he mumbled.

I lay across my bed, head hanging over a laws textbook.

"I wonder what Force control will be like. Tina said Professor Fellblue's methods are unconventional." Ruby stopped writing to ponder for a second.

"That'll be fun." Sephy danced around the room, checking every corner for her hat.

"You would say that, wouldn't you? Anything unconventional seems to take your fancy."

Sephy was unbothered. "I also like conventional. I'm off to one this evening. It's a fairy convention. Want to come?"

"Why are you going to a *fairy convention,* Persephone – you're not a fairy." Ruby pulled her brows together.

"Out of interest." And she was out, no hat.

We went back to working on the essays. *Bang,* something crashed against our ceiling from above. Ruby and I exchanged a look but continued working. *Bang, bang, bang,* the sound rolled across the ceiling, paint and dust falling on my bed. Someone was making a hell of a racket in the room above us.

Bang.

"That's it, I'm going to report it." Ruby sat up.

Bang, bang, bang.

"This is *unacceptable.* Some of us are trying to work down here!" she shouted at the ceiling. "I'll find my brother, Ross, he's the school councillor now – he'll tell them off."

"Look, why don't we go there and ask them to be quiet?" I disliked confrontations, but I was more afraid of becoming known as a snitch. Seeing that Ruby wasn't any braver than myself about ending what sounded like a seniors' party, I offered, "Let's give them one chance. We'll go, and if they don't stop, we'll get Ross." If we were lucky, it was Vince or Bertie.

Our dormitory was on the fourth floor of the right-hand staircase coming off the common room. With no further stairs to fifth floor, we decided the entrance to the dorm above ours must be off the left-hand staircase. Yet it turned out that the left staircase was only three stories high. Back and forth we went searching for the mystery noise, across the common room, where a group of boys sat on the sofa, sniggering. So much for a simple affair.

"You all right there, ladies?"

A boy I recognised from class as Dean Strange eyed us curiously. He was excessively at ease, already friends with everyone across the years.

I glanced at Ruby, who looked like she was about to run, so I did the talking. "Someone in the room above ours is having a party," I began.

"Looking for a party, are you? Well come, join ours," he enticed.

The other boys watched attentively.

"Thanks, but – it's just that we were studying, and someone is being very loud on the fifth floor."

"Fifth floor? There's no fifth floor."

"Come on, we'll just report it." Ruby dragged me away.

Climbing the stairs back to our dorm, the noise persisted and grew louder.

"How can there be no *fifth* floor? There's clearly someone there!" Ruby whined.

"Rubes, wait." I ventured past our room, where the corridor led to a dead-end around the corner. "Look, there's a door here." It was small and up a few steps, perhaps leading to a supply cupboard or…

"An attic." Ruby looked over my shoulder. "I'll get Ross, nobody should be up there."

"No – wait, please." We both jumped at a voice behind us. "Don't report it."

It was the sheepish boy with glasses and limp hair, buttoned shirt and creased trousers hanging over his lanky frame. Having followed us from the common room where he sat with Dean, he now looked lost for words.

"Do you know what's behind that door?" I tried, as Ruby froze, mouth open and eyes wide.

"Yes, um, there's a sort of attic, not used by anyone," he mumbled.

"Well, *someone* is clearly up there, and they're making a lot of noise," I insisted.

"Um, not someone, I suppose."

"Well, what then?" I raised my brow – smooth fibbing wasn't his strong side.

He pushed a pair of thin-rimmed, round glasses up his nose, searching for an explanation, apparently not used to being pressed like this. "Okay, here's the thing – but you can't tell anyone."

He produced a key and neared the door. The noise strengthened, something clawing at it from the inside. Ruby hid behind me, though whether from the noise or the boy I could not tell.

Instantaneously as the door released, out scurried a four-legged ball of white fur. Ruby shrieked.

"Hey there, buddy." The boy bent down, picking up the creature. "This is Flip," he announced, and for the first time his features pulled into an earnest smile. "He's always been with me, we go everywhere together. I couldn't just leave him at home, so I brought him here. And I couldn't keep him in my dorm," he said apologetically. "I didn't know what the other guys would say. They'd laugh at me, that's for sure. And I couldn't risk that they'd report him – Arden would make me send him home." Flip cuddled in his arms, the racoon-like face smitten. "Please don't report him," the boy begged.

"Of course we won't," I said automatically.

"Stars! Is that a squidrel?" Suddenly, Sephy ran towards us. "May I?" Without waiting for permission, she took Flip from his owner's arms. "Adorable, aren't you!"

"I think he likes you," the boy said with deepening enthusiasm.

"I think so, too." Flip returned Sephy's cuddles with a lick of her cheek.

"How was the fairy convention?" I asked, stroking Flip's white, fluffy fur.

"Oh, they didn't let me in. I'm not a fairy," Sephy dismissed, seemingly lacking the foresight.

"He was just saying…" I was about to recount for her, when I realised we hadn't introduced ourselves. "Sorry, what's your name? I'm Lilly, this is Ruby and Sephy, we live next door," I said, reaching out to shake his hand, as I thought was customary.

Ruby's jaw dropped and she stared, aghast.

The boy hesitated too, unsure or unaccustomed to being asked this question. "Kindegory, hi. But I prefer just Kin." He shook my hand, then reached out to Ruby, whose knees trembled as he lightly squeezed her hand.

"Lilly lived on Earth." Ruby unfroze for a moment, only to blurt out an apology on my behalf.

"On *Earth?*" he repeated, shocked. I was getting used to this reaction and the question that followed. "Are your parents diplomats? Sorry, we might have met already."

"No – I just lived there." Not wanting to go into detail, I steered the conversation. "Anyway, what are you going to do about Flip? He doesn't seem to like being locked up."

"No, it's no good," Kin sighed. "I don't know what to do, he can't stay here, and he can't stay in my dorm."

"He can stay with us!" Sephy beamed.

Ruby's horrified expression suggested otherwise, but no words came out of her.

"We're all here, we're all in the know – he can stay with us," Sephy concluded.

And so it was settled.

*

"Do you *know* who that was?" Ruby screamed as soon as we were alone in our dorm.

All the while as Kin took his time settling Flip into his new home, Ruby looked about to explode with nerves.

"That was Kin." I expected there was more.

"That was *Kindegory Spells*." She leaned on the back of the door, aware her knees might give way. "I can't believe we just *shook hands* with *Kindegory Spells*." I wasn't catching on, so she added, "He's the lawkeeper's son!"

The lawkeeper, she proceeded to inform me, was basically the interworld president, Head of the Authority, and replacement of the queen.

I let that sink in, but Ruby was already ahead with her thoughts.

"And now we're going to get expelled because of him!" she cried.

"What? Why?"

"Pets aren't allowed! Section 7.3 of the school handbook: under no circumstances are students allowed to bring, keep, or otherwise endorse animals in accommodation. If they find out—"

"Nobody will find out, because we won't tell," Sephy assured, arranging a nest from duvets and jumpers at the foot of her bed.

"Yes they will, Persephone, they will tomorrow when the pixies come in to clean! We're going to get expelled!" Ruby's mind jumped from packing up already to a salvaging excuse. "I know: it was blackmail. He pressured us into it."

"That's hardly true, Rubes, he didn't even ask us to do it," I protested.

"And besides, nobody will find out. I'll take care of Flip tomorrow," Sephy promised, as Flip settled in her lap, ears laid back, pleased as she groomed his fur.

Ruby slumped onto her bed, defeated and quite unconvinced.

"Just look how adorable he is," Sephy begged, brushing Flip's fur in gentle strokes.

Flip's cuteness was hard to resist, even for Ruby, whose affection was threatening to cross the hard-set line.

"Persephone, is that *my* hairbrush you are using?" Ruby suddenly realised.

"Oops."

CHAPTER 6
BEATRICE GOLDTEAR

I finished the test early, so for the rest of the time in laws, I was free to watch him. He sat in the row below me, within easy reach out of the corner of my eye, more comfortably if I turned my head slightly, subtly. Mate Grim. Was that really his name? He was quiet, withdrawn, distrusting of everything and everyone. Likewise, everyone of him. Mate Grim was avoided like the plague.

I saw his eyes flicker above the deep, sallow, shadows of his cheeks. Did he ever sleep? He ran his fingers through the tangle of golden-brown hair, leaving it in an even more perfect mess. It suited the red details on his jumper well. He pressed the end of a pencil against his lips, parting them slightly. He was thinking. The test wasn't hard, but I guessed he wanted to do well. Artsback gave him a tough time already, Mate couldn't spare another fail. Strands of hair fall on his forehead and turned up at the ends around his neck, a haircut due. His hands were covered in fresh scabs from duelling. Why didn't he just heal them up like everyone else? I could offer him a healing spell or two, though I'm sure he knew those well enough.

Mate was a very private person, not speaking unless spoken to, and even then only offering minimal responses. The only thing that seemed to bring him alive was duels, yet even after a successful match, when celebrations ensued (celebrations he had every right to be the centre of) he withdrew into the shadows.

His silent, bold presence was for me spellbinding, his mystery I ravished in; the cornerstone exciting my mundane, school life.

He was strange, and this strangeness I found irresistible.

Ever since we'd joined the school last year, I'd spent my free time watching him, all too painfully aware that this was where things would have to end.

"Oi, Mate." One of the other lads *pst pst*'ed in his direction. "Oi, got the answer to number four?"

A tiny pause in his movements, I knew Mate had heard, but ignored.

"Don't bother – he'd have to know the laws in order to keep them," another taunted.

Was it true, what people said about the Grim brothers? Anyhow, nobody would dare say that to Mate's older brother, the mighty Alastair Grim. I saw him sometimes in Champion Hall – who didn't? Alastair Grim was a magnet, attracting everyone's attention. Unlike Mate, however, he knew well how to play the rumours to his advantage. And when Alastair's formidable presence wasn't felt, Mate was quickly the butt of every joke.

"What's the matter, Matey? Never learned to speak, or did your mother knock that out of you as well?"

I saw his jaw clench in that instant, the marble lines of his cheekbone harden. Pencil lead snapped, crushed by his grip pressing it into the page. Underneath the benchtop, his other hand rested on his wand holster. Mate was ready.

"Shut up!" I hissed.

"Quie-t," Artsback tutted from the front of class.

They backed off. I had some leverage – telling people off for bad behaviour ran in the family, after all. I stared at Mate quite openly then, heart racing. For a moment, more smoothly and faintly than a gliding ghost, I thought I saw his eyes flicker at me, head bow slightly, an acknowledgement from this perfect stranger.

CHAPTER 7
ORLE GIGGLY LOBBSTER

He who seeketh to find me, must follow the seeds first. Each little seed of my reputation I plant, carefully, to mark the way. Each little seed grows, pulling them back. And as it pulls them back to me, it also directs, pollinates new minds.

Foundlings who stray their way to find me must first pass the test: the test of my trust. My trust hath certain conditions attached. Needless to say, if those conditions are not met, those who seek my services can piss off, even if they are willing to pay.

My spine pushed back against the rails of a chair. I settled uncomfortably; back of my body to back of chair. I waited, adjusted my hood. The Lair was crowded, bodies crammed inside the gut-shaped room; human pulp digested by the day, rowdy and intoxicated by the mere thought of an overpriced drink in the famous pub. The last flocks of tourists before winter, playing local in a place accommodating their charade. A perfect anonymity.

I sunk in.

I spotted the client right away. He looked nervous, out of place, too aware of what Loon's City was really like to share the tourists' charm. The Lair was ideal, in this respect: too obvious a place for my business ventures for anyone to think I'd risk it.

The Lair was also the last place in Loon's City from which I wasn't barred. That and The Nest, but the team liked to hang out in The Nest, so I couldn't pull off any funny business there. I once nearly did, and then *nearly* got barred, but I just about stopped myself, so I didn't – didn't get barred, that is. I was already banned from entering Vedder's Club, on account of toppling the drink bottles on the top shelf behind the bar. They were too neatly lined up, if you ask me. I was also unwelcome in The Centaur's Head, due to once setting half the place alight. It was an exaggeration anyway because only the tablecloth caught flames, and besides, I was merely trying to prove that they watered down their drinks. It turned out the drinks had a high spirit count all right. So now I'm unwelcome, if they have a good memory for faces, anyway. The owners demanded to take my name, said they're going to press charges. They never did. Or at least I wouldn't know because I said my name was Eugenius Haunt. That's how Eugenius Haunt got barred from most watering holes in Loon's City. Not that he ever visited such places anyway. Eugenius Haunt was the groundskeeper at Sapphy's, and he was about two hundred years old. Well, over sixty-five, at least. He probably would have minded me giving his name, if he knew, but he didn't. He didn't know, that is. Good ole Eugenius. But you never met a man twice as dumb.

I say good ole Eugenius, but actually I don't like him very much. Nobody does. I slightly hate him, in fact. He was the kind of groundskeeper who put up signs forbidding walking on the grass and reported you if he as much as saw your big toe tread on it. He set bird traps, didn't fix the showers for ages, and locked doors that didn't need locking just to make you go the long way round. Once I dropped my favourite glove walking across the pitch. I realised a few yards later, but he'd already mowed right over it. I bet he sprinted to mow over it too. So the next day I farted on his lunch when he ate it in the cloisters. I didn't plan it, I just happened to be walking by.

Right now I happened to be waiting, and the waiting was really starting to irritate me, among other things. I also hated how the napkins on the next table over weren't properly lined up.

Rod – my client – moved through the crowded Lair. His name wasn't really Rod, or at least I don't think so. I never asked. But tension kept him upright, and the name fitted perfectly, so I named him Rod in my head.

My legs danced a little dance under the table. I crossed them at the ankles, trying to force an interlude. It was a little while yet before Rod noticed me, and my legs' dance moved up my spine. Muscles tensed, I bounced. Tiny twitches of the arms, neck. Stars, how I wished he'd hurry up.

Rod edged closer, pretending to examine the various paintings on the walls. The Lair was too nice that way, too neat. Fake paintings of the city's fabricated past, neat square tables with drab, cream tablecloths, little vases with a single evergreen poked inside. Useless sconces on the walls giving needless light.

"Orle?" he half-coughed out, leaving scope to pretend it was an accident lest I not reply.

But I must have reacted – perhaps I told him to sit down – because he pulled out the chair opposite, and his arse touched down.

"Are you sure this is safe? I mean meeting here, of all places? It's so busy," his voice was blabbering.

I told him I'd cast a protective spell and nobody could really see us. It wasn't true but it calmed his nerves. He repeated his woe: one more bad grade and he was going to fail astrology. I grasped my throat to hold back a laugh. Why would anyone take astrology as an option in the first place? Rod wasn't wearing uniform – wise – but I took a guess that he was a Theorist. A good guess because I saw him some time later wearing a golden crest. So I named my price, and once the heads rolled across the table, gave him the formulae. They clearly worked well, if later on he was still wearing the golden crest.

That day, I also fashioned a spell to mend a bold patch in facial hair – very successful, judging by my own trials – and whipped up a love potion, half an ounce. Some twit also enquired about an invigorating spell, but those

I didn't sell so lightly.

Spells are a precise science, you see. Everything has to be taken into account. And everything is a lot to think about. If a phoney asks for a recipe to have some fun, I can guarantee it, but there's no one-size-fits-all. I am a tailor: judging dimensions, lengths, depths, heights, to coin the syllables of spells. But once I sell a special spell, that's it, it's out there, free to use repeatedly. Some of my clients were brave enough to attempt modifying what I'd sold them, searching for something new. Yet spells can easily go wrong, if the formula is imprecise. That's how Bulky – who bought a spell to tone his muscles up – overdid my formula, suspecting I had lessened it so that he'd have to come back for another one. Bulky added some more firmness to my spell, and sitting down in private, found that things had turned too brittle. Most of his tendons snapped; he couldn't get up off the loo. Sulky Bulky spent two turns re-growing tendons in the infirmary, and I had to shut business for a while.

A lesson learned, I now only sold to those who passed my test of trust.

My spells had a tried and trusted guarantee. I always tasted first the recipe I'd cooked up.

But my spells had a caveat. "Use exactly as instructed," I said to Rod. If the buyer got their ingredients slightly wrong… well, I can't be blamed for that.

Rod memorised the formulae – no writing down – though I had to repeat myself damn near three times. Together with the formula, I planted a little seed inside his mind; a seed of my vision that would grow with time.

Other clients were simply stupid enough to forget the recipe they bought. They returned to me, following the little whisper-seed path my successes had laid out. I couldn't make myself too easily found, you see. Those who forgot, I made them pay twice. Higher price, for stupidity was an interest to me.

I might have been a spellsmith, when I grew up. I might have graduated from the best school in the interworld, in which I was currently a student, then qualified with the guild, and got an official stamp. When I got older, I might have sold my spells officially, as authorised, at triple the price; worn a fancy velvet cloak, written a spellionary, stars – even a spellbook with worksheets for kids to fill out. I might have done all that in a few years' time, but it was too late to start me on that path. Growing up was a joke, and I was having quite a laugh.

Unfortunately I discovered my calling for this art too soon. Sorry Mum. Formulae to change the state of things cobbled together too easily in my head. Spell components oozed out freely from between the folds of my brain – I once nearly sliced it open just to check exactly how. They amalgamated before my eyes, tailored to whatever I was looking at. Sometimes I had to twist my tongue just to stop them coming out.

With each glance at the worlds, improvements materialised before my eyes. They layered up, a stack of imperfections sticking to the wet eyeballs' glaze, imperfect filth obstructing vision. The defects were so striking – in fact, they were all I could see, watching the worlds through thick, dim glasses of irritability. Why put in extra effort, why worry, why spend so much time on something that could much more quickly get done? These daily struggles frustrated me, oh stars they did, itching, burrowing under my skin. The worlds were so sluggish, it truly bothered me.

It bothered me because anything could be changed, amended, improved if you had the right spell. Anything could be made up if you found the right words; the right words in the right order. Stars, you could even make up whole new worlds if you knew how to spell them out, give a logic to a sequence.

But that's a lot to think about.

In answer to my ailment, I couldn't simply spell everything around; everything that existed, everything I knew. That was hardly fair, and anyhow, it was too big a task. Still, it was an unequal relationship: while I couldn't change everything around me, everything was free to change me. Influence me, bother me, get under my skin and obstruct my vision with its fallibility.

So I spelled myself instead, became Orle. When I was Orle, nothing really bothered me.

I was a poet of sorts, you see; a spell poet, writing my life in verses of half-rhymes, changing the rhythm of time; a poet, stringing syllables together to somehow make the day flow by; a king of the superfluous, fallen in the battle of ambition, sentenced to seeing the sublime. I was a fool, a fool for trying to get away with that.

My shoulder struck the doorway when I left The Lair, patting it goodbye. Unlike spell components, doorway dimensions were a bit harder to judge.

I took a trip through the city that night, visiting three cul-de-sacs. Only the residents ever went down cul-de-sacs, and I thought it funny to visit places unvisitable by design. The city looked so different in the dark. Crooks and oddities hid in the shadows. I waved because crooks and oddities were familiar to me.

"Roasted toads, stuffed with brie," an invitation bounced down the street. "Last orders coming up!"

The vendor was just packing up. He was a gremlin, a gremlin in a boater hat. Perhaps he sailed across the shoal, loading his lifework on a little raft. Entrepreneurs without permits often arrived in Loon's City that way. On rafts by dusk, they made their hopeful way. Apparently the Authority couldn't see well after dark.

I leaned backwards, trying to see underneath the canopy of the little stall. Then I bent forwards, for actually leaning forwards made it easier to see.

"Wants a toad, son?" he asked.

I watched his lifework slowly spinning on the roasting stick.

"They's stuffed with brie."

No sir, I'd rather spare myself stomach problems of the third degree.

The toads revolved with a little fire burning underneath. I remembered that Earthlings thought their Islands revolved – revolved collectively as one, just as all the three toads rotated together on the stick. It made me laugh.

"Wants one or not?" he demanded.

Suddenly he became so much shorter, head barely sticking out above the makeshift counter. Shorter, though the more I thought about it, he was abnormally tall for a gremlin – even with the hat. He was suddenly shorter, but actually, he became more gremlin-sized. I bent sideways to see why. He kicked a wooden crate out.

I searched my pockets for some heads. My hands searched, actually, for the coins that I'd just earned. "You got a packet of Focus?" the words came out.

His face twisted into a grimace, as if that was not a question he liked to be asked.

"How old is you?"

"Eighty-five." My fingers traced the engraved portrait I rather liked. "With a spare one of these."

The vendor considered widening his merchandise. It was much too much, of course. A head for something of officially seven fingers worth. But it was his life's work, and it was only fair, to exchange what mine had earned for his. I handed him the coin, and he found a filthy packet in the used utensil compartment of his cart. Filthy, he assured, but still brand new.

"Whatever." Goodbye.

Fate kindly gave me a light, and I hobbled up the cobbled street. I hobbled because it was only right to walk awkwardly along a lumpy street. The packet of Focus crumpled too much at my touch. A few sticks were missing. So much for brand new. I supposed this was Fate calling in her debt for me previously stealing a few.

I took a long drag to fill me up for three slow steps. Or perhaps this was
Fate showing me what she always intended me to be: a fool, a divvy on the
borderline, an unsound writer of my destiny.

CHAPTER 8
LILLY-ANNE SKYROSE

Grabbing some breakfast in the buttery the next day, I prepared myself for botany. Alongside spacetime studies, it was one of the two classes we didn't share – Ruby ended up in the split with the Champions, I with the Theorists. Musing at the porridge, I waited for Sephy to turn up.

"Remind me again, what time does the class start?" I asked.

"You should get there for five beats to the ninth round." Ruby scoffed a spoonful.

I looked down on my watch, though it did little to decipher what she said. Timekeeping in the otherworlds took some getting used to: ticks were the equivalent of seconds, beats of minutes, and rounds were hours. The year (for at least we shared that much) was divided into twelve turns – when it came to the Thotun sun, anyway – with each new day called a rise. I always forgot the word for weeks.

"Seven rises makes a…?" I thought aloud.

"Set," Ruby supplied. "You're probably better off just walking there on your own," she added.

"Would be helpful if I remembered the way."

Ruby launched into a volume of directions. By the time she recounted the whole map, Sephy finally showed up.

"Lovely morning!" she beamed, quickly chopping up an apple. Instead of eating it, however, she shoved the quarters in her backpack.

Pushing through the busy corridors, I tried to keep up with the sight of Sephy's ringlets sticking out above the sea of heads, a bouncing ball of friendly snakes as she skipped along.

"Morning, hi." Kin appeared at my side. "How are you, how is Flip? You didn't leave him in your dorm, did you? It's cleaning day."

"Sephy said she'll take care of it." I gestured in her vague direction.

"Good, amazing. Thanks so much again. Headed to botany, are you?"

I nodded.

"Mind if I follow you?" An unsure blush fired up his roundish face.

"Nope, I'm following Sephy myself."

"Well, let's hope she knows the way."

We trailed her sight, the one-eyed leading the blind.

*

"Find a workspace, settle down," instructed Professor Caspar Meyer, our balding, middle-aged botany teacher. "We'll be making griffin feed today. You might be wondering: *what does griffin feed have to do with botany?* Well, not much, but the griffins need to eat, and I need to start you off on an easy task. So," he kept an eye on the door, unsure how many more we were expecting, "with the person next to you, grab a list of ingredients; instructions are on the board, but really all you need to do is mix."

Kin and Sephy took one workbench; I settled at the next one along. Sephy set her backpack carefully on the floor, taking time not to jolt it as she shrugged each strap off her shoulder. The person next to me turned out to be Charlotte Sinnerstroke, whom I had briefly met before in her grandfather's bookshop.

"Fancy seeing you here," she smiled.

"Likewise," I returned.

"So, *I've heard*," Charlotte tip-toed around the subject once we'd gotten the ingredients ready, "that you didn't just *visit* Earth – you lived there."

"And where did you hear that?" I prepared myself for another explanation, inventive answers to 'are your parents diplomats?' running through my head. *They're runaway criminals, actually. No, I fell through a portal accidentally as a baby, they never managed to get me back. What do you mean on Earth, I thought we were in Wales?*

"Oh, you know – in the Theorist common room, people talk," she said casually. "Also, the girls' bathroom, the buttery, a few times in the cloisters."

Oh no.

"Well, is it true, then?"

Before I could answer, something scurried past our feet.

"What was that?" Charlotte exclaimed.

I followed the scampered trail, only to see Sephy bent over her backpack by the workbench, clipping up the buckle. Her wide eyes skimmed the floor, while Kin kept watch above table-level in hasty contraband teamwork. *Persephone, you didn't*, I imagined Ruby's horrified voice and smiled.

"He's after the narma kernels," Kin whispered, catching onto my stare.

"You've spoiled him rotten, Kin. He won't even touch the apple." Sephy sat back on her stool, keeping Flip's kicks coming from inside her backpack at bay between her feet.

"Don't tell anyone," I turned to Charlotte. "Please."

"Don't worry, I won't," she laughed.

*

Reunited for lunch, Ruby and I sat with Vince, Bertie, and Tina, our Ranger uniforms flocked together around a table in the buttery. Vince no longer sported the jumper he wore in the summer; instead, being in their third year, the three of them now wore blazers. Bertie held a copy of the *Interworld Seer* over his plate, a newspaper I noticed he read every day.

"Senate on verge of accepting Technology Pass," I read the headline over his shoulder, but he was too engrossed to hear.

"Mum wrote that," Vince answered for his twin. "They've been debating this for years. It might finally be passed. Then we can share a little more with Earth."

"Technology Pass? Does that mean they're thinking of introducing electricity to the worlds?"

"Stars, *no*!" Vince laughed. "Just the devices. We'd run them on Force, actually. Theory is that Force and electricity have similar capabilities, so we'd be able to import the outer packaging without the substance inside, so to speak. But it's controversial."

"I can see that being very useful – I could phone home, at least."

"Ready already," Bertie suddenly joined in, producing a bunch of smartphones out of his bag. "Anyone wants to purchase, friends' rates available."

"Gilbert!" Tina nearly screamed. Apparently righteousness ran in the family. "Put those away, they are *still* against the law!"

"When the Technology Pass is accepted, my offer won't be so easily rejected," Bertie replied.

*

"Welcome Rangers, welcome to Force control," said Professor Fellblue, as we filtered into his classroom. "Please, take a seat."

I looked at Ruby and Kin, who seemed just as confused. The tables and chairs had been pushed to the side, stacked up against the wall.

"On the floor, find a seat," Professor Fellblue indicated.

We did as instructed, feeling silly to say the least.

"Now, first things first: when we say Force control," Professor Fellblue spoke with a certain calmness in his voice, "the word *control* is misleading. If anything, you'll be learning to control yourselves, your feelings, your intuition." He paced about in thick, flowery robes and matching hat. He was exceptionally old, moving slowly, though at ease, sometimes taking off his hat to think. "How are you?" He stopped in front of Ruby.

"Um, I'm well, thank you, sir," she replied, reflexively.

"No, how *really* are you? How is your intuition?" He leaned in, and when Ruby returned all but a frightened stare, he addressed us all. "Always be honest about your intuition. It's normal to feel nervous – after all, we're not acquainted. You don't feel at ease, then say so. True intuition stems from true feelings, everyone."

We exchanged puzzled glances.

"Now, Force. Not all of us will channel Force – the sooner we accept that, the better."

"But, professor, surely every respecting person has Force in them?" someone butted in.

Fellblue thought a while. "As far as I'm concerned, Fate has a grasp over all of us. Whether you feel this grasp, whether you listen to Fate and succumb to her, is a personal matter. And if Fate gifts you with the ability to materialise her power – as Force – well, that's another matter. Some of us will be gifted already, others may need practice. And others still… well, Fate may have other plans in store for them than chucking bundles of fire."

He paused for a moment, sweeping his eyes across us all.

"Let's begin then," Fellblue continued, perching on his desk. "Put your books away. I tell them every year you won't be needing those, and yet they always end up on the reading list. Now, sit comfortably everyone, relax. Search inside your consciousness, listen out for Fate."

I braced myself for another bloody procedure, the signing quill still fresh in my mind.

"Now, let's meditate."

Looking around, at least I wasn't the only one who didn't understand what was going on.

"Close your eyes, Lilly, it's easier that way," Professor Fellblue instructed.

I closed my eyes and tried to focus on my thoughts. I didn't recall ever telling him my name. I guessed he was intuitive that way.

*

That night I had the same recurring dream: the forest, the meadow, the garden, the fortress, the hall, the tiles, the stairs. Everything was the same, until I reached the terrace. For the first time, someone joined me in this dream. Uncle Bill waited for me at the terrace, his kind face pulled into a smile, speaking to me. His lips moved, but no sound came out. It then followed the usual course of events: the silence, the screaming, and the nonexistence.

"Show them what you're made of," Uncle Bill's words rang out just as the sound returned, against the screams; the same words I heard him say the last time I saw him. Then we were both sucked into the light.

*

Within a few weeks, school days started racing past, though the novelty never really wore off. Through petty mistakes, things I'd said that clearly lacked an understanding of the wider context or, soon enough, through my general presence in and of itself, my reputation was soon sealed: I was the Earthling. Not even an Earthen or an Islander, which were polite terms. And yet, I had never felt so alien. Sometimes I wondered when I would wake up from this strange dream, for everything still felt so unbelievable it must have been one, long dream. Perhaps I fell into a coma with my blood disease. Perhaps I wasn't ever going to wake up. If that was the case, I decided to learn to live in my new reality.

Hidden among the novelties of this strange world – worlds, I kept reminding myself – were gems of seeming familiarity, landmarks on which to orient myself as I navigated the fabric of this landscape, pulling at the threads to see how they wove together. Sadly, not all of these familiarities were welcome; memorable horrors of PE lessons remained, for instance, disguised under the name of sport duels.

Our class gathered on the pitch, a Champion-Ranger mix in two distinct huddles on the frosty grass. Ruby started her litany of woes before we had even dressed this morning, and her complaints were not exhausted yet.

"This is utterly absurd," she whined. It was also pointless, unnecessary, and cruel. "I just don't understand why they would make this class compulsory. There's no *need* for duels anyway, it's merely an extravagant, foolish indulgence for those who clearly have no talent elsewhere. I, for instance, have *no* intention of joining the sports team."

"Morning, hi," Kin piped up alongside us, more cheery than his usual timid self. His very presence was enough to hush her up. "Are you all excited? I've been looking forward to training ever since we got here. Duels are my absolute favourite! Go to the interworld cup every year, been practising too since I was a kid."

"You must be naturally gifted with Force, then, Kin," Sephy complimented him, rolling up the bottom of her joggers, her frame drowning in the oversized shape.

He blushed and pushed his glasses further up his nose – a nervous gesture, for they weren't falling down. "I mean, I guess you could say that – I could spark by the time I was twelve." He demonstrated, snapping his fingers, at which a little, white flame appeared.

"I suppose talent fares well when supplemented with a private coach." Ruby couldn't help herself.

The confidence creeping up Kin's face immediately vanished. He fiddled with his glasses again, and mumbled, "Yes, I suppose."

Kin stuck around with us a lot, not just in class, but in the evenings too. The official reason, voiced every time we heard a faint knock on our dormitory door, was to see how Flip was doing. That he did, sat on the steps by Sephy's bed. Flip dashed around the dorm, ecstatic about the attention and range of makeshift toys Sephy had created: sock on a string, ball of scrunched-up homework, wand fetch-stick. The unspoken reason that hung in the air, however, was that Kin felt comfortable with us. Apparently not many others saw beyond his surname. We, on the other hand, didn't brag, didn't nag, and the conversation never steered in the direction of political intricacies, perks, or scandals. Or rather, I was too clueless to even try, and Sephy too wholehearted and blissfully unaware. Thus, the lawkeeper's son became friends with the traveller-showman's daughter and the Earthling. To be friendly with the blacksmith's youngest pride, he certainly tried. But Ruby found it harder to be comfortable around Kin. Too diffident to speak to him, when she did, the remarks were quite unrestrained and peppered with bitterness. Although no such judgement was ever passed on his side, Ruby seemed to translate everything Kin ever did into a comparison between his life and ours.

"Sour grapes," Sephy winked at him.

"Gather round, everyone!" Coach Dweegan made her way across the pitch to meet us, frost crunching at her feet. "Today you lot get to start duel practice – everyone's favourite! As you know, historically duels were the noble, honourable means to settle disputes. Now that we have our amazing judicial system, that's no longer necessary, so duels have moved into the wonderful realm of sport – both individual and team. And it is on this sport that we shall focus. If I catch anyone duelling outside of friendly remits, I'll have their head."

The look on her face was so stern that I wouldn't have been surprised to discover she had a display case full of severed heads.

"As it's still early days for your Force abilities, we won't be lighting up," she continued. "And anyhow, it'll only be the select few of you," Dweegan passed her scrutinizing gaze across us, "who are already gifted. Otherwise, we have lots of work to put in. So there's no point in us trying to practice duels just *yet* – instead we'll build up your stamina. Now, ten laps around the pitch, everyone!"

Ruby and I both sunk in on ourselves with dread. The pitch was a huge, grassy stretch located on a hill. By the third lap, as soon as we were out of Coach Dweegan's sight at the bottom of the slope, Ruby and I began to walk, breathless. This was everyone's favoured strategy, it seemed, for two figures were stationary at the bottom of the hill.

"Is that Kin? What is he doing?" I said, confused, recognising his lanky frame knelt down on one knee at the feet of the Champion girl with sleek black hair. I remembered her as Damsel Goldtear.

"I can't believe she made Kindegory Spells tie her shoelace!" Ruby gasped, trying to catch her breath.

Damsel's hearing was better than anticipated.

"*Kindegory* had offered to help." Damsel turned to us with an icy stare, though the pleading look on Kin's face suggested otherwise. "You should have dinner with us tonight, Kindegory. We'll be sat at the *higher* end of table." Damsel reached to tuck a strand of Kin's hair behind his ear.

He flinched, though said nothing.

"I think our company will suit you better. Lower table is more for those… deprived… of Fate's blessing."

"We're not deprived of anything," Ruby snapped back. "What kind of name is *Damsel* anyway?"

"Clearly a longer one than your parents could afford, *Ruby Jones*," Damsel sneered. "Sticking with the Earthling too, are you? Sink any lower? That's unlawful, if you didn't know, sharing our ways with the unknowing."

"I'm not unknowing," I threw back. "I know everything I need to know to see that you're just mean and insecure."

Damsel laughed. "Insecure? I'm just looking out for the *safety* of our worlds! Anyway, you better know how to count at least, Earthling, because your days here are *numbered*. I already told my daddy about you being here – the Authority are making plans to remove you as we speak! Exposing our worlds to the unknowing, how obscene! Whoever meddled with the list to get you here is going straight to Carcery! You just wait—"

"Skyrose!" Damsel's monologue was interrupted by Coach Dweegan's booming voice. "Which one of you is Skyrose?" She approached down the slope, flanked by two cloaked figures.

"There, see! They're here already!" Damsel exclaimed.

I gulped. There ends my dream. Yet as they neared, I recognised the two cloaked figures to be Vince and Bertie.

"I am!" I ran towards Coach Dweegan, glad to be rescued.

"The Globesglories here, they've just informed me of… uh… Anyway, take her away. I'll see you two at practice. Vincent, I hope you have a good strategy for the Rangers this year." Coach Dweegan turned to Ruby, Damsel, and Kin. "Why aren't you running? Stamina! Chop, chop!"

"Phew," I grinned at Vince and Bertie once the others had gone. "Thanks, both! You just pulled me out of something nasty!"

They exchanged a troubled look, not sharing my enthusiasm. "We're so sorry, Lilly." As Vince spoke, an odd sadness spread across his face.

"Sorry about what?" I still grinned. "Don't be sorry for saving me the running!"

"Oh stars, you've not read the letter," Bertie sighed. "It's Uncle Bill."

*

Checking the post had totally escaped me. Excused, perhaps, by the fact that the post room was located far out of the way of any classrooms or places I'd frequented. Fourth in the line of crooked towers fringing the school grounds, with uneven steps encircling its outside and blustering gusts of wind, not only on the ascend but also draughty through the top, the post room was not a pleasant place to be. After Tina pointed it out on the first day, I hadn't bothered to come again.

By the time we'd reached the top and I found an Authority-sealed letter amidst a stack of other makeshift envelopes with my name on it, I already knew. Vince and Bertie took turns explaining on the way. I was silent, incapacitated by shock and dread. Signing my name in blood underneath the Authority's seal, I didn't even quiver. Much worse things materialised before my eyes.

'Dear Miss Skyrose,' sorrow spread across the page. *'We write to inform you that according to our records, Fate has claimed back Force from Mr William Skyrose, and thus with Fate he is reunited. May Fate treat us kindly until our time is called.'*

"What does this mean?" I mumbled, though they had explained clearly on route.

"Uncle Bill died, Lilly."

*

I sat on the sofa in the Ranger common room, numb. If things up until this point seemed unrealistic, this was beyond comprehension. The facts were slowly sinking into me, though a mental barrier clouded their true shape. I refused, no, denied the truth from taking shape. It couldn't really be.

"But why?" I whispered. "He was healthy, I only saw him a few weeks ago – you saw…" I turned to Vince and Bertie, sat beside me.

Several others hovered about: Kin, with a hopeless expression, Ruby, who offered to get her brother Ross, the counsellor, for she struggled to find the right words herself, and Sephy, sat cross-legged at my feet, holding my hand. Tina, and Vince's girlfriend, Melanie, showed up for support. Francesca Jackson, a Ranger in our year, loitered too, but only to see what the fuss was about.

"I know, I still can't believe it." Bertie shook his head, flipping a flame across his fingers as if it were a coin.

"Mum thinks maybe being away from Fate for so long made him ill… I don't know, it's just a guess, no reliable evidence behind it," Vince added, his voice much quieter than usual. "She got a letter this morning too, wrote to us straightaway. The Authority notifies all close relatives and friends – they have a sort of register, with everyone who has ever been introduced to Fate on it. But Mum's had a feeling for a while now…"

"What feeling?" I sobbed.

"Uh, it's hard to explain. A feeling – like Fate was letting her know that we're going to lose him. Perhaps in a dream—"

My thoughts muted Vince's voice then. Uncle Bill was in my dream recently. Tears rolled down my face and snot dripped from my nose. I wanted to scream. Did I know? Did that thing, *Fate*, that I wasn't even sure existed, slip it into my nightly consciousness, that Uncle Bill was dy— No, I refused the word – that he was unwell?

Bertie handed me a tissue. "I'm sure Bill knew too – he was good with Fate, like old pals. Fate wouldn't just take him without a bit of notice," he said, as if it was meant to comfort us.

Did Uncle Bill know he was… dying? The word sunk in, crushing my chest. I felt heavy, with bewilderment and grief, and at the same time numb, with incomprehension. Was he really ill? Was he ill with the same strange blood disease? Why didn't he seek treatment? If all of this was real, if being on Earth really made him ill, why didn't he come back to the otherworlds? Why did he move to Earth in the first place?

Why did he take me there with him?

My head spun, sucked into a vacuum of questions.

"… a Lilly-Anne?"

"What?" I snapped out of it, hearing my name.

It was Fabian La'dore, followed by Rupert Risefaith and Dean Strange. The first two were Kin's dorm mates.

"I said, there's a big bloke at the main gate, giving Sesame a headache, trying to get in. Says he has to see a Lilly-Anne." They filed in, surprised to find this peculiar scene in their usual evening spot. "Empyrean-looking fella at first glance, but not a native."

Without a second thought, I darted out of the room. Running down to the school gate, I could already make out his shape behind the twisted iron bars. He leant into the checkpoint window, easily at eye level with Sesame, clearly arguing with him. Then he spotted me and moved to stick his arms through the iron bars.

"Lilly!" Gabriel yelled as I sprinted towards the gate, pushing one wing open and falling straight into his arms. "I came as soon as Dad found out. I'm so sorry." He held me in a bear embrace, and I let him, burying my face into his chest. For a moment, everything felt fine.

Then the tears and snot started up again.

"I knew he was going to die, Gabriel, I knew. I mean, I didn't know, but I had a dream, and I could have done something, I could have helped him, could have stopped it somehow, but I didn't realise – and in the dream, he was only briefly there, and I—"

Gabriel smothered my face back into his chest to shut me up. "*Shh*, don't beat yourself up about it." Gabriel stroked my hair. "Nothing you could have done anyway, none of us could have. Dad had a dream too, he thought something might be up. But there's no cheating Fate, remember? She takes who she wants."

"Centaur's hoof! Is that little Gabe Hale I'm seeing?" Bertie's voice caught up with us before the twins did.

Gabriel quickly released me, leaving only a wet mark on his t-shirt where my face was pressed.

"I don't bloody believe it!" Bertie looked him up and down.

"I heard about your uncle, very sorry for your loss." Gabriel nodded to him.

"Thanks, we appreciate the kind words. And you… came out all this way to say so? Blimey." Vince measured Gabe suspiciously. "Thought we'd be seeing you around Sapphy's by now. Didn't you have a place reserved?"

"Yeah, well, things change," Gabriel dismissed, avoiding the subject. "Anyway, I'm here to ask Lilly if she'd like to go back to the Empyrean with me – just for a few rises, I mean," he smiled awkwardly. "Might help to take your mind off things."

Taken by surprise, I lacked a quick response. The twins swiftly filled in the conversation.

"The *Empyrean?* And what in the worlds are you doing in the Empyrean?" Bertie blurted out.

"I live there." Another one Gabriel wanted to avoid.

"*Phhwwhht*," Bertie whistled, "much has changed, then."

Stood there, it dawned on me what a normal person under such circumstances should do: when your parent (for that's what I suppose Uncle Bill was to me) dies, there are things to do, to sort, to comfort, while the other one still lives. I should be with Lynne.

"I should go home," I whispered.

"I really don't think that's a good idea," Gabriel said straightaway.

"I think you should take the offer, take a break, Lills," Vince said after a short pause.

"Empyrean invitations are pretty rare. Better take the offer while it's still there," Bertie added.

Their encouragement was a blessing; a sanction, to hide away from something I quickly realised I didn't want to do. I should go home, be with

Lynne. I should, but I really didn't want to. Not only did this mean facing up to the facts, for Bill's absence would be a stark validation of what I'd just come to learn, but also because I'd never been close with Lynne. She detested me, I knew; tolerated, but resented. I was an unwelcomed intrusion into Lynne's life, as far as she was concerned. Somehow now, the prospect of facing her alone in the absence of the only person who'd glued us together, made my guts tighten in fear.

"Okay, Empyrean," I finally decided. "I'll just need to grab some things, a jacket." Rushing out, I hadn't even grabbed a coat, and by now the chill was starting to bite.

"Uh…" Gabriel scratched his head, his lips pulled into a nervous line. "Actually, I kind of booked return tickets for the portal already – special request is a bit pricey, you see, so I bought a return for two straightaway, and it… it kind of opens in ten beats."

"Never mind all your gear and bring us back a souvenir!" Bertie called, already on his way back to school.

Vince waved goodbye, chucking in, "Come back earlier if you need."

Then, we were alone.

CHAPTER 9
LILLY-ANNE SKYROSE

Seizing the narrow alleys in brisk paces, we reached the terminal just in time. Gabriel handed over two crumpled tickets.

"Kah-a'miss, this way," the conductor nodded. "Opening now."

Gabriel pulled me along, stepping through the hazy, charged opening at the end of platform three. My stomach flipped, and we were on the other side.

We emerged out of the Kah-a'miss terminal, if it could be called that, for it was no more than a wooden shack, loosely held together with some nails. Gabriel kicked open the shabby door, unleashing the warmth of sunshine on our faces.

"Why is it still light?" I squinted. It was long past sundown in Loon's City, an early winter settling in.

"Suns are still up – they rise and set here, so we get the most of them."

Outside was very warm; the air was saturated with moisture so thick it felt like we almost ploughed through it.

"It's a bit of a walk back to Matriah's house, I'm afraid." Gabriel glanced to check my reaction.

"I don't mind," I reassured, and though 'a bit' turned out to be almost two hours, I didn't mind at all. It was perfect, to take it all in.

The Empyrean truly was a different world. As far as the eye could see, everything was covered with luscious hues of green: fuzzy mosses, knotted shrubbery, and ferns covered the rolling hills, giving way to darker shades of foliage deeper within the trees and sharper drops of valley cliffs, dotted with brilliant blues, reds, and pinks in bloom. Every now and then a bird squawked nearby, a glimpse of bright feathers as it fled. The forest was wild, ferally sublime compared to the straight rows of pine I saw in my recurring dreams, but just as serene. Trees with trunks the size of towers, firmly rooted in the ground, boughs extending to the sky, reigned over the valleys; others twisted among them, leaning, dancing, interwoven with lianas and roots like a tangle of bodies with limbs untraceable to each. It was magical, untouched, and I submerged myself in its allure so completely, becoming wholeheartedly enchanted, that I forgot, for a while, about the reason I was here.

"How's school, then? Slayed the dragon yet?" Gabriel searched for something to say.

"Many times, but its head keeps growing back," I said sarcastically.

Gabriel laughed, and his sincere laughter did the job, calming the whirl of grief that eddied up inside me.

"Stars, I wish I was at Sapphy's," he mused.

"Why don't you transfer over? You've still got a few years of school left, don't you?" I said, hoping to find out how old he was exactly. Besides, I wanted him to keep talking, to draw me into trivial conversation.

"A couple, yeah. But Dad would never let me – he doesn't like us going away. It's a miracle he let me fetch you."

"I can talk to him if you'd like, persuade him – or try, at least."

"Thanks," he found that funny too. "But it's not just that – it's the funds for tuition. We don't have those."

"Ah."

"And I'm not bright enough to try for the scholarship," he added, answering my thoughts. "I did have a place reserved though, once. Things were different when we lived on the Continent. Mum and Dad worked for the Authority, we could afford it. They were going to send me and Billie to Sapphy's." Gabriel pulled a leaf off a shrub we passed, grinding it between his fingers, trying to collect his thoughts. "But then Dad remarried, and we moved here. Had to buy our way into the clan – they don't just let you in without an offering. That's not how they phrase it, of course – they called it 'parting with your old ways'," he put on a mocking accent. "Empyreans don't use coins and currency internally, no sir. Only for dealings with the Continent. Anyhow, it's all collective here, so I've said goodbye to my tuition fees."

"And your mum? Can she not intervene?"

He looked at me kindly, the way a parent looks at a clueless child before explaining something touchy. "My mum's with Fate."

I took a while to process what that meant. "Oh God, Gabriel, I'm so sorry!"

"That's okay." The corners of his lips turned up mechanically. "Mum died many years ago. I was a kid, though just big enough to understand. It was the bombing," he continued, massacring another leaf. "After the Rachthawnian Murders, when the Senate quickly formed out of what was left of the Authority, Mum and Dad stuck around a bit in politics, trying to hold it all together. It was chaos then, across the worlds. They caught the murderers pretty soon, they were inconspicuous after all, but the poison had spread already. A lot of people were unhappy, they turned away from Fate, poisoned by Hate. There were attacks all around, especially on the Authority, but civilians too. And it was in one of those that Mum was killed. Dad was injured too."

I remembered Harry did walk with a cane.

"And you know what's worst?" Gabriel asked, tossing the leaf remains. "It was a side-swapper who did it."

"A who?"

"A side-swapper." He stopped to look me in the eyes. "They pretend to be good, converted back to Fate, having *strayed* the lawful ways." The voice I thought incapable of anger suddenly edged in latent rage. "But it's all a mask. They're poisoned. Once poisoned, they won't ever be redeemed. Underneath the lies, they're all white blood."

"I see," I said quietly.

"And they're everywhere! They say they've rooted them out, shipped the lot of them to Carcery, but don't trust that, oh no sir, don't trust! You need to keep your eyes open, Lilly, stay vigilant." Gabriel moved closer, taking my hands in his and holding them to his chest, stiff with tension. "Promise me," he leaned in, resting his chin on the top of my head, "that you'll never trust a side-swapper."

"I promise," I mumbled to his neck, unthinking and slightly overwhelmed.

"The Empyrean is much safer, of course." He released me, his tone again carefree. "Empyreans don't get involved, so side-swappers and lawbreakers have little business here. That's why Dad decided on the move. That's why he had me fetch you."

"Wait," I processed, still dazed by the closeness. "What? Why would Harry want me here?"

"To keep an eye on you for a little while. Come on." He pushed through an overgrown path.

"And why does he need to do that?" The answer seemed as clear as the trail before us.

"Well… I'm not meant to say, but Dad will probably moan about it anyway." He stomped on a bramble so I could pass.

"Gabriel," I stared at him, silently demanding answers.

"Aw all right, all right: he wants to make sure they don't get to you, like he thinks they got to Bill."

"Uncle Bill? Who got to Uncle Bill?"

"I don't know! Side-swappers!" He released the bramble and it hit his arm, swinging. "Like they got to us!"

"And what reason would they have to go after Bill?" I pushed, though I felt myself sucked back into the vacuum of questions circling like undefined dust in my head.

"These people don't need *reasons*, Lilly – they just destroy. They stand against everything that's good in these worlds, anything lawful. I told you Bill was in the queensguard, many moons ago – do the maths yourself." He pushed aside another limber branch.

Pieces of an awful puzzle fell together in my head. The floodgates released too, a roaring wave of misery gushing in to blight my pretend-ignorance. Uncle Bill was gone, he really was. And not only dead, but killed; murdered by past ghosts, ghosts he'd ran away form, ghosts who finally caught up with him.

"Hence Dad suggested you stay with us for now, just as a precaution. Plus, it really might help to take your mind off things. *And* you get to see me. So, here we are, it's a winner."

We emerged into a clearing. In the midst stood a small cottage and several outbuildings, cobbled together from various materials: wood mostly, bits of corrugated metal, and chipped stone. Resting on his cane, by the door stood Harry; in front of him was an imperious-looking woman, no hint of warmth on her stern face. Her features were markedly different to those of Harry and Gabe. She was highly ornamented too: metal trimming on her dress, greying hair roughly pinned with jewelled clips, and stacks of rings on each finger. Behind them, in the shadows of the door, lingered someone else.

"Geez, a whole welcome committee," Gabriel grumbled. "Bow your head a bit and wait for Matriah to speak."

That I did, and once we'd neared, an awfully long moment passed before she spoke.

"No Fate, in her," Matriah finally pronounced.

Suddenly petrified and not daring to look up, I felt her scrutinize me.

"Well, but no Hate either. Please, we've discussed this. Lilly is the daughter of my friend, so she is our friend, too." Harry tried his best to ease the tension. "Now, can we all come in?"

Matriah nodded. "We will eat."

Inside the cottage was cosy, modest, and sticky with humidity despite the glass-less windows. Heavy air was saturated with the various cooking smells from the corner stove, no draught to push it out. Drained by what I'd just learned, nauseated by the sultry space, and anxious not to break some protocol – *uh, a drink of water or I might throw up.*

And as though my thoughts were heard, water did appear, handed to me by a young girl, who I only guessed was Billie. A younger, rounder-faced, and freckled version of Gabriel's features, she was dressed in a homespun, tattered jumper and culottes. How she wore those in this heat I don't know. The only difference was the hair, for hers was ginger, though similarly frizzed and pulled into a ponytail.

The walls were lined with drying herbs, ornaments, and other things I could not name. Matriah picked a bunch of dried leaves, lit it with her Force, and paced around the table, the smoking bundle in hand, chanting as she did. Gabriel set the plates; Billie brought a pot of stew. I looked around, unsure of what to do with myself. Should I help? Should I sit? Smalltalk, conversation? From what I knew, the Empyrean was a world of rules, customs, and formalised conventions that should not be broken lest you mean offence.

"You can sit," Billie offered, without looking at me.

I pulled out a chair.

"Not here, that's Matriah's."

"Sorry," I mumbled, and chose another chair.

Dinner was a pretty silent affair. Harry asked how I liked the food, to which I politely replied that it was delicious. Billie protested at once, that I really thought it was too spicy, only to be kicked by Gabriel underneath the table. I tried to raise the topic of Uncle Bill, anxious to know what Harry had dreamt and why he suspected – I barely allowed the thought to keep myself together – that he'd been attacked, only to be sharply reminded by Matriah that the dead ought not to be discussed at dinner.

After that it was soon nightfall. The suns set almost instantly, smothering the small room in darkness. Harry and Matriah retired, bidding us goodnight; Gabriel went to light some candles while Billie washed up, and I sat awkwardly amidst their bustling.

"Where would you like to sleep?" Gabriel asked.

"Um," I looked around, counting the doors leading out of the main room. There were three, one for each bedroom, I presumed.

"You can take my bed," he offered, indicating me to follow.

Gabriel's room was compact. In the corner stood a dresser, drawers spitting out his clothes, above which was a shelf with a tarnished mirror, shaving brush, and folded razor. Opposite, on the floor, was a grass-stuffed mattress covered with a quilt.

"It's not much, but – well, there's none that's better, I'm afraid." He seemed embarrassed.

"No, that's great. Thank you, Gabe. Where will you sleep?"

"Here." He pointed at a skin-rug on the floor. The stunned look on my face made him laugh. "I'm joking – I'll take the kitchen bench."

"Oh no, Gabe, I can take the bench then—"

"No sir, no way. I know that much about hospitality not to let my guest have the crappy bench." He grinned the sincere, warm Gabriel-grin which washed away any traces of dinner's hostile reception I'd received. "See you tomorrow, up nice and early." He closed the door.

I scoped out the tiny room, investigating the material tokens of his character, slightly flushed by the fact he'd said *my* guest. So much can be said of a person through their possessions. Every corner was crammed with things Gabriel had collected: tools, spears and arrows, sports gear (or at least I guessed), rocks and driftwood placed in disarray. He was curious, it seemed, appreciative of natural forms and the outdoors, though his curiosity ended there, for not a single book was in sight.

The night was warm and humid, despite a drop in temperature. I decided to sleep in my underwear and vest, peeling off the clothing layers appropriate for the chill back home. *Home*, I caught myself. By this point, I already considered Loon's City to be home. That thought only sent another suffocating wave of grief to drown me. I should go *home*, I should be with Lynne. Uncle Bill was gone; murdered, perhaps. A flash-flood of pain crushed against my chest, unleashing bouts of tears, and then slowly faded out as I drained all of my emotions, only to come again when my mind remembered him. Finally, I was submerged. Exhausted, and with the quilt pulled over my head, I cried myself to sleep.

*

I dreamed of a domed room with chiselled walls that night, rough stone, darkness. The only source of light – a narrow beam seeping through an opening in the rounded ceiling – illuminated a stone altar in the middle, on which some flat object was placed. I knew it was a dream because Uncle Bill was there. He didn't seem to notice me. He wasn't as aged as I remembered him, the first signs of grey sneaking into his hair, no beard. A woman was also present, the hood of her black cloak concealing her face, exposing only long wisps of dark brown hair. Intently, she examined something on the altar. Bill looked lovingly at her, with such concern and devotion I didn't realise his face was capable of showing, for he never looked at Lynne that way. She caught him looking, and returned a smile, though that soon faded into worry. Bill opened his mouth to speak then, but instead of words I heard a knocking.

"Are you up yet?" The words didn't fit Bill's mouth.

I woke up just in time to find the door creak open. "Don't come in!" I jolted up. "I'm not dressed!"

"That's okay." Gabriel's head poked around the door. "Come see the sunrise."

"Gabriel, *don't!*" I pulled the quilt up to my chin.

"Hurry up, get dressed then, it's dawning already," he said, no intention to close the door.

I stared at him.

"Okay, fine, but hurry, sunrise doesn't last long." Gabriel withdrew, and I heard his back slump against the closed door.

I jumped out of bed and pulled my jeans on, one eye on the door.

"Take my t-shirt, there's a clean one on the chair," I heard.

"No thanks," I objected automatically, though I wished I'd been allowed to pack at least a few belongings. The Empyrean climate meant yesterday's clothes were far from fresh.

"Go *onnn.*" The door creaked open slightly, giving way as he released it from his weight. "We don't like smellies over here."

"Gabe—" I grabbed the t-shirt as the door creeped gradually more ajar. "Fine," I snapped, pulling it over my head just before he came in.

"Ready now? Let's go," he grinned.

Sunrise truly was breath-taking. A giant, fiery, crimson halo emerged behind clouds stretched thin on the horizon, swiftly passing upwards, where it seemed to slow a bit. A few other giant orbs accompanied, a dance of blazing giants burning hues of red and pink.

"Hmm, red suns mean it's gonna rain," Gabriel grumbled.

And rain it did, a gentle seeping that soon intensified, reaching a torrential downpour. Sat underneath an awning of a shed where Harry kept the firewood, we hoped to wait it out.

"Gabe!" We both turned at the direction of a voice. "Gabe, news!" Someone ran towards us through the downpour.

"It's Ryeleigh." Gabriel stood up, making room underneath the shelter.

"What's the news, Rye?" he called back.

Ryeleigh slid into the dry, nearly slipping on the mud. Water dripped from his black hair and down his face, his features easily recognisable as Empyrean.

"They accepted it! It's been passed!" Ryeleigh reached inside the leather pelt draped loosely over his boyish shoulders, his clothes thoroughly soaked through. "I got this from Catrina, who got it from Sarwell, and apparently Mychel gave it to Sar – well, you get the idea." Ryeleigh produced a damp copy of the *Seer*, holding it proudly up for us to see. "Catrina says that's what it reads!"

I cocked my head to read the caption, for Ryeleigh held the newspaper upside down. 'Breaking news for disposable wand investment' it read.

"Who's this?" Ryeleigh only now noticed I was present.

"A friend." Gabriel took the paper, turning it the right way up and over. And sure enough, in big, bold letters the caption stated: 'Technology Pass accepted'. "You better show Matriah – she'll go mad."

*

"*Sacrilege!*" The damp paper slapped against the table with the force of Matriah's fury.

We edged away from the various curses she'd already thrown about, standing by the walls, as far away as the little room allowed. Poor Ryeleigh bowed his head as humbly as he could, no longer excited to be the bearer of such news. Billie fiddled with the thumb-holes in her jumper, not there by design but rather worn through nervous use. Even Harry seemed to shy away.

"They will turn us into the unknowing! Poison us, they will!" she roared, each word accompanied by a jangle of her metal earrings. With each word, Gabriel also grew tenser. "Blasphemous! Profane! To insult her holiness the all-knowing mother, Fate - bless us with your favour - in this way, to use her powers so carelessly! Had our ancestors not been so *weak*, had they resisted Rachthaw's rule, no such decisions of the Senate would damn us now!"

"More like if *you* were strong enough, you'd represent the clan in Senate and actually have some say," Gabriel muttered.

She heard. "I have no business in that Continental snake pit!" Matriah bellowed, picking up the *Seer* and aiming it at Gabriel's head.

He was quick to duck; it splatted on the wall behind him.

"Well, I think it's a good thing – the Technology Pass. Equipment will run on Force, and Force is Fate's gift to us, isn't it? It's our tool, our means of thriving – it's only natural that we should progress, keep up, make use of all the means available!" Gabe grew confident, irate. "And anyhow, electricity," Matriah shuddered at the word, "is similar to Force. Tell her, Lilly, tell her it's not bad!"

I opened my mouth in horror at having been dragged into this, but before any words could come out, Matriah erupted into flames – quite literally. Every inch of her burned white, fervent flames of fury.

"Out, boy! Get out!" she roared.

Gabriel didn't wait around, sprinting out the door, myself and Ryeleigh after him, narrowly escaping fiery gusts of Force she chucked in our direction. They landed in the yard, fighting against the rain.

Stomping off towards the outbuildings, Gabriel lashed out at an overflowing water butt along the way. "Ha! She'll eat you alive in there, Lilly!" he bawled when he saw us following.

I wondered how literally he meant it.

"That's *real* Empyrean hospitality for you!" he yelled specifically towards the house. "No offence, Ryeleigh," he added, now more calmly as we settled a safe distance from the house.

"Oh, none taken, Gabe. I'm quite excited about this myself," Ryeleigh said enthusiastically. "I heard there are these things called teller-phones, where you can talk to people at a distance. Not in dreams, but in real time, like a portal – but for voice. And automobiles, like bears to ride on but faster and with spare parts!" Ryeleigh clearly looked up to his friend, keen to agree with whatever was Gabe's opinion. "I heard from Catrina that Mychel knows someone," he lowered his voice, "who's already got one – Troby of Viak'mul, his name is, he has an automobile. I'm hoping to go down and see it. Just the electricity business scares me a bit – what if there's still some left in those devices?"

"Well, you shouldn't be scared of electricity, no sir. It's all blown out of proportion, anyhow. Designed to spur contempt for the *unknowing*, their *false gods* – what a load of tosh! The unknowing *know* their stuff, let me tell you, sir. It's similar to Force really. Tell him Lilly," Gabriel nodded at me. "Lilly lived on Earth."

"*On Earth?*" Ryeleigh exclaimed. "So you know about electricity? Can you channel it, like we channel Force?"

"Uh, I guess so. It can travel through you – but you'd be electrocuted." That word made no sense to them, so I explained. "It would hurt to channel it."

"So it *is* bad!" Horror struck Ryeleigh's innocent expression.

"No! No, you just need to learn to use it safely," I backpedalled.

"That's beside the point," Gabriel weighed in, taking a penknife to sharpen up a stick. "It's just the devices we will use, they'll be empty shells, we'll run them on Force, make them our own. No electricity involved."

Ryeleigh nodded, though he appeared not to fully understand. "Anyway, I got to dash. Need to catch some dinner. Want to join the hunt, Gabe?"

"Not today, my friend." Gabriel handed over the unfinished wooden spear.

"Next time, then." Ryeleigh turned to me. "Nice to meet you, Lilly of Earth."

"Does Matriah always take to news so lightly?" I asked, as Ryeleigh's shape faded among the foliage.

Gabriel let out a full breath, appalled. "You heard her – it's blasphemy. The old Empyreans, they think running technology on Force will somehow spoil the sacredness of it, of Fate's gift, turn it into Hate maybe, or worse: electricity. That it'll make us forget our ways, like on Earth." He picked up a new stick, drawing mindless patterns in the mud. "But that's just Empyreans, stuck in their old ways. They'd have a greater say in the worlds, the Senate, if they didn't focus solely on being bitter about the Rachthaws and the Continent getting a better deal with Fate than they did. They had their own ways with Fate, you know – thousands of years ago, but then the Rachthaws subjugated them, the clans, and persuaded them that the Rachthawnian way was better. And they're still bitter about it!"

He paused, though I sensed he was working up to release more thoughts which normally didn't have a verbal outlet.

"The Empyrean Federation could be something if it wasn't purposefully trying to hold itself back. There are resources here, oh sir, plenty of! The Fed. Could get rich on trade. Some forward-thinking clans, they've begun to mine. They get involved in the Senate, they have a say, trade in heads. But not Kah-a'miss, no sir. Matriah – she's a clan elder, all this in Kah-a'miss falls under her jurisdiction. Not a single tree gets cut down without her knowing. But she won't go to the Senate, no sir – most of the Empyrean seats are empty there. Only the ones who permit mining get involved." He chucked the stick into the bush, absent-minded with frustration.

Maybe I'd got the wrong impression of him yesterday, reading through the things he had collected in his room. Maybe Gabriel was interested in the wider picture – an interworldly one, in fact – beyond outdoor fun and games.

"Perhaps the Empyrean could regain its sovereignty now that the Rachthaws aren't around – I mean, maybe the clans are able to govern themselves?" I tried.

"Oh, they're able to govern themselves all right," Gabriel half laughed. "That's the problem. The Authority doesn't intervene here enough. And the clans, they aren't exactly begging for the Authority's attention. But you see, the interworld has changed too much. You're either with the Authority, or you're nothing. That's the times. And the clans, they don't keep up with the times, bar a few. Stars! They'd have a greater say in the interworld if they actually learned to read!" Gabriel sat down with a *humph*. "You saw poor Ryeleigh there, he's a good kid and all, but he's illiterate! They won't teach them to read, say it's not needed – *Continental tricks*," he said in a mocking accent. "Fate was kind and Mum taught me to read and write. You know, they didn't even have proper schools here until a few generations ago – they'd pass down stories at home, is all. Now they've got these measly things where you're taught some Force control, a few basic spells, and tradition – oh yes sir, lots of tradition. But it's not worth comparing to something like a thousand-year-old Sapphy's…"

It was strange to see Gabriel so resentful. The Empyrean maybe kept him safe, but it clearly touched a raw nerve. Were the clans not merely demanding their own rights?

"Anyway, I think it's a good thing – the Technology Pass – and moving forward, generally. Automobiles – we could use them, there's not many portal terminals here, and now that spacetime travel is monitored and you can't just open up a portal as and when you wish, travel here is pretty difficult. It's a huge land…" he trailed off. "Have you used one?"

"Yes, yes I've used an automobile."

"What's it like to travel on one?"

"*In* one. You have to learn to drive it."

"There are commands?" he enquired.

I shook my head.

"Spells?"

"No, there's a steering wheel and gears. We pass a test to drive. They can be dangerous, many people are killed in crashes every year."

"People are killed by spells and Hate too." Gabriel leaned back on a tree, more relaxed now.

"Yes, but road crashes are accidents, careless driving."

"There are no accidents, everything is fated," he looked at me. "Besides, Fate would keep us safe when driving. Or not – if it's our time to pass."

Not keen on the turn our conversation was taking and feeling a subtle wave of pain lap over my insides, I steered the subject. "We call them cars, actually."

"*Carrrs*," Gabriel purred, pleased. "I'd like one. But there's no way Matriah's letting me get *carrs*. They're big, I heard, too big to hide," he mused, a mischievous look across his face.

"You could try a motorbike – they're smaller," I suggested.

"Mo-ta-bike. That could work." And it was back, the Gabriel-grin that ameliorated everything. "Want to see the clan lands?" he suddenly perked up.

*

The rain subsided, then picked up as we hiked around. I doubt we ventured far – as far as it was reasonably possible to walk – and although my hopeless sense of direction didn't help, Gabriel knew well when to turn back. Crossing meadows, jungle forests, pastures, and streams (I refused the rope bridges, slung over wild and rapid rivers), the day passed pleasantly. We were in good spirits, all grievances of this morning passed, soaked by the rain, dried by the warming suns, and then soaked again.

Gabriel showed me around the various outbuildings once we returned; not because there was much to see, but I guessed he didn't want to go back into the main house.

"And this is Dad's workshop. Oh!" He opened the door, only to see

Harry cleaning up some tools. "Hi, Dad," he said, a tad embarrassed.

"Hi, kids, did you have a good time?" Harry asked amiably, then looked over our drenched state and frowned. "Gabe, go fetch some towels."

Gabriel went, leaving me with Harry. I took a deep breath. This was my chance. A chance to ask Harry about what he'd dreamt, about Uncle Bill, about his fears of lawbreakers and side-swappers. And as silly as the latter label seemed to sound, Gabe had done a good job of instilling a fear of them in me. I needed to know why Harry thought Bill had been mur— attacked.

"Can I ask you something, Harry?" I began, but the words then dried up in my mouth.

"Sure, shoot, kid," he said, looking at me only when no questions followed. "What d'you want to know?"

I cleared my throat, picking up a metal ingot off the worktop, only to put it straight back, realising it wasn't mine to handle. Normally, I would be shy, mannerly, restrained; Gabriel's carefree attitude had clearly rubbed off on me. Yet I still couldn't voice the M-word. A different thought escaped my mouth.

"Was Bill with anyone? You know, before he moved to Earth… before Lynne," I said, my face slowly turning red.

Harry laughed. "Well, that's not the question I expected. No, not as far as I'm aware. And I'd like to think I knew him well. Why'd you ask?"

I shook my head. "No reason, just want to understand him, I suppose." *Understand my dream, if dreams were meaningful.*

"No, Bill was only devoted to one person, and that was the queen. Took his role extremely seriously. The queensguard, they weren't allowed relationships, you see, celibate." Harry hobbled over to sit opposite me, indicating that I take the other stool. "We used to laugh about it – why would anyone make *that* choice? But it was a calling, fated. That's why none of us could believe he quit, just upped and left. Just before the Murders too."

"Bill left just before the Murders? You don't think he was… involved…

somehow?"

Harry looked at me with an expression that suggested I was mad to even hint at such an accusation.

"Not the man I knew. He resigned, said it got too much for him. But that's a big, fat lie, if you ask me," Harry mused, and a twisted grin suggested he relived the astonishment felt then. "I suspected Bill was on some secret mission for the queen. Something he couldn't even share with us. He disappeared, and the next thing I knew, Dianne said he'd moved to Earth, and *then,* next I hear, there's you. Out of the blue. I thought if any of our shared acquaintances had given up their child, I'd hear of it. But it was nobody that we knew. I was going to press the old bugger about it, actually, in Loon's City. After all these years, I hoped he'd finally say."

"And did you?"

"Oh yes, I did."

Harry's weathered face pulled into a smile, and I felt something heavy envelop my shoulders. Gabriel draped a towel over me. I wrapped it around myself, instinctively.

"But he wouldn't say a word."

"So you don't know who my parents were?"

Harry shook his head. "Not a clue."

CHAPTER 10
BEATRICE GOLDTEAR

"And as for homework, there's a worksheet for you to complete, but you'll need to partner up for this one." Professor Sprause wiped her dirty hands down her lab coat as she spoke. "Quickly now, find a partner, don't fuss over it."

"Are you free, Bea?" one of my girlfriends asked across the room.

I rummaged in my bag strategically, long enough for her to decide I didn't hear. Carefully packing up my things at the end of class, I didn't look up lest I catch anyone else's eye. There was only one pair of eyes I wanted to notice me, but of course, he wasn't looking.

"All right then, everyone partnered up? I'll see you all for class next set," Sprause concluded, and we were dismissed for lunch.

"I don't have a partner still, professor," I timed to say just as everyone was leaving.

"Oh, Beatrice. Are we odd?" She counted students under her breath. "Even number, who else doesn't have a partner?" Sprause scanned the room. "Mr Grim?" she caught him just as he approached the door.

My heart pounded.

"No, I don't have a partner, professor." Mate slowly turned back, the rare sound of his musical voice a sweetness to my ears.

Mate Grim. Mathaniel, it turns out; Mate for short.

"Very well then, there you go. Work together."

His dark eyes dashed to meet mine briefly, and I swear I saw his jaw tighten. He turned on his heel and promptly left. My girlfriends loitered, feeling sorry for me already. I dismissed them with a wave and tried my best to force down a grin. I made excuses to return library books.

"I'll see you all after lunch," I reassured.

I hurried past the library, however, to the place where I knew he spent his lunchtimes. And sure enough, he was there, sat alone in the great hall. The place was near-deserted, as everyone else crowded in the more informal buttery. I took a deep breath. We'd have to talk at one point, he couldn't run from me forever. I made my way over.

"Hello," I waited to be acknowledged, but he continued to chew unapologetically, eyes on his food. "I'm Beatrice—"

"I know who you are." Mate sat up, piercing his gaze through my soul. "Why did you do that?"

"Do what?" I felt the hairs on my arms rise.

"Ignore your friend, wait until everyone else had partnered up, and then bring it to the teacher's attention just before I walked out." Not a hint of the sweetness left, Mate's voice was sharp, just as his observances.

We measured each other across the table, him sat and me standing awkwardly on the other side.

"I didn't... it was a... coincidence," I finally managed.

"I'm not stupid." Mate released me from his gaze, scrunched up a napkin, and threw it into a plate of barely-touched food. Without another word, he got up and left.

"Wait!" I hurried after him. "Wait, what about the worksheet?"

"What about it?" He walked fast, purposefully.

"How would you like to do it?"

"Here's what we'll do." He stopped abruptly, turning back on me. The purple shadows under his dark eyes seemed even more so today, defining the contours of the stern, chiselled face. "You'll tell Sprause that you found me unmanageable, and that you'd like to work by yourself. You're clever enough, it shouldn't be a problem."

"What? No – but I want to help!"

"I don't need your help," I heard as he walked off, indifferent.

"Okay, fine, I want to work with you." I chased after him again, nearly dropping a few textbooks.

"No, you don't."

"Yes, I do. Stars, I don't have bad intentions. Are you honestly unable to trust someone, just for once?"

"Whatever your intentions, you'd better just leave now."

"*Fine*," I fumed.

For two years, I'd imagined having his attention. The mysterious Mathaniel Grim. In a desperate attempt, I even borrowed fancy earrings from my little sister, thinking that would make him notice me. Soon enough I realised he cared not for material tokens and shiny things. Sometimes I imagined us exchanging a few words, rehearsed what I'd say, something worthy of captivating him. I imagined us as friends, whole dialogues in my head. Not one ended up like this.

"I'll just do the work and hand it in on your behalf!" I fumed.

That seemed to throw him off. Mate stopped, pulling his brows together underneath the slick, brown locks stuck to his forehead. He sucked his cheeks in, thinking.

"Why would you do that for me?"

"Why wouldn't I?" I whispered, hooked on his every move.

Spacetime stood still for a moment then, as he held me in his stupefying gaze, and I looked up to him, transfixed, unable to help myself.

"The worksheet then?" he finally asked.

"What?" All of that escaped my mind.

"Shall we get on with it?" He unlocked a door, and I realised I'd followed him into the depths of Champion Hall, past the common room and underground, to his dormitory. "After you," he pushed the door open.

The room was well-furnished, spacious, and very neat. So neat, in fact, one would never think it was shared by two teenage boys, for I knew Mate lived with his brother. The main door led to a sitting area – a spacious parlour with a sofa and fireplace. Either side, doors led to bedrooms, I presumed. It was one of the nicest, biggest dorms in the hall – as should have been expected, really. Alastair Grim wouldn't settle for less than the best.

Mate followed me inside, indicating the sofa and lighting the fire with a snap of his fingers. His hands were covered with fresh burns, cuts, scabs – a testimony to his duelling prowess. Many times have he and Alastair carried the Champion team to victory. I knew, I attended every match. *Why don't you heal those?* I yearned to ask. *Let me heal them for you.*

Instead, I sat down on the sofa. Mate sat at the other end, as far away as the space allowed. We sat in silence, until I remembered the reason I was here.

"For the worksheet, then." I pulled it out of my bag, carefully placing it between us, hesitant as to what was too close for me to reach near him.

Mate looked straight ahead, perhaps questioning his decision to let me in.

"We're looking at precious substances, and how they react when mixed with various kinds of dark matter."

He didn't move, so I continued.

"For question number one, I think the answer is, substance X will bind to Y, attaching permanently, irrevocably."

"I think you're wrong," he finally said, still avoiding looking at me now that we were inside, alone.

"Oh." I flipped through my notebook. "I'm pretty sure that's right? If substance X is—"

"I think you're wrong to be here with me." Mate turned to face me, and I felt myself sink into the sofa. "What would your father say if he knew that you were here, willingly spending time with me," he paused, his voice a sweet melody again, "a side-swapper? What would he say?"

So it was true then.

"You'd have to give up your summer internship, if he lets you off easy. If not, you'd be disowned."

"I don't care," I'm not sure I said out loud.

He was right, I wasn't being wise. But if there was a turning point, I'd passed it a long time ago. There was something about him, something that perhaps Mathaniel was not consciously aware of. It drew me in so forcefully, that the inner barriers of self-preservation, the hierarchical walls built by the Authority, collapsed.

"I'm not very good at this," Mate said softly, reaching for the worksheet, reaching towards me, so much so that from half a foot away, I almost felt his touch on my skin.

"That… that's fine, we can take it slow. I mean, I'm not experienced either. It's just… I just – I just want to know you," I stumbled over my words. The inscrutable complexity that was the person behind the eyes that stared at me now upended everything I ever was, renewed me.

His dark eyes focused on mine, as he digested what I'd said. "I meant alchemy," he clarified.

"Oh," was all I could return.

"But we can try, I suppose," he said, delving into the ambiguity.

CHAPTER II
LILLY-ANNE SKYROSE

I kept myself occupied, and homework to occupy my mind was plenty. Not just to stop myself from noticing how everyone (okay, *most people*) thought I was an Earthly freak, but to stop myself from thinking about Uncle Bill. It wasn't just his absence, which I somehow still refused to see as permanent, that bothered me. Each new wave of pain that washed over me deposited a sheet of silt: yet more unanswered – unanswerable – questions layered up inside. Who really was the man I knew as Uncle Bill? William Skyrose of the queensguard, who swore and broke an oath to protect the queen; William Skyrose, who chose the unimaginable it seemed, by relocating to Earth. And Uncle Bill, who took me from my parents in the otherworlds, and brought me with. I had previously asked about my parents, of course, I wasn't so immune to questioning. But conversations always turned sour when I tried, especially with Lynne around. Now it seemed the answers had disappeared forever.

The dubious silt of secrets was speckled with guilt too. What kind of person was I? I should be with Lynne. There were arrangements to make, surely, grieving to live through together. Part of me wanted to go back to Cley just to check he wasn't really there; that part of me which, being so far removed from everything… *geographically*… refused to accept the facts.

Geographically isn't the right word, and indeed, there are no good words to describe the otherworlds in Earthly terms. *Otherworlds* is my word, too. Spelled together in my head, I coined it to describe everything other than what I thus far knew. I made the other worlds mine that way.

I should be with Lynne. But even if I did go and visit, I wouldn't plan to stay. And if I didn't plan to stay, I would need to know how to return, request a special portal opening, and buy a ticket, especially on the Earthly side. I had no clue how to do that. So I reasoned with myself, the practicalities of it all outweighing the righteous call in my moral bargain. Still, all that was beside the point – I simply didn't want to do it.

I didn't want to face Lynne. Despite my good intentions, I frankly feared how she would react. Ever since the rudimentary payphone was put up in Sapphy's, I queued up to phone her regularly. Watching groups of students sniggering at the receiver, surrendering fingers, even heads to phone the few numbers that by now existed across the otherworlds, I debated with myself, mostly abandoning the cause by the time it came to my turn at the receiver.

Once, I convinced myself to dial.

"Who and which location would you like to connect to?" asked the fairy operator.

I gave her Lynne's name and our farmhouse number.

"*Where?*" came the reply.

"In Norfolk… on Earth."

"Listen, hun, I've honestly had enough with you kids trying to play tricks on me. I can connect you to someone on the Continent, but at this time, I can't even guarantee they'll be up to take the call."

There was no point trying to convince the operator that my intentions were legitimate. Thus, being the coward that I am, and careful so as not to disclose any information unsuitable for an unknowing, I wrote letters instead. I doubted a single one of them reached Lynne's Earthly address, as pixie post didn't seem to regularly deliver into the UK. At least I felt a better person for it.

Soon I was running out of things to say. So I struck another bargain with myself: each time I wrote to Gabriel, I would write to Lynne too. A pleasure for a pain, I forced myself to do the righteous thing.

"Actually write back to me this time, will you?" was the last thing Gabriel said to me, as I departed Kah-a'miss. Feigned irritation in his voice, he forced down a playful grin.

Turns out the Authority's notice of Bill's death was not the only post I'd missed in the first half of the semester. Back in Loon's City, I scribbled an apology to Gabriel straightaway, starting a string of regular correspondence.

Gabriel always wrote back promptly, a blessing and a curse. We bonded over being outcasts, each in a place we didn't quite belong. We shared absurdities, the highs of boring, daily life, reassured each other we weren't the crazy ones at all. The level of sincerity was unsettling at first, but he started it, and I couldn't help but go along with it. Behind his stories, no matter how mundane, I could almost feel the beauty of Empyrean lands, the warmth of the Gabriel-grin, and determination, the 'Oh yes sir' determination to improve in his every spelling mistake. He crossed the line sometimes, I thought, with teasing. So I accused him of being immature, and he retorted that I must have lost my sense of humour on a hike. I caught myself – not once – realising that Gabriel's letters were the highlight of my day.

Ever since I returned from the Empyrean, the semester dragged a bit. My reputation grew, not least thanks to the Technology Pass, which although provoking no outbursts to match Matriah's, remained controversial. Professor Meagles took the news as a cue to start the *Island Understanding* module early, and soon enough I kicked myself for thinking he was nice.

"And that is why the Earthen false god is inferior to Force," Meagles concluded, smug, leaning on his desk.

The reason given? Microwaves. They produced heat – like the burning of Force – but needed to be plugged into the mains to work. Without a physical connection to the *false god*, microwaves couldn't function, unlike

Force of course, which needed no physical connection to Fate, and could be spontaneously produced at the hands of any individual *inducted* (I laughed privately at the choice of words) into Force control.

*

One day in the lower library, where quiet talking was permitted, we sat around a table, our noses buried deep in *Proper Use of Magic: Pragmatics Vol. One* and a worksheet on domestic spells.

"So if…" Kin frowned, then sighed, seemingly defeated by his own question that he tried to ask. "If I have a plate to wash up, and there's also a bowl in the sink that I don't want to wash, how do I distinguish between them in the spell?" he tried again, slowly, checking the sense of every word.

"Which question are you on?" Rupert leaned over, frowning too.

"Sink scenario, number two."

"Well, it'd be the roundness that distinguishes them," Rupert said triumphantly, and Kin nodded.

Like all types of magic, pragmatic spells were mental formulae. Aside from the wand flick, the resemblance to maths was uncanny. My talent for spells was similarly comparable; maths had never been my forte. In spells, instead of numbers, syllables were joined together, divided, multiplied, or subtracted with precise effect. Each spell was unique, tailored to the actor, recipient, distance, intent, sometimes I thought even time of day.

"Never use spells during a full moon, for they will backfire," Professor Flashmight repeated over and over again in every class.

Ruby cleared her throat, and we all looked at her. "You'll want to multiply the relative flatness as a key component of your spell."

She was unwilling to draw attention, but unable to stop herself. Sometimes I thought she was physically in pain, listening to us butcher what came so naturally to her.

120

"The plate is flatter, while the plate and bowl are both… round."

"Oh! Yes, of course." Kin scribbled down the answer before he could forget. "Thanks, Rubes."

Ruby's face then turned the colour of her name, like it did every time Kin spoke to her, and especially when he called her Rubes. He'd picked that nickname up from me.

There were two ways to succeed in spells: memorise the lot (impossible) or learn the patterns of the formulae. Ruby seemed to have cracked the latter, quickly grasping the mysterious grammar.

Truth be told, the idea of putting meaningless syllables together in your head, coupled with the waving of a stick, was silly and theatrical to me. To think it could be consequential… Perhaps magic was like Force: you had to really believe it for it to happen. Perhaps that's why Force wasn't happening to me: I wasn't so convinced about the whole Fate business. That's also why, when one evening last week I reversed the order of a packing spell and *whooshed* my wand around aimlessly pointing it at Ruby's bed, I thought nothing of it. My ignorance shattered with a loud *poof* as the pillowcase ripped open, exploding into a million feathers covering the room.

"Thanks for that," Ruby remarked with a grim smile, and with a flick of her recycled wand, easily put the damage back together.

Rupert and Ruby then began a fierce discussion, each voice controlled to a low hiss permissible in the library, about the specificities of spells. The plate was green and chipped in the scenario, and it was best to involve this in the formula. Over-scrupulousness was a good habit to get into, Ruby insisted, despite here being unnecessary. It's just more work, and such details were only needed when the spell recipient was *really* undistinguishable from others nearby, Rupert dismissed.

Rupert Risefaith was a Ranger in our year. He was self-assured and buoyant, usually with little substance to back up his expertise, except a fair amount of appetite to confirm his plump appearance. In the bastion, Rupert and Kin lived with Fabian La'dore, who was with us in the library. Fabian was friendly and his temper rather muted, thus he was much less tiresome than Rupert. Fabian's features were recognisably Empyrean. Francesca, who apparently knew everything about everyone, later confirmed that Fabian's dad was indeed an Empyrean banker, moving to the Continent to secure his children's schooling. Kin, Fabian, and I listened to the debate intently, and I was glad not to be the only one whose brain struggled to keep up.

"Good morning, Kindegory."

We all jumped at the voice that cut into the dispute. Damsel stood by with her entourage of friends, all dressed in Champion red.

"I hope you're not bothering yourself with *domestic* spells. It's not like you'll ever need to use them."

"It's afternoon," Ruby muttered gloomily.

Kin tucked a strand of limp hair behind his ear, dislodging the glasses from his nose. He searched desperately for some response to make her go away, but his wit – naturally weak at best – failed him.

"Anyway, I have an invitation for you." Damsel handed him an envelope. "Only for the select few. You're invited. See you there."

"Thanks," was all that Kin said, looking like he wished he was invisible.

Damsel turned and left, not without throwing, "Hope you've packed your bags, Earthling," in my direction.

Kin quickly stuffed the ridiculously decorated –perfumed, even – envelope between random pages of his textbook.

*

After the events of Force control that afternoon, I considered taking Damsel's advice to pack up and leave quite seriously. Most of us were still hopeless when it came to sparking the white flames. Not everyone was gifted with Force, Professor Fellblue reassured, but for me the doubt was deeper. Although I'd witnessed others do it, I could not imagine ever doing it myself. Be it little playful flames handled out of boredom or to brag, or big gusts of fire like Matriah's, channelling Force was to me a circus trick – amazing, magical, and beyond something I could ever do. Often, we went to watch Vincent's duel practice, for he was captain of the Ranger team. Thanks to Kin, we spent hours on the grassy pitch, watching opponents hurl fire orbs at the defender strategically, while the latter tried their best to deflect those from the target board behind their back; the rest of the defending team scattered on the pitch to put out the diverted shots – all with their bare hands.

It was surreal, to think all this started here, in this class. It was also pointless (I began to side with Ruby on this one) that all this effort into channelling Force went into a game. Professor Fellblue disagreed, emphasising that in Force control we learned to be in touch with Fate, to be intuitive. This was the prerequisite to Force, and it was this prerequisite that mattered.

Professor Fellblue had us meditate again, though this time he insisted we lie down on the floor. Stunned looks and awkward grunts echoed in the classroom. The only eager student, Sephy, was at once stretched out across the floor, arms and legs moving to make dust-angels on the wood. Everyone else followed more or less unwillingly.

"Close your eyes now, relax everyone," Professor Fellblue's calming voice sounded as we settled. "Open up your mind, your heart, feel Fate inside your veins, feel her talking to you, listen to her."

That was the whole problem: I couldn't hear Fate. Anyhow, I didn't know what I was listening out for. I couldn't imagine myself handling Force because I lacked the prerequisite: faith in Fate. Fate was all-important in the otherworlds, I'd grasped that much. Everyone obsessed about it. It was supposedly an energy that directed your entire life. If you did as it pleased, if you were a good servant, it would tell you what it had in store for you through dreams. It would also let you materialise itself as Force – a small bonus, it would seem. If you broke the laws, this displeased Fate, and the Authority banished you to Carcery on Fate's behalf. All that was well and good, but how the hell was I supposed to keep the laws, if Unbreakable Law one was doing what Fate wanted me to do? Or at least *not* doing something that conflicted with Fate's plans for me. And to know what Fate had planned for me, I would have to hear it. Or *feel* it, somehow. The problem? I didn't.

I wondered if anyone could tell. Up till now, I'd sort of gone along with things, bluffed my way through the otherworlds, assured by Uncle Bill that it is here, rather than on Earth, that I belonged. Some people treated me suspiciously; others, like Damsel, took every opportunity to point out that I was an Earthly spy among their midst. If Fate was real, I just hoped I wasn't breaking any laws. An ignorant delinquent, me.

If Fate was real, did Uncle Bill fall ill due to being away from it? Or was Harry Hale right in thinking something far worse happened?

"Open up your mind, feel Fate within your heart, feel her strength in you," Professor Fellblue's soothing voice continued, interrupting my bleak thoughts.

Typically in Force control, I fought against sleep, meditation and boredom the perfect foundations for a nap. Lying down was even harder, and my eyelids fell heavy, my body going numb and still. It was an overwhelming feeling, the verge before an onset of an intense dream. I felt the blood slow inside my veins, limbs numb as if already asleep, so much so that to move them would require conscious effort to awake them. Yet with my mind still active, ideas racing through my brain, seeping in from the unconscious, I drifted into the dreamy borderlands.

Then suddenly, I was falling.

In an instant, I felt my body plunge, as if plummeting through air, dropping, sinking. I sunk into the floor.

I woke with a huge jerk and a slight scream, breaking the silence of the class. Everyone stared at me, confused or alarmed, myself included, for I could not explain what just happened to me. I *felt* my body falling. Then as soon as I established I was fine, I was terribly embarrassed because they all stared at me. I wished I could *really* sink then, sink and disappear.

I'm fairly certain that it was a dream; one of those dreams experienced bodily, where you physically feel your body fall in a terrifying instant of a sensation running through the flesh. It lasts a second, then your heart jerks you awake.

"All right, everyone, I think that's enough meditating for today," Professor Fellblue smiled as he dismissed class.

Looking at my watch, I was surprised to find the hour had nearly passed. We scrambled to our feet and grabbed our bags. Whispers were exchanged about what had just occurred. Earthling freak strikes again.

"Lilly, may I have a word, please?" Professor Fellblue said just as I was leaving.

I hung back awkwardly. Fellblue sat behind his heavy desk, the only usable piece of furniture in the room. All the other tables and chairs were still stacked up against the walls.

"What happened?" he asked, though his expression remained friendly. He wore long, patterned robes, blue-green jacquard this time.

"I'm sorry, professor, I don't know. I uh… I think I fell asleep. It won't happen again," I apologised, anticipating trouble.

"Asleep? Well, that's okay. At least you weren't snoring, unlike Mr Risefaith," Professor Fellblue smiled. "What did you dream about?"

"Uh… I dreamt that I was falling, like *really* falling. I could feel my body…" I shook my head trying to describe the feeling. "I could feel my stomach squeeze and the air rush past, like I was falling from a height. Sinking, actually. I felt myself sink into the floor."

"Interesting," Fellblue nodded, more to himself than to agree with me.

"And why do you think that is?"

"Uh… I don't know, really."

"And if you were to take a guess?"

"I'd guess it was my blood, then." That seemed to shock him, as he grasped his hat. "I mean, usually before I fall asleep, I know I'll have an intense dream because my limbs feel so numb – almost like my blood slows, and my arms and legs – they fall asleep. But my mind is still so active, I feel detached from myself, from my body. And I wonder if it's just my blood disease."

"Well, Fate be kind! Blood diseases are very serious, Lilly-Anne!" Fellblue got up and began pacing by his desk. "Are you sure?"

"No, I mean, it's just what the doctors said. There was something skewed about my blood tests. It wasn't serious – it's just what I am, it seems." I fidgeted with the notebook in my hands, rolling the corners between my thumb and forefinger.

"Hmmm…" Fellblue looked lost in thought. "Perhaps the Earthly doctors just couldn't see Fate in your blood."

"Really? You think there's Fate in my blood?"

"Yes, blood is the conduit of Fate, and Fate has a grasp over all of us."

"So you think it's not strange that I was… summoned… back from Earth?"

"No, of course not. Everything is fated, in Fate's hands. If you're here, it's because she wanted you back. I trust that you originated in our worlds. Earth was temporary. We are glad to have you back."

The way Professor Fellblue spoke seemed almost like he knew me well, despite the fact we had never spoken before in depth. My reputation as the Earthling was clearly widespread. Unlike everyone else, however, it didn't seem to bother him. In fact, he seemed determined to allow my presence in the otherworlds, to induct me in their ways.

"Indeed, I would hazard a guess that your dream of falling, sinking, was

Fate calling you," he continued. "You mustn't resist. You've been away for so long, Fate is asking to be let back in." He paused. "Do you know the building well?" he suddenly asked.

"Pardon?" I stumbled, perplexed.

"The layout of the school, do you know it well?" Fellblue clarified.

I shook my head.

"Do you know what's directly underneath this classroom?" he asked, then continued without waiting for my answer. "It's the chantry. It's the oldest part of the building. Built by the Rachthaws themselves, when they inaugurated the school. They consecrated it with Fate's blessing, so we could teach students about Fate's ways."

"I see." I pressed the edges of my notebook between my fingertips, disfiguring them beyond repair.

"Fate is present there, materially." He paused, reaching to check a reference in a book lying open on his desk. "The chantry has a hearth – a 'socket' in Earthly terms, I suppose. You can plug yourself into Fate directly there. I heard that's how electricity works. Perhaps a bad comparison. Perhaps it's better to call it a shrine? Anyhow," Fellblue took off his hat, "I think Fate was calling you, in your dream. You were sinking because Fate pulled you in. Dreams are important, Lilly-Anne. It's how Fate communicates."

*

"What do you think is in that envelope?" Ruby asked, as we all lay in our beds that night.

The dormitory was pitch-black, only the moonlight glow entering through the turret windows. In love with the moon, Sephy refused to draw the curtains for the night.

"You know, the one Damsel gave to Kin," Ruby went on.

"No idea." I lay on my back, arms tucked behind my head. Perhaps it was the full moon, but I couldn't fall asleep. "Is that what's keeping you up at night?"

"We could go and ask him," Sephy chimed in.

We were all awake, apparently.

"No, and *no*." Ruby pulled the duvet up to her chin, lodging her arms firmly on top of the covers.

"Uh, I can't fall asleep," I couldn't help complaining. Tomorrow morning was sport duel practice, and I couldn't bear to face that normally, let alone after a bad night's sleep.

"What's keeping you up at night, then?" I heard Ruby ask through the darkness.

"I'm not sure. Dreams, maybe. I might be overthinking, but I've had a weird few."

"Oh, dreams *are* important."

"So I heard."

"But it's hard to know which ones matter, really. It could be Fate talking, it could just be a dream."

"Funny how you have to focus on the details," I mused. "And then once you know something, you look back on a dream, and it takes on a whole new meaning."

"Like Kin's nostrils," Ruby said.

"*What?*" I almost got up to ask.

"Kin's nostrils open up real wide when he takes a deep breath. But only when he's nervous."

"Right."

"He's got a big nose anyway, but his nostrils are quite slim. And when he's nervous they swell up." Embarrassment about the observation was almost tangible in Ruby's voice, though it sounded like she simply *had* to share.

"Is that what keeps you up at night?" I teased.

"Shut up."

"The worms keep me up at night," Sephy's voice sounded from the turret, a Flip-shaped bump settling by her feet.

"*What?*" Ruby and I said simultaneously.

"The worms." Sephy's duvet shuffled in the dark. "When I close my eyelids, but I keep my eyes open underneath and stare up, I see the worms moving in the dark, underneath my eyelids."

"There are no worms underneath your eyelids, Persephone," Ruby assured.

"But there are!" Sephy shrieked. "They're colourless outlines, and they move – but only in the dark. I see them when I close my eyelids and stare up, so they must be there."

*

I dreamed again that night, like I'd feared I would. The same domed room, sharp, chiselled walls of flint. The only beam of light coming through the ceiling illuminated an altar. I was alone this time, neither Uncle Bill nor the woman present. My perspective was different too. Through the dust motes that flickered in the beam of light, I edged closer to the altar. Atop it was an ancient book, fragile parchment unfolded at the spine. There was writing on the page, an old script unknown to me. But it was writing, I'm quite sure. Light pulsed through it, like pulse passing through an ECG. Flashing, passing, flashing, it pulsed through the script.

I reached out to touch it, only to hear a faint voice whisper, "You've had a nice dream."

CHAPTER 12
PERSEPHONE BUTTERBLESS

"You've had a nice dream." I couldn't help announcing it.

I sat cross-legged, clutching at my feet. It was safest, to hold onto your feet; you never know when they might run away. That's what feet do – run – so it's a good idea to hold onto them, just in case.

I sat at the foot of Lilly's bed. Beds don't really have feet, at least not ones that run away. It was still pretty dark inside. Not so much outside; dawn was breaking, Lilly was waking.

Lilly propped herself up in bed.

"I didn't mean to wake you," I reassured. There was something special around Lilly whenever she dreamed. I could feel it, an aura hovering nearby.

"Are you okay, Sephy?" she asked.

"Oh yes! I think you had a good dream!"

"Umm… I did dream, I guess."

"What about?" I crawled forward, towards Lilly. I put myself beside her. A truly potent feeling evaporated off her skin.

"I don't know, a domed room, stony, some book."

"You dreamt about the Cradle!" *I knew it – knew it, knew it, knew it. It was so potent, it had to be.*

"What's the Cradle?" Lilly asked.

"Don't be ridiculous, Persephone. Lilly can't have dreamt about the Cradle, nobody knows what the Cradle looked like." Ruby-roo had woken up too.

"What's the Cradle?" Lilly asked again.

Some questions are so important, it's best to ask them twice. I snuggled up to her.

"The Cradle was the Rachthaws' sacred place, where it all began in Fonsland. It's where the first Rachthaw talked to Fate, and it was kept as a sanctuary until it was destroyed during the Murders. Its exact location was a secret, but it was likely near the palace. As to how it looked, there are only guesses," Ruby said.

"You have a really nice aura today." I reached out to Lilly's neck. I wanted to rearrange her hair, a soft, messy strand across the collarbone. Not wanting to disturb the aura, I decided to leave the arrangement in place.

"What in the worlds is this *aura* of yours, Persephone?" Ruby-roo was getting ready to take on a class or two.

"It's just in the air. A feeling, sometimes only a glimpse of a feeling. The mood in the room, the little things."

I floated my hand around Lilly's hair. It was so tempting to rearrange a strand. Ruby went to grab her socks. I placed them specifically under her bed.

"No! Don't move those – they're contributing to a friendly atmosphere."

Ruby's eyes looked swiftly up and then rolled back, as if she was looking for some reason on the ceiling. "They're contributing to me being late to class, so thanks for hiding them."

*

The very special feeling of this morning had stretched so thin I could barely sense it now. We hung around the cloisters after class, sat on the wall between the colonnade, facing the grass court. I swung my legs, I let them swing free. At least they were having fun; I wasn't. A thin sheet of frosty crystals covered the wall and the grass court, and soon enough if we didn't move, it would cover us too.

One part of me was sad. I wanted to do *something*, but moving meant I'd crush the crystals. At the slightest touch, they melted, disappeared. Destruction followed every step; the crystals perished. Another part of me was inundated with their magic, each and every frosty shape unique. I wanted to see them all, take them in and appreciate them. I felt torn apart. Too bored for my own good, searching for something to do, the slightest thrill, anything to distract me from the tragic beauty of the melting frost. Just a subtle escape. I wasn't used to staying in one place.

"Let's move, let's do something." I pushed off the wall. A sad crunch echoed underfoot.

"What would you like to do?" Kin looked up.

Sometimes I think he is the only one who hears me speak.

"Let's go to the waterfall," I suggested.

"The waterfall is out of bounds, Persephone."

Oh, Ruby-roo heard me too.

"Chancellor Arden said so specifically, we are not to go to the waterfall in winter, it's too dangerous."

"We'll be careful." I pulled my way in this verbal tug of war.

"It's out of bounds." Ruby stood her ground.

"That'll be perfect then – Flip needs a roam. There he can roam free." My backpack nudged at this idea. I picked it up carefully, and Flip's fluffy ear poked out from an opening in the zip. I searched my pocket for a snack, but Kin already had some berries to hand.

Flip crunched eagerly, I set off cheerfully.

"Wait up!" Kin chased after us.

Squeezing through a hole in the fence on the far side of the pitch, I wondered why someone had tried to cover up this entrance. We followed up a narrow path through the woods – adventure! I set Flip free from his carrycase. He loved to run around, sniffing at the various woodland smells: a patch of rosy flowers, a grubby shrub, a lost shoe. Was that mine?

Kin talked about this or that, mostly duels, some society he'd been invited to and didn't want to go, his little sister Clementine, though I'm afraid I hadn't paid attention. I'll feel sad about that later, not appreciating my friends enough. I was too busy now, pointing out lovely lichens and paw prints in the ground.

It felt soothing to be away from everything, to glimpse the real magic of the worlds, beaming off every little plant, encapsulated in every curious bug, and brewing in the stinky, rotting mud. Perhaps the worms lived in that mud, those worms that kept me up at night, swimming underneath my eyelids. They seemed like the mud-dweller kind.

"Look, Kin! The river, look!"

"Huh?" he said, but I already left his voice behind.

"Over there!" I was running. Flip ran ahead of me, suddenly aware that we were in a race, though what we raced for he probably didn't understand.

Stopping just short of the shore, Flip's little ears perked up as if to say, what was all that about? Kin caught up right behind.

"Wow, it's all frozen," he wheezed, pushing his glasses further up.

And it was. The usual gushing of the angry waters stood still, frozen underneath a thin sheet of ice. A noticeable chill lingered above its surface, attune to the serene stillness, the calm. Intricate patterns wove through the ice, wrapping around each other, hugging each other gently, singing a visual melody of delicacy and chilly chime. The patterns were so beautiful, inviting; I longed to get closer, to sing with them.

Then – an idea: I *could* sing with them. One step forward, one foot on the ice. *Crack.* New patterns emerged around my foot. I was invited to be a part of this mosaic. A further step, a further *crack.*

Crack, crack, crack, I sung in symphony with the ice.

Veins spread across the ice-sheet, an energy that flowed straight from me, from my veins into its icy, venous cracks. I united with the river-being, who stopped momentarily in its usual hasty tracks so that it could say hello to me.

Then a hand gripped my arm and yanked me back.

"Stars, Sephy! You can't do that!" Kin pulled me back, Flip anchoring Kin to shore with a bite of his trouser leg. "You'll fall straight through! It's freezing underwater."

I stared at Kin, Kin stared at me, different expressions crossing our faces. He was concerned, and I (judging by what reflected in his glasses) looked like I was underwater, like I had really fallen through; like the worlds that I was seeing were warped to those stood above the surface.

I wanted to explain the song, the patterns, the beauty and the thrill, but his nostrils flared wide. He was nervous, frightened.

"Ruby was right," I mumbled.

"Gee, well..." He relaxed a bit, the nostrils slimmed, allowing his glasses to slide somewhat down. "Ruby's usually right. It's not safe around here, and Flip's had his share, so let's head back."

Head back we did, back into the mundane, leaving the magic of the forest, mud, and ice behind.

"Are you going to be in spacetime studies this evening?" Kin asked as we neared the bastion.

"Of course, it's my favourite class." Flip hopped gleefully into my arms; I packed him into my backpack.

"Cool. Well I guess I'll see you there, then."

We walked inside, past the gremlin on the door. Kin's glasses steamed up, reacting to the warmth inside.

"Ah, this always happens." He reached up to take them off, but I stopped his hand.

I have a gift for seeing through people you see, seeing *right* through them, inside-out, to who they really are. Kin was a good person, kind, and all he wanted was acceptance in return for that; acceptance for being Kin, not Kindegory Spells the lawkeeper's son.

I drew peepholes in the steam on his glasses. Blinded by the steam, he missed my finger reaching for his eyes, and then when he realised, it made him laugh.

From behind the steamed-up glasses, a pair of happy eyes focused on me through the vision-openings I drew. I hoped that way, perhaps he'd see as I see, through my magic-misted eyes.

CHAPTER 13
LILLY-ANNE SKYROSE

This morning started like any other. In Force control, Professor Fellblue greeted us with an encouraging smile. Several of my classmates had managed to concentrate their Force after just a few tries. Kin was at the forefront of that group, a natural. A small, white flame danced across his fingers whenever he willed it into existence. Spontaneity, reliability, control, and speed were the desirable components when it came to using Force in duels. He had it all.

Thankfully, we weren't lying down today. Sat in a circle on the floor, those who could spark already took turns to do so. Then we meditated until the end of class, and I fought hard to resist any kind of sleep. I wasn't going to embarrass myself again. Having had two cups of coffee at breakfast and some kind of spell to keep me alert from Bertie, I was buzzing. Deliberately focusing my mind on everyday tasks, I kept it busy and shifted my body slightly once in a while, altogether resisting myself from wandering into the dreamy state.

After class, we all headed out for lunch: Ruby, Francesca, myself, and Sephy with Kin in tow.

"I had a look at past exam papers for Force control, and I really don't see how we're going to answer questions about permissive use of Force when all we do is meditate in class," Ruby complained.

"I'm sure we'll get to that," I offered, unsure if dry theory would be more or less fatiguing.

We pushed through the busy corridor, headed for the buttery. Sephy mused about what to feed Flip today, Kin ran through a list of favourite snacks, while Ruby wondered (mostly aloud) how long we could keep Flip a secret when Sephy kept taking him to class.

Suddenly Kin's voice trailed off, and we turned to see he'd stopped some paces down the corridor, staring ahead. Following his gaze, I noticed her at the entrance to the buttery: Damsel with her entourage. They were fully dressed in fancy uniforms, Champion red from head to toe, rather than the usual black with coloured accents. Such uniform was required only for special occasions, and I wondered if I had missed the memo for some school event today.

"I uh... I just remembered I need to see Fabian." Kin's voice was muffled against the bustling of the crowd. He pushed his glasses up, threw us a louder "See you later," and swiftly left.

As if in a mirror image, Damsel left too, though not before giving us a scowl.

"Honestly, who does she think she is, scaring him like that?" Ruby huffed once Damsel's scarlet robes were safely out of sight.

"*Who does she think she is?*" Francesca echoed, as we settled by a free table in the buttery. "She's Damsel *Goldtear*, for stars' sake."

"Thanks, Francesca, I know that," Ruby said sarcastically.

I looked from one to the other. Eagerness to gossip flushed across Francesca's face, waiting to erupt on the right cue.

"And what's that supposed to mean?" I offered her the bait, which Fran willingly took up.

"She's Justiceman Goldtear's daughter, of course," Fran said.

Reading the blank expression on my face, she continued.

"Justiceman Mortimer Goldtear? From the Order Department of the Senate? He's in charge of Hate eradication. Big name. He's the one responsible for rounding up lawbreakers, gaining intelligence on their connections – basically all means necessary to root them out. It's thanks to his efforts that they're brought to judgement in front of the high judge. You've heard of the high judge, right?"

I shook my head.

"Oh, but you *must* have, come on! High Judge Percival Potts – acts on behalf of Fate to pass judgement now that the Rachthaws aren't around to do it. Advisor Globesglory is his left-hand man." Francesca raised an eyebrow.

I perked up. Jacob Globesglory – Vince and Bertie's father, who I knew worked for the Senate still. Francesca was then explaining Lawrence Dodge, the high judge's right-hand man, but I shut her out.

Despite the infinite expanse of the otherworlds, everyone seemed connected here. Damsel's father headed a team responsible for sniffing out criminals, brought them to the courts and justice, where Vince and Bertie's father advised the high judge, and all was orchestrated by Kin's father, Lawkeeper Montgomery Spells. I wondered what percentage of my classmates sported such a pedigree background.

The connections extended further, of course. I thought of Gabriel and his family: Justiceman and Justicedame Harry and Nadine Hale, chief advisors of the queen and later mentors of the Senate. The flip side to the pedigree was clearly damage, the damage left by murders and chaos, the repercussions of which imprinted on my generation. Being orphaned was unfortunately not uncommon for people my age.

I mused over my sandwich, lost in thought about my own heritage, when the bitter taste of confusion seeped into my lunch. Where did I fit into all of this?

*

Sat on sofas in the Ranger common room that evening, I wrestled not with confusion but with anger; anger at Professor Meagles and his stupid *Island*

Understanding module in history, to be precise. I entered the classroom that afternoon dreading only another rendition of *Head, Shoulders, Knees, and Toes* as an example of Earthen culture; I left fuming about the absurdity of telephone lines.

Meagles noticed all too soon that I didn't have a textbook: his own *Understanding Islanders* – his life's work, it turned out; also the only one I didn't buy. He wasn't pleased.

"I take it that you are so confident in your knowledge of the Earth Islands, that you don't require the set text, Miss Skyrose?" he asked.

"I guess I have some first-hand knowledge to draw on, professor," I defended myself with a weak smile. For once, I thought I could work my background into an advantage.

"Perhaps you'd like to explain to the class then," Meagles said smugly, "how telephone lines work."

Nope. Not a chance. "Uh… there are signals… wires." Stumbling for words, I felt stupid and caught off guard.

"How does a stationary telephone – the so-called *landline* – know, when one human dials a number, that a device on the other end is connected to *that* precise number and the human they wish to speak to?" he pressed, but before I could even think about it, he went on. "A brand-new device has no number inherently assigned. The number is assigned to the human, or homestead. So how does a telephone know it is connected to that number? And how does it know that a device in another's homestead is assigned to the number being dialled? It's not the telephones that communicate after all – it's the humans. So how does the signal know where to go along the line?"

I shook my head, my cheeks burning red.

"Well, you'd know if you had my textbook," Meagles rebuked.

Idly, Charlotte slid her copy across the desk for me to look at.

"Ah, thank you kindly, Miss Sinnerstroke. It's good to see other students are prepared. Would you like me to sign the front page?"

"It's already signed, thanks. A limited edition."

I imagined Charlotte had taken it for free from her grandad's bookstore.

"Wonderful! Well, I'd be happy to sign it twice – it'll be worth twice as much."

History was a mixed class, and my punishment was reading the whole paragraph aloud to Rangers and Theorists alike. The correct answer? A Chinese-whispers-style chain of ants with maps who worked tirelessly to relay the messages along the telephone line.

Thus, come evening, I was still sulky; sulky and mad.

"I bet half of the stuff we learn in history is bollocks, so don't take it personally," Dean tried.

Dean Strange was another with a pedigree. He had friends across all years and affiliations, as well as no apparent permanent place of residence, for he seemed to spend each night with a different set of friends, old and new. That meant only one thing: if Dean was aware of the reason behind my sulking, half the school was probably laughing at me now.

"Yes, I tried to corroborate some of the sources for our earliest essays between Meagles's textbooks and the wider literature. Meagles's story is typically dumbed down, an unequivocalness hyperbolised – nowhere near the real intricacies and historical facts…" Ruby added, and Dean looked at her as if long words were going out of fashion.

"Yeah, and some of the stuff I hear my dad talk about doesn't fit one bit with the histories that Meagles teaches in class," Kin echoed.

This time Ruby eyed him with suspicion.

"What?" he mumbled, slighted that he was again being looked at as Kindegory the lawkeeper's son. "I hear some stuff, big deal."

"Heard you're not that good an Earthling after all, Earthling," I heard behind me. It was Constantine Dartwood.

I rolled my eyes. Who else? Bertie had already made that joke earlier, albeit in less awkward terms. As had Rupert, some random strangers in the cloisters, and no doubt Gabriel will too.

Constantine moved around the sofa to face us. He was big and bulky, though of an athletic build that would put many rugby players to shame. It was hard to believe he was just sixteen (or seventeen – Sephy and Dean organised his birthday party recently).

"A bad Earthling," he said in a slow, drone tone that matched his intellect.

"Oi, put that attitude away, Stine," Dean tutted at him, keeping his expression playful.

Mine wasn't; I'd had enough.

"Is that supposed to be a compliment, Constantine? *A bad Earthling?* Because if I'm bad at being an Earthling, I must in fact belong here, rather than on Earth," I snapped at the mountain of flesh – no brain – dressed in Ranger robes. That confused him.

"What's that you got there, Stine?" Rupert asked. A simple question that Constantine understood.

"From Damsel." Constantine held up a gilded envelope.

"What, not you too? Has everyone got one, then?" Rupert folded his arms in a strop that matched mine.

Dean fished out the same envelope, though very crumpled from being folded and sat on, from the back pocket of his jeans. "Invite only, Rupes." He waved it around.

Ruby folded her arms too at the sound of *that* nickname Dean had decided to honour Rupert with.

"What's all this about?" Rupert looked from Dean to Constantine, ending up on Kin. "You got one too, didn't you, Kin?"

Kin adjusted his glasses in response, his lanky frame looking like a thin dividing line between his friends, both taking up much space either side: Dean, laying all sprawled out, and Rupert, who couldn't help his size.

"Yes," Kin eventually admitted.

"What's inside, then?"

"Nothing." Kin's envelope was still playing bookmark in a textbook on his lap. "It's just some stupid society that Damsel has set up. Don't bother being jealous."

"What society?" Rupert pressed. "I'm not jealous, anyhow."

"*Purgers*," Dean laughed, setting his feet on the low table between the sofas. "First dinner is tonight. Are you coming, Kin? Stine?"

"I hope they don't make you vomit up the meal," Ruby muttered, then retracted, feeling the eyes that fell on her. "What? Have you not noticed how silly small their posh, little portions are at lunch?"

"No, I'm not coming. I like to eat my fill," Kin returned what was perhaps the first attempt at a joke I ever heard him make.

Ruby blushed.

"Ah, but it's about a lot more than food though, buddy. And you know that well." Dean leaned back, putting his arm around Kin and shaking him a little.

"What is it about, then? I still don't understand." Rupert pulled the envelope from Kin's book.

"The Purger Society," Kin sighed. "Damsel thinks she's carrying out Fate's work. They aim to seek out any lawbreaking activity within the school, reporting to the Authority – ridding our worlds of Hate and all that. Anything suspicious, they want to know about it. If you ask me, it's a pathetic excuse to stick their noses up."

"Is that why you're not coming, Kin? Too good for all of us?" Dean teased.

"*No* – I just don't think it's necessary."

"Think your designer robes will put us all to shame?" Dean shook Kin's shoulders a bit more with his one-arm embrace. "That's real kind of you, pal."

"*No*—"

"I've got an Arabella suit myself, mind you," Dean grinned. "Perhaps we can outfit match."

"Okay, that's enough." And Kin was off, only a few rude gestures to say goodbye.

They fell silent then, perhaps wondering if they'd pushed him too far. Sephy was sure to find Kin though, as they always seemed to gravitate towards each other, and she was sure to soothe him. Kin would be all right.

Rupert studied the invitation still in his hand. "Do you reckon they'd let me in with this, if Kin doesn't want to go?"

"Sorry, Rupes, it's invite only." Before Rupert could react, Dean had snatched the envelope, chasing out of the room.

Rupert followed with an awkward jog, leaving only Constantine with us, who in turn looked lost in our all-girl company.

"Bye, Earthling," he finally said, after staring for a while.

CHAPTER 14
ORLE GIGGLY LOBBSTER

Orle diddly doo, I've got a personality or two.

Stars, I'm losing it.

*

Dingy room, and in it bodies crammed side by side, red and blue, arranged in formation for a chemical demonstration. Student dominos, perching on uncomfortably tall stools around uncomfortably hard tables. Though I suppose tables are intended to be hard, sturdy, not to fall apart. I wish I was a table.

My shoulder leaned over to the shoulder nearby. Like a domino piece, I wondered – one push – could I start a cascade? A laughing cataract? A tempting fact, to start a giggling pact.

"Oi, can you not? I can't see what she's doing now," the shoulder said.

Dingy room – a classroom, actually, because it held a class. A pungent smell, the clink of glass, a hint of smoke. I hope it's not my sleeve burning. One bottle up, another vial down. Professor Sprause mixed ingredients, like some game of shuffled cups and ball. Students gaped at her hands, hopes high to pass this class, expected to endure this shell game.

My eyes gaped too, not because I cared so much, but because the order mesmerised. I liked an order, sequence, formula. So I gaped, staring from behind my eyes. I was somewhere in there, deep inside my head, swimming in my thoughts, I swam. The spells I took were precisely calculated to work like that, to hide me – shelter me – from the dim and boring world that unfolded outside the thin film barrier of my eyes.

When the recipe was finished, we, the minions of the class, set about recreating the creation. The classroom fizzled up with chatter.

"How much barking nut did she add, did you see?" the same shoulder asked me, or rather the voice belonging to its mouth; the shoulder's body, its mouth, that is.

Half an ounce, I thought, too preoccupied to say it out loud.

Still mesmerised, I was busy counting the little droplets of moisture in the air. Three hundred and seventy-one, they glistened. Heavy smoke, wet smoke, coming off the vials; wet, heavy smoke that settled as little droplets of moisture on everything around. Or maybe it was moisture from a heavy breath, Sprause's heaving breath, laboured in the smoke.

"Did you see? How much barking nut—" the same voice went on.

"Do you see how the moisture settles, on Sprause's little chin hairs? Makes them all stand out?" Little, wet pine needles on Professor Sprause's face. A wrinkly, hairy apricot in a steam bath.

"That's gross," said someone else.

"That's gross," I echoed in a silly voice, for no other reason than trying to entertain myself.

My toes wiggled and my face pulled into squished pulp. I drove my eyes to settle elsewhere in the dingy room, on something, someone, more respectable, satisfying, *gross* – gross, in the obviously-stands-out sense of the word. I like words and their meanings very much.

A pretty face. I think she was pretty, anyway. My cheeks pulled into a face again, and I crossed my eyes. There were two of her now, two Jolie Andersons, sitting on the Champion side. And the two Jolie Andersons noticed me and scowled.

"Freak," said the two Jolies from across the room.

"Hey, try not to make her mad," said the voice coming off the shoulder by my side. "Grim might think that it's *me* messing with his girlfriend – and I don't fancy getting beat up on your behalf."

If Jolie whines to Alastair, what I've started might end up being your load to bear.

Except Alastair Grim wasn't here, of course. Alastair had better things to do than be in an alchemy lab. I filed the threat away for later, as something to forget about.

"Sometimes I wish we didn't look so alike."

"Nah, you don't. I don't. Mel gets confused all the time, don't you, Mel?" I said.

"Again – gross."

*

Walls narrowed and moved in, ceilings stretched up, the corridor flooded with a sea; a sea of bodies in an uneven flood. Some hurried, limbs moving, the backpack-limb attached to the shoulder or spine; others loitered, still, confused, a bit put out. A sea of students swimming in the corridor as the class doors opened and released the flood.

"Give us a hand with the magic homework, will you? You're good at spells."

Good? Honestly brother, please. *If that's all I am, allow me to demonstrate my humble magical expertise. With a simple trick, in a moment I will conjure up the worlds' greatest miser, and of my magic he will be none the wiser.*

"That'll cost three fingers," I said.

"Yeah? Well, you can shove them, then."

"Up yours, if anything."

"Oh honestly, grow up," Mel butted in.

Grow up. I always found it hilarious when people told me to grow up.

What did she think I'd do, stop aging just in spite?

Then things started calming down – I started coming down. I wasn't calming down. I sat my arse on a comfy seat, a sofa seat, taking in the surroundings that have changed. Even higher ceilings, big chandelier, blue diamond shapes that lined the walls – so neatly put together, so well arranged, diamond side to diamond side, floor to ceiling on the wall.

The floor started quaking as more people peopled the Ranger common room. My eyes swam across the space, still quite fluidly, though quivering, trembling, dimmer with each quake.

My whole body moved in fact, starting with a tremor in the floor, my pelvic floor, zapping all the way up my spine. There they reached my head, each spasm shaking me awake. Pulsing, dimmer, pulsing, dimmer. The diamonds looked so ordinary now – a wallpaper.

The room wasn't quaking, it was just me. I was shaking. My head dropped between my knees, my body folded in. More comfortable, less to look at; the less to look at now, the less disappointing the worlds seemed. Each spasm dimmed me further, pulling me back towards the surface, the surface of the ordinary, closer to my eyes. And soon enough I would be seeing right through the barrier of my eyes, my treacherous eyes, which saw with clarity the infuriating dullness of the worlds. All the inadequacies, the faults, the crimes against efficacy designed and existing to ensure I noticed them. Stars, sometimes I really hated having eyes.

I sat folded on the sofa, arse plonked on the seat (though sliding down), with my head between my knees. Something else briefly caught my eye, and I was so thoroughly folded up, that it really was unfair I glimpsed it. About two yards away (though he might as well have slapped it in my face) was the big, stupid, shiny captain's badge. Though I admit, it wasn't really big, and it was kind of worn down – passed down through generations of grubby hands – pinned lopsided to his blazer threads. But it really set me off. It was too much.

At the end of last school year, just before summer, when Teethers graduated, he picked Vince as the next Ranger duel team captain, and for no good reason, if you ask me, because we both stood equal chance. Teethers was our last captain. His real name was Tithers, but he had big teeth – so big they made his jaw all funny – so I called him Teethers. He thought I couldn't get his name right. But that was not the reason. The reason he picked Vince was because when we went on one of those rare away matches, they charged me with looking after our kit on the way. And let me be clear, they *picked me*, I didn't volunteer. So I can't exactly be blamed for losing all the kit at the portal terminal, but they all blamed me anyway. We had to play in school uniform – blazers, jumpers, formal trousers and all – and none of us were feeling the vibe to play that way. Naturally, we lost – big time. It was in the papers, even. They all hated me after that. So Vince inherited the captain's badge from Teethers, and I only got the half-empty packet of Focus that he left behind in his locker, which I don't think he meant to leave, anyway.

The memory of this punched me in the lungs, and I folded a bit more. Here's another thing that frustrates me: pity, pity for my poor fool's soul. Vince did a whole lot of work to keep me on the team after that. Stars, I wish those memories could be disposed of.

A shimmer; my spinal disks stopped holding hands. I knew my options. I knew which I preferred. I didn't want to take too long deciding, not right now, not when I felt like this, not when a solution was within such easy reach. Soon enough that solution would go up in price – moral price – because sense and reason would take hold of me.

I could be sensible for a while, come off the spells, wallow in frustration, try to live with it, with the dirt covering my eyes.

Sense and reason would take hold of me, I could handle that. But they had a sister, and she always followed them, haunting me whenever I planned to allow myself some magical relief. Sense and reason had a sister, and her name was guilt.

Another spasm through my spine – the spine that couldn't even hold me upright now.

I could be sensible for a while, but I couldn't stand the guilt.

Why do you keep doing this to yourself? You can't go on like that, guilt whispered in my ear.

I knew my options because I'd been here about a hundred times, though the choices only started to get tough at the end of last school year. I might be a fool, but I learned fast: it was easier to avoid the guilt.

My hand reached to my shoe – it wasn't far, when I was sat all bent like that. It found a pencil tucked into a sock against my shin. Emergency makeshift wand. *One last time, then I'll stop.* A quick calculated whisper and a gentle flick sent me back. Back into my head, and again I looked from behind Orle's eyes. *Relief,* at last.

Beyond the timeframe of a spell, Orle knew no consequences. Thus naturally, guilt could not take hold of him.

"What are you doing?"

"Tying my shoe," my mouth offered an excuse.

"Cor, that's taking you a while."

"Shoelaces run for miles."

The head that held my vision slowly panned back. I unfolded. My eyes were on a journey, from floor to ceiling until I was looking at the wall behind me upside down. The diamonds nested side by side, fitted so perfectly together. Upside down, they were, but looking rather normal because diamonds look the same upside down or downside up.

"Shall we go and practice duels?"

I ignored the question.

My head hung over the back of the sofa. Bodies came and went, hovering like fruit flies around a rotting fruit; a rotting fruit that was Loon's City, its core here in the school, the school that spawned more and more of the aimlessly wandering, hovering, student fruit fly kind.

"I want to have some kind of training schedule nailed down before we even start the try-outs, so that I know exactly what it is we're looking for in new players."

I giggled.

"What's so funny about that?"

I giggled because they were all moving upside down.

"Are you coming then, or have you got better plans?"

That's when I saw her. And I mean *I saw* her, saw her from behind my eyes. I've seen her before, of course, but not like I was seeing her right now. She filtered through my vision, integral, *whole*, moving so gracefully despite being upside down. A person among the fruit flies, she glistened, dazzling, so full of life.

"But I'm telling you, there *are!*" she squealed.

"I repeat: there are no worms behind your eyelids, Persephone."

"Yes, there are. I see them."

She was a visionary, exceptional and wild.

"You're seeing things that aren't really there. Or they're just bits of miniscule dust that stuck to your eye. But they're not *worms*, and they're nothing to worry about."

"I think they're trying to show me things – and for this reason they moved into my eyes."

"Moved in from *where*? You're not making any sense, Sephy."

"They live in the mud, too. They like watery places, I think. I could show you."

"Whatever."

She spread her wings and took flight, wings flapping and dazzling as she moved by. Her wings – glittery and bell-shaped flowing down her arms – waved me goodbye. I watched her leave, skipping along the ceiling – the ceiling that was actually the floor because I was still watching upside down.

Then I watched the place that was now empty of her, and it wasn't the same place as before. It wasn't the same because she'd changed it, and I changed watching her, and it was empty now. Something rippled through me, trapped me like an avalanche. *Oh for stars' sake. I think I am in love.*

"Duels, then? Or are you just going to sit like that?" a voice said to my stubbly chin, for the rest of my head was still hanging back.

"I gotta take a piss first," were the only coherent words I could find.

*

High walls and windows became trees and waterfalls, the chandelier now a faint moon in the sky. My legs carried me out, left right, left right, they took two steps at once. Outside was muggy, foggy – I think I was groggy. I think I was groggy because I swayed a bit, and Haunt – in perfect groundskeeper guise – was yelling something, yelling at me, in fact. My legs picked up speed. I sped along an invisible string trail that she left, the fleeting presence of her light.

The scenery stopped racing past when I spotted a thick, puffy jacket. When I spotted her jacket, I stopped racing and calmed down. Perched over a puddle and cocooned inside was the vernal visionary; the Acaulescent Dreamer, as I thought I'd call her. She was a baby-bird now, eyes wild, fingers poking in the mud, no longer dazzling, sequins hid underneath the down, stowing her light underneath three jumpers and a puffy coat.

I watched from behind a bush, from behind my eyes – anyhow, a lousy disguise. I stalked her like a preying cat. I didn't want to harm her, though – honest. I just wanted to chat.

"Hello, Orle," said Daffodil. This seemed a better name for her because she was the first sighting of her kind, and seeing her was surely a sign of better times to come.

She spoke as if speaking to an old friend. My back arched, mind jumped to high alert. How did she know what Orle looked like? I'd never fashioned her a spell. Had she somehow stumbled upon my work? Birdfeed was mainly seeds, after all, and I did put a lot of seeds into my work.

"How do you know me?"

"Oh," she cocked her head to the side, and the gold coils springing from it followed suit, "I know everyone, once I take a look."

And she was looking at me now. No point in hiding.

"Well, here's me." I swirled and bowed.

She laughed, and the sound moulded to the folds inside my brain. She looked at me with a sort of admiration and curiosity. I looked right back, and I must have looked a while because I realised her laughter stopped, echoing only in my head.

There was a silence. I didn't know quite what to do; what to do about a lack, a lack of words, how to work with something that's a gap.

I took too long deciding. She straightened up, rose as a heron to her feet, supporting her puffy roundness on those silly stick legs rooted in the marsh. Was this it then, will she fly away? I thought about spelling her, prolonging the moment just to make her stay.

No! You can't just spell people, force them that way. Ask her a question, moron, she'll stay to answer – that's the normal way.

Right, yes. "How do you do?"

"I'm rather bored. How about you?"

"I've seen the light, and I'd like you to see it too."

She considered this request. "Thank you, friend, that's very kind," she smiled. "I'm an adventurer of sorts, I travel far and wide to leave the boredom behind."

"Pleased to have crossed your path, adventurer-of-sorts. I'm a wanderer myself. I seek the extraordinary, the brilliant, to escape my mind."

"Well, you're in the right place. The extraordinary is all around," said Dawn, as I had decided I would call her because she brought light into my life. Or maybe I would name her Irn-Bru, simply because it was something outlandish that I really liked.

"Ordinary, extraordinary," I babbled, "hidden from view, yet always in plain sight. Beyond vocabulary, revealed at the right cue. I help myself to see it, that's true. Formulae to keep the worlds bright, merry, for adventurers like me and you. I'm a poet – a spell poet – you see."

"A spoet," said Springtime; in her presence I was truly brought alive.

"A *spoet*, I agree."

She took me on a journey then, a journey through the forest, through wonder, through the mud. A timeless, space-less journey to appreciate all things small, all the little things around. We trudged and drifted, slipped and swam. The worms lived here – the worms I couldn't quite see, but trusted she would find.

"Why?"

"Because they dwell in places where the ordinary is transmogrified. Like my eyes. And like the mud – mud is ordinary dirt transmogrified. You just need to see it right."

I listened to her words most intently, but they skipped my ears, etching straight onto my brain.

All of a sudden, and I don't quite know when or why, she became my soulmate, Orle's only real pal. I was addicted – to spells, yes – but more so to her charm, the mirror image of me that reflected in her eyes. Adequacy, she could have called me if she handed out names because in her eyes apparently I looked just right; her eyes that burrowed through my brain irreversibly, sure to leave a hole at the back of my head if she ever took her gaze off me; her eyes that credited me with a bit too much. Our visions collided, merged, magnified. I wanted to look through her eyes, to see the worlds through her appreciative gaze. Indulgence – perhaps a better name to give her, as appreciation came so naturally to her. And hearing her talk about it, like a maximum strength verbal de-greaser, it wiped the filth off my eyes.

Perhaps she was my Remedy.

No, Remedy wasn't accurate enough.

Panacea, I finally decided, would be her name, because to put it simply, she took all those things that bothered me and made them quite all right.

She hadn't followed Orle's seed path, it turned out. Orle hadn't fed her fantasies. I had no hold on her, but she certainly captivated me. I was truly trapped, with no intention of breaking out. For this captivation, I had naught to offer in return; naught but spells, and for spells she didn't ask.

"Please hold onto me," I said.

Panacea smiled and took my hand. Orle quickly calculated her parameters, and I bit into my lip to stop the binding spell coming out. Please, Fate, please don't let her take flight.

*

"Where in the worlds have you been? You've been gone for ages!" I saw myself say.

Or rather, said the one who looked like me. A mirror image – physical resemblance, the same bad posture, pathetic facial hair.

"Had stuff to do, to realise."

"Honestly, what is up with you recently? Thought you were only going for a piss and then we'd go to practice duels."

He was watching me, no cosy appreciation in his eyes. Instead there was suspicion, scrutiny, icy pins and leash. An anticipation. A guess, for what I might mess up next. Stars, I hated being watched like that.

"Took a detour," I shrugged.

"Gee, what a lengthy detour that was."

Longer and more astonishing than you could ever know. And those I met along the way, I never will let go.

CHAPTER 15
LILLY-ANNE SKYROSE

"Try to let Fate reach you," Professor Fellblue reminded me. "I have a feeling that you are trying hard to shut her out. Give into intuition."

I promised I would try, though if he was right, I didn't particularly want to succumb to the sinking, dreamy feeling that sucked me in each time we meditated in class. Not only that – since the *incident,* my dreams became more potently vivid and terrifying, transporting me more often into the dark, domed room.

Whether strolling through the grounds in matching velvet robes and hat, making unreciprocated small talk with the gremlins at mealtimes, or paying a quick visit to Ranger Bastion to ensure all was in order – as he did now – Professor Fellblue congratulated and spoke individually to his students as Head of the Rangers. In general, he was pleased with our first-year progress, hopeful that our talents would bloom as the years passed.

"Ah, Mr Globesglory!" he greeted Vincent in the common room. "I trust that preparations for this year's duel team intake are well underway?"

"Yep, professor, all in hand. We're going to smash some games this year." Vince was sporting his team captain badge.

"Very well, very well. There's some splendid talent to choose from in the first year," Fellblue commented as he straightened up a painting on the wall – the testimony of Dean's little party from last night. "Good morning, Miss Jones!" his words caught Ruby as she hurried past. "I hear from Professor Flashmight that you have a natural talent for spelling. Keep it up."

"Thanks, professor," she blushed, textbooks tucked under her arm.

"Perhaps you'll look to join the spelling circle? We have some splendid potential among the Rangers, though our presence in the club is rather slight," he offered, but before Ruby could reply, his attention shifted to Sephy skipping by. "Persephone! It's good to see you. May I take this opportunity to remind you that there are classes going on today. I appreciate you must be busy, but do make an effort to turn up."

"Will do, Professor F," Sephy returned his smile.

Increasingly more often now, Sephy didn't show up in class. Ruby had of course already given her a telling off for that, unamused by the excuses that varied from 'I forgot' to 'it wasn't worthwhile'. Unamused, too, by having to look after Flip in Sephy's absence.

Sephy pranced around the room now, bobbing unevenly with each step. She checked under pillows, behind curtains, and was about to sift through the ashes of the fireplace, when Professor Fellblue asked:

"Have you lost something, Persephone?"

"Just my shoe." Sephy frowned, pointing at her left foot, which, unlike the right, lacked a heavy lace-up boot.

"Might it be the one that's hanging from a window in the first tower?"

She smiled, guilty, and skittered out.

"Mr Strange," Professor Fellblue turned to Dean. "Perhaps you'd like to escort Persephone to her shoe. I believe I saw some of your belongings there as well. Ah, good morning, Rebecca! Lovely performance by the choral group recently."

Fellblue stood in the doorway now, bidding each of us good morning as we left the bastion for the day.

"Miss Jackson, good day… Rupert, hello. I hear the head chef has a spectacular pudding lined up for tonight… Constantine," he shouted after Stine, "uh, Mr Dartwood, the laws classroom is that way."

Finally, he turned to me.

"Keep an open heart for Fate, Lilly-Anne," he simply said, his features composed into that same kindness with which he awarded everyone.

*

Shuffling along the bench into the middle of the row, I snagged my tights.

"Shoot," I muttered to myself.

Seeing me examine the petty damage, Ruby rolled her eyes. She knew what was coming – I'd asked her for a mending spell three times last week.

I got ready for laws, taking out my notebook, pencils, and textbook – the heaviest of them all. Thanks to Ruby, we were always early to class, giving Professor Artsback an extra five minutes to concentrate his aversion on us before his disgust could disseminate more evenly across the class.

A few more students filtered in. Professor Artsback scanned the room conspicuously. Black jumper next to black jumper, a blue dragon crest on each, we sat in rows scaling the lecture hall. His gaze reached the one that obviously stood out, Sephy in her already holey school jumper and sparkly dress underneath. Somehow she got away with it, though Artsback looked about to put an end to that. His gaze then quickly shifted, finding a pricier victim.

"Nervous, Miss Skyrose?" Artsback raised a brow.

He commanded his eyebrows separately so well, Bertie told me Artsback's brows had their own minds.

I panicked, looking up.

"Is there something you're concerned about? I notice you are always wearing your ayutum to my class," Artsback added in a dry voice. Like a raven, he stood by the blackboard with folded arms wrapping his black cloak tightly around.

"M-my what, sir?"

"Your necklace," Ruby whispered. Thankfully, the classroom started filling up, and Artsback's attention shifted. "The symbol: it's an ayutum. I

157

thought you knew."

That morning I learned that my most prized possession – the necklace that I always wore – was a common good-luck charm in the otherworlds.

"I have one too, Fate be kind to us." Ruby pulled out a flimsy, battered metal keyring from her pencil case.

It was the same eight-pointed star, red paint peeling off the centre, where a red gemstone shone on mine. Parents gave ayuta to babies at birth, she explained, for good wishes and success. It was a symbol of the Rachthaws, the common folk believing that wearing it will bring them favour with Fate.

That morning too, I learned more about the Carcery. Professor Artsback took pleasure in watching us wince at the very graphic explanation – prints and paintings included – of what exactly happened to condemned lawbreakers. The Carcery was a barren world, uninhabitable, I knew that much. There was no fertile land on the rocky, frozen landscape; fresh water was hard to come by. Paintings depicted slumped, ragged bodies battling the frost, and where rags did not reach, skin was lacerated and blotched from frostbite. Toxic air silently filtered through the lungs of those who were banished to spend the last few of their remaining months there, for nobody lived long once they found themselves in the Carcery. Apart from Senate-sanctioned, one-way portal openings that delivered more lawbreakers to their destiny, no other transport of food or supplies was delivered. The Authority did not execute directly of course – that would be against the laws. Instead, High Judge Percival Potts, relying on his supreme intuition, passed the judgement of Fate. If Carcery-bound lawbreakers didn't die of starvation, they suffocated, breathing in the toxic air.

Artsback waved his wand, and another painting floated in front of the blackboard: court proceedings of those directly involved in the Murders. Ruby flinched as the well-known criminal faces stopped just a few feet in front of us. I strove to find the reason for her reaction, for they looked so normal, like any neighbour or passer-by. Only their faces were burning with the perceived injustice they received.

"Abhorrent, rabid on Hate, erratic, they exist only to destroy what is so dear to us," Artsback's raspy voice echoed through the stillness in the lecture hall.

And in the stillness, there was fear; fear so tangible it verged on horror, an ingrained conviction that, despite the Authority's efforts, mindless evil still lurked in unexpected places across the worlds.

"They called themselves the Legion. Sixteen years ago, the Legion launched an attack on Fonsland, their numbers and Hate so fervent, it left the world practically destroyed. Hundreds of civilians, celebrating by the Rachthawnian palace, perished. The attack was planned to coincide with the queen's announcement. They thought they could destroy all that which held our worlds together. And where are they now?"

Another painting drifted in to replace the court proceedings: darkness, with rips of faint blue and white. Smudged behind the colours were figures, their shapes contorted, warped.

"Locked forever – safely – in the eternal, unmelting ice."

My hand reached automatically to fiddle with my necklace. It didn't escape Artsback's notice, and again, he raised a brow.

"Yet we must remain vigilant, for although the Legion has been… incapacitated…" Artsback continued.

That was putting it lightly. Members of the gang responsible for organising the Murders were literally frozen, perhaps still alive, in a secret location somewhere far away in spacetime.

"… Hate has spread its roots, possibly infecting far and wide. Never take your safety as a given, or your intuition for granted. You must all fortify your minds, abide by the laws, stay true to Fate, and *never* forget that someone, somewhere may attempt to infect you with Hate."

What exactly was Hate? A clear answer was hard to come by. I imagined it was like a virus, which turned the peaceful-minded into fervid killers and physically turned the blood white. How it spread was another matter. Some said physical contact was needed, that infection was transmitted through contact with a lawbreaker's burning Force. Others said it was a substance that materialised inside the mind, rewiring the brain when someone disobeyed Fate's plans. It then spread through persuasion, a whisper of false promises – a better life, if only you cut off the puppet-strings that Fate attached to you.

"The Authority has already uprooted a great deal of those infected so they can do no further harm. Still, we must all play our part. And thanks to the initiative of a new student society that has been set up, we will now be able to keep a closer eye right here, in Sapphire Dragon's, on anything that…" Artsback looked at me, "… isn't quite right."

My fingers traced the edges of the eight-point star, each point a different length and width to the rest. I knew these contours off by heart. It was supposedly my mother's, and if that much was true about my past, then there was one thing I could be sure about: I belonged to the otherworlds. I was born here, and perhaps my mother gave it to me for good luck, to keep me in Fate's favour. I could only hope that it was working now. If Fate *was real*, then I hoped that I was doing whatever the hell Fate had planned for me. *Unbreakable Law one: do not cheat Fate.* But how was I supposed to know whether, inadvertently, I wasn't doing just that, breaking this law? Did the Authority send people to Carcery for unknowingly breaking laws? I thought about piercing my finger just to check my blood hadn't turned white. Or, could they decide that I was truly an unknowing Earthen who'd already seen too much, sending me to Carcery just for that?

I snapped out of it when Artsback dismissed class.

No, I mustn't scare myself like that. I wasn't even too sure if Fate was real, if Hate was real. Was that a crime? The substance of the otherworlds was tangible enough, though the cosmology evaded me. The Authority *sure was* real, but I hadn't done anything wrong, and I doubted they would sentence me to death just because I wasn't shooting fire out of my hands.

Or could they?

I chewed my sandwich unwillingly at lunch. Ruby argued with Rupert about the configuration of levitation spells. It was advanced, third-year material. She waved her wand and moved a cup of water above his head, threatening to spill it over just to prove her point. Fabian boasted he'd saved up three wholes to buy some event ticket. Constantine was showing off to Vince how quickly he could materialise a spark, snapping his fingers to produce a white flame, while Bertie used his Force to brown a cut of meat on his plate, for he liked it more well-done. A gremlin shuffled past. A group of giggly girls asked *Kindegory* for an autograph, which he only found the courage to refuse when they specified that they wanted it in blood – for authenticity.

Although several months had passed, sometimes I still thought that this was all a dream, and soon enough I would wake up in the small bedroom of our Norfolk farmhouse.

A trail of lost sequins on the floor marked the path Sephy left behind. She picked up fruit for Flip, leaving in a hurry, the broken threads of her dress dropping sequins as she skipped out. Besides the fact that she smuggled a squidrel in her backpack, her disarray and trifling bustle was the most familiar, *Earthly*, of all things surrounding me right now. And Flip, well – Flip could pass for an albino racoon, perhaps.

A tiny domestic pixie flew past, picking up the sequins – and with them all traces of my secure familiarity.

It was impossible to know if I had broken any laws. Would I be able to prove my innocence if the Authority accused me of lawbreaking? I suppose there was one way to do that. *Try to let Fate reach you*, Professor Fellblue's words rang in my head.

CHAPTER 16
ORLE GIGGLY LOBBSTER

"Well done, full marks again." Professor Flashmight's arms were handing quizzes back. "You really ought to think more seriously about joining the spelling circle."

"I'm afraid the duel team takes up the majority of my time, professor."

"Well, if you ever change your mind, we'd love to have you." Paper down to desk, Flashmight's fingers pressed it down, trying to look nonchalant.

That look never suited teachers well. There were two kinds of teachers, I noticed, and Flashmight was of the first kind: the passionate devotees and the second-hand-career-choice ones. Artsback was of the second kind. I knew because I'd once heard Dad say he applied to work at the Authority every time a mind invigilator position opened up. They turned him down repeatedly. Asset Artsback; never a benefit to the team.

Flashmight's hand flicked back to the stack of quizzes cradled in his arm, then added (his voice added, that is, coming from his head rather than his arm), "Have you thought about what you'd like to do after graduating? I could put in a good word for you with the guild, you know."

There it was again, the nonchalance reaching out like a third arm.

"Thanks, professor. I'm still making my mind up."

My mind was a mess that couldn't be made up, like a puzzle missing pieces, so I found it funny he phrased it like that. My brother, pretending to be me.

"Watch your dreams, then," Flashmight smiled, distributing more average grades down the aisle. "I'll be damned if Fate wastes a talent like yours."

The piece of paper with full marks swung back into my face; swung, attached to an arm, an arm that flopped over the head belonging to my brother's body sat in front of me.

"He got us confused again," said the voice belonging to his head – or at least I so assumed, for I could only see its back. Half its back, actually, because half was obscured with the quiz being handed back to me. "This is yours."

"Cheers," I said.

"Congrats."

My mind was a mess that couldn't be made up, but for the near future, I'd set a clear map – a map leading to the only treasure I hoped to find; a wandering, wonderful, treasured remedy that was constantly on my mind. We'd pick a new meeting place each time, a starting point of a new adventure, so I had a stack of maps layering up in my brain. I'd stashed them away as keepsakes of a friendship bound not to last.

I left the building thinking about how they ever managed to build a place so big. You have to leave in order to truly appreciate a building's size – imposing from the outside, hard to grasp when you're too close to it. Stone on top of stone, one after another, and suddenly, an educational fortress rose up. Similar to individual words being arbitrary until you put them together right. Halls and classrooms, corridors, rooms with purpose and rooms without; a cellar or storeroom – quite indistinguishable, unless you have the words to tell them apart. An academic stronghold guarding intuition, carefully distributing it so that access was kept intact, with a fake dragon on the top to keep a dead watch over everything with its fake eye.

Wind was wild outside, pushing against the stones, trying to topple them. But the stones withheld, proud, laughing and gluing themselves together tighter. Or maybe it was the wind that laughed. A hooting through the mortar gaps, cracking up – cracking open – a window with a flimsy latch.

This time the map led me to the forest. I thought I glimpsed my treasure, hidden inside a golden, windswept fuzz. Hidden too, behind a wide tree with too many arms. I went around the tree – my legs went, quicker now – but she was nowhere to be found. So my legs continued, pacing around the tree once, twice, thrice. I went around like this a few times – a few, I think, because it's hard to know exactly where a round tree finishes and starts. And each time I glimpsed her, once I got there, she was nowhere to be found. But trees are hardly roundabouts, so I turned back on myself, and my body bumped right into hers.

"Do you think you're funny?" I asked Panacea; she had been hiding, hiding right behind my back.

I guess she thought she was because she pressed her face against the bark and laughed.

"What would you like to do today?" she asked the tree – or asked me, rather – but she whispered against the bark. The tree wiggled its fingers in return – its little branches – trying to catch onto the fleeting wind that bothered it.

"He looks busy." I patted the tree, trying to encourage it in the windy fight. "But I've got two tickets to the orchestra, if you'd like to come."

"I'd love to!" she called out, or at least that's what her face looked like because the wind stole her words' chime.

We watched the orchestra from afar, from a balcony above rather than up close, but it wasn't an issue because music isn't a sight. Like smoke, music rises up, food for the celestial beings in the night sky. Food for Fate. Except that it wasn't yet night, and the music only rose up to the ceiling; the ceiling of the chantry, to be precise, the most purposeful room here in the school. So purposeful, in fact, that its purpose could be divvied up, and the chantry was sometimes repurposed as a music room.

My tickets to the orchestra were a lock-picking charm, honoured at the side door. Today's performance was a rehearsal of bad notes, followed by Professor Phigg's 'ensemble out of tune' as the orchestra sought common ground with the choral group.

I watched the music for a while, seeing it rise and then, disappointed to be trapped, unfold across the ceiling and trickle down the walls. But since music isn't a sight, I started listening instead. And as you listen, attuned to the things around, words to match the sound seep in and thoughts materialise. Food for Fate. Food for thought – Panacea's thought, to be precise.

Her head rested on a shoulder – my shoulder, actually – as if needing more surface area to fully sit down. She was a dreamer, dreaming even when she didn't sleep. Fate gave her a gift of dreamy vision through open eyes. Or at least that's what she thought.

I thought having to sleep in the first place is really so tedious, pointless even, when the next morning all you needed to do was to wake back up.

"In sleep, we are alone," she said.

I freed my hands so I could take her words in. A wrinkly apple rolled by my feet. She temporarily left my shoulder to bend and hand the apple back to me.

There is a certain energy – an aura, she said – that comes with being alone. And this energy is not always a good one. I agreed. Sleep was wasted time.

"That's not what I mean," Panacea corrected me. "In dreams we are alone, and I dream all the time."

The solitude she talked about was a stinking, lonely pit that opened in her stomach, burning with a yearning to share life's wonders with others, but having no one to share them with. A master of self-propelled entertainment out of need, she filled each crevice of the loneliness with new ideas. These ideas, they hid among her curls, I'm pretty sure. Where else would they come from? Ideas had to spawn close to the head.

"Rebecca keeps looking at you," Panacea whispered to my shoulder.

"Which one is Rebecca?"

"The one in blue." She pointed a verbal finger to the choir below.

I didn't quite follow, but figured it didn't matter because there were several of them wearing blue.

There is a different kind of energy – intoxicating, charged, almost like pure Force hanging in the air – that comes with being alone *with someone else*. I was hardly ever alone, or I hardly noticed being alone. The worlds are full of things to notice, especially frustrating things that jump out, scream, and layer across my eyes. So I call Orle into being. Or whisper, more like. Orle sees past the drudgery, and I see with clarity with Orle behind my eyes.

The worlds are full of things to notice, and even with six senses, it's hard to notice them all at once. Being alone with others is not something I've ever cared about. But stars – I felt it now. It was a strange feeling, pleasant but nauseating at the same time. I'm not sure I can spell it out for you, but it was very real, though too ephemeral to be captured into words. In this big room full of people, Panacea and I were alone together. The three of us.

Panacea's vision – appreciative vision – was my remedy. She saw through things without their underlying beauty having to be spelled out. This was funny because she said she saw right through me, and behind Orle, I was just pathetic dirt, social trash. She wiped the filth off my eyes, but as she did so, underneath she must have seen the real ugliness inside.

Past Orle, I feared this friendship wasn't built to last.

*

As soon as Panacea left, my stomach rumbled, and I started craving more of her company. But she had things to do, her moss collection needed sorting out. I did too – have things to do, I mean – but I no longer felt like doing them. So I went back to my dorm, planning to sleep. Everything was doubly dire when she wasn't around.

Pace, pace, pace, hop – over an empty tin lying on the floor – pace. My legs carried me back to the dorm. The tin kind of knocked me out of rhythm though, steps became longer strides. Notwithstanding the fact that I started booting the tin down the hall.

Once I'd started kicking it down the corridor, my legs couldn't quite match pace with the tin. Steps got awkward. My legs did not agree, unable to communicate among themselves. Bodies are so cloddish. Stars, it really bothered me.

I switched to not stepping on the cracks instead, but that was even harder, for apparently my strides were precisely crack-length apart. That really set me off. *Stars*, why are the worlds designed to taunt me?

I thought I'd go to sleep, waste some time. Be alone, as Panacea said. Alone, with nothing to torment me.

I walked in to find the dorm full of bodies, all piled up in heaps on beds, the floor, chairs. Human debris of the school day. Fate was really having a laugh.

"What do you want for dinner? We're ordering a take-out."

I hated take-outs. They always disguise the dishes in the names, and you should know by now that I'm a person who savours the clarity of words. You order one thing, something completely different turns up. The discrepancy always made me itch; itch so badly. An allergy to inaccuracy. And don't even get me started on spelling mistakes.

"Hopes and dreams," I said.

Chief roommate scowled. He always did that, when I was being funny, and again he was *watching* me. For stars' sake, how I hated being watched like that. Especially when the spells wear off (and they tapered off a while ago, only being with Panacea I hadn't realised), and I feel so rotten. Filthy like the worlds around. Stars, I really felt rotten now.

Deep breaths, ignore the itch. Ignore the twitch. Ignore it because if there's one thing I hate more than being watched with pity or mistrust, it's registering that I'm feeling rotten. Worse still if anyone else mentions it.

"In a mood, are you?" Vince asked.

I might as well explode.

I fell back on the pile of bodies – the pyre – that I kind of wanted to set alight; the people gratuitously sat across my bed. I jumped on them. Groans squeezed out from the sacks of skin.

Fate – I'm begging, honest, claim me now.

CHAPTER 17
DAMSEL GOLDTEAR

I looked through each little drawer of my dresser again. They weren't there – my diamond earrings – a present from Daddy, straight from an Empyrean mine, that went perfectly with the dress I picked out for tonight. Damn domestic pixies. I always suspected they had an eye for shiny things. I would report this to Haunt tomorrow, though I doubted he had enough brains to bring the pixies into line.

The door opened – silently now because I had the gremlins oil the hinges recently. Marisol came in. There was a third bed in our dormitory, but I didn't like it when things got too crowded, so I refused to share with a third. Besides, I needed the extra wardrobe to myself. Marisol was enough to deal with.

"Have you seen my diamond earrings?" I smiled at her sweetly. I'll bet my prophecies that she was the one who took them, actually.

"Hmm…" Marisol pouted.

My suspicion rose.

"Didn't you say that your sister borrowed them?"

Oh, yes. My older sister, Beatrice. I remembered now, Beatrice borrowed my earrings a while back. It clearly escaped me that she never gave them back. The last time I saw Beatrice, she seemed unusually giddy – strange, for her usually shy self. There was determination and excitement in her tone, which I suspected had little to do with good grades (which is usually all she cared about) because she asked to borrow my diamond earrings. I remember thinking, *Beatrice, dressing up? What for?* Who was she trying to impress, and why?

There was a good choice of fine boys among the Champions, I supposed she hoped to bag one up. Despite our family connections, Beatrice was apparently unwilling to tug on the strings. Being a Goldtear, and a Champion of course, she practically had a career lined up. Yet judging by her lack of enthusiasm when Daddy said she could do a summer placement at the Senate, you'd think her career choice was housewife. That was my goal, actually, so I hope for her sake that she wasn't going to make it a competition. I should probably claim my diamonds back before they help her snatch someone off the top shelf.

I swung my cloak around my shoulders, ready to find Beatrice, when I realised: she wasn't after Kindegory Spells, surely? No, he was too young. By one year, but still. Besides, Kindegory was mine.

Damsel Spells, it's meant to be. I see it very clearly, so there's no doubt it's fated. Kindegory and I first met at an aurochs racing event a few years ago. We sat in the sky lodge with our parents – the most expensive seats, from where we couldn't smell the awful beasts. We struck up a conversation. He spoke first – a clear sign. 'Excuse me', he'd said to me, trying to get past. It was obvious he knew who I was. I caught him looking at me from the side before he decided to make a move. There were at least two other ways he could have got to his seat, but he chose to squeeze past *me*. I then asked if he'd placed a bet on the winner. He said no because he wasn't interested in aurochs racing. That's something we had in common already: I hated the stinking animals, but Daddy invested in the race, so we came to watch it every year. Kindegory said his dad probably did too, but that he didn't really know. Must have been confidential detail he couldn't share.

Walking through the corridors of Champion Hall, I caught my reflection in the gilded mirror that covered half the wall. I stopped a while; seeing how good I looked always put me in a splendid mood.

We then met again at his mother's premiere fashion show. I wore my best hat, and Arabella – Mrs Spells – complimented it. Another sign: I practically belonged in the family. It was at their summer house, and I got a good look around the place. Arabella Spells may have a superb taste in gowns, but the dining room curtains certainly need to go. Kindegory wasn't easy to find, but that's just to do with the size of the house. I *did* make acquaintance with Clementine, however, my future sister-in-law, who claimed her brother's really hiding. What a strange sense of humour. She had a peculiar tone too, as if she thought she's better than me, the child. I felt as though our personalities may clash, but I let it go and told her that her hair looked nice. Finally, Fate led me to Kindegory, tucked up on the sofa in a drawing room furthest from the show. The care in his voice when he asked if I was lost was charming, though he looked very mediocre, not particularly well dressed for the event. He then showed me back to the main hall, where the gowns were being modelled – too much a gentleman to have me alone, of course. Only that he disappeared soon after.

I crossed the Champion common room, passing paintings of alumni, trophy cabinets, and antiques. Kindegory would have liked the hall. Why didn't he – his parents – protest when he was made a Ranger? Affiliations aside, I prayed that he would show up at the Purgers' dinner tonight. I can't stand another evening pretending I enjoy Dean Strange's company. The way that boy chews, you'd never guess he's a third cousin once removed of the Rachthawnian line. Good riddance about the Rachthaws – otherwise Fate would have surely had me tied to Dean. I'd rather fall off the Continent and drown in the spacetime sea. What self-respecting parent gives their child such a short name anyway? *Dean* – for someone of his standing, the name was an equivalent to drinking champagne out of a mug. Perhaps it's short for Deannard. Deanovich. Deannopole. *Kindegory* – now that's a grand name, important, lavish. I still hated my parents for investing more in *Beatrice*.

No matter how much Dean repulsed me, we needed to stick together – Daddy always said – build an allegiance of trust in times when Sapphire Dragon's awarded increasingly more scholarships. Scholarship students were of another kind, Daddy said, and it was troubling to see the school trying to force intuition out of merely *anyone*. Laws exams should be compulsory for everyone, especially the Empyrean savages, but everything else ought to be more restricted. Only for those with the right means, and scarlet blood of course.

Which reminds me: why, *oh why*, did Kindegory feel the need to spend his time in such awful company? The Earthling was an abomination, and how she managed to swindle her way into Sapphire Dragon's was an unforgivable crime. I wouldn't be surprised if her blood was in fact green. An unknowing, beyond Earth – it made me sick. I'd written to Daddy about it straightaway, and he thanked me – said he was proud – but at the moment, he had more pressing matters at hand.

The Earthling was high on the Purgers' list. Then there was the Jones girl, but she wasn't a threat as such, unless poverty was a crime, and the travelling showman's girl, the freak. Was Kindegory trying to rally up support of the mindless masses, as his father had done? Or perhaps he was gathering evidence against the Earthling. That made me smile. I'll bet my prophecies he is.

I tapped a little melody onto Beatrice's door. Her roommate answered shortly.

"Beatrice isn't in," she informed me.

"Well, tell her I want my earrings back, fast because I need them for tonight."

"I would, but doubt I'll see her. She hardly ever comes back here, only sometimes to fetch more stuff."

"Oh." I quickly straightened out the confusion in my brows. "Why?"

"Haven't you heard?" the roommate jeered, as if I was oblivious to some news. "She's kind of moved out."

I'm not surprised, who'd want to share a room with you, I wanted to say, but instead I forced a flattering smile. "Is she living with Catherine now?"

The roommate shook her head. I ran through a list of Beatrice's other friends I knew, and each time she shook her head, growing more amused.

"Where will I find her, then?" I resented being treated like this. *Hope your family have paid their tax this year.*

Finally, she gave me directions. I followed the way she indicated, taking stairs and corridors I never imagined myself taking into the depths of Champion Hall. It was unsettling, to be so far underground. My perfect outfit jarred with the unornamented, cold, stone walls, grimy mosses growing here and there, sprouting from leaks in the low ceilings and somehow surviving with no natural light. Nobody chose to live down here, surely? All the best rooms were in the top staircases – spacious, light, and grand.

Standing in front of the door she indicated, I presumed she lied. I *tap, tap, tapped* my little melody, suddenly so unfitting for the gloom. Silence – a confirmation of her lie. Most likely I'd been tricked to come knocking on a laundry room. *You lying bit—*

Suddenly the door snapped open. I stumbled back. Holding it open beside him, so that I could barely look inside, was the one who everyone always talked about. We weren't acquainted, as he was older, a third-year, and besides, it was best to keep my name free of acquaintances like *him*.

People talked about Alastair Grim because he always accomplished something. Usually, it was a victorious Champion match, and just as frequently it was a new girlfriend, frenzied that she had his attention, even if for a little while. Or some deal he'd brokered to suit himself only, some revelry he had organised, a bet he won at impossible odds. A master of persuasion, strategy, and charm, Alastair Grim was the hidden hand orchestrating everything he considered worthy to care about. Less gripping were the stories about his immaculate academic record partnered with the fact that he was (apparently) always ditching class.

Most compelling – and up close I could see why – was just *him*, the way he looked. Very tall – yet not ridiculously so – lean, but substantial. Kindegory could use a bit more of his height.

Confidence in his own success for just about everything Fate had lined up in his path was written into Alastair's features, like some unspoken bargain he had struck. It was there, in the turned-up corners of his mouth; in the spark of triumph lighting up the gunmetal eyes; in the stiffness of his shoulders and the way he held them back. The innateness of this success, the way it came so naturally to him, was even woven into strands of golden hair, which, by evening, fell slightly out of a neatly combed-back line. I bit my lip. *Stop looking, Damsel*, now.

It took him less than a tick to figure out I wasn't a threat. His contoured, bold features relaxed into an indifference with which he treated everything and everyone he held in disregard.

"Can I help you?" he asked. His voice was smooth, velvety, with a natural coaxing edge.

"I… I'm looking for—"

"Oh." He didn't let me finish, turning inwards into the room, and called "Bea?"

I stole a glance into the dormitory as he left the door ajar, disappearing inside without making further conversation. The room was *huge*, like a private hall within the hall, and suddenly I understood the thrill in people's voices when they hoped to be invited to a private gathering Grim had organised. A little get-together, they always said. I'll bet my prophecies these weren't very *little* at all. How was it possible that such grand dormitories existed, and *I* didn't know about them? Then I realised, *of course*, it had to be underground because there was another edge to Alastair

Grim that people whispered about. The rumours, about how he *really* managed his success in all domains of life. And when he heard about it, he laughed, never confirming nor rebutting the claims.

Accusations of lawbreaking were more easily slapped on to the other Grim, the one in second year with an absurd name. Without looking under his skin, I was sure that Mate Grim was a whiteblood. He was just below the Earthling on the Purgers' list, though untouchable – at least for now – because nobody dared cross his older brother. It made me grind my teeth together, that none of the Purgers or teachers alike were resolute enough to stand up to Alastair. I stood here even more furious now, that I let myself be so dismissed by him.

Laughter echoed inside. I recognised the voice, and soon enough, Beatrice appeared at the door.

"Oh! Damsel, hi." She was surprised to see me. "What are you doing here?"

Beatrice looked nothing like me, and for that I was glad. We had similarly dark hair, and perhaps there was something in our features that excused a resemblance, but my mother must have been glad to see I grew up looking so much *different* (to be polite) to her first child.

"What are *you* doing here?" I snapped.

"That's hardly your business, Damsel." Beatrice stepped out into the corridor, pulling the door nearly shut.

"Your roommate said you moved out," I accused.

"Don't make it sound so dramatic, it's hardly like I moved worlds."

"Well, what are you doing here?"

A worst-case scenario was forming in my head: Beatrice had fallen victim to Alastair Grim's charm, and he now toyed with her. Then again, I remembered hearing that Jolie Anderson claimed Alastair's girlfriend status these days. Was he a cheater? I wouldn't be surprised. Regardless, whatever Beatrice was up to with the Grims, I could not allow it – not when we had the same surname and Daddy's reputation to keep up.

She sighed, understanding that I wasn't going to give up. "I'm spending time with my… friends."

"*Friends*? Beatrice, are you *insane*?"

Mate Grim suddenly appeared behind her then, looking more disgusting and sick up close than my memory held. His pose echoed hers, like a shadow that took too long to follow her.

"Is everything okay?" His words were a concerned whisper, aimed only at her.

"Yes, don't worry." Beatrice reached to cup his jaw and cheek, stroking the ghoulish bones that stuck out.

I felt nauseous, sick, watching her do that.

"Is there anything else, Damsel?" She finally peeled her eyes off him.

I stared, aghast. Beatrice hadn't simply fallen for Alastair like every other girl. The situation wasn't bad, it was *dire*. My sister, a Goldtear, was in love with Mate Grim.

I must have asked to have my earrings back because she went to fetch them. In the short while she was gone, Mate stayed behind, blocking the doorway and – to my discomfort – acknowledged that I was there. *You foul, filthy, cunning side-swapper scum*, I wanted to scream. *How dare you?* He held me in his sullen, sickly gaze, apparently matching my contempt. *How dare you hijack a Goldtear like that!*

Beatrice handed me a little pouch with the earrings inside. "I never wore them, in the end," she smiled, then nestled back into his frame, as if he was the last puzzle piece her existence needed to be complete.

His face pressed against her head, dark eyes assessing what might happen next. No longer a shadow, he was a hunter hovering to protect his prey.

I stormed off down the corridor – nearly ran – towards the upstairs, towards airiness and light. My heart was pounding. This wasn't right. Was she poisoned? Did Beatrice fall victim to Hate? Did he *infect* her? This was dangerous, beyond words.

Stopping only when I reached the toilets, I leant over a sink, unsure if my stomach was about to return everything I'd eaten today. The cool ceramic felt good under my fingers, but it was of little help. Nausea turned into fury, letting uncontrolled temper run wild. I felt my hands burn in white flame. Soon enough, it engulfed my whole arms. I pushed away, reining myself in only when burn marks spread across the sink.

More rationally, I thought through the options. Mate Grim was a rumoured side-swapper. If the rumours were correct, he had a history of Hate, inherited from a lawbreaker mother. A side-swapper, by definition, was a (suspected) lawbreaker returned into Fate's service. Though a side-swapper, by definition still, continued to be a threat, for you never truly knew if those people harboured Hate. My jaw began to ache, and I realised I had been clenching my teeth tight. How could the Authority allow people like this to roam free, to give them another chance? They clearly had nothing on him to make an arrest – *yet*. I failed to see a reason beyond trickery and hateful hypnotism that had lured Beatrice to him. I'll bet my prophecies that the rumours of his past were actually correct.

Should I tell Daddy? Perhaps there was hope, some means to exorcise her, purify her blood before it was too late. Hearsay had it that such procedures were sometimes carried out. Hate was a powerful poison, after all the only one strong enough to meddle with Fate's plans, to stray us from Fate's chosen path. If there was some means of turning Beatrice back to Fate, surely it was worth a try?

On the other hand, there was Daddy's reputation – and with it – the Authority's, and most importantly, mine. Justice was justice, and Fate had to be obeyed. If my sister was poisoned, damned by Fate's judgement, then so be it. A tough stance on Hate is the only means to root it out.

The options were therefore to keep this absolutely quiet, or to let it explode and let harsh judgement be passed. I looked up into a mirror above the sink. My mind was set – praise be to Fate – and my reflection returned a smile. Another side-swapper will be exposed, judged as hateful, and condemned. I'd ensure the Purgers saw to that. All that lawful effort with only me to thank. Another would be punished for collusion, for I wanted to see how Alastair Grim claimed oblivion to his brother's state of blood. Most likely both Grim brothers were side-swappers, as the story said. And if my sister went down with it – well, that would only make me martyr twice as much.

CHAPTER 18
LILLY-ANNE SKYROSE

The semester was gradually drawing to an end. Waves of doubt still ebbed and rocked me from time to time, though three constants kept me afloat: friends, homework, and a steady stream of Empyrean-stamped envelopes. Scaling the steps to the post room in the fourth tower, a momentary current of panic always passed through me, threatening to draw me into a whirlpool of irrational pessimism that remained in the depths of my consciousness, growing stronger each time Damsel, Professor Artsback, or anyone else insinuated that I was an Earthly threat. Retrieving Gabriel's letters from my post box, I always half-expected to find an arrest warrant too.

I pushed against the angsty current, focusing on the trivial day-to-day. Whatever was fated will become clear in due time.

That's just a saying, though, that I had picked up – people always said this and that was *fated* in the otherworlds. *Fate* itself I wasn't all too clear on still, and despite forcing myself into attempted intuition, could not feel. Failed attempts only strengthened my conviction that the idea of some power that predetermined everything in life, was inescapable, and moreover, which run in my blood, was silly. Just another part of the charade shrouded by the magic of the otherworlds.

Then again, the Authority was real. The Carcery – or at least the threat of it – was real enough.

Back and forth I swung, between careless disregard of and anxious panic over breaching Fate's plans for me.

The semester would soon end, however, and more immediate storms brewed on the horizon. As soon as the posters were put up, there was only one thing everyone seemed to talk about: winter ball. Apart from the opening dance and meal, it wasn't an excessively formal event, though everyone was keen to dress the part. 'What are you wearing?' and 'who are you going with?' were the questions that abounded. Marking the end of the semester, and as such prematurely marking winter solstice – the most important Continental event – it was the biggest celebration of the academic year.

So big, in fact, that listening to conversations about which table my friends were going to sit at, who to buy tickets off (since they instantly sold out), and which shoes coordinated best with what dress had quickly become tedious. Despite the limited number of tickets, and rather unrealistically, everyone hoped to be there: Vince and Melanie, Bertie, Tina, Francesca, Dean (of course, that boy was simply everywhere), Charlotte, Constantine, Fabian, Rupert. Even Kin seemed to entertain the idea, though his enthusiasm visibly dwindled when Sephy announced she had more important plans that night: a rare stellar conjunction, unfortunately she couldn't make the ball. Ruby was intrigued by the hype that the event created, although looking at the ticket price, she quickly decided that it was not for her.

With neither Rubes nor Sephy confirmed for the ball, my choice was much easier. I wasn't planning to go, but I endured the surrounding conversations, and regardless of how repetitive and boring they got, I strove to find enthusiasm for my friends. I vented to Gabriel about it, and he offered to lend me his t-shirt in return, in case my ditching of the ball was because I didn't have anything nice enough to wear. His t-shirt suited me well, he wrote, and if I wore it, I was sure to be crowned ball queen.

Partly, I endured conversations about the ball because something even more dreadful followed it: end of semester. I would have to go home and see Lynne – unless I was rescued with an invitation to the Empyrean, though at present this didn't seem to be forthcoming, and I was too much of a wimp to just invite myself. Matriah had apparently not taken too well to my last visit and associations with Earth. Thus, my reunion with Gabriel hung around awkwardly among the words of letters we exchanged.

*

I took my usual seat in botany and waited for Charlotte to turn up. She too was going to the ball, but at least she was cynical about it; I looked forward to laughing at her eye-rolls and snide comments. Getting her hands on one of the few tickets that were cheaply raffled off – a new initiative to make the ball more accessible, a cheap raffle ticket that could win a ball entry costing several times as much – Charlotte was going with her girlfriends and wearing an old hand-me-down. She didn't care, looking forward to the unlimited food and drinks.

Professor Meyer had a practical lined up, re-potting and pruning the various courtyard plants. It was better than the last practical, at least, that involved separating gravel into colours.

"What does colour-sorting gravel have to do with botany, you may ask? Not much, unfortunately, but Chancellor Arden wants a gravel mosaic laid out in the cloisters, and someone has to get that done," was the excuse last time.

"Hello, Earthling." I looked up to find Constantine planting himself down in the seat next to me.

"Ur, hi."

This was unexpected – and unwelcome, I must admit. Constantine wasn't exactly a friend; he seemed determined to pick on me, though I struggled to find malice in his words. It was as if he half-heard what everyone else said about me, misread the room, and constructed arbitrary sentences from the mishmash that the process produced in his head.

"I see you've chosen to sit with me today," he said.

"Uh, no, actually. This is my usual spot. You just sat down next to me."

"That's fine, I don't mind you sitting next to me."

Charlotte skidded into the room, winking at me upon finding that her usual seat was taken. I shrugged back. She sat behind us, Constantine's mountain of a body obscuring her from view.

I decided to give up reasoning with Constantine, and we got on with the re-potting. Soon enough, it became apparent that even the simplest of tasks was beyond his capabilities. I watched as he struggled with the pots, the ensuing root damage causing re-potting to do more harm than good.

"Look," I finally snapped, taking the pot from his hands and squeezing gently on the sides to loosen soil. "You don't need so much strength, just ease it out. It's not difficult." I imagined this is how Ruby felt watching me butcher spells.

"Of course it's not difficult, otherwise you wouldn't be able to do it, Earthling," Constantine returned.

I stopped trying after that. We worked in silence for a while.

"Are you going to the ball, Earthling?" The surrounding conversations filtered in through Constantine's ears, passing quickly through the empty brain and out his mouth.

"I don't have anyone to go with, so no, I'm not."

"Well, I am. Perhaps someone will take pity on you and invite you," he said.

"I don't need *pity*, thank you very much. None of my close *friends* are going, so I decided to skip this year." I wondered if he was clever enough to make the connection between *friends* not going and the fact that *he* planned to go.

"You need more friends then, Earthling."

I didn't bother responding to that.

*

In Force control, to nobody's surprise, we meditated. Professor Fellblue also invited anyone who felt the need to do so to come forth and discuss their intuition. Sephy raised her hand.

"Yes, Persephone?"

"You said, Professor F, that Fate reveals things to us in dreams. And that blood is the conduit of Fate. Well, I was wondering," sat on the floor, she drew her wobbly knees up underneath her chin, "is it possible that Fate runs through the eyes as well? That Fate reveals the true nature of things – of people – by laying a lens over one's eyes?"

I heard Ruby sigh. This was about the worms again. It was all connected, in Sephy's mind: blood, vision, Fate, dreams, and the worms – that she now thought might be Fate materialising underneath her eyelids. She claimed the worms – or Fate – lived in everything now, not just mud, transforming the ordinary into miracles. Through Fate laying this lens over her eyes, she got to see everything in a special way.

Professor Fellblue stared at the ceiling, taking off his hat. He apparently did this to think more clearly. "Yes, I suppose that's possible. Fate works in mysterious ways, after all, and she is all around us. There are also blood vessels in the eyes. Do you think Fate has put a lens over your eyes, Persephone?"

"Yes, it's almost like there is something in my eyes that makes me see through people clearly – how they really are – and see the true beauty of things. Like you would normally in a dream," she clarified.

Ruby sighed again, this time in relief that *worms* were not directly mentioned. In my world, doctors would have told Sephy to get her eye pressure checked out.

"I suppose we might say that you are living in a woken dream, then." Professor Fellblue smiled.

Rupert's hand went up.

"Rupert – please, share."

"I think I've been feeling very intuitive lately," Rupert straightened up.

"That's very good."

"Well, professor, the thing is… it kind of hurts."

"Oh?" Fellblue didn't quite know what to make of that. "How so?"

"It starts in my stomach, a kind of burning – I think it must be Force burning in my blood. Then it spreads to my core, between my lungs, but it's quite uncomfortable and it leaves a bitter taste in my mouth."

"Oh dear, Rupert." Professor Fellblue put his hat back on. "I think that's heartburn you just described."

*

Professor Fellblue asked me to stay behind after class again.

"Have you tried the reflective exercises I suggested, Lilly-Anne? To build up intuition."

I clutched my notebook nervously. There were two ways out of this: I could lie, saying that I have, then fail miserably to materialise any evidence of greater intuition, for there was no way that I could willingly produce a white flame across my palm, or, I could say the truth, and risk my lack of faith being exposed.

"No, I haven't, professor. I'm sorry, I'm sure they are good exercises, it's just that… you keep repeating that intuition and feeling Fate are the prerequisite to materialising Force, and I…" I trailed off, the crux of the truth getting stuck in my throat.

"You're not sure if Fate is real," he said calmly.

I nodded, surprised at the casual tone in his voice.

"Well, you won't be the first, and certainly not the last. I'd hazard a guess that this question has crossed most people's minds. And given your

184

upbringing, it's hardly a surprise – you're only getting used to the concept, after all."

I almost shuddered with disbelief. "But I thought... I thought everyone believed in Fate? That believing in it was written into the laws..."

"Well yes, I doubt the majority of people would have the confidence to ask this question out loud." He leaned back into the heavy chair behind his desk, while I stood on the other side. "Personally, I think Fate *is* real, she is all-knowing and all around. We cannot escape being in Fate's reach, unless this is what she wants us to do. And even then, our escape is her wish. It is a paradox, the greatest one of all. But you must decide for yourself how you feel."

"But what about the Unbreakable Laws? And the Carcery?" I gulped. "How am I supposed to do what Fate wants me to, when I don't *know* what she wants?"

Fellblue laughed. "I believe everything you do is fated, Lilly-Anne. What time you get up, what you eat for breakfast – it is fated to some degree. You might not be aware of it, or make such choices by consciously following Fate's wishes, but it is. That's not to say that Fate will contact you directly and tell you to choose orange juice instead of apple. What it *does* mean, however, is that you should be open to signs, which mostly come in dreams. If Fate is kind, and if she has some higher plans for you, there is likely to be forewarning. And then, if you are a loyal servant, you will obey and carry through the plan. Most people go through their entire life without ever noticing a grand revelation. Then again, most people don't have access to resources that may help nudge their intuition – schooling, for example – such is the predicament of our worlds. They may carry on looking out for Fate's signs. Or, they may falter, stray, and decide that Fate doesn't exist. They may become jealous, covet that Fate has been kinder to others, or feel that the whole concept is nothing but a scam."

"Isn't that the third Unbreakable Law? Do not covet," I asked.

"You have been paying attention, very good," he smiled. "Yes, the Authority dislikes it when the common folk question why access to Fate's blessing is so exclusively centralised. Not to mention that superior intuition of our justicemen seems to correlate with wealth. I must stress though that I think intuition is a personal matter – only you will know if Fate has reached out to you."

"And the lawbreakers – do they purposefully go against what Fate had planned for them?" I asked, since it seemed like we were speaking frankly.

"That is difficult to say," Fellblue sighed. "Sometimes I think it is more helpful to separate out the concept of laws from Fate."

"But they are judged, aren't they? They are deemed to have cheated Fate and sentenced to the Carcery."

"Yes." A thoughtful sadness crept into his voice. "You must understand, Lilly-Anne, that you have entered these worlds through a door that is relatively high up in the interworldly ivory tower. Sapphire Dragon's is no ordinary place – there are strong links to the Rachthaws, the Authority – the hands which for millennia have held the worlds in a tight grasp. And to maintain such power, one must convince everybody else that you have something that they all lack. The Rachthaws were supremely intuitive, Fate's most loyal servants – I don't doubt that. But we can all be intuitive, if Fate reaches out to us and if we listen. And I do believe that Fate has an equal grasp over everyone, including lawbreakers. Yet the intricacy with which her grasp is tied to laws and to who has the *power* to construe what Fate really asks of you..." he mused. "Well, it is up to you, to decide where you stand."

"I think I prefer to play it safe, professor; stick to the laws, rather than risk a slow and painful death," I mumbled, still trying to make sense of his words.

Fellblue chuckled. "Yes, that's very wise. I see Asset's classes are as effective as ever in ingraining the Authority's message. Though I doubt you have very much to worry about. Even if the Authority have an issue with you, it is Fate's judgement in the end."

"And if Fate sentences me to death?"

"Again, I recommend not worrying about things outside of your control. I believe that whatever Fate has planned *will* be. There is nothing we can do other than accept the plan if it is kindly revealed to us."

The logic of it all spiralled in circles in my head, a never-ending paradox formulating. "But you said, *if* you are a loyal servant, you will obey whatever plans Fate has revealed to you. That leaves a possibility of disobeying."

"Yes, and the Authority would call that cheating Fate. The first law."

"But how is it even *possible* to disobey, when you said whatever Fate has planned *will* be," I protested.

He sighed again. "There are two answers to that. The Authority would say that lawbreakers disobey Fate because they are poisoned by Hate; that Hate is the only concept strong enough to change Fate's plans. But in this understanding, Fate's plans are always aligned with what is best at keeping the Authority intact. In this official understanding, *if* you are Fate's loyal servant, you will obey – obey Fate, or rather, the Authority's translation of Fate's plans. When one sees the concepts of laws and Fate as so intertwined, the worlds appear black and white, right or wrong."

"And the other answer?"

"The other answer is less commonly spoken aloud." Fellblue took off his hat. "And some of our justicemen would say that the other answer is precisely the crux of Hate. We are speaking purely theoretically, of course." He looked up to make sure I understood. "The other answer is that it is not possible to cheat Fate, ever. It therefore follows that there's no such thing as Hate, and those apparently poisoned by it are simply doing whatever Fate had planned for them, meaning that lawbreakers are Fate's puppets, her servants, just as you and I. Such an answer would therefore render the laws and Authority quite useless."

Fellblue paused, gazing out of the window, before returning his eyes to me.

"I believe Fate works in intricate ways, Lilly-Anne," he continued. "But how we *use* the *concept of* Fate, is another matter entirely. It is a tool for those in power. It is a comfort and solace to explain unfortunate events. At the same time, it is an injustice. It is a devotion, a guiding path in one's life. By the same token, it is also an excuse – if everything is fated, we hardly need to feel responsible for our actions."

I stood motionless, sensing that there were further questions to ask, but lacking the words to put them out. Professor Fellblue was saying that it was possible that Hate did not exist; that Hate was just an excuse, made up by the Authority on behalf of those who did not comply with their laws.

Then again, he said some people decided that Fate wasn't real; that Fate was nothing but a scam by those in power who disseminated this story in order to keep their privileged position, for they sold themselves as the only ones capable of *truly* knowing what Fate had planned. And because they had painted Fate's power (and by extension, their translation of it) as absolute, there was no escape. If you tried to escape, you were deemed poisoned by the (also possibly bogus) power, Hate. The only option was subservience.

Yet Professor Fellblue didn't think that was the case. He thought that Fate *was* real, it sounded like, and that it – she – truly predetermined everything. It would follow that all these intricacies and power schemes, Fate simply made up for her own entertainment.

The otherworlds' shape refused to stabilise; it was something different, depending on who you asked. And in the overlap of their words, their stories, I found myself in a kaleidoscope of understanding. Each meaning as transient as the last, the otherworlds' true colours surfaced, reformed, then blurred again.

In that moment, something caught my eye, only partially visible under various papers and instruments scattered on Professor Fellblue's desk.

"What is that?" The words slipped out without any politeness attached.

Professor Fellblue followed my sightline, reaching to retrieve a paperweight that I instantly recognised. The glass ball, palm-sized and flat on one side so that it could stand, had etchings and crystals in a constellation embedded inside.

"A gift." He held it up, where it caught and refracted beams of light. "From one of the most talented students of mine."

"Unc— Bill Skyrose," I mouthed.

The paperweight always sat on Uncle Bill's desk at home, the same one I always wanted to play with as a child, and he only moved it higher up outside my reach. By the time I was tall enough to take it, I'd lost interest, dismissing it as another strange object that he hoarded. Most of those had otherworldly uses, I knew now.

"Yes. William called on me at the end of summer. It was very flattering of him, I must admit, to remember that I was still alive," Fellblue smiled. "He told me that you'll be matriculating, asked me to keep an eye on things. I'm very sad to hear of his passing. He was one of my best students. I even recommended him for the queensguard myself."

Resentment simmered up inside me; overwhelmed with questions, the answers to those at the core of my existence, Uncle Bill took with him to the grave.

"Well he clearly didn't do a very good job, seeing that the queen is dead."

Ignoring my bitter remark, Professor Fellblue stood up and began pacing the room. "William was very intuitive, Lilly, answering to Fate's every command. And with regards to the Murders, some might say that it was Fate's plan all along."

"Why would Fate plan to destroy the institutions that spread her message, kept everyone in line on her behalf, and upheld the bargain? Why would Fate kill off her most loyal servants?"

"Fate works in intricate ways, Lilly-Anne."

I remembered Uncle Bill similarly suggesting that Fate had also *planned* to cut off the Earth Islands from herself.

"I don't understand."

"It is not our right to demand an understanding of that which is not revealed to us," he said. "Besides, rumour has it that the queen was aware that the Murders were going to take place. It makes sense, after all, that Fate would be kind enough to let her most loyal servant know."

"Then why didn't she prepare for the attack?"

"Perhaps she did – albeit not in a way we would expect. The Rachthaws commanded armies enough to easily defeat the Legion. Not to mention the queensguard who would have eagerly perished if only it would have saved the queen."

"And yet Uncle Bill resigned," I pressed.

"I wouldn't be surprised if he was *sent* away." Professor Fellblue held up the paperweight to a beam of sunlight. It refracted a multitude of rays around the room. "Sometimes intuition comes at a price. What you learn, what Fate has in store for us – it may not be pleasant."

"You think that Fate ordered the queen to stay and die? And everyone else with her?"

We briefly learned about the scale of this attack; hundreds of people died. Fonsland was nearly wiped off the map. The Legion attacked on a day when large crowds had gathered by the palace – civilians, almost all members of the Authority – awaiting an important announcement from the queen. I shuddered. Did the queen schedule all this knowingly?

"Sometimes, Fate demands a sacrifice," Professor Fellblue answered, and the words rang through my brain.

For some reason, I had a feeling that I would come to hear their awful sound again.

CHAPTER 19

PERSEPHONE BUTTERBLESS

In, through, and out the other side. Then on the reverse: in, through, out. And again: in, through, out. Only several more to go. In, through, out. Reverse – in, through, out. Across, and pull it tight. The gap closed.

"That's better." For a first attempt, it was looking rather fine.

"Are you sure Ruby won't mind?" Kin asked, tilting back his head.

He sat on the steps at the bottom of my bed. I sat on the bed, and he tilted his head back to look at me. He was more than welcome to sit next to me, but the floor felt safer, I guessed, grounded. You can't fall off the floor.

"No," I said. Turret windows reflected in his glasses, transforming them into his own little, private windows to the outside world. "But there's only one way to find out."

"Will you make one for me, too?" he asked.

In, through, out. In, through, out. I was getting the hang of this; the needle almost worked itself.

"Of course."

"You could just spell it and spare yourself the work." Kin chucked a ball of yarn, and Flip scurried after it.

"That's not the same." I placed the stiches in a precise composition, guided by what felt exactly right at this particular time, sewing the moment right into the fabric.

"If you say so." Flip returned the yarn and wagged his little tail excitedly. "Are you sure you're not going to the winter ball?" Kin looked like the question was costing him too much.

"Sadly, I simply can't miss the two blue moons conjunct – they do a little dance. And I can't be in two places at once."

The needlework stopped as I thought a while. Were these events really on the same day? I'm getting my days all wrong recently.

"You could watch it from the ball – it's still the same sky." Kin's head tilted back to smile at me again.

I dropped a depleted bundle of yarn on his head, and it slid into his lap. Half of the winter ball was going to be inside – the meal, the dance. There were also tents, stalls, and activities outside. A big one-night funfair. I will be sad to miss it. But I couldn't be in two places at once. Or… could I?

"Aura at the ball won't be right for watching the blue moons conjunct, it'll be too bright."

"Yeah, I guess you're right." Kin tossed more yarn across the room. "Want me to come with you then, to see the moons?"

"Of course, we'd love to have you there."

"*We?*" Kin seemed a little disappointed. "Many people, or…?"

"Not more than at the ball." In, through, out. I was getting close to finishing the last one.

Kin laughed, but the laugh was just a mask. "I guess you're right again. Do I know them?" Kin was so shy, no matter how hard he tried.

I wanted to hug him tightly, to reassure him. Instead, I dropped more yarn onto his head. "Some you know, some you don't. They all know you, though."

Kin would prefer to sink into the anonymity of the ball. Attention at personalised gatherings was a bit much for him, that's why he wasn't at the Purgers' meeting tonight. That, and because he was too kind.

"Right, perhaps it's best I pass on the moon party, then."

He took the yarn off his head and chucked it.

Where I was going to be in a few sets' time, there wasn't going to be a crowd, just two persons. Two persons in one body, one familiar to Kin, the other a transmogrification of him. I'd already made a promise for that night. Orle wanted to spend time together, promising he knew a place so high that we would almost reach the moons and dance with them in the sky. We would watch the misty raindrops falling to the forest floor, search for mosses, and listen to the little bugs snore. I enjoyed his company too much – it would be a heartbreak to decline.

Proudly, Flip returned the yarn, tugging on Kin's trousers when he didn't react.

Kin was busy looking up, up and back, back at me. I peeked through his glasses, held by his happy-sad eyes. They pleaded for a promise too, a promise for care, support, and love. I wanted to love everyone, and Fate was kind because love came easily to me. People were just so wonderful, too beautiful in their oddities not to indulge in knowing them. Kin needed my support that night; Orle needed my company. I couldn't be in two places at once – or could I? Perhaps Orle would know a formula for that.

The door opened, and the last of our little family returned. Lilly came in but her mind had been left behind elsewhere, and my brows furrowed trying to deconstruct the aura that she brought with her. A concoction of determination and confusion hung in the air. Ruby followed right behind, her mood diffusing into the aura as she saw my work, and… oops.

The aura fell heavy. I guessed Ruby did mind.

CHAPTER 20
LILLY-ANNE SKYROSE

After Force control, I went to see Charlotte in her grandad's bookstore. The doorbell of Sinnerstroke's Texts and Tales rang as I pushed open the door.

"What was *that* about?" Charlotte greeted me enthusiastically, referring to Constantine's usurping of her seat in botany.

Her question brought me back down to earth – however unfitting the expression is. The conversation with Professor Fellblue left me out of balance, detached, perplexed.

"Don't ask," I shrugged. "I honestly have no idea. He seems determined to talk to me for some reason."

"Huh." Charlotte carried on restocking shelves, hoping for business during winter break to pick up. "Constantine Dartwood, some would say he's quite a catch."

"It's not like that," I objected, picking up a box to help her out. "He's not very nice to me."

"Perhaps he's never talked to a girl before," she laughed. "Maybe he wants to ask you to the ball."

"Fat chance, I told him I'm not going."

"You're welcome to come with us if you can miraculously source a ticket and fancy listening to pointless philosophical debates," she offered.

"Yes, I've heard the Theorists are a real fun bunch," I retorted.

Charlotte stuck out her tongue. "Or, perhaps Constantine is just a cocky bastard. He's telling everyone he made the Ranger duel team already," she said.

"I thought the try-outs aren't until after winter break?"

"They aren't." She shoved a book onto the shelf. "But he's overly confident that he'll be on the team. Which is bad news – I don't particularly fancy standing up against him on the pitch. Have you noticed how *huge* he is? One blow and he'll knock me out."

"I didn't realise you were hoping to be on the Theorist team."

She shrugged. "Free merch. Gets you out of classes for practice when matches are coming up."

The doorbell rang again, and we peered around the bookshelf to find Francesca and Ruby coming in.

"Saw you two through the window." Judging by the look on her face, Fran was already eager to get out – books were not her thing. "Want to come dress shopping with us?"

"I've hardly got the heads to spare for a new dress," Charlotte said without breaking from her task.

"That's okay, Ruby's just coming to browse too."

Ruby nodded in agreement, though cast a pleading glance in my direction. It was obvious she would much rather spend her time browsing here.

"Sorry, Fran, I've got work to do," Charlotte declined.

Francesca pouted, then turned to me. "How about you, Lilly? Are you getting a new outfit for the ball?"

"Oh no, I'm not going." I picked up some more books to hand Charlotte.

Ruby spotted one she liked. "How much for *The History of Continental Trade?*" she asked.

"Four heads," Charlotte answered without looking.

"And for a friend?"

"Four heads."

"What do you mean you're not going, Lilly? I thought you changed your mind. Constantine said he was taking you to the ball." Francesca sounded genuinely confused.

"*What?*" the three of us chimed at once.

"When?" I added, staggered.

"Just now. I bumped into him and Rupert. I'm going with Fabian, though Dean will probably tag along," Fran rolled her eyes. "Constantine said he's taking Lilly, and Rupert is thinking of asking you, Rubes – sorry, I kind of spoiled the surprise."

Ruby's jaw also dropped, and I swear I heard her mutter an almost silent, "Oh no."

"I am *not* going to the ball, and certainly *not* with Constantine," I said through clenched teeth.

"Well, you better let him know that." Francesca hooked Ruby by the arm, already engrossed in the gossip the scene I was about to make would provide.

I looked for Constantine everywhere: in the Ranger common room, the buttery, the great hall. I circled through the cloisters and grass pitch in the pouring rain, even checked the library (though that was unlikely), but now that I actually wanted to speak to him, Constantine was nowhere to be found.

Then it occurred to me that Kin was handed another one of Damsel's perfumed envelopes. A Purger Society meeting was on tonight. Constantine was always invited too. Furious, I stomped through the corridors until I found the designated meeting room. How *dare* he tell people that he's taking me to the ball when I *specifically* said otherwise?

Laughter and the clink of glasses echoed from inside one of the meeting rooms in the main building, a thin rim of light around the heavy doors edging into the darkness of the corridor. Unable to make out the individual voices, I lingered by the door, trying to listen in. Hearing Dean's hearty laugh, I decided that this was the right place. The Purgers' meeting was inside. I took a deep breath.

Did I have the guts to willingly walk into a snake pit? No.

Was I furious enough to do so? I pushed down on the handle and opened the door.

About twenty pairs of eyes turned to stare at me as the revelries died down. I gulped, suddenly feeling very small. Most of them were sat around a long table lined with heaps of silverware; others retired to armchairs pulled around a lit fireplace, and a few hovered in between. All were dressed in Sunday best.

"Oh, look who's here!" Dean got up and put his arm around my shoulders, tiddly, judging by the smell of his breath. "We were just talking about you!"

Traitor, I thought. Scanning the scene, which looked like it belonged in a frivolous costume drama, I expected to see Damsel at the centre of attention, being the gorgon who organised it all. Instead, the now-fading energy seemed to gravitate towards someone else. With neatly combed blond hair that parted to one side, grey eyes, and a pristinely pinned tux, he sat at the head of table, leaning back and drumming his fingers lightly on the wood. An arrogant – almost accomplished, like he had just outsmarted everyone in the room – look branded on his face.

Damsel sat to one side, stiff and almost too upright, her lips pulled into a tight line. Next to her was—

"Constantine, a word please," I said, still through clenched teeth.

"We've had so many unexpected guests tonight – first Alastair, now you," Dean blabbered, then stumbled as I shrugged his arm off me.

"Constantine, now," I repeated.

"Why, where's the fire?" Constantine finished off his drink. "Oh wait – certainly not on your hands, Earthling."

Everyone laughed.

"I'd like to know why you're telling people that you're taking me to the ball," I snapped, and the laughter turned into a hooting chorus of *oooh*.

Constantine's chair screeched as he stood up, making his way over.

"Because that's the case – I decided to take pity on you and take you to the ball, Earthling."

"I don't *need* your pity, and you never asked me to go with you."

"Thought you're just too shy to ask, Earthling." He grasped my hand, lifting up my arm in a victorious hold. "My ball date, everyone."

Fury over-boiled inside my blood, my free hand clenched, a fuse blew inside my mind. Never before had I felt a deeper conviction that I had been wronged, humiliated, and taken over to such degree. This wasn't *right*.

"Ouch!" Constantine recoiled and dropped my hand. For a moment, I thought I saw something bright flash across my palm.

Taking a deep breath to calm myself, my eyes fixed on his and slowly, I spelled out, "I'm not going to the ball with you, Constantine."

He froze, leaning back, chin tucked into the enormous shoulders either side, bewilderment across his face. Stillness in the room was broken in that moment, as Dean tripped and flew into the table. Attention turned to rescuing the spilled cups.

"You can't do that now, I already told everyone," Constantine managed to breathe out.

"Too bad. You won't see me at the ball." With that promise, I turned and left the room.

*

My legs carried me so fast through the stone-lined buildings and across the grounds to Ranger Bastion that I almost ran. What just happened had caught up with me, disbanding my calm.

I darted through the bastion's entrance without acknowledging the gremlin porter, then ran across the common room and up four flights of stairs. There, I caught Ruby, also on her way back to our dorm.

"Rubes!" She turned at the sound of my squeal. "Rubes, I think I just burned Constantine!"

"What? How?" she matched my tone, baffled.

I relayed the events to her. She blinked several times, alongside a few *wows*. Then her brows pinched together and nose wrinkled.

"Wait, *that's* what the Purgers' meetings look like?"

We made our way back to the dormitory. Delighted for this whirlwind day to finally end, I was unsure I could stand anything else happening tonight. I pushed the door open, and at that instant, a ball of yarn landed at my feet. At the launch of its trajectory sat Kin, with Sephy on her bed just behind. The horror in Ruby's gasp was audible as she processed what was going on.

"*What* are you doing with my school jumper, Persephone?" Ruby huffed.

Sephy hopped off her bed, holding up her work proudly. "I've made us all matching ones."

"They *were* matching, Persephone. That's why it's called a uniform!"

I moved closer to examine the collection of four jumpers laid out on the little turret steps. Sephy had sewn a little pocket by the bottom hem onto each. On each pocket she embroidered a thick, wiggly line.

"Kin helped – takes after his mum in fashion design," Sephy beamed. "It's no Arabella Spells, but we tried."

Kin pushed himself off the turret platform steps, adjusted his glasses, and pursed his lips thinly in a guilty smile.

Ruby picked one jumper up, scrutinising the damage. "What *is* that?"

Sephy looked across our faces, some big revelation building in her eyes. "It's what Lilly was looking for."

My face must have been puzzled, and perhaps she noted I was way too drained to guess.

Sephy held up her work again. "A slug pocket, for each of us."

I tossed around in bed that night, unable to sleep. Too hot under the covers, too cold if only I stuck a leg out. The day's events raced through my mind. I retraced the conversation with Professor Fellblue – or as much of it as I could remember, for each time I went over it, the reasoning made less and less sense. Replaying the image from this evening, I posed the same question over and over again: had I *really* burned Constantine? Is that what made him drop my hand? Was the bright flash of white – white fire, Force – across my palm something I imagined? If it hurt him, it didn't hurt me, that was for sure.

With one finger, I gently traced the lines across my palm in the dark. White light, where did you go? Fate – hello… are you there?

CHAPTER 21
ORLE GIGGLY LOBBSTER

There were those who waited to grow up, those who waited for solstice night or a new power-flick wand model to come out. There were those who waited for lunch. Others waited for their friends, for their bodies to take shape, for *the one* – or merely someone – to notice them. The moons waited for the night, nibble bugs waited for the hyacinths to bloom. Professor Meyer, I think, waited for us to leave, for the earliest reasonable moment to dismiss class because his face looked awfully fed up.

I waited for you because my whole life changed whenever your shape came into view.

"Are you all right there?" Meyer stopped his monologue to ask.

He stopped to ask – ask me, I realised – because I gagged. The thought was too corny. I still waited to see you. But the thought was so corny, it made me gag.

"Yessir." Too corny to be ever said aloud. Putting things into words makes them real, you see. Especially if they're said aloud. And I still couldn't believe such a friendship was happening to me.

Meyer's head raised a brow, his tongue licked the end of a chalk stick, and hands carried on writing on the board. I don't know why he was writing. To give the impression of teaching, I suppose.

"Next time, we'll be calibrating scales." *Scales*, he underlined. "It's not botany per se, but the alchemy department needs them calibrating, and if we ever need to weigh yield – they'll be ready for us to use."

"Three years in this class, and we have never grown anything successfully enough to have to weigh yields," whispered a voice behind my back.

"Did you have a point to raise, Miss Jones?"

"No, professor."

"Very well. Class dismissed, enjoy your lunch, everyone."

Chairs shuffled and bags packed – were packed, by students and their arms, I should clarify – and the herd funnelled through the door, galloping across the fields into the sty. Feeding time. I funnelled out with them, but then turned around, heading for the garden instead because I was quite full.

Full of hope. For seeing you.

The muscles in my throat clenched again, and instead of saying hello, I gagged a greeting out.

Oh, you itsy-bitsy loved up fool, do you honestly not know how to keep your cool?

Thankfully, Panacea didn't mind. Or I guessed so because she smiled. She never minded me apparently – perhaps she put up with me because she was attuned to seeing magic everywhere, and I was full of spells.

She sat in the school's walled garden – salled garden, as I thought of it – behind the botany lab. In a big chair, she sat. Or rather, on the thick, low branch of a chair-shaped tree. Exactly where I'd asked to meet her. I knew she'd understand the instructions that I'd passed to her:

At the corner that leads nowhere, take a right.
Carry on until the angry roses (beware, they bite).
Here you should turn back on yourself, preferably twice,
And follow the litter trail left by the spotted mice.
This will lead you to the chair-shaped tree,
Where you can sit and wonder, waiting for me.

"Thanks for waiting," I said to Panacea.

"It's hardly waiting when there's so much here to see," she clarified.

"Thanks for watching, then," I adjusted, and Panacea's face returned a grin.

"Oh, I think the show has just begun," she said eagerly, drawing her legs upwards and sitting cross-legged on the tree. "What's on the menu today?"

Reins of realisation pulled me back. I froze, but my neck nearly snapped. There it was again, a little, innocent hint. A reminder, that there was no reason for her to spend time with *me*. Because when I wasn't Orle, there was nothing likeable about me. Not until I jacked myself up on spells and became Orle. And when I *was* Orle, well – they might not have liked me still, but at least I didn't care. Yet there was one reason people returned to Orle, and that was the spells that I'd cook up.

The spells that so far she never asked for. This realisation was killing me. It weighed about four hundred tonnes, and it was pressing down on me. Her order was coming, and sooner or later, it would arrive. Once she had what she wanted, she wouldn't come back. Or at least not for me. She'd come back for the spells, like they all did, once a seed grew inside their minds. I knew that well because my own mind was a thicket, I confess, an overgrown hash of magical wilderness.

"I mean… what's the plan?" she corrected, as if sensing this.

"Well, we can watch the plants grow." I sat beside her, trying to push the thought back. But not too far back, lest I fall off the tree.

"Do you have a favourite?" She scanned the garden.

Like my mind, the garden was a mess. It belonged to the botany department, but Meyer didn't look after it. Only Professor Sprause sometimes ventured in, desperate for some ingredient. I only know because she once walked in on me, and politely pointed out that the entrance said (not literally, as doors don't speak) that entry for students is not allowed. I panicked then and told her that I couldn't read. It wasn't my finest moment. I got detention, mopping the library corridor for a good while . Haunt would come in to check on me, every half a round – come in with his muddy boots on, especially.

"Over there, in the corner by the music tree," I said, when I remembered Panacea was waiting for an answer. Music trees were a second favourite, as they grew only to the sound of music, faring best in fast beat.

"Is that a— "

"*Concentracia stimulata.*"

"The focus plant."

"Indeed, I planted it myself." I listened out for distaste, but none followed, so I figured she was okay with that. Like the vendors and peddlers that lined the city streets, focus plant cuttings came to Loon's City without permits, on shabby rafts at dusk. Unauthorised, so you had to know where to ask.

"Have you picked any of the leaves to dry?" she asked. Dried, rolled leaves sold officially for seven fingers per twenty in a pack.

"Nope, it's a little too young for that."

"When did you plant it?"

"'Bout this time last year."

"Wow, it's already so big." She studied it from across the garden. "You really are multitalented, you know. A spellsmith, a dueller, and now – a green thumb."

Her eyes filled with wonder, lit up to the brim, leaving no room for contempt, and as such, no room for me. A laugh erupted from my chest; I could not reply. A laugh – a cramp – locking uncomfortably my ability to speak into the horsy sound. For it's when she saw me like this – and her opinion was horribly sincere – that words failed me most, and to Orle's vision, nor to her vision of me, I could no longer adhere.

"I was wondering." Panacea let a nibble bug crawl up her hand, and I wasn't sure if she was talking to the bug or me. "Is it possible to be in two places at once?"

Me. "Course it is."

"Well, do you think you could show me how?"

Reins of realisation reigned over me, issuing commands. This was it: a goodbye. "You need a spell?"

She nodded. "I guess that's what I mean."

There was a tearing sound. I felt something break and checked to see if the tree we sat on had snapped.

Now, now, lad, stay strong. You can't risk her getting a spell wrong. "Come on then, I'll write it down for you." My arms pushed off the tree bough – still intact – and legs ordered themselves back to the botany lab. Flowers turned their sad, little faces at me as we passed. I took apart my broken heart, for that's what must have torn, swept it into a pile, and left it by the door.

A desk with a forgotten notepad invited us from across the empty room. My hands worked up each other's arms, rolling up the sleeves – each in turn, for I couldn't do both at once. Tears threatened to come out. I blinked them back, forced them to flow inside the hollows of my cheeks. Only one escaped out through the nose, but my tongue was long enough to claim it back. My stomach played a melancholy symphony.

"Want to grab some lunch soon?" Panacea hovered nearby.

"Not really." My guts struggled as I swallowed back my pride. "Hold this."

She took the wristwatch that my hands unstrapped. I didn't work well under the pressure of time.

"I need some details: who, when, where, why."

"Me," she clarified. "Do you know my dimensions?"

"I've got them etched into my brain." *Blimey laddie, that honesty was much too straight. Though actually, who gives a shooting star right now, it's already too late.* "When and where?"

"Two rises from today. I need to be wherever you will be to watch the moons, but I also need to be at the winter ball that night." She started explaining the *why* next, but I wasn't listening because the reins of realisation steered me another way.

"Wait a tick," my insight interrupted her. "I need to be at the ball too." *Well, well, laddie, someone clearly hasn't thought this through. Did you forget, what happens at the winter ball? Upon your absence, your position on the duel team is bound to take a toll.* "Or else they'll trade me off the team at the rounds."

I scratched my head, unsure of what to do. Had it been covered in curls, perhaps I would have found a solution lingering there. Instead, ideas slid down the straights of my hair.

Panacea supplied one herself, however. *You should be proud, boy, she really is clever.*

"So double the recipe, if you can."

"Two consciousness multiplication spells, that's the plan."

I picked up my hopes from the door on my way out, the pieces of my broken heart, but it wasn't quite the same. We would be together still, though half apart. I worried it was this friendship's end about to start.

CHAPTER 22
LILLY-ANNE SKYROSE

I woke up to a chilly draft wrapping around my neck, and instinctively, pulled the duvet tighter around my head.

"Look everyone, snow!" Sephy's voice chimed.

"Will you please close the window, Persephone – it's freezing," Ruby moaned, her voice muffled by the covers as she too hid from the frosty breeze.

It was true. Overnight, the weather painted Loon's City black and white. As far as the eye could see, white fluff settled on every surface, crocket, and parapet, filling every stonework niche, spandrel, and tracery. The dazzling white contrasted deeply with the blackness of wet stone, the mosaic of rooftops, even the deadened, black branches of trees. As far as the horizon stretched, the sky was milky white too – a blanket of thick, white cloud obscuring any blue. Rows of forest in fading shades of grey crept up the hills on the other side of the shoal, which too, turned monochrome – a murky, frozen black.

Suddenly wide awake, Ruby jumped out of bed, getting dressed in a flurry unfitting for a Saturday.

"What's your hurry?" I asked her, wrapping myself in the duvet like a human Swiss roll.

"I 'eed to get au' the bast'on 'fore Rupert gets up," she said through the toothbrush in her mouth.

"You think he will still try to ask you? That's leaving it a little late, the ball's tonight."

Ruby spat the toothpaste out into the washbasin in the corner of the room. "Don't want to risk it." Ever since Francesca's warning, she zealously avoided Rupert. "I'm going to hide in the library."

"Try something less obvious, maybe – if there's one place he's sure to find you, it's the library."

"True…" Ruby grabbed her textbooks. She was always in the library. "The reading room, then."

The long-dreaded moment had come: the end of semester. Unwillingly, I got out of bed and wrote a lengthy one to Gabriel now that I finally had the time. Compensating for the lack of classes over winter break, Professor Artsback doubled the homework load. Professors Meagles and Flashmight were not too kind with history and magic either; the last couple of weeks had quickly passed.

A fortnight ago, I hastily wrote to Gabriel about how I *think* I materialised Force. He quizzed me about the circumstances, of course, and found it hilarious when I wrote it's because Constantine believed he was taking me to the ball.

Wow, Gabriel wrote, *I'll make sure to have some healing spells ready for* ~~when~~ *if I ever ask you out.*

I penned a quick one to Lynne too.

Dear Lynne,

How are you? I won't be coming home for winter break, but perhaps I'll see you soon. Love, Lilly.

In my neatest handwriting and vain hope that it would somehow help pixie post deliver, I wrote Lynne's lengthy address, even adding 'Earth' on the end. If this ever reached her, I hoped she'd dismiss it as a bad joke. The other address was much simpler: Gabriel Hale, Kah-a'miss, Empyrean Fed.

By early evening, I wrapped up warm in a hat and scarf, ready to post these off. The night was icy, still, with no wind. Snow covered everything securely with no threat of melting anytime soon. Unable to cross directly through the grounds, I edged along the temporary fencing lining the perimeters. Like the majority of the main school building, the grounds were only accessible by ticket tonight. Music and a merry hubbub coming from over the temporary fence indicated that the ball was now well underway. Why anyone would want to spend this icy night outside was beyond me, though Charlotte said she'll have a warming spell written on the back of her hand, just in case.

Dropping the envelopes off in the 'outgoing' box at the top of the fourth tower, I climbed down the stairs until I reached an arched doorway about halfway down. Normally, I ignored this little entrance, which led to a rampart connecting the five towers. Usually, I simply climbed all the way down to the bottom of fourth tower, taking the shortest route back. For lack of better things to do, I decided to take the long way home. Merriment coming from the grounds echoed at the heights, at odds with the silence and stillness of Loon's City, asleep at this time of year. The rampart soared above the city, offering a brilliant view. A monochrome patchwork of rooftops unfolded below, only an occasional street lantern or stray breathing life into an undisturbed city. Beyond, frozen shoal waters glistened in the moonlight. Watching over this conjunction from the fifth tower was the motionless sapphire dragon, its tail wrapped around the drum, the tail's end a blazing beacon of moral righteousness of the otherworlds.

I trailed the rampart, grasping at the merlons of the battlement lest I slip on the ice, passing an archway entrance into the third, second, and first towers. At the last, I stopped, spotting someone sat on the steps inside. Perched, he looked through the lancet window on the festivities below.

Hearing my approach, the familiarly lanky frame – on which hung

several layers of white tie attire underneath a heavy winter cloak –
straightened up and turned to me.

"Oh, evening, Lilly, hi," Kin muttered and pushed his glasses up.

"Hey, Kin. Aren't you supposed to be at the ball?" I went to sit beside
him, and he shuffled along the step to make room.

"Yeah, I guess I am," Kin smiled sheepishly, holding up a crumpled
ticket he clutched in his gloved hand. "But not sure I feel like it anymore."

"Aww, Kin, why not?" I peered over his shoulder at the dance below;
music was louder here, reverberating through the air and heights. A group
of students spilled out from a tent as a giant inflatable orb rolled past. I swear
I saw Professor Meyer link arms with Sprause as they walked towards the
hall. "It looks like fun."

"Yeah, I guess, it's just that…" Kin gazed out of the window too. "Look
over there," he nodded.

I followed his sightline and spotted exactly what – who – he meant.
Easily recognisable in a glittery gown and nest of golden ringlets on her
head, Sephy danced, cloak wrapping around her as she spun.

Then it occurred to me. "I didn't realise Sephy planned to go."

"Neither did I. She said she wasn't going, that she had other things to
do." Kin dropped his gaze to the floor, milling his ticket between his fingers.
"I'm starting to think she only said that because she didn't want to go with
me."

"Kin, no, you mustn't think like that," I tried to cheer him up. "You
know how Sephy is; maybe she just forgot, or she changed her mind – you
know she's unpredictable at best." He finally smiled at the latter. "Perhaps
this is a surprise, you should go join in."

"Maybe you're right…" Kin's sadness waned a bit. He looked up, and
then alarm crossed his face. "Shoot, Lilly, I have something for you." He
reached inside his jacket, struggling to pull something out while wearing
gloves. "I was meant to pass this to you about a set ago. I'm so sorry, I

totally forgot.”

He finally fished it out, and I grimaced as the yearbook picture of Constantine came into view, teeth flashing and head turned to the side in some misjudged attempt to allure. It was completed with an autograph.

“Don’t shoot the messenger,” Kin laughed, noting my grimace. “Did you really burn him – Stine? Dean came back that evening saying that you did, but his speech was so slurred, I didn’t really understand.”

“I’m not sure,” I admitted. I turned the picture over to find a personalised message written in handwriting worse than a doctor’s scrawl, the only recognisable words of which were ‘Lilly’ and ‘ball’.

“I think this was meant to persuade you.” Kin poked the picture.

I sighed theatrically. “If only you remembered to give it to me, Kindegory.”

Panic flashed across Kin’s smooth face, but soon enough he caught onto the joke. “Whoops, don’t arrest me, looks like I cheated you right out of what Fate had planned to be,” he teased.

“Too bad I just informed on you to the Authority,” I gestured towards the fourth tower.

“Sending another letter to Lynne?” Kin asked, more serious now.

I nodded.

“I could have a word with someone, if you’d like, make sure they get delivered.”

“It’s fine, thanks, Kin.” I stared at the lights below, absentminded. “If they make it, they make it. If they don’t, they don’t.”

“So have you got anywhere to go for winter break? I mean, are you going back to Earth? Because if you need somewhere to stay, you’re welcome to stay at mine – there’s room enough, we could probably house the entire batch of Rangers and Mum wouldn’t notice.”

“That’s really kind, thanks, Kin. I’ll be at the Globesglory’s for winter break, though.” Dianne’s invitation, relayed by an overly excited Bertie, saved me at the dreaded semester's end.

"Oh yes, of course, I forget you're family. I'm sure solstice is going to be really fun with them."

"Are you looking forward to solstice?" I asked, unsure what the traditional celebrations entailed.

It was Kin's turn to grimace now. "Not really. Dad probably won't come home, Mum will have a hundred strangers over for some grand do, and Clementine will only want to show off."

"Who's Clementine?"

"My baby sister." He tucked a strand of hair that dislodged with the face he pulled. "I mean she's fifteen, but she's still my baby sister. Hey – do you think I can ask you for a favour?"

"Sure, go ahead." I couldn't possibly imagine what Kindegory Spells might need from me.

"With the duel team try-outs coming up next semester, do you think you could… you know… put in a good word for me with Vince and Bertie?"

I couldn't help but laugh.

"What?" Kin asked, laughing with me now.

"You could just *state* that you would like to be on the team, Kin, and I'm sure they'd let you."

"I know, I know." He pushed his glasses up. "But I want them to know that I'm *good*. And I'll show them that I am, at the try-outs – but just to prime them. I don't want to make the team just because I'm a Spells. Will you, please?"

"Of course," I reassured.

"Thanks."

We both turned to look out of the window at the sound of Sephy's chiming laughter ringing through the chilly air.

"Will you join the ball, then?" I nodded at the lights. "I bet she's wondering where you are."

"You really think so?" Kin perked up.

"Totally, I bet she turned up to surprise you."

Kin jumped to his feet, almost tripping over his cloak as it caught his foot. "Maybe I'll go then. Thanks, Lilly."

"Anytime," I mumbled, but Kin was already too far down the stairs to hear.

*

We crowded by the school gates, waiting for another Brightwood-bound carriage to turn up. Unlike the journey to Loon's City – where I boarded a carriage picking up the last remaining students – everyone was now going home at the same time. Griffins screeched and huffed, ready to take flight. The gremlin driver whom I recognised from last time pulled up and scanned his list, relieved not to have to request a special portal permit to Earth this time.

The carriage took flight just moments after we sat down inside. The journey wasn't long, and conversations about the previous night soon filled the gap.

"Did you see Professor Meyer go off with Sprause?" Tina began the stream of gossip.

"Gee, they were already flirting at the meal," Vince made a gagging sound.

"How do you know?"

"Saw them sitting at high table. It's near to where the duel team captains and their dates sat."

"Oh of course, towards the high end of hall. How were the captains' rounds?" Tina asked.

"Boring," Melanie butted in.

Vince rolled his eyes. "Promising, I think. We're in for a good season, we brokered some good deals with the other captains, came to mutual understandings." He nudged Bertie in the side, who was falling asleep and looking rather ill. "Bertie did the honours and drank most of the rounds himself," Vince laughed.

"You looked stunning at first dance, Mel," Tina added.

"Aw thanks, I didn't think anyone noticed me, not with Jolie Anderson also there," Melanie smiled.

"I noticed you there." Vince gave her a quick peck on the cheek. "Only have eyes for you."

"That's good to know, Vince," Mel retorted, "seeing that you were the one I danced with."

"I think I'm gonna puke," Bertie groaned, and we all leaned away.

Much to Ruby's embarrassment, Metalsmiths District was the first stop. I knew she hoped they would be dropped off last, so that nobody could see where they lived.

"Right, that's us." Tina reached for her suitcase. "Have a good solstice, everyone. See you next year."

"It's a pretty deprived neighbourhood," Vince explained once we'd said our goodbyes and the carriage rolled past the Metalsmiths. "But it's not that bad, there's much worse places in Brightwood – Glass District, for example. Look." He pointed out of the window.

I held back the flimsy curtain just in time to see the fronts of red brick tenements give way to grand, detached houses one might expect to see in rosy suburbs. The stately houses of the Glass District, however, were overgrown with vine, unlit in their bay windows, which were boarded up or smashed, half-burned and otherwise dilapidated.

"What happened here?" I turned to Vince.

"They had a real problem with Hate, not long after the Murders, spread like wildfire. Nobody lives here now."

I only guessed at what happened to the residents.

Sat on the edge of the sofa in the Globesglory's living room, and despite Auntie Dianne's enthusiastic reassurances that she was *so* glad to have me here, I now felt like an intrusive third wheel as Vince and Melanie cooped up next to me.

It was a warm welcome. Dianne hugged me tightly, showering me with questions: how was school, did I settle in, did I like it, were *these two* helpful in showing me around? Could I give her some help with an article she was writing on motion pictures and video cameras? She was having trouble understanding what made the pictures move – was it in real time? Jacob Globesglory, Auntie Dianne's husband whose stressful job certainly made him show his age, was glad to see me too.

"We're so sorry about Bill – taken too soon," he said, shaking my hand with both of his.

Dianne and Jacob were in the kitchen now, obscured from view, though their agitated voices carried a vivid picture through to the living room.

"I'm so sorry, honey, I'll try my best to get back quickly." Jacob was shuffling into his mac.

"But it's solstice night," Dianne protested. "You took this day off especially, surely they appreciate that?"

Jacob sighed. "Yes. But it's an emergency hearing, news just came through."

"Is it about—"

"Yes," he cut her off.

Dianne exhaled deeply, and irritation rang through her voice. "They really have us in a double bind, you know. And it's times like this when I feel it the most."

"I know, I know," Jacob soothed. "I hate it too. But I dare say I wouldn't be advising the high judge, nor you, writing for the *Seer* – and I don't mean to undermine your talent – but something tells me you wouldn't get to report on *these* kinds of stories either, if they didn't feel like they could control what news leaks through. I know you want to write the truth – but that truth is theirs. Everyone knows you get inside knowledge from me. And regardless of whether you report the *real* truth, or what the Senate wants everyone to think is the truth, or a truth that they want everyone to think *isn't* true – they've got us trapped."

There was a short silence.

"Go, then," Dianne sounded resigned. "But I'd say the *real* emergency is *here* tonight – I'm cooking."

There was some more shuffling, then Jacob popped his head around the door. "Bye boys," he said reflexively, then added, "and girls. Save me some cake."

"Will do, Pops," Vince answered for everyone.

We heard the front door unbolt, and Jacob left.

Bertie swaggered into the living room then, sprawling himself between myself and Melanie.

"Dad's just left," Vince informed him.

"Can't even give them one day off for solstice," Dianne's voice rumbled against the clutter of kitchen pans. "High Judge Percy Potts clearly has no concept of family time."

"That's a news headline right there, Mum," Vince said, and we heard Dianne laugh. "I wonder what the emergency is…" he mused.

Bertie clicked his tongue and produced a sheet of paper from his pocket. "Exhibit A." He unfolded it, displaying it to each of us. *Wanted*, it read in big letters, with a drawing of a woman underneath, together with a hefty reward sum. "They put these up around town last night."

"Hardly any point in putting the posters up, if you're just going to tear them down, Bertie," Mel scolded.

"They're after the last Rachthawnian murderer," Bertie ignored her.

"How do you know? It doesn't say that here." Vince took the poster from his brother, scrutinising the details.

Bertie clicked his tongue again, swung his arms in a loop through the air, and pointed both towards the location of his dad's study. "Exhibit B: Dad's desk."

Vince raised a brow, so Bertie continued.

"I may, or may not, have looked over Dad's shoulder when the message appeared on his instant ink pad. I then may, or may not, have read it after Dad left and before it disappeared. They've arrested some wee lad, were about to sentence him to Carcery, when he wiggles his way out of it, saying he's got information on the Legion."

"And the last murderer still being on the loose...?"

"You're looking at her right there," Bertie nodded at the poster. "Drawing is based on the lad's description."

They sat in comprehensive silence for a minute, and I guessed this was big news.

"About time... Only took some sixteen years," Mel finally said quietly.

"And you know what else?" Bertie could hardly contain the excitement. "The drawing's hardly accurate."

"How so? Thought you said it's based on the description that the arrested lad gave," Vince interrogated.

"*Based*, yes, but Morty Goldtear put a lot of edits in. According to the wee lad, she's a *demon*," Bertie's voice hushed and eyes widened at the word.

"Oh, Bertie, *please*, don't start," Mel groaned.

"What are demons?" I asked. I've heard demons mentioned only once before, in history class.

Bertie spun around, eager to have someone's attention. "They've got horns," he stuck a finger up either side of his head, "and tails, and scales –

like fish, but they don't live underwater – no! They live where they please. They're unnaturally fast – too fast for human eyes – and exceptionally strong, strong enough that spells and Force can hardly damage them. They're smarter and more cunning than any of us. And they've got fangs." He shifted his fingers to his mouth, sitting very still. "Do you know why, Lilly?"

I shook my head.

"Because they exist to feed on your blood, drain you dry and leave you dead."

"*And* they're also a myth," Melanie added, leaning over Bertie to clarify. "Don't let him scare you. There are ancient texts that mention demons… and dragons… and centaurs. They're just stories, written at a time when fact and fiction were rather intertwined."

"They're ancient texts *written by* the Rachthaws," Bertie protested, intending to add credibility.

"Yes, but the Rachthaws had to win over populations somehow, didn't they? *Hey ye, we got rid of the demons who were apparently eating you, now worship us.* Anyway," Mel looked at me, "the last *apparent* demon sighting was hundreds of years ago, and after the very, very ancient times, they're seldom mentioned in texts at all."

"She has the horns and tail! Wee lad said so himself," Bertie butted in, irate.

"Next, you'll be saying there's immortals hiding among us in the worlds." Mel rolled her eyes, turning to me to explain further. "Ancient texts talk about a hierarchy, a food-chain, as it were. When Fate first revealed herself to Rachthaw, a bargain was struck, whereby Fate gave Rachthaw a weapon powerful enough to defeat the demons that were supposedly eating everyone. This weapon was the *immortal* – a being whose body had pure Force pumped inside its veins, and who was the only one able to kill demons. But these are just stories. In whatever way the bargain was struck, its origins are a myth."

Bertie was about to object, when Vince finally weighed in. "The Senate can hardly afford to go on a wild goose chase after a myth, brother."

"Oi, that's enough." Dianne popped her head around the door, frying pan in hand. "No more meddling in your father's business. Those were private messages, Gilbert. What's intended for the justicemen needs to stay that way until official press release," she scolded, but her words rang with a scepticism and the faintest hint of distress. "Now why don't you boys go and do something more appropriate – go practice duels or something. I'm having a nightmare enough with this salad as it is."

"Need any help, Mrs Globesglory?" Mel got up and headed for the kitchen.

"Oh yes please, sweet, if you wouldn't mind. The ingredients just won't mix properly." Dianne's voice was muffled by water running in the sink.

Vince pushed off the sofa too, holding an arm out to help Bertie up. I followed Mel into the kitchen, hoping to make myself useful, and put off by the idea of watching the twins hurl balls of friendly fire at each other in the frosty night.

CHAPTER 23
IONA JAKE

I had copious amounts of patience, as every master huntsman does. But my patience had been spread thin over centuries, and it was running out. It is pathetic, an abomination, a vulgar violation of my superiority that I should find myself in this position; ridden to live underground, to feed on the decaying flesh that was the only sustenance in this land. At least there was a regular supply.

To find that after centuries of my existence, and despite all my strained efforts thus far, I must still hide lest *she* tracks me down. And she was still present, I could sense it, even though she has not made her presence known for hundreds of years. Perhaps she was satisfied – for now – with so few of my kind left, that her work was done.

One of my claws ripped through the cartilage at the thought. I looked down to examine the severed ear I toyed with. I'll have to get another; these were exceptional playthings to fondle as I thought. And I did a lot of thinking these days.

Fennel cleared his throat when he walked in. Unnecessary, I heard his approach from a mile away. He was nervous, rightly so. The only reason he was still alive was because gremlin blood tasted foul, and I was too proud to sink so low.

"There is movement, your abhorrence, on the Senate front." He moved so ungracefully, a jarring, awful sight. His voice was a screeching in my ears. I ripped fully through the cartilage at having to endure all this.

"Continue," I ordered, leaning back in my nest. This was my private chamber, I did not like to be disturbed.

"A warrant has been issued." The smell of sweat running down Fennel's back filled the air. "Here." Fennel staggered closer, holding something out.

I snatched it and not a tick later, a laugh ripped through my core. "*What is this supposed to be?*" The pitch made the cave shake, as even the stalactites laughed with me.

"You, your abhorrence." Fennel backed away.

I shredded the paper in my hands, disfiguring the image that was already so imprecise. Even the name was fake, for I did not have a name. My kind had no need for names, just as we had no need for air, water, warmth, or rest. We had a need for blood, breeding, fear, and worship in the momentary gaze of our prey.

We had no need for language either, but I learned because there were so few of us left now. In desperation, I bartered with humans rather than drain them dry. I learned their language and I took a name (two names, after two random meals I ate) because that made humans more comfortable, a point of reference in their minds.

I was not sentimental, and I cared little for avenging those perished of my kind. I was indifferent to the dark, cold, supposedly unpleasant surroundings. But I *was* hungry, hungry and fed up of feasting on meals that others had chosen for me. It infuriated me that my meal choice was determined by the humankind, by those in uniforms who dropped off a fresh meal every once in a while. For while *she* persisted, I could not freely roam the worlds, choosing my prey as I wished. While she persisted, I was no hunter – I was her prey. I lingered underground, venturing out at night to snatch whatever despicable human happened to be nearby. There was a steady supply of them, here in the barren lands, but they did not fare well in this climate and their white blood – usually so exquisite in flavour, so potent and rich – developed a sour edge when their health declined. And in their decline, was mine, for I was not as fast and strong feeding on rotting flesh.

I have seen others of my kind – so few of them left now – wither and decline lacking good nutrition.

We cannot go on like this. We will not survive – another century, perhaps.

There was therefore only one solution: get rid of *her*. She, who was neither human nor my kind. She, who hunted my kind down, who was responsible for my decline. She, without whom my kind would once again be unstoppable, doing as we pleased across spacetime.

I couldn't simply kill her; I couldn't crush her skull or easily outrun her. She was invincible against my strength, it seemed. So I watched, deduced, learned. A plan materialised, and I nearly put an end to her.

Her existence is tied to humans, specific humans – a lineage dressed in fancy clothes. My tongue ran over my lips reflexively – I liked a well-dressed snack. So I put an end to that lineage. I could have done it by myself, of course, but why expend the extra effort when willing humans gathered to help out? They too wanted to end the lineage and, being human, were stupid enough not to understand that helping me would result in their demise. For once the lineage was annihilated, whatever force held *her* in place would disappear, and my kind could freely hunt humans again.

Or so I thought. The logic had no flaws. Yet despite the fact that my human Legion destroyed the lineage so many years ago now, my instincts told me that *she* was still around. This could only mean one thing: the lineage was not fully destroyed; the ties holding *her* to it still persisted.

"Call on the Legion to come forth," I ordered the gremlin.

Fennel was a loyal hand, believing in the promise that once my kind were superior again, gremlins would no longer find themselves in human servitude. We had common interests, in this respect: showing humans their place.

"They won't come," he screeched and dodged the remains of the ear I threw at him. "Those who survived the battle are now locked in ice. You need fresh soldiers, your abhorrence."

"I will do it by myself, only then will it be done right."

"Forgive me, if I may? That will take a lot of time – to find the Rachthawnian heir, to finish what you started. The heir could be anywhere, your abhorrence."

I left my nest so fast he did not see me coming and lifted him by the throat. So small, perhaps he could make my next plaything, now that I was out of ears. "Then I shall sift through every dwelling until I find what I am looking for."

"That is… sure to… make you… her target," Fennel choked out.

Yes, *her*. I could not risk going above ground for long and doing the dirty work myself. I dropped him to the ground. The cave shook again with my roar. To be so powerful and *yet* so powerless!

"Bring me fresh soldiers," I ordered.

Fennel scrambled on the floor, long arms and legs so easily breakable. "They will require payment, your abhorrence."

I roared again. *Humans!* So disgustingly materialistic, as if any of that made a difference to their puny lives. Humans boasted morals, standards, devotion, and yet all of that was futile unless they were given shiny wholes and heads. I liked wholes and heads too, but I liked them fresh.

"An opportunity has arisen, to secure the funds," Fennel murmured.

I loathed having to listen to this.

"There is a monetary reward set," he continued.

"Set for what?"

"For you, your abhorrence, your captivity." Fennel's deep-set eyes dashed to meet mine. It was thrilling to hear that humans thought they could capture *me*. "There are no humanly means to imprison you, of course, but this leaves the reward wasted. If you could perhaps… collect it. The reward is meant *for you*, in the end."

I saw it in the gremlin's eyes then, the same thing I was forced to tolerate in my human soldiers: greed. I saw past it, too. I remained safe from *her*, decaying in the shadows. But her and I were both safe in the shadows, shielded partly by our supreme abilities, and partly by the limits of the human mind – the myths of our existence, the myths that so few knew to be true. If I were to step out, would she follow me?

Returning to my nest, I stretched out, and a finger dug into the scales running down my leg. "What do you propose, Fennel?" I pointed the finger at him, and he cringed for it wasn't one of my own.

"Turn yourself in."

Fennel jumped to dodge a falling stalactite, as the cave shook with my laughter's chime.

CHAPTER 24
ORLE GIGGLY LOBBSTER

My mind shrunk outwards, then exploded inwards on the ride. My mouth fell through the ceiling and my back shot through the floor. Teeth danced, guts spilled through my side. I was seeing backwards, reliving it once more.

Strap in everyone as I swallow back my pride, for this is a story of how a spell went wrong and Gilbert Globesglory nearly died.

*

"Now, why don't you boys go and do something more appropriate – go practice duels or something," Mum suggested.

Like a trained puppy, Vince got up, holding out his hand. I followed, since none of them were going to believe me. I could waste five hundred years trying to persuade them that I'm right. Nobody ever takes Bertie seriously. But let me assure you that, in this instance, I was right.

Out in the icy night, I watched my breath puff out, but it was a boring breath, not the glistening unfolding of personal mist that Orle liked. I sighed and another disappointing breath appeared. How was I going to cope with that dullness, when I had to breathe all the time?

I clenched my teeth and thought, *no Bertie – not tonight*. Tonight was merry, cheery, *family time*. We climbed a grassy hill overlooking the estate – a favourite duel spot, where none of the neighbours could complain. 'This is a respectable neighbourhood, I'll have you know,' Mrs Carp said once, when we tried to duel too near her house.

All the suns were at their lowest over the Continent today. Now they hid under the spacetime sea, and when they rise tomorrow, things were bound to improve. Another new year. I remember saying this last time. And on it goes. The same old, boring crap. Every year.

He got me in the side then, when I wasn't looking. A friendly shot but it stung a bit.

"Oi!" I yelled across the hilltop. "A bit of warning would be nice!"

"Stop whining, princess!" Vince shouted back, shooting another one. It got me in the neck before I could react.

I retaliated but my hand trembled and the trajectory faltered, missing him by several feet. My hand trembled nowadays when Orle called it back. My body responded to this latent transmogrification, as did my mind. Perhaps my body had a mind of its own, for recently it was trembling so much. I ground my teeth and repeated to Orle, who begged to take shape inside, *no Bertie – not tonight.*

"Cor, you're really out of form, aren't you?" Vince laughed.

"Shut up!" I yelled. I was quick then, materialising, aiming, and *bam* – it got him in the leg.

"Hey!" Vince patted out the flame and rubbed the sting. "All right, let's do this properly. Ready?"

He bowed and before he straightened up, I hurled another few shots, missing him entirely.

"Gee, I said let's do this *properly!*" Vince was angry now. "What is *with you* recently? First, you're out of shape, now you're out of line!"

My aim was better then, but he saw it coming and rebounded the shot so that it hit the icy grass where it smouldered out.

"How do you expect me to share the captain role with you if you can't even stick to the rules? Why can't you do something *right* for once?"

His words stung more than any shot I'd ever taken. They ricocheted inside my brain, snapping something on the way. That's it. I wasn't going to be pathetic anymore. I *was* coveting however, I'm well aware. Vince had it all: he had friends, good grades, more facial hair, the stupid captain's badge, and now he even had a girlfriend. Not that I was jealous of Mel specifically – in fact she kind of irritated me. It was the principle that bothered me. He was half an inch taller too. Being born first, he snatched all the good things that Fate had lined up for us to share. Even Mum had a surprise seeing me pop out – a nasty one I'm sure – for she only expected one of us. And that was Vince – I, the unwanted runner-up. Now he had it all together, while I was torn in half. A quick formula and Orle could have anything. If I was Orle, I needn't worry about coveting. As Orle, I wasn't bothered by anything.

A quick recipe for precision, speed, and strength formed inside my head. Turning my back to Vince, I slid the wand out of the holster on my arm. Letters rearranged inside my head; I muttered the formula to myself. Orle's vision was forming, but in the midst of this, something caught my eye – the eye that still recognised the city's skyline unfolding below the hill. It was the Senate House, looking not quite right.

"Fire," I said out loud, realising this.

In that instant, Orle moved my hand. The wand drew circles in the air. The last circle ended in a tiny flick. A spell materialised.

The two extra syllables dislodged the formula, binding to the spell in unintended ways. What I had observed of the Senate House moved its destruction to my flesh. The effect was immediate: a warmness exploded in my stomach, I buckled to my knees. A fire ripped through my insides.

My lungs gasped for breath but found none. My body collapsed, convulsing, and I screamed a silent scream.

"What's wrong?" a panicked voice shouted in my ear.

I tried to answer, I tried to see. But all of that was suffocated, smothered by the flames, the fire engulfing me underneath the skin.

Icy pins dug into my back. It felt good, but good was not enough. Vince must have turned me over and it was the icy grass digging into me.

Tears ran into my ears, a trickle each side of my head; my body's only attempt at extinguishing itself. I lay there burning, barely seeing the night sky. Flames ripped through my insides, burning, kneading, and smelting all organs into one. Vince unloaded a litany of healing spells on me, all the ones he could remember, most repeated twice.

Finally, when the flames stopped, my lungs drew an ashy breath. I heard Vince exhale deeply too. I lay there still, watching the stars in the sky. I guess they decided it wasn't my night to die. I lay still and lay some more. He put his arms underneath my pits, trying to sit me up. I coughed out a cloud of ash.

Vince managed to sit me up eventually on the once-frosty grass. He put half my body weight over his back, secured it with one arm. With the other, he held onto my arm, which he put around his neck. Like this, he dragged my body home, and in the corner of my eye – before the hill obscured it from my view – I swear I still saw the Senate House looking not quite right.

I was dragged upstairs, finding what energy I had to help out with the climb.

"Is he okay?" somebody asked.

There was no screaming attached, so I guessed it wasn't Mum.

"I hate you," Vince concluded, putting a glass of water by the bed.

I couldn't reach it anyway. My muscles were stiff, my throat charred with thirst.

That's how he left me, with my body all wrong across the bed. It was wrong because it was sideways, and my feet hung off the end.

I fell asleep, ungrateful, defeated, and unsure if Fate would waste her efforts to ever wake me up.

CHAPTER 25
JACOB GLOBESGLORY

I hurried up the lengthy portico steps, taking two at a time. A hawker trying to sell souvenir ayuta paced between the pillars of the colonnade. The three-storey marbled entrance hall of the Senate House was already exceptionally busy when I arrived. Everyone got the message. I made my way across the crowd, and up the three flights of zigzagging stairs, whispers of conflicting opinions to the left and right. In the centre above the final flight of stairs, where the balustrade met to encircle the balcony around the hall, hung a huge ayutum, its centre a shining red. A red carpet ran down the stairs, and red curtains obscured the pitch-black night outside, giving the impression of a normal working day inside the torch-lit building. All were coloured tokens, of the Authority we once had.

From there I entered a portal corridor, heading for the courtroom. The Senate House was so large we used internal portals for quick access. Lawrence Dodge appeared by my side.

"I see you managed to make it, Globesglory," he said.

"I see you made the decision to print wanted posters without consulting me," I replied. I had a particular dislike for Dodge, I must admit. His decisions were hardly driven by intuition, unless in his veins flowed career goals.

"Is that bitterness I sense?" Dodge kept up pace, looking straight ahead. "Besides, I merely suggested it, lawkeeper signed it off himself."

We took our places in the courtroom, either side of the high judge at the tribunal, myself on Potts's left and Dodge on the right. The long room was unusually full tonight, the stands lining the walls almost spilling to the brim. Only sixteen years ago – edging closer to seventeen now – court proceedings were instead held in the throne room, where Queen Adalma the Rachthaw sat and passed her judgement. The sole reminders of these times today were Percy Potts's red tippet and the few of us who survived. Today, Lawkeeper Montgomery Spells sat in a tribunal above myself, overseeing our work in the courtroom, nodding, signing where necessary – a figurehead.

"Silence! Order, now!" Potts banged the gavel. Chatter in the room eventually died down. "Justiceman Goldtear will now present the case."

Mortimer Goldtear stood up in the stand, bowing to each side. He looked eager and fresh, abnormally so, like he had nothing else in the worlds to do but work.

"Justicemen and justicedames," he began, "as you will already be aware, we made a successful arrest yesterday. It goes to show that our hard work, our strategy and persistence, our intuition, pays off. Fate is kind to us."

"Hear, hear," echoed up and down the stands.

"Get on with it," I couldn't help but mutter under my breath.

"The arrest and subsequent interrogation led us to obtaining extremely useful, albeit alarming, information," Goldtear continued. *By what horrendous means?* I thought. "The detained lawbreaker, a young man of twenty-six, has confessed to awful crimes whose details would be inappropriate to recount on solstice night. We have also uncovered that this lawbreaker has ties to the so-called Legion."

Gasps and whispers rose up around the courtroom as he mentioned this.

"Quiet!" Potts banged the gavel again, then leaned his head towards me and grumbled quietly, "Are you writing all this down, Globesglory?"

"Yes, sir."

"Good." Potts straightened up in the tribunal. "Continue, justiceman."

"While the organisation itself has been thoroughly disbanded, rightfully judged, and the spread of Hate associated with it immobilised straight after the horrific events – we thank you Fate, for the intuition then and now – it is possible that individuals previously connected to the Legion are still at large." Goldtear added a dramatic pause, then went on to praise his department's (and mostly his own) efforts at uncovering said individuals.

I tuned out for that part, hearing it often enough as it was.

"Our work therefore continues, justicemen and justicedames. The decision to issue wanted posters was made last night. This is to simply serve as a reminder to our populations to remain vigilant, to reassure that we continue to serve Fate's justice on her behalf. Several candidates have already been brought forth and will be interrogated, although I personally doubt that the portrait we printed refers to *a specific* individual at all."

"Meaning?"

I was startled by the lawkeeper's voice echoing above us, interrupting Goldtear. It was rare that Spells paid enough attention to ask follow-up questions.

"*Meaning*, lawkeeper, that the portrait is based on a description provided by the lawbreaker we detained yesterday. He claims they were both involved in the Legion. However, the description he provided was… absurd… to say the least, and thus has been revised for print. We therefore have reason to believe that the young lawbreaker, although we do not doubt his former connections to the Legion, has lied to us regarding the portrait *per se* in an erroneous attempt to save his skin. For that he will be judged."

I held my breath; they offered the laddie a way out if he cooperated, now they're going back on their word.

"That being said, we will continue to work upon the description he provided to see if it proves fruitful underneath the surface… absurdities. For now, the posters remain a reassurance to the populations and a deterrent to those within Hate's easy reach."

"And what absurdities are these, exactly, justiceman?" Spells asked.

Mortimer Goldtear was silent for a while, deliberating how best to phrase his words. "Krebbles, perhaps you would like to explain," he turned to a junior member of his team.

Krebbles jumped to his feet, searching through a stack of papers. Finally, he found a transcript of the interrogation. Clearing his throat, Krebbles read aloud, "The detained said, I quote: 'I tell you – it is no lie, I beg you, please, please have mercy. No! No, please! Fate – I know Fate is kind—'."

"Just the general gist will do, Krebbles," Goldtear snapped. "No need to recount the whole interview."

"Yes, of course." Krebbles's face turned pink. "The description provided by the detained depicts a female of undetermined age, abnormally tall, with blue skin covered in scales, a tail," Krebbles's voice now struggled against the groans sounding all around the hall. "… crooked horns… fangs… sharp claws… unruly mane."

"Quiet!" Potts banged the gavel four times.

"What about wings?" someone asked.

A wave of laughter passed through the room.

"And how is this… blue female… linked to the Legion precisely?" Spells pressed.

"As I said, lawkeeper," Goldtear took over again, "we believe the description to be a far-fetched attempt at—"

"How is she linked to the Legion, justiceman?" Spells repeated.

"The detained claims that she was one of the main perpetrators responsible for organising the Murders," Goldtear said slowly.

The courtroom erupted again.

"The detained is twenty-six now, meaning he was what – ten years old – when the Murders took place?" someone shouted from the stand. "You expect us to believe, justiceman, that a ten-year-old was involved with the Legion?"

"Hear, hear," echoed others.

Distressing as it was, I have witnessed precisely such cases in the past; the Legion had a habit of recruiting young, indoctrinating, poisoning the mind.

"Sounds like a child's imagination running wild!" came an accusation across the room.

"*As I said*," Goldtear tried to make himself heard above the uproar, "we will work tirelessly to see if anything useful can be discerned from the description he provided. For now, we should rejoice that another lawbreaker has been arrested and will be judged."

"Absurdities aside, surely it is *not* good news, Justiceman Goldtear, to learn that individuals with previous connections to the Legion are still at large. What if the organisation regroups? Surely your effort should have uprooted *all* of the Legion by now," someone countered.

I wondered if Goldtear would make a point about his department's funding needing to be upped, but before he had a chance to respond, someone (an Empyrean elder, judging by her accent) spoke out.

"Justicedames and justicemen, do not so hastily dismiss the picture painted by the young man." The uproar gradually died down as her words sunk in. "We must not blindly dismiss the demon rumours as untrue."

We all stared at her, the only one brave enough to put a name to what the detained laddie described.

"That is what they are *precisely*, justicedame, *rumours* – old wives' tales – and nothing more," High Judge Potts addressed her directly. "I will not have the Authority's resources or time wasted on deliberating vainly."

The room fell silent.

"Wrap it up then, Potts," the lawkeeper finally said. "Your judgement on tonight's hearing, please."

"By the power invested in me by Fate, I hereby pronounce my intuitive judgement on tonight's hearing as such." High Judge Potts recounted the formula in a quick monotone. "The twenty-six-year-old lawbreaker will be subjected to a judgement – a separate hearing is to be held. Justiceman Goldtear and his department will look to decode the description provided by the detained, though we must equally entertain the idea that he is lying or insane—" He suddenly stopped, and we all looked around at each other.

The building trembled, a faint quake, I'm sure of it. Judging by the perplexed expressions around the room, others felt it too.

"The tremendous effort put into Hate eradication will continue as usual—" Potts's speech was interrupted again by another tremor.

This time the chandelier shook visibly, torches flickered.

Potts tried again. "I hereby announce tonight's hearing number…" he leaned towards me.

"Two thousand and twenty-one," I prompted.

"Number two thousand and twenty-one as dismiss—" Potts did not finish.

The courtroom door burst open with such force it flew off the hinges. Blazing flames and smoke gushed inside. Screams came from every direction, disorientating me. It all happened so fast then. My eyes barely made out the abnormally tall figure nearing through the flames; coiled horns growing from a long mane, graceful, silent steps, an agile tail swaying at her back, and bony wings folded by the arms. Blue scales covering the body glistened in the flames.

The next instant, the creature was in front of me, leaning on the tribunal. A snarl escaped her mouth, revealing a set of razor teeth. Fixing her animal glare on High Judge Potts's face, she slowly slid a sheet of paper towards him across the desk. Frozen with terror, Potts still managed to recoil as he noted the severed finger that she used to push the paper with.

"Hello, Mr Authority," the creature said, in a jarred accent and voice so unfittingly soft. "I believe it is me you are looking for."

CHAPTER 26

LILLY-ANNE SKYROSE

What began as an innocent celebration of solstice night turned stranger and stranger as the evening progressed. Melanie and I helped Dianne prepare dinner – and help was truly appreciated, as it was clear Dianne didn't often cook. I was setting the table in the dining room when a cold draft wrapped around my ankles. Stepping out into the hallway to investigate, I almost had a heart attack seeing Vince drag Bertie through the front door.

"Is he okay?" my voice was a strained whisper.

"Yes." Vince let out an angry sigh, shifting more of the lifeless, limp Bertie onto his back. "Just stupid. Do me a favour, Lilly – make sure Mum is busy for a while."

I nodded, suddenly feeling the gravity of whatever was going on. Without thinking, I went into the kitchen and turned up the heat on a soup Dianne had going on; soon enough it over-boiled, capturing her attention. I then chatted to her about video cameras, only vaguely aware of the background thuds as Vince dragged his brother up the stairs.

We didn't have to worry about making excuses for Bertie over dinner because the grand dinner Dianne had planned never happened. Jacob Globesglory didn't return that evening. Dianne was going out of her mind. A neighbour came to ask if we'd seen the protective dome that suddenly appeared over the Senate House. Apparently there had been a fire.

Jacob returned in the morning, and when I briefly saw him while fetching porridge for a now conscious though still rather ill Bertie, Jacob looked paler than a ghost. Dianne threw her arms around his neck.

"What happened?" she sobbed.

"The one on the wanted posters... she... it... came to us," he said emotionlessly, as if he was still processing exactly what went on.

I left then, to give them privacy.

Not long after, Dianne ordered the four of us to pack up, marched us personally to a portal terminal, and waited to ensure we stepped through to Loon's City safely.

Back at school, there were still a few days left before spring semester started. I spent my days with Charlotte, as she stayed behind in Loon's City to man the bookstore over winter break. Business was slow, however, and she had plenty of time to chat. I relayed the events of solstice to her. A wanted poster, already obsolete, was still plastered by the doorway. According to official reports, the fire in the Senate was a minor accident – a portal malfunction, overheating.

"You know what the strangest part is," Charlotte mused, cashing up the meagre takings. "They haven't sent her to Carcery yet. I don't understand why they're holding out – she turned herself in, so what? Usually it's a quick affair."

In the evenings, I moped around Ranger Bastion, the only (miserable) company being Vince and Bertie, who practically refused to speak to each other, and when they did, they jumped at each other's necks.

"I'm telling you: one more time, and I'll throw you off the team!"

I walked into the common room to find Vince jabbing a finger at his brother.

"So much for your promise of sharing captain, then," Bertie said wryly, avoiding his twin's gaze.

"You're hardly fit to be a striker, let alone captain. Oh hey, Lilly." Vince crossed my path, leaving already. "Maybe you can talk some sense into him."

I slid onto the sofa beside Bertie. "Talk some sense into you about...?"

I asked.

"About nonsense," Bertie grinned and crossed his eyes.

Hoping they may have some insider information from their parents, I tried asking the twins about what happened at the Senate, and why the woman from the wanted posters wasn't sentenced yet. They didn't know. Or at least, that's what I deduced, for Bertie maintained it was because the *woman* was really a demon, and the Senate didn't know what to do with her. I dismissed that as Bertie being Bertie, his imagination running wild.

The day before semester started, Sephy arrived first, and I knew she had arrived before I even saw her. Coming back into our dorm, I found the room looking like a tornado had just passed. Clothes, potted plants, talismans, potions, sketchbooks, mosses, and odd socks were strewn around the floor.

"Sephy?" I called. Her head poked around the corner by the washbasin, ringlets springing in every direction.

"Lovely Lilly!" she chimed, running to hug me. "You'll never guess what I got!"

"What did you get?" I didn't bother guessing. Her hobbies – just as her character – were so wildly unpredictable, my guesses wouldn't stand a chance.

She skipped around the corner, beckoning me to come with. On the little cabinet next to the washbasin, in the corner between her turret and Ruby's bed, was an old transistor radio.

"Now we can listen to stellar constellation updates in real time!" Sephy beamed.

"How are you going to make it work?" I asked, quite sure these required batteries.

"Watch," she said, pressing her fingers against the back casing. A heat haze appeared around her fingers, melting the plastic slightly. "Gently does it," Sephy mumbled to herself, adjusting the pressure. Something stirred inside, and the radio buzzed to life.

Ruby arrived later that night, losing hope as soon as she opened the door.

"I should have expected that she'll only acquire more weird stuff over the holidays." She cast a pleading look at me and brushed some moss off her bed. "Urgh, what is that constant monologue?"

"There's music sometimes too." Unbothered, Sephy went to collect her moss off the floor.

There was a faint knock on the door.

Despite being furthest away, Sephy was there to answer it in no time. "Kin!" she shrieked, throwing her arms around his neck.

"Evening, hi," Kin managed, his round face perched on Sephy's shoulder, framed by curtains of his flimsy hair.

"Come," Sephy led him in by the hand. "I must tell you all about the poddlywonks I met over the holidays."

"What's a poddlywonk?" I whispered to Ruby, whose memory held more atlases and taxonomies than I could name.

"No idea," she shrugged.

I never did find out. We sat on our beds (Kin on the turret steps) chatting about this and that, but the subject of poddlywonks never cropped up. Perhaps they did not exist – I wouldn't be surprised. A while later, there was another knock on the door. Sephy and Kin scrambled to hide Flip underneath the curtain hanging over her bedframe. Ruby went to answer it this time.

"Yello," we heard, as Ruby looked over her shoulder to briefly cringe at us.

"Hello, Rupert." She moved aside to let him in.

Rupert sat awkwardly on the edge of Ruby's bed, and in turn, she moved to sit with me, stubbornly keeping her head turned away from him. Conversation soon regained pace following the setback. Refusing to be kept out of the loop, Flip made an appearance too, provoking a high-pitched shriek out of Rupert, much to Kin's amusement. Despite reassurances of

Flip's friendly nature, Rupert sat with his legs up safely on the bed for the remainder of the night. This, in turn, set Ruby even more on edge. When she finally turned to look at him, the only thing she saw was the dirt on the bottom of his shoes. Sephy made Rupert pinky-promise not to tell anyone about our fluffy contraband. Satisfied that such a promise could not be broken, she concluded Flip was safe.

Another knock on the door interrupted us. I pushed off the bed to get it, though before I was even close, Dean invited himself in.

"Heard there's a party going on in here." He strolled in, ignoring Ruby's instant negations. "Who's this little guy?" He bent down to stroke Flip's head.

Dean was made to pinky-promise too, and I felt the last of Ruby's hopes for an orderly semester evaporate into the frivolous mood that filled the room.

Night fell and we lit candles, in no humour to go to sleep. Dean fiddled with the tuner on the radio, looking for something more upbeat, and I wondered if it was possible to pick up the BBC. Kin ran his hand over the length of Flip absentmindedly. I looked for more candles to hand Sephy, when I noticed the familiar eureka look creeping up her face.

"Let's divine!" she suddenly cried, making Ruby jump and drop the book she pretended to be reading. Filling a large, flat bowl with cold water, Sephy placed it in the middle of the room, where we gathered round. She then handed us a lit candle each. "Pour wax onto the water," she instructed.

"Are you sure Fate would want us peeping at her plans like this?" Ruby approached, cautiously.

"Shush," Sephy interrupted. "Pour."

Ruby tilted her candle over the bowl of water, and with a quiet hiss, the melted wax settled over the surface in a large, round blob.

"Wonderful!" Sephy announced. "You'll join the spelling circle."

Ruby rolled her eyes. "That's hardly a divination, Persephone. I already signed up."

"Kin, you next." Ignoring this, Sephy invited Kin closer.

He passed a candle over the water in a zigzag.

"Hmm, looks like you'll need a lot of abhorawort," she interpreted.

"What's abhorawort?" I asked.

"A common meadow plant," Ruby answered quickly. "A very useless meadow plant – it has no botanical use and smells awful."

Kin shrugged.

Rupert went next – according to Sephy's reading, he was going to spend a lot of time around books. "What a joke," he frowned, as did Ruby.

We took turns pouring wax into the water. Dean was going to lose his wallet, and I was going to get a fancy chair.

"But you're not going to like it, I'm afraid," Sephy pouted, feeling sorry for the reading she provided me.

"It's fine, Sephy, I'm sure I can handle a chair," I reassured her.

Lastly, Sephy swirled her candle over the bowl. It settled on the water in an indistinct shape.

Kin peered over her shoulder. "I think it might be a dog… Hey, maybe you'll get a puppy – it can play with Flip," he said.

Sephy cocked her head to the side. "Mmm, yes it could be a dog. But it's something more than that, I can see that here." She pointed to a bend in the wax, and it bobbed on the water where she pressed. "It's not a very friendly dog either way."

CHAPTER 27

IONA JAKE

I had patience, but patience to savour a meal was one thing, and patience to sit around waiting for the humans to work out what to do about me was quite another. Though, I admit, it was quite thrilling to listen to them debate, wonder, to hear their little minds squirm and struggle to wrap around concepts they had so hastily dismissed. I heard it all upstairs in the big room, smelled the fear sifting through the air vents, while I sat cooped up in a diminutive cage clearly not built with someone of my size in mind. Patience for the latter ran out. I broke free.

I leaned back in my nest now, drinking through a straw straight from a neck. The blood was hot, fresh, and scarlet – this gave it a sweet taste. Too soon the supply ran dry, and the empty vessel fell to the ground. I put my feet up on the head that now lay on the floor; an obsolete bottle cap for the drink I had just enjoyed. I liked to keep tokens, little souvenirs, especially after the well-dressed ones. I kept the head as a footstool.

Weasel eyed the drained container eagerly. He edged closer to it, then finally found the nerve to strip off the outer label – a red uniform jacket belonging to one of the Senate prison guards. He tried it on, and it fitted him, for Weasel was a human.

"You don't look good in red," Yolanda criticised, lingering by the outskirts of my chamber.

"Find the heir," I ordered.

They froze. A delicious scent filled the air – fear, adrenaline pulsing through their veins, underneath the flimsy shell that held it all in place.

Yolanda and Weasel were both so new to this, and as previous experience some years ago had taught me, humans required to be trained. They feared me, and that fear should remain.

"A-are you s-sure the heir exists?" Yolanda stuttered.

The Rachthawnian heir, as they liked to call it – humans and their insistence on names.

Fennel had been quick to organise their service, and the lowlifes were quick to take the materialistic bait. They believed – or were led to believe – that destroying the heir would put an end to institutions they called the Authority; the Authority that so readily rounded up lowlifes and criminals like them, and unknowingly packaged them off as ready meals for the remainder of my kind.

They failed to see past this intermediate outcome, however. For sure enough, destroying the heir would lead to an end of the Authority. But destroying the heir would also lead to an end of all dispensable human affairs altogether because destroying the heir meant destroying *her*, the immortal who was somehow tied to the heir's lineage, and who stopped my kind from roaming free. Yolanda and Weasel were my soldiers for now – a meal that I was putting off for later. For now, they had their silver heads and wholes, and I had mine – fresh. I took both from the Senate on my way out.

A laugh ripped through me. Being well-fed always put me in such an exalting mood! I'd like to see *her* try to come at me now. I was fed, I was stronger. I could outrun her at the very least.

"Do not," I got up and had them cornered in an instant, "question me."

They both fell to their knees, shaking their little heads up and down. This was a human gesture of understanding, I'd learned.

Fennel warned that a much larger army than last time would be necessary, to sift through the human masses of the worlds until the heir was found. A grain of sand in the desert, he said. He estimated that the heads and wholes I took from the Senate would suffice to pay the mercenaries. But I cared not for money, and I had a plan to ensure the loyalty and strength of my new troops through much more cost-effective, binding ways.

I dug my claw into a portion of my skin uncovered by scaled armour. The liquid substance of my existence oozed out in little drops, the most potent substance in these worlds, the source of my speed, strength, effective senses. The substance that flowed through me, thanks to my nutrition, contained the purest energy that sustained these worlds.

"Drink," I ordered, and drink they did.

CHAPTER 28
LILLY-ANNE SKYROSE

"It was seven hundred years ago today, that the Ranger duellers first went to play!" Bertie cried, jumping from sofa to table.

We cheered.

"And we have waxed and waned, but through experience we have only gained!"

More cheers.

"Now let me introduce to you the candidates our hopes and dreams rest on for the next year!"

The common room erupted in hoots and applause. Those hoping to make the duel team filtered down the staircases on the left and right. Most were eager first-years, dotted with seniors who missed out on the chance in previous years and had never given up the dream.

The try-outs group was large, competition would be fierce. Out of the nine places on the team, only a couple needed to be filled for those who graduated last year. A few others might be chosen as reserve.

The exaggeration of a personality called Constantine appeared on the steps. The little crowd that gathered applauded louder. He flashed the stupid smirk and waved. No gloves – of course. Constantine liked to pretend that burning didn't bother him. I folded my arms tightly.

Behind him, nearly falling down the stairs as he struggled to find his gait, was Kin – tripled in size by all the padding strapped to him. I joined in with the clapping and cheered.

Vince began organising everyone. Kin waddled over to us.

"I look stupid," he accused, aiming at Ruby.

"No, you don't." She reached to fasten the buckle under his hardhat, then stopped short, realising the proximity this involved. "You look safe."

"I doubt we'll get killed out there, and it's not like the others have to wear all that," he protested, but lifted his chin up.

Ruby reached up again, securing the buckle this time. "You don't *have* to wear it, it's only being sensible and precautionary," she scolded.

"Go, Kin!" Sephy chimed, planting a sticker over the padded vest across his chest. "I have a feeling that Fate wants you for striker."

"Good luck, Kin," I added, then remembered luck was not a concept they were much familiar with.

"Thanks, both." He tried to smile, though nerves were getting the better of him.

We followed the existing team and candidates outside. Champion try-outs were coming to an end, having secured the morning spot on the pitch. Rangers reserved the afternoon, and Theorists had theirs in the evening after sunset.

"They don't need daylight 'cos they don't know what they're doing anyway," Bertie said.

Stood on the sideline, waiting, we got a glimpse of the last Champion round. One after another, Champion team candidates lined up to defend a huge target board. One after another, they failed as the shots hit the wood successfully. Only the bravest, fastest few reached out to smother or rebound them, leaving the post with scorched hands, arms, shoulders, or whatever body part was used to defend the target. Hurling the shots was the Champion captain himself, and they flew mercilessly out of his hands. The rest of the existing team lingered in the vicinity, looking rather bored, ready to smoulder the few shots that candidates managed to rebound.

"Are you sure you want to be up against *that* on the pitch?" Ruby whimpered, clutching harder onto a copy of *Emergency Healing Spells* at her chest.

"Shush, Rubes, I haven't even made the team yet," Kin retorted all too quickly, looking less convinced that being on the team was all he ever dreamed of anymore. Then he sneezed so hard his glasses fell onto the ground. He bent awkwardly to try to pick them up, obstructed by the various pads tied to his legs, grasping hopelessly at the grass through a ridiculously oversized glove.

Another Champion candidate moved to defend the target board. The shot hit him perfectly in the head. We all cringed as he fell down with a loud thud.

"Somebody please patch him up," the Champion captain said, offhandedly. With a sigh, he ran his hand through his hair, pushing it back into line.

I recognised him then – no tux, the blond hair parted more scruffily – but it was the same bloke I saw at the Purgers' meeting, I'm sure, acting like he owned the place.

"Here you are, Kindegory."

Watching the resuscitation scene unfold, I started to find Damsel next to us. She put Kin's glasses back on his nose, lopsided.

"Are you hoping to make the Ranger team?" she asked.

"Yes, thanks, hi," Kin said all in the wrong order.

"You should have said, I could have arranged it for you, no hassle of try-outs," Damsel replied.

"Is that so, Damsel?" Dean put his arm around the bulk of padding on Kin's shoulders. "Have some insider sway over duel teams, do you? Now that your sister is dating Mate Grim?"

Damsel stiffened, and her lips pulled into a tight line. Over her shoulder, I felt the sudden weight of a dark, deadly stare on us, coming from across the pitch.

"Do not," Damsel said through clenched teeth, "say that name around me."

There was a short pause, as we tried to figure out how to get rid of her.

"Mate Grim!" Ruby suddenly yelped.

Damsel stared at her, perplexed to be contradicted.

"Mate Grim!" Ruby barked, a little terrier at Kin's side.

Damsel's brows lifted unevenly and her forehead wrinkled at the unexpected childishness.

"Mate Grim!" Ruby cried.

Utterly baffled, Damsel almost ran away.

"What in the worlds just happened?" Kin broke the silence that followed.

"I have no idea, but it worked better than a spell," Ruby breathed out.

Dean and I burst out laughing. I creased and almost cried, until I spotted him, marching across the grass like some devil we had just summoned – Mate Grim, on his way to beat us up.

"O-o," the sound escaped me automatically.

There was something simply terrifying about him, the way he moved like a ghost, the way he looked like a zombie brought back to life. Deep shadows hung under his eyes, crept up underneath each sunken cheek, and upheld his locked jaw. The others caught onto the deathly stare. We stood, frozen, as doom marched closer to us.

With one swift movement, an outstretched arm, the Champion captain halted Mate Grim in his track. They were still for a second, then Mr-who-owns-the-place turned his head to assess us from the corner of his eye.

"Don't bother," he said, dropping his grip.

Mate Grim didn't drop his deathly stare, however. He breathed deeply, judging by how much his shoulders moved up and down.

"Next!" the Champion captain yelled, and another forthcoming casualty moved to defend the target board.

Mate Grim turned on his heel and returned to needlessly defending the pitch.

*

Ruby sat with the newspaper unfolded at full width in front of her face. I peeked over her shoulder to see what had captured her attention so unanimously. Up until lunchtime, and persistently over the last few days, she was busy scolding Kin for getting hurt at the try-outs, as if the burns and bruises were his fault. The injuries weren't major, of course (Vince was easy on them, ensuring that the day was fun instead of deadly), and Ruby had escorted Kin down to the infirmary straight after, leaving him with only a few scratches and scabs.

Major incident at Senate House, I tried to read further below the headline, but in that instant, she thrashed the newspaper down.

"Do they have any idea where she might be?" she directed the question across the table, at Kin.

"I know as much as you do, Rubes. The woman from the wanted posters turned herself in, then escaped before they sentenced her." He pulled the newspaper's corner out of his plate.

"But *how* did she escape? I thought the Senate House had the best security systems in the worlds," Ruby wailed.

"I don't *knowww*," Kin mimicked her tone.

"How dangerous is she really?" Ruby demanded.

"Stars – I don't *know*!" Halfway to another bite, Kin put his fork back down. "Do you honestly think my dad gives me daily updates on intelligence? I haven't spoken to him in a long time."

"Have you told your dad that you made the duel team?" Sephy asked, her voice airy-light. With her rucksack on the bench beside her, she ripped an omelette with her fingers, feeding pieces to the bag.

"Yes, I did write – doubt the message got past his PA though," Kin answered with a sigh.

A group of girls flittered nearby then – seniors or third-years, judging by the uniform – on their way to the lunch queue. "Look who it is," they whispered among themselves. "Hello, Kindegory," they piped as they passed.

"Um, morning, I mean afternoon, hi." Kin pushed his glasses up, a blush spilling across his cheeks. Ever since he made the Ranger duel team, the attention was getting slightly out of hand.

Someone who handled the attention very well, however, was Constantine who, annoyingly, also made the team. When a small photographer's studio opened in Loon's City, the owner's worries over capitalising on the new technology and flocks of tourists turned out to be unnecessary, as Constantine supplied half the business himself. Amidst a stack of anxious letters from Gabriel telling me to be careful given the recent Senate incident, I found a new photograph. Looking serious and dressed in blue duel gear, Constantine scribbled a short message for me this time: *Any regrets? I may consider giving you another chance.* I tore it up, letting the pieces fall from the fourth tower.

In spacetime studies that evening, I scooched up next to Charlotte on the bench running around the internal perimeter of the observatory. She was waiting for me, apparently preferring my company to her own Theorist friends. I was glad to see her because, as in botany, she was my only hope for a partner after Sephy and Kin paired up in the mixed Theorist-Ranger class. As in botany, Ruby ended up in the Ranger-Champion split. The classroom was an attic room, cosy (or, as Ruby described it, crammed), topped with a glass dome for observing the night sky. On the outskirts of school grounds, it was closer to Theorist Keep than any other building and maintained by none other than the Theorist Head, Professor Deborah Phigg, our teacher.

We'd spent the whole of last semester learning how to open spacetime portals (in theory, of course, not in practice) only for Professor Phigg to realise it was third-year material. Halfway through the chapter, we moved onto a new topic. Hardly anyone noticed, as hardly anyone paid attention. I only realised when Sephy pointed it out, pouting in disappointment. This was her favourite class and, unlike our other classes, which she didn't always feel like attending, she always turned up to spacetime studies.

"The aura isn't always right for studying," she winked at me, her only explanation for regularly ditching class.

Today, we were identifying constellations in the sky. Each pair was given a diagram to locate through a telescope. I took my turn viewing, locating roughly the area we were looking for, then passed to Charlotte to find the details.

She swung the telescope in a complete other direction.

"What'd you do that for?" I complained.

"There's something else I want to find," she said, squinting through the eye piece. "It's one that keeps cropping up in my dreams."

"Have you tried a sky atlas? Might be easier than looking aimlessly around the sky. The one you want might not even be visible tonight."

"Huh," she answered, then left the telescope to sketch out the exact star alignment she was looking for. "Do you recognise it?"

I picked up the notepad to study Charlotte's drawing. It looked familiar, sure enough, though I couldn't quite pinpoint where I recognised the constellation from. I dismissed it – they all looked similar enough.

"Looks like a set of dots and lines to me." Then I remembered I had a message to relay. Kin was out of earshot, but I muted my tone anyway. "Ruby said to ask you to take it easy on Kin in the upcoming match."

Charlotte rolled her eyes. She managed to secure a place on the Theorist duel team, which she claimed wasn't hard, despite her lack of real talent.

"I hope you will say the same to him about me. He really is good, you know – quick."

Professor Phigg was making rounds to check on our work, getting increasingly closer to our station.

"You better put the telescope back to where I had it," I frowned at Charlotte.

"Oh, Phigg won't notice," she smirked.

Charlotte was right. Professor Phigg glided towards us. "Any success with the Giant Paw, girls?" she asked.

"Yes, it's over there," Charlotte pointed vaguely at somewhere in the sky.

"Very good!" Phigg shrieked, veiny hands balling up into excited fists. "Very good," she muttered, walking away.

*

As semester unfolded and spring came into full swing, Loon's City too began to bloom. Lively energy once again returned to the alleyways and boulevards. Shops of every kind, cafes, merchants, guest houses, offices, and halls came alive, the pulse of the city's human and non-human traffic drifting through their scores. Street vendors, pickpockets, and peddlers flogging whatever they could find sprouted from every corner. Students increasingly ventured past the gates and downwards into the awaking city whenever a spare hour allowed. I ventured too, drawn by the energy and magic of the walled maze, reliving the wonder of my first steps here. Birds nested on cornices and stone canopies where the snow once lay. Sullied remains of winter lining the city streets were swept into crevices and drains by rousing footfall. Over the murmur of the shoal, the forest once again greened.

Inside the school grounds, bands of first spring flowers poked through the grass, only to be mercilessly mowed down by Haunt, in preparation for duel season.

Duels were kind of stupid, Ruby was right. I could hardly make sense of the rules, let alone the point. In team matches, two teams played against each other. One on the offensive, the other defending. The defending side nominated a keeper – guarding the target board – while the rest of the team scattered strategically to field the pitch. Players on the offending side took turns to 'bowl' – as was the analogy to cricket in my mind – hurling Force at the target board, which the keeper attempted to extinguish or at least redirect towards the pitch, where the rest of the defending team stepped in to put them out. Points were scored for hitting the target board directly, or if the shot was diverted, for how long it took for it to be put out. A striker was outed once their shot was successfully extinguished. This meant they could carry on shooting as long as they hit the target board each time. Once all strikers on the offending side had been outed, they swapped with the defenders, and the process was repeated. The game ended when both sides were out of players, and the points were tallied up.

There was another way to duel, one-on-one rather than as a team sport, which made a lot more sense to me. Instead of a target board, the opponent simply served as a live target. We didn't play this at school, unless it was for practice purposes, and then it wasn't very serious. Historically, however, this was *the* way duels were resolved, a one-on-one deadly match that ended when one of the opponents died. A traditional way to settle disputes, it was obsolete now that lives belonged to Fate by law and High Judge Percy Potts decided who was in the right.

Clustered in the spectator stands with Ruby, Rupert, Fabian, Sephy, and Dean (as well as just about all the other Rangers, including Professor Fellblue, dressed in embossed regal blue for the occasion and waving a little flag) we cheered our team on. I tried my best to get into the spirit. Making just as much noise across the pitch, with golden flags and banners, were the Theorists.

Barely distinguishable from the top of the stands – a safe distance, according to Ruby – I noticed the reason we bothered to be here today emerge into view. Lining up to take his shots as striker, Kin exhaled deeply and shook his shoulders out a little.

"Go onnn," Dean yelled. "Bullseye!"

Vince patted him across the back, and Kin jogged up to an allocated striker's spot on the pitch. The other eight players watched eagerly from the sideline. Defending the target board was an experienced Theorist keeper, Fabian told us, while the other eight Theorists took their positions fielding around the pitch, calculating where the shot might ricochet if the target was successfully defended.

The keeper bounced from side to side on the balls of his feet. Kin mirrored the steps unsteadily. Despite the lack of real investment I had in the game, a little lump rose in my throat. They danced like this, like two peacocks trying to outperform each other or, more accurately, a peacock and a penguin, for Kin's steps were wrecked with nerves. Then, *bam*, the crowd erupted!

Kin's movement was so fast, I must have blinked to have missed it.

"Eighteen points!" Coach Dweegan measured the damage on the target board.

"Gosh, he really is fast!" I shouted towards Ruby, struggling through the noise.

"I know!" she called back with pride, her cheeks pushing upwards into the happy-crescents of her eyes.

To think that only a few months ago, Ruby had reduced Kin's talent to money and access to a private coach, was almost impossible right now. It was almost as if, similarly to my own approach towards the otherworlds, Ruby had eventually convinced herself that her dream of meeting the lawkeeper's son was not a dream after all. She was still aware of Kin's background, of course – sometimes all too much – but most of the dividing line had blurred when, again and again on the daily, our friendship group willingly came together.

Kin took four more shots before he was finally outed, hitting three on target and the fourth gaining only three points as it was quickly extinguished by Charlotte in the field.

It all went downhill once our team swapped to the defending role, however, judging by the booing and creative strings of insults Dean directed at the pitch. Bertie was charged with defending the target board. His reflexes were always a second too late, however, and the Theorist striker pelted shots on target one after the other.

"We need to swap keeper *now*," Rupert groaned, jabbing a mini blue flag through the air.

"They can't swap Gilbert over until the striker is outed. Keeper swaps are only allowed between players," Fabian explained. "I don't understand why Vince made him keeper in the first place. Did you see last practice? Gilbert's not in top shape."

The rest of the match was quite hopeless, in this respect. While all of us began to mope, the game continued to hold only Sephy's attention, for she remained standing, wide-eyed, wand in hand, lips parting and pressing tightly back together as if she was debating on whether to say something.

Once the striker was *finally* outed – a shot that Bertie just about managed to deflect into the field – Vince swapped his brother over with Constantine. Though the match was already lost with the amount of points the first striker managed to rack up, at least Constantine was big enough to physically cover half of the target board.

After the disaster ended, we waited for Kin outside the changing rooms. As in the stands, the mood inside the changing room was sullen, with only Vince's hollow words of reassurance attempting to lift team spirit.

"Good effort, everyone! We nearly got them," I heard from inside, followed by grunts. "Kin – thank you for today, really great, I love what you did with the spin – he absolutely didn't see that coming. Constantine, high five! Dana – on it as always."

"Some of us have to be, don't we?" Dana's voice answered sarcastically.

"Yeah, thanks. Bye, Dana."

We moved aside as the players began spilling out. Kin appeared shortly, and both Sephy and Ruby stepped in eagerly to greet him. Oblivious to the latter, Sephy threw her arms around him, locking Kin in place where the boys also attacked him with high fives and friendly punches. Ruby retreated, loitering to the side of the commotion.

"Cor, showed them their place, you did." Rupert fist-bumped Kin's shoulder, knocking him a bit.

"Good game," Fabian echoed.

They headed back towards the bastion then, and I promised to catch up, wanting a private word with the twins. As ignorant as I was about the intricacies of otherworldly politics, the news about a wanted criminal breaking free from prison was unsettling. Newspaper reports mentioned casualties, and the thought of Jacob Globesglory being anywhere near the events had me worried. I hedged one step into the changing room to ask.

"What in the worlds was *that* performance about?" Vince almost shouted.

I backed out.

"That was your *chance*! I asked you to be keeper so that you could redeem yourself, and you went out there to do what? Give everyone something to laugh about?"

An answering sigh was all the response, until Bertie finally choked out, "You said yourself, one more time and you'll have me off the team."

"Yes but... stars! Pull yourself together! Is that *all* you're worth when you're not all spelled out? Do you need help? If you need help, I'm here for you, but this... this isn't you!"

"That's the problem, Vince – I am *meee*," Bertie mulled the words in a low hiss tormented with guilt. "I am nothing but my pathetic, useless, sorry, little self today. Are you pleased?"

"You know I don't mean it like that." Vince backed down.

"Yes, you do, Vince, yes, you do. Take a good look because this is all there is to Gilbert Globesglory." Bertie stretched his arms out, surrendering, and spotted me lingering by the door.

Vince followed his twin's gaze. "Hey, Lilly," he said, resigned.

I searched quickly for something to say – good game? No. Well done? Not really. It'll be better next time? Hardly – they were up against the Champions next.

"Um, hey," I finally managed. "Sorry, I didn't mean to interrupt."

"What's up?" Vince prompted, forcing a smile.

I stepped into the changing room, feeling awkward. "I just wanted to make sure your dad was okay, you know, given the jailbreak from Senate," I asked them both quietly.

"Yeah, he's fine, thanks," Vince answered, though there seemed to be no substance in his words. "He wasn't there when it happened."

CHAPTER 29
GILBERT GLOBESGLORY

I went to sit in the alchemy department supply cupboard because that's where I liked to go when things were getting a bit too much. Or when I wanted to borrow something, with no intention of giving it back. But right now, things were simply overwhelming, and I wanted to hide.

Professor Sprause kept the place tidy, neat. She lined up little vials with leftover potions, muddled-up ingredient jars, spare equipment, and outdated tools. Sprause was a hoarder, and by hiding junk in the supply cupboard, she thought she could get away with not binning it. And all this rubbish, she still kept neatly organised.

Among the cracked glass cylinders, dried up pastes, and leaking thermometers, I settled down. I settled down because I fitted in. At least here in the supply cupboard, junk wasn't pretending to be something else. It was just that: ordered rubbish. I let its imperfections stand out to me, and it wasn't frustrating as such (not like elsewhere in the wide outside worlds) because here there weren't improvements to be made. Nothing could really be done to help these broken, useless bits. But that was fine because they were already ordered in their uselessness, and anyhow, as I said, they weren't pretending to be anything else but that.

It was nice to sit and stare at an order, however obsolete, when everything else was in disarray. So I sat on the floor and stared, momentarily forgetting that I existed, pretending that I was just part of the forgotten junk.

Nothing could really be done to help me either, but the problem was, for the last few years, I had to a large extent been pretending to be something –

someone – else.

There was a shuffling behind my back, and I thought maybe Sprause had come for something, though it was late at night. She did have a habit of sleepwalking however, or so she claimed, when I once caught her scraping out the alymthium from Phigg's time-telescope. Alymthium is the crucial, rare substance that makes time-telescopes work, by the way. I told her I'd come to the observatory to do my spacetime homework, and she left me that way. I was there for a bit of the alymthium myself, actually, though I didn't take any in the end, feeling bad for Phigg having two attempted robberies in one night. Regardless, Sprause had a habit of sleepwalking, especially down to Meyer's chambers recently. I only know this because sometimes I went down to the botany lab (and he lived nearby) to rearrange the labels on the plants. There was this young music tree sapling that he had. I swapped that label with an evergrowing shrub. Those things took centuries to grow a foot – the evergrowing shrubs, that is. Meyer never noticed anyway, not knowing how to properly recognise young plants.

The latch of the supply cupboard gave way. Or perhaps Haunt had followed me. That guy never slept, which was kind of admirable, until you realised he didn't sleep so that he had more time to get on everybody's nerves. I was on the verge of thinking up excuses for my presence in the cupboard, when I realised the steps were too light.

"Hi." Panacea stepped in. "What's wrong?" she immediately asked.

She sat beside me on the floor because I didn't stir.

"Is it the game?"

The last thing I wanted to be reminded of was that damn game.

How did you find me? Why did you bother, anyway? I'm not fun company right now. The laughter has left me, I said, and Orle pinched my spine in reply.

"It really wasn't so bad," she prompted.

I realised I hadn't been speaking aloud. Sometimes speaking aloud took too much energy, so I responded only with silent thought-words, getting annoyed when people couldn't hear what I thought-said.

"I'm so stupid."

"Aren't we all?" Her head touched down gently on my shoulder. "Life's a bit stupid, if you think about it too much. We're here, and then suddenly we're gone, Fate claims us back. It's all a bit tragic, but it's wonderful too, if you take it a moment at a time."

"No, it's not."

"It is. Think about it, what would you be doing if you weren't alive?"

"I don't know."

"Exactly," she smiled, and I tried my best not to notice it. "So you might as well make the most of it. That's where the wonder comes from, from living, from within."

I guess you're right, it does come from within, but only when I've got Orle at the forefront of my brain, when he rearranges my vision. Only then I can see things in this light, and—

"Orle's not here right now," I said, out loud, I think, because she scrutinised my face as if expecting it to shape-shift.

"Well, I know that, Bertie."

"And…?"

"And that's all right, I like both of you," she beamed.

No, it's not, I disagreed. *Nothing ever goes right, unless I spell the common sense out of me, take myself apart and rearrange the pieces of my brain so thoroughly, senselessly, that there's nothing of me left not transmogrified.* My hands started shaking, excited by the thought. Panacea, Persephone, Sephy, my only friend – I'm not sure which because the sights were fading, and I was being pulled back in – put her hand over mine. Pulled back into my head, I was, tempted to put things right. Oh, how easy it was to remedy. One little spell, just one. I closed my eyes and saw the formula on the back of their lids.

Sense and reason were screaming.

Guilt rubbed her grubby hands.

Don't bother, I said to myself, wedging my hands underneath my arse and pressing my lips tight. *It won't help. No matter how many spells you put over yourself, you'll always come back; come back to being Bertie, pathetic Bertie, configured to get annoyed with the inaptness of everything around.* And if that was a cruel joke on Fate's behalf, then I was truly the butt of it: the most inapt of them all.

"I want to help, you're my friend," Sephy pleaded, forced to remove her hand.

I laughed, though it came out more like an angry cry. It was her pity that set me off this time. Pity was disgusting, as if I could somehow help being a moron, as if I already wasn't trying hard enough. And here she was, taking unsolicited pity on me, when I'd specifically removed myself out of everyone's way to sulk.

"I don't want your help," I told her. I needed to face Orle alone, and boy, he was putting up a fight.

She curled up on the floor, staring at me with those big, sad eyes that shouldn't be allowed. I'll have to add this friendship to the list of things that I'd messed up.

"Perhaps we can just spend time, then…" she mumbled, but my whole body was shaking now.

My body shook as Orle called on it, longing for the comfort of floating in magical abyss; a fragile eggshell, yearning to crack open and break free the juicy yolk inside, to break free my carefree enjoyment of life, before it hardened and over-boiled. Before I grew up.

"I'm afraid I'm out of time," I said. I was a merchant after all, and as far as merchandise was concerned, right now it felt impossible to buy me any more of this particular line. I was breaking, caving into my cravings inside.

"Please, just a little while," I heard her say past the commotion in my head.

Yes, any tick now. I was unstable, like an explosive with a timer attached, except that the timer wasn't predictably ticking down. "You need to leave," I told her because I really thought I would explode. Explode with frustration. Frustration with the worlds, with myself, with the ease of putting an end to it; with knowing that it's not *right* to relieve it so – spelling myself unconscious and uncaring – but wanting to do it anyway.

Stars, how I wished Fate would just hurry up and make my mind up for me. I kind of screamed, and Sephy shuffled back into a corner. I wished she'd transfigure me into one of those obsolete, broken cylinders, sit me on the shelf, and leave me to collect dust. Or into some old parchment, to be torn up into pieces and put in the bin as she left to get on with her life.

But she wasn't moving, just staring with those big Sephy eyes. So instead, I got up, threw the door open and ran. I ran because I couldn't stand myself, and more so, I couldn't stand letting her down.

CHAPTER 30
LILLY-ANNE SKYROSE

Having decided that we were intuitive enough to meditate without supervision in our spare time, Professor Fellblue announced that the class would move onto a new exercise. No – it wasn't theory. Ruby took a deep breath and her lips pressed into a hard line. We would try to focus while balancing on one leg with eyes closed.

"I fail to see how any of this will prepare us for exams," she couldn't help herself. Thankfully Professor Fellblue's hearing wasn't too good.

Awkwardly, I lifted one foot off the floor and wedged it on the inside of my other thigh. Instead of Force, I focused on willing my balance and abdominal muscles into existence. Ruby's foot hovered just above the ground – not for lack of balance, but for lack of zeal – while Kin lifted his knee high up in front of him. Sephy positioned herself gracefully, a bird or angel, one leg outstretched behind her while she leaned forward effortlessly with her arms spread wide. Rupert swapped feet often, wobbling whenever one left the ground, as did Dean and Francesca. Fabian was more steady, composing his balance whenever it appeared to give way.

Suddenly, a loud bang sent us toppling like dominoes to the ground. Startled eyes searched for its source: the classroom door, thwacked into the wall. Holding it open was Haunt, a dripping trench coat over his shoulders, withered strands of grey hair mangled in the mess, and a crooked tooth jutting outside his bottom lip.

"Skyrose," he sneered in a heavy accent, and his lip curved to reveal more gnarled teeth. "Chancellor's office, now."

My muscles froze in place with a determination that my body was incapable of just moments before. Professor Fellblue looked amiably from Haunt to me.

"I think Eugenius wishes to show you to Chancellor Arden's office, Lilly-Anne," he said. "You are excused from class."

The expression on Haunt's face made me wish I wasn't.

"Do carry on the exercises as homework, if you like."

Ruby shot a panicked glance in my direction, while alarm in Kin's eyes only refined when he pushed his glasses up. Francesca began to pay attention for the first time in class.

What did the chancellor want from me?

I followed Haunt's dragging footsteps to Chancellor Arden's office, running through a list of possible wrongdoings in my head. Had Professor Flashmight finally realised that Ruby practically did all of my homework for me? Surely this wouldn't warrant a meeting with the headmistress. Was it Flip, had domestic pixies finally discovered him? Was I just the first one of our group to be summoned? Had Constantine told on me for *possibly* burning him? Would his pride even allow it? It would be easy enough to disprove, at least. It was my word against his, for I doubted any of the Purgers saw me do it, and even if they did, they wouldn't admit that I was capable of channelling Force – not the *Earthling*, not me. Or—

I stopped mid-stride.

The weight of my next thought glued me to the ground.

Or the situation was much worse, and the Authority had finally decided that I was an Earthen threat, just as Damsel predicted. Perhaps Damsel ensured of my demise personally. *We were just talking about you*, Dean's words from the Purgers' meeting rang in my brain. Perhaps my letters to Lynne had been intercepted, perhaps I'd written about something that I shouldn't have.

Realising that I wasn't following, Haunt turned back with a grunt. "This way," he spat over his hunch.

My feet uprooted unwillingly, and I hauled myself towards an execution.

Haunt escorted me rigorously to the heavy, double-arched door reinforced with ornamental metalwork. Two stone gargoyles above the doorway turned their lifeless heads at our approach. The door creaked open of its own accord.

"Come in," said a clear, female voice inside.

I slipped through the doorway, catching my tights on the frame and feeling the threads bunch together into another snag. Chancellor Martina Arden was a tall, thin woman, her face composed and lined with deep-set wrinkles recording every matter she'd ever had to worry about.

"Mr Krebbles here from the Order Department of the Senate has some questions for you," she said calmly.

Order Department. Senate. Authority. My knees buckled and she indicated that I sit down. My body obeyed thoughtlessly. I moved to one of the free armchairs.

Krebbles finished off his tea as I sat down, preparing to announce whatever ordeal he had lined up for me. My mind detached, painted scenes of the Carcery uncontrollably invading my sight. How long could I breathe in the toxic air? Would I be alone, alone among *real* criminals? I debated a less painful outcome: slowly die of starvation, or be killed by one of the mindless murderers who occupied this land.

Krebbles cleared his throat. "In light of the recent events, as a precautionary measure…"

We are arresting you for breaching unknowing rules binding Earth, I finished his sentence in my head. Maybe they could just erase my mind and send me back to Earth. I practiced the most persuasive way to beg inside my head.

"… we are cleaning out safe boxes at the fairy banks, held in the names of those now deceased. Who knows what they might have stored inside?” He directed the latter musing at Arden.

She nodded in agreement.

“We have come across a safe box registered in the name of William Skyrose,” Krebbles continued.

The words directed my attention back into the room, and for the first time, I looked up at Krebbles’s face. He was young, a junior justiceman, perhaps. Acne still riddled along his jaw and around a laboured smile, which stretched uneasily along his lips as if he’d been relegated to do a job below his rank.

“You are familiar with the deceased?”

“Yes,” I muttered.

“Very well, we thought as much.” He plonked a briefcase onto the edge of Arden’s heavy desk, sifting through the contents. “Mr Skyrose’s safe box was almost empty, bar one little thing. My instinct was to return it to Mrs Globesglory, née Skyrose as I understand, who we believed to be the sole inheritor. Only then did I stumble upon correspondence that was sent out upon his passing. Notices were sent to Mrs Globesglory, a Mr Hale, and… yourself – Fate knows how, for you, Miss Skyrose, figure nowhere in our records. Anyway…”

Underneath a stack of papers, Krebbles finally found what he was looking for: a small bundle, wrapped in silky cloth. He snapped the briefcase shut and unfolded the bundle, stuffing the handkerchief wrapping into a pocket by the lapel of his suit. He turned to me, clenching the bow of a golden key between his thumb and fingers.

“There we are.” Three golden wards protruded from the stem of the key he held out for me. “That’s everything as for your inheritance, I’m afraid.”

“Thanks.” I stood up, taking it from him.

Something seemed to catch his eye then, as his gaze paused for an unnecessarily long second at the hollow of my throat.

"That'll be all from me," Krebbles recovered quickly, picking up his briefcase and turning to the door. "Thank you, chancellor."

"Anytime, justiceman," Arden's words were a valediction. "You may return to class," she said to me once Krebbles left.

Pocketing the key, I didn't waste time doing as she asked.

"Oh and, Miss Skyrose," Arden's voice caught me by the door, "please remind Mr Spells that no animals are allowed in school accommodation."

*

I went back to class, but class had been dismissed early in preparation for tonight's Ranger versus Champion match. Ruby waited by the classroom door with my rucksack. I recounted the events to her. Almost immediately, her posture relaxed, and the panic faded from her features with a deep exhale. Or perhaps, I was just seeing myself through her eyes. Relief flooded through me: the Authority was aware of my existence, of my ties to Earth (most likely), and it didn't seem to bother them.

I was safe, I realised. No Carcery for me.

"What's the key for?" Ruby asked.

"It's for Uncle Bill's desk." I shrugged, though I couldn't understand how or why it suddenly found its way to a safe box at an otherworldly bank, for Uncle Bill always kept it on the same split ring as the rest of his farm keys.

"Huh," she dismissed the subject, some other topic clearly on her mind. "We better hurry, I think the game might have started already."

Sure enough, cheers and a steady rhythm of chants carried through the grounds, their words blurred by the distance. Deafening thudding pitted the spectators' clamour, each thud sparking a new explosion of cheers. Ruby and I ran towards the stands. An ecstatic bouquet of every pitch producible by the human vocal cords erupted from the blue side, only to compete with disgruntled booing from the red side of the pitch.

"*Annnd* he strikes again! How does he do it? Where does he get the energy from?" the commentator yelled. "Gilbert Globesglory, everyone – unbelievable! *Annnd* – yes! He's done it again!"

Another thud reverberated through the air, accompanying the commentary. I looked to ensure that what I was hearing was correct. Across the pitch, in the striker's spot was Bertie, shaking his arms out. Without warning, he spun three-sixty on his heel and – *thud* – a perfectly round sphere of white flames formed at his palm, leaving it in a fraction of a second, and landing near-centre on the target board. An unsuspecting Champion keeper almost jumped out of the way, apparently bewildered by the turn of events. Judging by the scoreboard, Bertie had been at it for a good while.

"Another nineteen points for the Rangers! Unbelievable everyone, un-be-lie-va-ble!"

"They've closed off the stands, we can't get in!" Ruby shouted above the uproar, pointing to the barriers that had been put up to protect the pitch as the game went on.

I spotted Francesca and Sephy waving at us from the front row. It wasn't far. There were no fielders nearby. "Come on, we'll just sneak past." I grabbed Ruby's arm and towed her towards a gap in the barrier.

"Here he goes again and – *ooooh* – it rebounds!" the commentator screamed; the red stands erupted in excitement. "How many final points can Globesglory get before he's outed? Count with me!"

I slipped through the barrier; Ruby followed suit. We edged along the inner rim towards the stands.

"One! Two! Three!" the commentator counted the seconds it took Champion fielders to extinguish the shot. Each extra second was an extra point, to a maximum of ten. "Four!"

I was just at the edge of the front row, when suddenly something –

someone – crashed into my shoulder, knocking us both to the ground.

"Five!"

I fell backwards, landing on my backside.

He fell too, and the velocity of the collision made him roll over his side several times.

"Six!"

He stopped the tumble, crawling forward at speed.

"Seven!"

A fiery ball of light landed and burned just yards ahead. Pushing his weight half off the ground, he hurled himself to reach and slammed his bare hand on it, smouldering the flames.

"Eight! Eight points!" Coach Dweegan yelled.

"*Annnd he's out!* Globesglory's outed!" the commentator shouted over her. "Despite some, urr... minor inconveniences... Grim saves the day again!"

He rolled onto his back then, the one who'd crashed into me, lying still for a second to catch his breath. Then, tipping his weight to the side, he propped himself up on his elbow to search for the source of his collision. His grey eyes locked on mine.

I recognised him instantly: no tux – a charred, red sports kit instead – the same haughty look across his face. Mr-who-owns-the-place. *Grim* saves the day?

"Watch it, little girl!" he snarled, then cursed and spat in my direction.

The commentator rumbled on, the crowd turned to background noise, and something tugged me by the arm. So he was a Grim as well; the Champion captain, the Purgers' ringmaster – Grim.

Grim (the other Grim, not his devil brother) released me from his gaze and pushed himself up to his feet. I realised then that the tugging was Ruby, struggling to pull me up.

"Come *on*," she whined, fully red in the face.

"Are you all right?" Fabian asked as we stumbled to our places in the front row of the stands.

"Yes," I nodded, though my whole core throbbed with the pain that Grim's impact had inflicted on me.

"I can't believe he didn't even apologise," Ruby shouted through the crowd.

"Well, you did kind of invade the pitch, cross his path," Rupert butted in from the row above. "I bet he'll demand an apology from *you*."

I'd like to see him try, I thought, clenching my teeth. We may have *invaded* the pitch – though what a gross hyperbole that was – but still, he did not apologise. Hell, he nearly spat on me! Something tingled through my palm.

The remainder of the match, I spent watching him through fury. Grim. I analysed his every move, every refined stir of his muscle, every fluid movement, every calculated fielding run, the smug – no, arrogant – expression on his face. Beneath the arrogance, however, I saw something else. Fury, I decided. Grim was furious too. The fury jarred his motions, surfaced momentarily in his eyes. Something wasn't going quite to plan for Grim. It disturbed his confidence, intruded into his control over things. It made me smile.

This Grim looked nothing like his devil brother – lighter eyes, blond hair, now not so neatly parted. The off-centre parting was still there, I noted, though the arrangement was ruffled from exercise. Sticky, golden strands fell out of line and stuck to thick brows. I caught myself and looked away.

My eyes wandered back every time. The way he shook his hands out after extinguishing each shot was almost funny, so unfitting compared to the rest of his composure, the way he stiffly held his shoulders back when waiting. And after each burn he suffered, his lips seemed to part slightly, ebbing with inaudible sound. Was he murmuring healing spells to himself? The action was unthinking, as if ingrained, so it did not impact on his concentration. I knew from Kin that duellers liked to compare injuries after the game – a twisted kind of trophy-taking before they healed themselves up or headed to the infirmary. Grim didn't have a wand in hand either. Were these healing spells? I tried fruitlessly to read the words off his lips. Ruby once said that spelling without a wand was unpredictable, potentially very hazardous. Was Grim someone so confident in his abilities that he dared to play with the figurative fire as much as he seemed to enjoy playing with the literal one?

Mud was smeared across his cheekbone from when he landed on the grass. His face wasn't ghoulish nor sickly, not at all, though I suppose it was chiselled enough to find resemblance to Mate Grim, whose deathly, bleak stare still haunted me. Mate Grim was on the pitch too, fielding. I paid him no attention now, just as I paid no attention to the rest of the match. My eyes seemed willing to follow only one thing. I studied the way skin stretched over the hinges of his square jaw as he shouted commands, the way veins and tendons protruded when he projected his strength, the way little droplets of sweat fled down from his hairline when he stood still, outlining his contoured face and pooling in the hollow of his collarbone, as if there for this purpose by design. No, I decided. The other, older Grim was unlike his devil brother. He was much worse; he was a devil in disguise.

The last Ranger took her shots and was outed. The game ended. Coach Dweegan tallied up the score on her clipboard. I watched from the front row as he strode to stand by her right – long, confident strides, shoulders rigidly back, fury, more fury than before, in his eyes. Vince slogged to stand at her left.

"With a score of two hundred and eighty-six, to a very close score of two hundred and eighty-four, the winner of today's sport duel contest is…" Coach Dweegan announced, a hint of surprise in her voice, "the Rangers!"

The stands erupted around me, flags, hats, and scarves waving in the air. Dweegan lifted Vince's arm victoriously to the sound of fanfare. My group of friends shrieked and jumped excitedly. Rupert hopped on Fabian's back from the row above, nearly causing him to tumble. Dean looked ready to jump on the pitch and celebrate with the team. Sephy was on her tiptoes, stretching a banner she prepared, triumphant. Only this morning, Dean insisted the banner was a waste of time – there was no way we could win against the Champions in first match.

All this was background noise because I was still watching *him*.

"Congratulations, Globesglory, give that brother of yours a pat on the back. I've never seen anything like his performance today." Dweegan shook Vince's hand, then turned to her right. "Well played, Grim, tremendous effort. Yet what a difference two points make." She looked from one to the other. "Be nice, now that you're off the pitch."

Vince thanked her and Grim merely smiled, holding tightly onto his unshakeable charade. Dweegan walked away, confident that she had formally dismissed today's rivalry.

"You're going to pay for this," I read the words clearly off Grim's lips, which otherwise remained turned up at the corners, composed and calm like the rest of his posture. The fury now only surfaced in his eyes.

I forced myself to check Vince's reaction, and to my surprise, Vince was nervous, as if displeased by our victory. "I'm sure we can negotiate a suitable solution," he answered wryly.

"Humour me," Grim said through his teeth and left to join the rest of his disgruntled team.

And as he left, I too was forced to return to the reality of everything around me.

*

"Waheeey!" Dean yelled across the common room, hands clapping above his head. "Here he comes!"

"Here he's brought forth, more like," Ruby countered.

We sat on the back ridge of the sofa, watching above the sea of Rangers, still high from the close win. The team entered to everyone's applause, carrying a ridiculously exhilarated, giggly Bertie on their shoulders. Vince followed close behind, apparently not as thrilled about the turn of events as everyone else.

They let Bertie down, and immediately he jumped on the low table between the sofas.

"Who says we can't beat the Champions in first game of season?" he yelled, arms outstretched like a victorious eagle, basking in glory. "Not I!"

The room broke out in approving cheers again. Fabian calculated that Bertie alone scored over one hundred and sixty points.

"*Globes-gry, Globes-gry, Globes-gry,*" chanted the crowd around Bertie.

Vince slumped down on the sofa by my feet.

"Congratulations." I slid down from the top to sit with him. "Was that an unexpected win?" I prompted, when he didn't reply.

Bertie jumped down from the table in that moment, planting a big kiss on Rebecca Charlie's face. She blushed but wrapped her hands around his neck.

"My hero!" Rebecca cried when she could finally get some air.

The crowd hooted.

Vince rolled his eyes. "Unexpected *and* unplanned," Vince eventually answered. "Alastair's going to have my head for this."

"What do you mean?" Alastair – that was his name. Alastair Grim. Suddenly I realised something terrible. "Is it because I intruded on the pitch?"

"Nah," Vince laughed, relaxing a bit. "Though the barriers are there for a reason – you could have got hurt. And you probably did stall him for a couple of ticks."

I did the maths quickly in my head. A couple of ticks, a couple of seconds: a couple of points. A winning score of two hundred and eighty-six to… two hundred and eighty-four.

Across the room, Bertie popped open a bottle of fizz that someone handed him, half-spilling it over himself. More cheers followed.

"So let me get this straight: Bertie thinks he almost singlehandedly won the match, and yet the two point difference… the two seconds – I mean, ticks – my intrusion stalled… *Grim*… for…" I lowered my voice to ask Vince, though we were apparently unnoticed below eyelevel of the ensuing celebrations.

"First of all, *Bertie* didn't win anything," Vince grumbled. "His stupidity only won us more trouble. Champions like to win all of their first matches of the season, you see."

"Well, they can *like* all they want, but surely it's a game, and it looks like the odds were in our favour tonight."

"It's not quite as simple as that." Vince's words were drowned out by the crowd.

"What does that mean?"

"That means," Vince paused in disapproval, Bertie's basking clearly getting on his nerves, "that each year the captains all get together to… discuss… how the season will work out. At the winter ball, actually – a silly tradition really, it's called the captains' rounds. Bertie was there, he sealed most of the rounds himself. Anyway, we discuss and agree on certain things, trade-offs."

I looked at him, shocked. "We weren't *meant* to win this game?"

Vince shrugged. "Usually, it just so happens that our training routine isn't intense enough for us to win the first match against the Champions. After that, we ramp it up, and the real fun begins."

"And the team, do they know…?" I asked, spotting my friends showering praise over Kin. Sephy clung to his arm, holding so tight as if letting go meant she'd somehow lose him, her big eyes glistening.

"No." Vince lowered his voice so that it was barely audible. "Well, maybe. Everyone knows about the rounds, just not the details of discussions. That's a captain thing."

I scowled at him.

"What? It's always been this way. Tithers, the Ranger captain until he graduated last year, taught me all about it. It's like that across the board: Alastair does it, Kornel does it – every captain before us has done it. Alastair especially – he loves a good deal."

"What's he like?" the words slipped out before I could stop them.

Vince grew a mocking smile. "Eye-catching, judging by your sentiment."

I scowled more, verbal protest building up – of course I didn't mean it *that* way. I was still angry with Alastair for knocking me over, I wanted to say, trying to gauge if lack of empathy was his norm. Was he just an arsehole, full stop? Though I decided he probably *didn't mean* to spit on me – nearly spit, anyhow. I just happened to be in the trajectory of a reflex bodily function. In his path once again. It was no excuse for being gross, but—

Vince continued before I could speak coherently. "He's stubborn. He's fast, almost one shot per tick at times, and he's strong. Stars, I have no idea where Alastair gets that strength from – it's like there's pure Force flowing through his veins."

I wasn't exactly looking for a run-down of Alastair's sports achievements either, but Melanie soon joined us, and I forced myself to bottle up the anger; the anger that I refused to call curiosity.

Bertie stumbled past us, nearly tripping at our feet, towing a very giggly Rebecca by the hand towards the left staircase.

"I give that relationship three rises," Mel pursed her lips.

"Twelve rounds, more like, until he calms down." Vince shook his head.

CHAPTER 31
LILLY-ANNE SKYROSE

Ruby sat with the *Seer* folded lengthways, looking only at the second page, the way she did most mornings now. I didn't have to peek over her shoulder any more to know what she was looking at. The macabre had become routine. She lifted her eyes off the page to peer inquisitively at Kin.

"I don't have any further details for you," he defended himself before she could ask.

Every few weeks, and soon enough every week, newspaper stories reported missing persons all over the Continent. Families pleaded for their return. Sometimes, they would be found – or rather, their bodies were found. Initial reports included graphic descriptions: drained, lifeless bodies, skin sunken and grey as if cursed. Reporters and officials speculated awful dark magic was at hand. Aside from an occasional missing ear or finger, the victims were otherwise physically intact.

As weekly reports turned almost daily, they were shortened and relegated to the second page, becoming informational and lacking in morbid prose. By this time, our imaginations painted the gruesome picture well enough.

"Demons," Bertie coughed the word out, and we all glared at him.

"This isn't a joking matter, Gilbert," Tina scolded him, taking the newspaper from her sister.

"Who says I'm joking?" he maintained.

Rebecca giggled and patted Bertie's head. He stole a chip off her plate in return, shoving it in his mouth. Rebecca giggled even more.

Melanie took the *Seer* next, offering it to Vince once she'd scanned the page. Vince declined this daily dose of terror we were all apparently so fixed on getting, shaking his head. It was as if each day, we all needed a reminder, a harrowing reassurance that the danger was still there. No details necessary, just another number to tally up the conclusion in our heads that something bad was going on.

Sephy poked at her food mindlessly, and I guessed that the disappearances and dark magic were ruining her aura. Ruby had strictly forbidden her to go out in the evenings, especially outside school grounds. To our surprise, Sephy submitted to this (usually unreasonable in her regard) demand without a fight, as if whatever forces that previously drew her oblivious mind on regular adventures had lost their pull.

Vince glanced at his watch. "We're going to be late for class." He got up without enthusiasm, gathering his things.

We followed suit, acting on the cue. Only Bertie and Rebecca stayed, play-fighting over the last remaining chips.

"Thank Fate, I swear I'll puke if I have to watch any more of this," Mel said under her breath.

Although mean, it was a sentiment we all grudgingly shared. Vince and Mel had both been wrong. Ever since the victory against the Champions, and to everyone's annoyance, Bertie and Rebecca had become inseparable. Inseparable *and* intolerable, as if having to purposefully make a show of their relationship – if it could be called that, for it appeared to lack any sort of serious undertone.

"Are you coming to magic, Bertie, or are you all *spelled out* for today?" Vince growled at his twin.

"Oh, I'll have some magic today, keep your sarcasm at bay." Bertie offered the last chip to Rebecca, her mouth open like a baby bird, only to shove it in his own mouth instead and kiss her while he still chewed.

Grunts from each of us echoed at the sight.

Sephy finished packing up her belongings just in time to see the smooch. "Don't forget to dip your chips in superficial sauce." She pushed a little tub of ketchup towards them. "You might choke, if the affection has too strong a real flavour."

Confusion crossed Rebecca's face. Bertie's hand meandered unthinkingly over his shoulder, to the back of his head, as if feeling around for something there. All the while, he stared at Sephy, a bit of chip still hanging from his mouth.

I waited for her to join me so that we could go to class, but Sephy lingered, holding onto that stare, trying to dig something out of her bag.

"Oh look, pumpkin – it's your watch you said you lost!" Rebecca piped excitedly when Sephy dug out a wristwatch from underneath her books.

Bertie made no move to claim it back, however, when Sephy dropped it on his plate.

"I hope you find the time," I heard Sephy say before she turned her back on them and joined me.

*

I woke up to find our dorm empty except for Flip, whose little ears perked up to the stirring of my movement. Intensity of sunshine and the length of shadows it cast over each little chimney among the rooftops outside the window indicated almost noon. It was Saturday, April fourteenth, or the fourteenth rise of Thotun's fourth turn.

Ruby was probably already at the library. Sephy must have cleared out for the day, perhaps to see the sunrise or collect acorns, pinecones, interestingly-shaped twigs, or whatever else the woodlands around Loon's City had to offer. Though her trips were daytime only and less frequent, her collection was getting steadily out of hand – domestic pixies now refused to clean our dorm, insisting that Sephy must first make room for them to do so.

I slipped out of bed and Flip scurried to my feet, poking his head up to be stroked. "Sephy didn't take you with her?" I asked, and he purred in response.

I reached for his snack jar, trying to wrangle the top open. The lid gave way with a jolt, spilling nuts all over the floor. Flip hurried after them, swiftly scoffing up the spill. I watched his little, fluffy paws pat over the floorboards.

"Dig in, little one."

Ruby would have hurried to beat him in mopping up the excess snacks, afraid of overfeeding. But it was hardly too much, I decided, and today was April fourteenth.

"We're going to have a field day today," I said to Flip, and his eyes measured me, fluffy ball of a tail quivering excitedly. I dropped a couple more nuts on the floor.

My mind was like clockwork, producing the same dream on the same day each year with the same increased intensity. Just moments ago, I stood on top of the familiar hill, which soon gave way to the forested valley beyond. I sprinted through the towering conifers, their size and stillness attesting to my insignificance in this dreamy realm on whose edges they stood guard. I drifted through the sea of dry grass beyond their border, seeing the sway of each blade against my skin, though not feeling it, not even feeling the wind that motioned it. I carried on through the grounds, the garden, into the fortress and the same empty hall with giant green tiles. I did not pause to study the scenes they depicted. My feet hurried up the steps, onto the terrace. The same faceless crowd gathered below. Sounds returned, applause changed to screams, my imagination turning up the volume just at the cusp of dream to nightmare. The blinding, white light was already on its way, encroaching, swallowing up the crowd. Just moments later it engulfed me too, distorting my confines, twisting me inside out, and pulsing through me.

The nightmare was familiar, though I hadn't lived through it in a while. On April fourteenth each year, however, the blinding white light held me in its nonexistence for much longer, refusing to let me wake, refusing to let me go.

I splashed some water on my face and straightened up to study the features reflecting in the mirror. Signs of the restless night puffed up under each eye. Otherwise, I looked the same: brown hair folded into waves, strands contorted ungracefully by the pillow, boring brown eyes, skin that longed to see more sunshine. I hadn't changed overnight in appearance, only on paper. Overnight, I turned seventeen.

The door creaked open. Moments later, Sephy's head reflected in the mirror above my shoulder.

"Happy birthday!" she shrieked, and I wondered why her arms weren't wrapped around my neck yet.

More commotion followed; Ruby and Kin came into view. I turned to see that Sephy's hands were busy, just about holding onto a plate with layers upon layers of spongy mess sloshed in pink goo.

"I baked a cake for you!"

I thanked her, taking the sweet array from her hands, and immediately she locked my neck in a tight embrace.

"I can't believe you baked this yourself, Sephy." I placed the towering arrangement on a bedside cabinet, examining the layers. Each appeared to be a different type of cake.

"I can't believe it either. She broke into the gremlins' kitchens this morning, and I spent the entire time trying to convince my brother Ross that this was an essential wellbeing activity. Anyway, this one's from me." Ruby handed me a package that she tried to hide behind her back. "Happy birthday, Lilly".

I unwrapped the brown paper to reveal a book, *Bouncing through*

"It's the only one that Charlotte had about the Islands that wasn't written by Meagles," Ruby continued with a hint of an apology. "I thought you might like something to remind you of home, since…" She looked to Kin.

"Since I thought you might not want to go home for summer," Kin smiled, impish. He handed me an envelope. "Happy birthday."

I thanked them both and carefully slid out the envelope's contents. "What's the Rachthawnian Royal Fonsland Show?" I examined the sturdy strip of card. A ticket, I realised, with *executive lounge* printed down the side and an eye-watering price of five wholes. "*Kin!* I can't accept this, it's way too much." I shoved it back to him. Though no conversion rate to pound sterling existed, I knew that Ruby found four *heads* to be expensive. Wholes and heads were incommensurable, though I suspected five wholes was roughly twice an average monthly salary.

"Told you so." Ruby raised her brows at him.

Kin knotted his hands behind his back, refusing to accept returns. "Look, if it makes you feel better, Dad has plenty of those lying around the house. I took one for each of us, thought it'll be nice to spend a bit of summer together," he countered.

"Kindegory, that is *theft*," Ruby frowned at him, and I sensed that this argument was repetition from one that had already taken place. "Fate have mercy, I don't want the lawkeeper after us for stealing his things."

"No one's going to be after you – it's all on me. And Dad will never notice anyway. The Royal Fonsland Show is a big event, trust me, it'll be fun. Have you ever been?" he asked me.

"To where?"

"The Royal Show."

"Of course not," I allowed.

"It's no longer in the Fonsland, obviously, because that world was deserted after the Murders. The Show's been held on the Continent ever since…" Kin began explaining, but I wasn't listening anymore.

A warm, tender feeling rose to a lump in my throat. This wasn't about money, pretence, or showing off. This was kindness, real and affectionate. I wanted so badly, for the first time in my life, to spend the summer with my friends.

"Have *you* ever been?" Kin turned to Ruby.

"Well, no, but…" She crossed her arms, looking to me to back her up.

Kin unknotted his hands and gently pushed the envelope back towards me. "Well, neither has Sephy."

She drifted to his side as if called, resting her ringlet crown on his shoulder and fixing her pleading eyes on me.

"I go every year," Kin continued, "but now I finally have the chance to go with friends." He smiled. "So don't break my heart."

And of course, none of us could break Kin's heart.

*

The doorbell above Sinnerstroke's Texts and Tales announced my entrance.

"Hey!" I called to Charlotte. It was early evening, darkness beginning to fill the store, though I hoped that the sole candle burning by the register and unlocked door meant she was still here.

I'd spent the day with Ruby, Sephy, and Kin, discussing our plans for summer and trying to make our way through the overly-sweet cake. Sephy insisted we eat each layer separately, rather than cutting vertically through all at once. Dean, Fabian, Rupert, Francesca, and later even Vince and Mel, as well as Ruby's eldest brother Ross, helped out with making sure that the cake didn't go to waste. Once we'd all eaten more than enough, there was still plenty left.

"Hey," Charlotte called back from somewhere among the shelves. "Give me a moment." She emerged from the shadows soon after, kicking a box along the shop floor into a bay still lit by outside streetlights and holding a pile of books in her arms.

"I'd help you, but…" I held up the plate with cake remains for her to see.

"What's this?" Charlotte struggled to make it out from behind the tower of books in her hands.

"Birthday cake," I said, putting it down on the counter, next to where Charlotte released her books.

"Aww, thanks! How did you know? And why is it half eaten?" she smiled, then frowned, turning the plate to examine.

"What do you mean? It's my birthday cake, baked by Sephy. I brought a slice – a layer – for you."

"*Your* birthday cake?"

"Yes."

"I thought you meant it's a birthday cake *for me*," Charlotte laughed.

"Why, when is your birthday?"

"Today."

"No way – so is mine! What a coincidence," I laughed with her.

"Happy birthday," we both said at once.

Charlotte decided that no more business will be made tonight and closed up early. She led me through the bookshelf labyrinth and through the back, up a fire escape exit (how ironic for the otherworlds) to a little balcony that was the upstairs' storeroom emergency exit. The night was warm, pleasant for the time of year. We settled on the damp clay tiles, digging into the remnants of Sephy's cake and taking in the view of Loon's City, each band of rooftops cascading down towards the next rampart wall that held it all intact. As the city's pulse slowed down and moonlight flooded empty streets, a chill ran through my spine thinking about the myriad of dark, empty alleyways.

"What do you make of the recent disappearances?" I asked Charlotte on the whim.

She chewed through a mouthful of cake before answering. "Kinda scary," she swallowed. "Grandad says this is how it all started about twenty years ago – people going missing, weird-looking bodies turning up. He doesn't leave the house now, just in case."

"Really?" I poked at the crumbs, trying to stick them to my finger. "You think it could escalate like before?"

Recent events had me unsettled, of course, though I had a feeling that they meant so much more to the people of the otherworlds. Gabriel's letters certainly conveyed this sentiment: *do* not *go out at night alone,* he wrote. A creeping feeling of unease hung in the air, a sense of pending dread, a return to chaos that had not so long ago characterised the otherworlds.

"Hopefully not," Charlotte said. "The Authority's got much better security measures in place, so they're watching out for anything suspicious. There's been an increase of gargoyles in town, for example."

I raised my brows at this, not following the train of thought. "The gargoyles on buildings?"

Charlotte swished her fork rhetorically. "They're always watching, and they're plugged straight into the Authority. The officers are watching through their eyes."

"Oh." I wondered just how much I had been oblivious to.

"It will be interesting to see how many measures they revert to, if people continue disappearing."

"What kinds of measures?"

"Well, spacetime travel is already closely monitored – each portal opening is recorded and checked if unauthorised. That was brought in after the Murders. Each new-born must be formally introduced to Fate and registered. There used to be rewards, Grandad said, for information on suspicious and hateful activity. We'll see if they'll re-introduce blood checkpoints at terminals, shops, etcetera, or even random stop-searches of the mind too—"

"Stop-searches of the *what?*" I couldn't help butting in.

"Right after the Murders, the Authority had a lot of mind invigilators on the streets carrying out stop-and-search checks of the mind."

My baffled expression must have amused her because she nearly choked on more cake while holding back a laugh.

"Mindreading, or mind influence, it's a thing – a discipline, in fact. You can take it up in third year, if you fancy spending more time with Professor Artsback and Professor Chambers, who's an even bigger witch."

"No thanks," I quickly decided.

"Yeah, not many students pick that option. Anyway, they used to halt random people on the street and check if they had any hateful thoughts on their mind."

"And if they did?" I asked quietly, though I'm pretty sure I knew the answer.

"Well, they were judged and sentenced accordingly." Charlotte bit into more cake. "You know, they say that the number of people killed during the Murders was high… My guess is that the number sent to Carcery since is far greater."

I chewed on a piece of dry skin on my bottom lip, letting the words sink in.

"Still, it doesn't appear to be enough given the recent attacks," she added casually.

"*Charlotte!*" I gasped. How could anyone wish that *more* people were sentenced to a living death – starvation, hypothermia, gradual asphyxiation?

"What? None of us are going to be safe until Hate is completely eradicated," she said, the words an ingrained mantra. "If even small hotspots are left, they will grow over time and continue to infect more and more people until the worlds are at a tipping point yet again."

I realised that *Hate* in her mind was inseparable from its vector, the humans in whose hearts and minds it apparently festered.

"How is Hate even quantifiable? How can the Authority decide if someone is infected?" I struggled to understand the seemingly immaterial, subjective, and yet incredibly consequential notion.

"If they've thought about breaking the laws, they're infected," Charlotte explained like it was obvious. "And their blood is checked. If it's white, then they're *definitely* infected, as they've already broken the laws."

"And the first Unbreakable Law is to not cheat Fate," I mumbled to myself, trying to fit the concepts together in my head.

"That's right." Charlotte scoffed more cake.

"What if the thoughts of those infected by Hate… of the lawbreakers… are exactly what Fate wanted them to think? What if their actions are in line with Fate's plans, motivated by what Fate has revealed to them, just like everyone else's?"

Charlotte looked at me from the corner of her eye with a hint of concern. "I guess you're new to this," she dismissed her suspicion. "That's not how it works. The laws are there for a reason, and this reason is because Fate's plans are in line with the laws. Stick to the laws, and you'll be sticking to Fate's plans. Everyone's been dealt a card by Fate, and if you don't *like* the card that you have been dealt, if you rebel against it and desire to take more, it means you have been poisoned by Hate. Fate has already decided your course long before you were born, so if you attempt to alter that in any way, you're cheating, coveting, and probably harming others along the way. That's why the laws are there, to make sure we all abide by Fate's plans."

I stared into the night, attempting yet again to make sense of the fabric of the otherworlds, trying to find a thread to follow along. Only that the threads had no ends. The logic was circular.

Could it really be possible that there exist two such potent, omniscient, and incompatible energies – Fate and Hate? And everything that exists, every action, every thought is governed by a battle fought between the two, with no scope for human free will at all? One energy that predetermines everything that has ever been, is, and will be; and another, a dark and evil power that worms its way into innocent, unsuspecting brains, usurping their designated paths, and driving them to change their course. *Everything is fated*, predetermined by Fate – unchangeable. And yet Hate has the ability to make people change their course. Moreover, regardless of the nature of this change, simply having the ability to do so – to change - is considered to be bad, evil, and unnatural – against Fate's plans. Yet if *everything* is fated, was the spread of Hate not fated too? How can it be possible for sane people to uphold these two incompatible beliefs at once?

"But if Fate has already decided your course—" *then how can people even attempt to change it in the first place*? I wanted to say.

The whole concept of Hate, which apparently tricks the innocent into cheating Fate, logically contradicts a life that's absolutely predetermined. *The laws are there for a reason*, Charlotte insisted. What reason? Logically, there is no need for laws in the first place because Fate has predestined everything anyway. I chewed the logic over, but it wasn't breaking down. No matter how hard I tried, I couldn't swallow it. I bit back my tongue, hesitating whether the words were safe to say aloud.

In that moment, as if by some miracle that prevented my thoughts from being verbalised, the little balcony on which we sat trembled.

The whole building briefly shook, in fact.

Light-speed fast, something big darted through the sky, a flash of glistening blue against the dark night.

My hands planted on the tiles automatically, trying to steady myself, heart pounded in fright. Charlotte dropped her plate, wide eyes searching through the night.

"Did you see that?" she squealed, trying to keep her voice down.

"What was that?" I could swear the blue flash originated nearby, in one of the alleyways below where we sat, its sudden movement causing the walls to tremble.

"A giant bird?" Charlotte breathed, just as terrified.

I replayed the brief image in my mind. The flash seemed to morph as it sped against the moonlight, folding and unfolding like giant wings. It disappeared just as quickly as it had emerged, much too fast to see properly.

I shook my head. "It was too big, too fast. Perhaps it was a shooting star."

"But it wasn't *falling*, it flew up!"

"We better get back to Sapphy's."

The reality of being alone in the city at night, especially given the recent unexplained disappearances, suddenly dawned on me. While I was busy worrying about ontological paradoxes and metaphysical threats, trying to untie the knot at the heart of otherworldly logic, I'd forgotten that much more immediate, *real* threats potentially loomed in the dark.

We raced down the stairs and through the pitch-black shop floor, pulling the front door open just slightly to check if the street ahead was clear. The doorbell chimed a muted ring. My mouth filled with an acidic taste of fear. My heart pounded so fiercely I could feel the throbbing in my veins, the thudding of pulse in my ears the only sound present in the night.

The street was deserted, unsettlingly peaceful, lit by warm lantern glow intermittingly reaching all the way up the ascent. School gates were just around the corner there.

We can make it, I repeated in my head. One last glance each way before we leave the shop.

Empty, all clear. I nodded to Charlotte, she nodded back.

We ran out into the night, sprinting to Sapphire Dragon's gates; the gates that promised safety from whatever lurked in the darkness and deserted alleyways.

We didn't pause until Sesame appeared at his post to let us in, alerted by the drumming of footsteps on the stone. By some coincidence, Professor

Fellblue was out taking a nightly walk. He found us at the gates, terrified, and escorted first Charlotte to the keep, then myself to the bastion. And as we walked slower now, my mind caught up with me, barely registering the scenery we had sprinted past. I mulled over what I had just seen, the light-speed blue flash. Out of the corner of my eye too, I thought I saw a glimpse of a satin, white gown flutter by.

CHAPTER 32

IONA JAKE

I had patience, though patience for humans to do things at their speed was strained. They couldn't simply *act*, they couldn't just get things done. Plans required to be exactly spelled out to them, and plans were delayed when humans slept, stuffed their mouths with disgusting organic mash, or otherwise attended to their needs. My army grew, though numbers were not compensating for accomplishments. The heir was nowhere to be found.

Some of the matters I took into my own hands. I ventured out more frequently, beyond the barriers of the barren land. I flew and sped and overturned, looking in places where the heir may be hiding. I fed along the way, for the temptation to feed on healthy blood across the spacetime sea was hard to resist. Having tasted the possibilities of freedom, it was increasingly harder to restrain myself, to force myself to return to the underground. For as long as *she* was not in sight to rip me to pieces, restraint was not something I cared about.

So I indulged. After centuries of abstinence, of feeding on the rotting flesh, to allow myself the pleasure of choosing my next meal as and when I pleased was truly welcomed. To feel the returning taste of my supreme power, from centuries long ago, was irresistible. And with every successful meal, I began to entertain more seriously the idea that *she* was no longer present, that *she* had truly been destroyed. What a waste of years in hiding that would have been!

One night, crouched between high edifices where the night light barely touched the ground, watching the fiery celestials reflect in my victim's eyes as the colour drained from the rest of his flesh, I heard dessert waiting for me once the main was done.

"And the first Unbreakable Law is to not cheat Fate," I heard somewhere nearby.

"That's right." A different voice said.

Two – there were two courses lined up for dessert. What a treat. My teeth dug in deeper, excited by the pleasure that awaited me.

It was one of my favourite moments, when the flesh turned grey and limp, when the life-force passed from my meal to nourish me, but their eyes still shone with wetness; frozen open by fear, they glistened like little mirrors for me to observe my brilliance in.

Yet that night I did not get to savour my meal, not to mention my dessert. That night I saw something else reflect in these dead eyes – not only myself, not only the stars. I saw *her*; a sway of white cloth (for she was vain enough to dress) almost too quick for my eyes to catch.

A tick didn't pass. Forced to abandon my unfinished meal, I raced back, back to hiding, back to the underground. Faster than I had ever done before, I sped back.

She did not follow.

Perhaps she was too proud, satisfied that merely her presence would achieve the intended effect.

I ripped my nest to pieces upon return, along with a few useless human soldiers who were unfortunate enough to find themselves too near. My rage ripped through the ranks that night, as confirmation of my predicament honed in.

She was still present.

She, the immortal being who still hunted me, was ready to end my existence if only I stepped out of line.

Was this her idea of mercy? Pity? Mirth, sport? Instead of finishing off my kind quickly, thereby exerting herself, she'd simply drive us to extinction, leave us in too few numbers to breed, feeding on rotting flesh, declining. Hiding. *Hiding* – that, I resented most. And I resented myself for running away from her.

It was run or die, however, at least for now, and I still had the patience in me to finish her off in a roundabout way, a way unconnected to my supreme strength, which (I hated to admit) was no match to hers. A human way, with my human army destroying the lineage she was tied to.

"Find the heir," I ordered. "And build me a new nest."

"Your lair will be rebuilt by the morning," the man I'd nominated as in charge of my human soldiers replied.

His voice was calm. I smelled no sweat, no adrenaline. Deceit wasn't his intent, though his lack of fear bothered me. Had he become desensitised to my monstrosity, or had I lost my monstrous touch?

"As for the heir, we have traced a good lead. I expect it won't take too long to follow through."

Joel Ruffus was a clever human, he didn't need precise directions to do the work I bid him to carry out. He was experienced too, knowledgeable, with connections he considered to be useful. I recruited him straight out of the barren lands – quite literally ripping him from under another supreme being's fangs. My kind didn't usually fight over our food – so few of us left, plenty of sickly humans to go around. My kind were solitary, uncommunicative, unless primal needs called for it.

Yet this human, Joel Ruffus, captured my attention. I noted his presence in the barren lands over and over again, and each time he'd disappear for a while, making his way back to civilisations across spacetime, only to be brought back again. Fennel advised that this particular man had been involved in my initial Legion, many moons ago. He kept to the sidelines back then, wasn't directly involved in the attack. Ever since, his suspicion had been aligned to mine: the lineage wasn't fully destroyed – an heir existed. The Rachthaw's heir, as he liked to call it. Thus, over the years, Joel

Ruffus plotted, organised, and scouted with whatever resources he could find. I didn't care to remember individual faces, but his resilience and initiative stood out to me. So I gave him more resources, putting Joel Ruffus in charge of my human soldiers, for my patience with their wretchedness was running out.

"Fate intends us to be liberated," Joel Ruffus said to himself.

Aside from being human, there was only one other flaw to this man: his tiresome musings about some supreme power. Incomprehensible nonsense, for there were no powers higher than myself or *her*. Like all my human soldiers, he held onto the idea that his fortunes were pitted against him by the humans dressed in red. The only explanation he could find for the Authority's continued power over him, was that the Rachthaws had not been fully annihilated. He was a visionary, however, insisting that some fate intended him to get rid of those in red. And to do that, he hunted for the heir. While superficial, this suited me, and thus our goals were aligned.

"My theory is that the Rachthaws hid their heir someplace safe," Joel Ruffus addressed me with an irritating lack of fright. "The Empyrean Federation, perhaps, or the atheist Islands – though this kind of blasphemy would surprise me. Fonsland would have been too obvious, though I have checked just to ensure. Fonsland is in ruins. There is no one there."

"I don't care where you look, as long as you find the heir." I recovered my new favourite footstool from the mess of nest remains, shaking dust from its hair. Knowing I could trust him to get things done put me in a better mood.

"Some time ago, we traced a consistent pattern of portal openings to the same insignificant location on the atheist Islands," he continued, unbothered. "It appeared promising at first, though in the end we found little of interest there, except—" He flinched slightly, when I ripped the footstool's ear off.

"Except?" I fondled the cartilage in my hand, though it had hardened and greyed, no longer the pleasant, pliable tissue my claws liked to dig into.

"Except a stubborn, unyielding man."

CHAPTER 33
LILLY-ANNE SKYROSE

The news spread fast. By next evening, it was everything everyone talked about. Or refused to talk about. Solemn silence or horrified whispers filled the common room, the classrooms, the corridors, echoing in the grounds. *Loon's City was supposed to be safe*, people said. *Dark magic*, others speculated, *lawbreakers on the loose.* A special assembly was called.

"Sapphire Dragon's is secure," Chancellor Arden reassured from her lectern. "You have nothing to fear."

Haunt nodded in agreement by her side, and his crooked teeth wobbled as he did so.

Last night, Dean said he saw a trail of blood, smeared across the stone floor from the main school door. He claimed that they had hauled the victim inside school gates just after midnight, taking him straight to the infirmary. Haunt ushered him back to the bastion soon after, Dean didn't see much. Bertie said he heard screams. Francesca disagreed – the victim was already unconscious when they brought him in, unable to scream. Regardless, the morbid news – the news we previously monitored distantly in daily newspapers – had hit too close to home.

Someone had been murdered in Loon's City.

Or at least that's what we all assumed, for none of the teachers would confirm what really happened.

What the teachers refused to verbalise, we pieced together in hushed voices among ourselves. He wasn't local – a middle-aged peddler, who'd recently come to town, trying his luck selling talismans and second-hand wands. Someone found him in an alley, barely alive, shrivelled and bleeding out what blood was left in him. They called on the school to help.

Officers sent by the Authority patrolled the city, scarlet cloaks fluttering in the streets, looking for the perpetrator. A few were stationed in the school.

The victim left Sapphire Dragon's the next day, shrouded on a stretcher. Despite Nurse Poppy's best healing spells, he was too far gone and passed away soon after.

"Where were you?" Ruby yelled at me as soon as I made it to the bastion that night.

I could see the accusations coming – we'd assumed that it would be Sephy whom we'd have to keep a close eye on, prevent her from wandering too far outside school grounds.

"What were you *thinking*? This could have been *you!*"

I didn't protest. I knew that she was right.

Ruby wrapped her arms around me, teary. I closed my eyes. More weight pressed down on the embrace, and I looked to find that Kin had also put his arms around the both of us, head pressed to my shoulder. Sephy did the same round the other side.

We stood like this, huddled close together, glad to have each other, and utterly terrified.

The magic I saw of the otherworlds, the brilliance and wonder of the place I had grown to call home, waned and warped before my eyes, masked by the real horrors that also dwelled in crevices of spacetime. Or perhaps it was the benevolent mask that had been so suddenly and violently ripped off, revealing their true colours.

I realised then, in that moment, just twelve hours after narrowly escaping the harrowing events, that I had simply turned a blind eye to the warning signs issued by just about everyone who had grown up in the otherworlds. Too caught up in swinging between trying to stay afloat in the novelty of daily life and pondering the metaphysics of an all-knowing power, I had too readily dismissed the immediate threats, the undercurrent that wove the conduct of these worlds together: Hate.

Charlotte was right, the laws *were* there for a reason. Faced with immediate danger, it didn't matter whether Fate was real, whether everything was truly, absolutely, predetermined. It mattered as much as whether I'd brushed my teeth that morning or whether I wore a t-shirt inside out. A cursory *belief* in Fate was enough. It was the substance of daily life, unthinking, its existence taken for granted in the face of life and death. And having treaded that line too closely, I did not dare question *why* the laws were there, or how exactly they tied into Fate. I didn't worry whether what I did was in line with Fate's plans. If anything, I was glad to be spared – to be alive.

I welcomed the Authority's presence in Loon's City, the sense of safety this provided, an assurance that last night's events were isolated. I appreciated – with much greater enthusiasm than Kin – his own personal bodyguard, sent to follow him around the school. And I realised why Uncle Bill most likely made the choice he did, moving to Earth: the otherworlds could be an arbitrarily deadly place.

Did it matter whether Hate was *real*, or how exactly it worked? Did it matter whether whoever committed last night's crime was poisoned by it? Having narrowly escaped what could have ended so badly for myself and Charlotte, I decided it did not, for what other explanation could there be to drive the perpetrator to commit the crime they did. Hate, whether a real evil power or simply a human explanation for it, had to be eradicated.

*

Spring semester droned on. The events of April fourteenth gripped us for weeks to come. The perpetrator was never caught, the 'unfortunate incident' making only a brief appearance in the *Seer* as the last of its kind. No new disappearances were reported. The Authority relaxed their presence in Loon's City after several quiet weeks. Kin's bodyguard was similarly recalled – much to his relief.

Yet an unspoken, latent fear remained. I feared resurgence of crime just as much as everyone else. An unsettled atmosphere of mistrust hung in the air – mistrust towards anything not quite conventional. Everyone kept their guard, watching out for anything that was just slightly out of place. Unfortunately, this also included the Earthling outside Earth – me.

I was an allergen, it seemed. Following the string of disappearances, my mere presence set off a reaction on the student body; an itching of suspicion, an inflammation of curiosity, bloated by my every move, and spotted with hostility. There were those who studied me, keen to report on every my mishap. Others still, were deluded with a fever that my oddity was somehow tied to recent events in direct, sinister ways. And the smallest group, who seemed to grow immune, who trusted that I was not a threat – my friends.

My contagious effect soon swelled and spread, affecting the apparently learned brains. Artsback was the worst and laws my greatest nightmare. Not a single class passed without a show of his contempt, now even greater than before. He disliked each one of us, of course, because those worthy of anything at all ended up in Champion Hall. But he picked on me especially, brewing up a question from the depths of legislature that caused every pair of eyes to wander, desperate to avoid eye contact lest they be called to answer. When he finally had one that made even Ruby's hand stay down, the familiar sneering, "Skyrose, what is the *sta-tute*?" made my blood run cold.

I felt a similar vibe in botany too, although what my interworldly trespass had to do with plants was hard to see. In history, not much changed; Professor Meagles had written me off long ago. Professor Sprause in alchemy was fortunately too busy with her potions and elixirs to care, while Professor Phigg of spacetime studies was too indifferent to anything closer to the ground than the sky to notice. Magic with Professor Flashmight I could handle, for he was a pleasant man, and besides, it was Ruby's trophy-subject, so there was no way she would let me go to class unprepared. Finally, Coach Dweegan was interested in only one thing, and that I didn't have: the ability to chuck white fire balls at will. In her eyes I did not exist. Against my expectations and despite the dreadful cardio, duel practice was a welcomed breather.

One day I woke up to find that the suspicion had reached the dragon's head. Having ran up to the fourth tower to check the post that morning, I flicked through the stash at lunch. Among student fliers and reminders (overdue books, spelling circle – Ruby still pleaded I sign up – a few caricatures of myself) was a handwritten note in the awful handwriting I recognised all too well by now. *Don't try to talk to me*, it read. Thanks Constantine, I was just begging to. I scrunched it up.

There was also a formal letter addressed to myself: pristine envelope, signed for, with a mighty seal.

The last time one of those arrived, bad news came inside. I shuddered at the memory and the now-faded obligations I once fought so hard to shake. *I should see Lynne.* Yet what good would that do now, after so many months had passed? I reasoned with myself. Now that I had thoroughly decided to make the otherworlds my home, I ought to focus on the future rather than the past. And in the immediate future, Kin's invitation for the summer meant I could put off facing Lynne that little longer.

Besides, the bad news from last year couldn't be matched – I had no other family left to die. No other family except the Globesglorys, of course, and I spoke with Vince this morning; apart from wanting to snap Bertie's neck, he was absolutely fine. There was therefore no way the Authority could be notifying me that Fate had claimed any more of my relatives. Without further thought, I took my signing quill.

"What does it say?" Ruby leaned in.

By this point in the semester, I was good at ignoring any curious, distrustful stares, though I noted that she had been anxiously watching the envelope. Kin too, seemed interested.

"Dear Miss Skyrose," I read aloud. "It has come to our attention that you partake in education at Sapphire Dragon's Respected School of blah, blah, blah. Our records indicate that no account of your introduction to her almighty Fate exists. As you have failed to supply the documentation supporting your fated heritage claim, you are hereby ordered to a judgement on the first rise following the Hueradiss full moon. Witness my hand this twenty-seventh rise of Thotun's fifth turn, on behalf of the Authority, blah, blah, blah."

No deaths, just as I suspected. Folding the letter back into the envelope, I returned to eating my lunch. Only when no response followed from either Rubes or Kin, did I look up.

Ruby's eyes had widened so much they nearly spilled out of their irises. Kin dropped his fork, taking his glasses off, unwilling to see.

A second passed, and Ruby was packing up her things at speed. Once all the books she consumed at lunchtime were securely gathered in her arms, she picked up the letter I had just read, my bag, and finally me, grabbing my arm to pull me up. Kin was forced to follow us merely by her commanding stare. Unfinished meals were left on the table as she marched us back to our dorm, barely dropping the grip over my arm.

Ushering us into the room, where Flip shook his tail excitedly at our earlier return, she only breathed out once the door was shut. I looked from Ruby to Kin, who had positioned himself hopelessly at the steps to Sephy's turret.

"Kin," Ruby whined, leaning back against the door, blocking it lest someone try to enter, "do *something*!"

Kin stared back. His mouth fell open and his shoulders slumped.

"*Kin!*" Ruby demanded, pleading.

"You know I don't have any sway over matters like this!" he wailed, resigned.

"But there must be *something* you can do? Speak to your father or… or something!" she shot back at him.

"Stars, I wish I *could*, but I doubt he's even aware of every judgement that takes place! I'm sure it's nothing major anyway—"

"Nothing *major?*" Ruby cried. "How can you just sit there like this when your best friend has been ordered to a judgement?"

Caught amidst the storm between them, the reason for it finally clicked inside my head.

"Wait," I interrupted, "what is a judgement, exactly?"

They looked at me, my question a reminder that I was also in the room. Ruby released her hold over the door and, putting her hand softly on my shoulder, led me to sit on the turret steps. She perched down beside myself and Kin. I shrunk between them, like a child who is about to have something unpleasant gently explained by her parents.

"A judgement is a…" Ruby searched for kind words, "is a… a… judgement." She gave up.

"It's an intuitive decision," Kin helped, "to see if you have acted against Fate. You haven't been breaking the laws, have you, Lilly?"

"Of course she hasn't," Ruby snapped.

"It must be because you've lived on Earth, then," Kin tried.

"*Honestly,* Kindegory, have you ever considered a career in mind invigilation? Because that is some *real* detective talent on your part," Ruby retorted. "Let's see the order again." I handed her the envelope. "It says that you have *failed to supply* documents. Don't tell me you've received a notice and ignored it, Lilly-Anne," she scorned.

"I haven't been asked to supply anything!" I protested.

"Well, there we go," Ruby said triumphantly. "All you need to do, is write to the Authority and explain that there has been a misunderstanding;

you have not been asked to prove anything, so you can't have *failed* to have done it."

"You write to the Authority yourself – I'm not doing it!"

"Oh for stars' sake, Lilly-Anne, don't be childish." Ruby picked up a nearby notepad and pen.

"I'm serious!" I pushed it back. "I wouldn't even know how to address it! *Dear misters of the Authority, I'm afraid there's been a mix-up.*"

"Well, I don't either!" Ruby squealed, though the pleading look I attached must have convinced her, for she passed the notepad to Kin. "You've got the most experience dealing with justicemen, Kin."

He took it unwillingly. "I'm happy to help you draft it, but you know I'm no good with words. My latest history essay, Meagles said it had the substance equivalent to what comes out of a centaur's backside."

Ruby sighed. "That's because you only wrote about four lines. All right, let's concentrate. It's just a simple explanation. The correspondence instructing you to supply documentation of your fated heritage never arrived. Problem solved: supply the documents they want, no judgement."

"What kind of documents might they want, anyway?" I asked.

"An introduction certificate," she suggested.

"A what?"

"Every child that is born must be formally introduced to Fate, thereby being registered in the Authority's records," Ruby explained, and I deduced that it was more or less a birth certificate.

That was a problem. Not one I had cared for much before, aside from a missed school trip to France, which I couldn't attend due to lack of passport. I had no birth records. I had no documents at all, in fact.

Ruby and Kin took my silence as an acknowledgement of the predicament.

"You have your ayutum, I guess," Kin offered.

My fingers reflexively traced the edges of the star.

"You know as well as I do, Kindegory, that she could have bought that anywhere," Ruby shot down the argument, then addressed me in a softer tone. "Is there anyone that might know about your parents?"

I shook my head.

"That might testify you were born here?"

I had no clue about the circumstances of my birth nor identity of my parents. There were the Globesglorys, of course, and Harry Hale, but neither knew. And with Uncle Bill's passing, the answers were as good as him: gone forever.

"My parents died of carbon monoxide poisoning shortly after I was born, and that's when Uncle Bill took me in. Neither his sister nor his closest friends have any idea who my parents were. He moved to Earth, married Lynne, and one day not long after their marriage, he left for work and came back late with me in his arms," I said flatly, staring at the pattern in the wooden floor.

"Your parents died of what, sorry...?" Ruby's gentle voice probed.

"Carbon monoxide poisoning," I repeated.

There was a short pause. "What's... carbon monoxide?" Ruby finally asked, her voice almost a whisper.

In that simple question, the conundrum of my existence crashed down on me with the weight of all the worlds combined. Of course my best friends – including Ruby, the Ruby who had lexicons, taxonomies, atlases and alchemic formulae memorised – would have no clue what carbon monoxide was. There were no concepts of gasses, or physics, or chemistry as I knew it in the otherworlds. Uncle Bill had lied to me: either my parents didn't die of carbon monoxide poisoning, or they weren't from the otherworlds at all. My whole backstory, the little that I knew of it, had been a lie.

There were two solutions that immediately materialised. Either I was truly born here, and Uncle Bill had lied about the gas because my parents died in some other, awful way – potentially illicit circumstances, which could not be named. That was *likely*, seeing that a man so apparently devout to servitude suddenly made a run for it. Or, solution two: my parents truly did suffocate in their sleep, murdered by an unserviced boiler, victims of unpaid council tax somewhere in Briston, or Norwich, or Lowestoft, with my birth records misplaced somewhere in the James Paget Hospital. That would make me an unknowing beyond the boundaries of Earth. Either way, I probably had lawbreaking on the back of my hands.

And now the Authority, the institution that I had come so blindly to trust in protecting me – now that I finally felt like I belonged somewhere – were after me for being a threat to *their* worlds.

My stomach twisted and my lungs shrunk. If my imagination was capable of dreaming all this time, this was a perfect moment to wake up.

*

Professor Fellblue read the order I received. The three of us crowded around his desk, fidgeting. He read it once, about to speak. We looked eagerly, awaiting his opinion on the precise state of my demise. He went back to re-reading the notice once again. Ruby shifted from foot to foot, lips pressed in a tight line. Kin took off his glasses to wipe them with his jumper's hem. I fixed my eyes on the glass paperweight, now sat on Fellblue's desk, and imagined myself smashing it to pieces.

Lies – everything Uncle Bill had ever told me was lies. If he wasn't lying about the existence of the otherworlds, he was lying about my past.

Ruby decided we should seek advice from Professor Fellblue. She figured if I could learn to channel Force in a matter of a few days, this would prove that I was intuitive and at one with Fate, therefore not a lawbreaker. Kin offered to help me train. I didn't argue, knowing the plan was already futile. If I hadn't learned to materialise the white flames in half a year, how could I do it in days? Besides, lawbreakers could command Force just the same, only theirs was poisoned by Hate. Aside from being futile, the argument wasn't even logical.

Not that logic was much adhered to in the otherworlds.

"Why now?" My thoughts suddenly escaped in anger.

Ruby and Kin started at the broken silence. I'd been here for nearly nine months. Why had the Authority just *now* decided that I was a threat, an incursion beyond the rules binding Earth? They had dealt with me before – correspondence of Uncle Bill's death, handing over the inheritance; I'd testified to officers in April, as did Charlotte.

"Why have they only now decided to judge me?"

"I imagine they have been too busy up until now, given the recent events." Professor Fellblue's words were oddly calm, a subverted reassurance.

Did he suspect I had it coming all along?

"Still, I think it is for the better," he added.

"Forgive me, professor, but this is a *judgement*, and it is unnecessary in all respects, so how can you say—" Ruby began.

"Well, given the spike in lawbreaking over the last few turns, I suspect the demand for judgements has been high. Am I correct, Kindegory?" Fellblue turned to Kin, who simply shrugged. "I think Fate must have you in her favours, Lilly-Anne. High Judge Potts is much too busy these days, he hasn't got the time to make each and every judgement personally. And this one has been scheduled to take place here, at the school. You won't even need to travel. We have received notice as well." He produced an envelope with the same official stamp. Professor Fellblue knew all along. "And better still, we won't have to rely on the high judge's own intuition for the verdict."

"Who will judge me, then?" I asked.

"My guess is that you will be judged by Fate herself," Professor Fellblue smiled, handing me back the letter. "So do not fear, the judgement will be the purest it can be."

*

Over the next few days, we spent whatever time allowed in the little reading room of the library, surrounded by piles of books – history, legislature, chronicles, even fairy tales, too many in total to borrow between the three of us – as Ruby pieced together information.

"It doesn't hurt," she deduced, having ran through the procedure for me.

"Tell me again, please," I sighed. It still wasn't making sense.

"Judgements by Fate herself are *not* common, so I'm trying my best to find out what to expect." Her words were a disclaimer. "They'll run through the formalities on the day – speeches, etcetera. In the presence of intuitive witnesses – i.e., a representative party of justicemen and justicedames… most likely spectators will be allowed, too…" She shot me a sorry glance. "You will be asked to step into the hearth, which is essentially a shallow pit marked in the floor of the chantry. There, Fate is materially present and will judge you."

Materially present. "A fire," I assumed. "I'll have to walk into a lit fire-pit."

"It won't be lit," Ruby clarified. "Not when you walk into it, anyway."

"So I'll walk into a grill, and then they'll light me up. Great."

"It won't hurt," she insisted.

Kin peered over her shoulder, concentrating on Ruby's notes assembled from across the literature.

"It won't hurt if you're innocent," he read.

I buried my head between my hands.

In an instant, Ruby plucked her notes up from the table, rolling them up into a paper baton. "Of course," she whacked it on Kin's arm, "Lilly… is… innocent!" She hammered the words onto his arm.

305

Kin rubbed the spot. "I know, I know. Sorry – it's just what you had written down."

Ruby slumped back into her chair, embarrassed and depleted. "The last judgement by Fate was many years ago, so it's hard to say what exactly it will entail."

"What happened at the last one?" I mumbled to my sleeve.

Ruby didn't answer, and I looked up to find her expression hesitant. A demanding stare finally got her talking again.

"Well, it won't *be* like the last time, not with you, so there's no point going into detail."

I didn't drop my stare.

She sighed. "Last time Fate judged herself was after the Murders," she admitted. "Those directly involved were sentenced."

"What happened to them?"

She didn't answer, so Kin read from her notes again.

"They burned – but not completely. They were then locked in the eternal ices of the Carcery."

I shoved my head back between my hands.

"But it won't be like that!" Ruby asserted. "Prior to this most recent case, a Rachthaw was judged about a century ago. Members of the Authority accused her of acting against Fate's wishes. The Rachthaw objected, claiming her intuition was aligned with Fate. She subjected to a judgement willingly. She wasn't hurt, and those who accused her were subsequently found guilty of an insurrection."

We fell silent. Neither of these scenarios were fitting for my case, we all knew that much.

"I have a feeling that everything will be all right," Kin whispered, pushing his glasses up.

He'd tried his best to teach me how to spark the white flame, to will it into existence, to have it dance across my palm. All to no avail – and much to Ruby's annoyance at playing with fire in the library.

I could try to run, I thought at first, back to Earth or to the perceived safety of the Empyrean. My questions were pre-empted: I would be stopped at any portal terminal, Ruby said, a judgement pending against my name. I was locked out of Earth. I wanted to laugh. Imagine opening a door straight to the moon, stepping through, only to realise that it's a one-way door. Which disappears.

"Maybe it's not too late to ask for one of the justicemen to pass the judgement," I wondered.

The thought of a sentient, empathetic, *rational* human deciding my destiny seemed less harrowing than it being decided by an immaterial, divine power, a power that, if real, would surely find me guilty for the mere baseline of doubting its existence. Less harrowing than walking straight into a fire-pit, at least.

"No!" they replied simultaneously, apparently trusting more in the will of Fate than in the Authority's intuition of it.

"You heard Professor Fellblue," Ruby said. "Fate has brought you here, previously she decided you should live on Earth. Fate alone knows best why, and if the Authority needs a little reassurance of that, then let them have it. Maybe Fate has set this judgement up to meet you personally."

I could only hope that they were right, that everything really *was* fated, and my adventure in the otherworlds wasn't an accident, an unintentional breach on my behalf. And if everything was fated, then I guess I had this moment coming all along.

If everything was fated, she'd set this up precisely so that I couldn't run.

CHAPTER 34
BEATRICE GOLDTEAR

Mate unlaced his long boots, pushing down on the heel of one with the other foot to get it off. It didn't budge. Duel boots were nearly knee high, thick leather. He retracted the laces through a few more eyelets, trying to pry the boot off again. His hands were covered in scorch marks, as they nearly always were. He let me heal them though, if they were too bad. He did that to humour me – pain didn't seem to bother him.

I slid off the bed – his bed, he had just come back to Hall from practice – and stepped lightly around the frame to kneel in front of him where he sat on the edge. He straightened up, retreating from the closeness. I began to encroach on his space, his time, his proximity with unspoken permission. He allowed it. But Mate was always cautious, unsure, as if protecting me from himself.

"Let me help," I suggested, taking one boot and placing it on my knee.

Dark eyes returned an acknowledging gaze from the shadows of his face. I undid a few more eyelets and the boot slid off easily. Patience.

Duel season had been suspended due to the recent lawbreaking in Loon's City. It felt inappropriate, Chancellor Arden explained, to carry on the games after such horrendous events and while an investigation was ongoing. Initially, while officers patrolled the city in dense numbers, we didn't go out. It wasn't safe for anyone while a lawbreaker was on the loose, and besides, I sensed a tacit understanding between the brothers that it was safer *for them* to keep below the Authority's radar.

I stayed inside with Mate, tiptoeing the line between two kinds of righteousness.

Moreover, it wasn't even a lawbreaker who was responsible for the attack, Alastair said. Whoever – whatever – did it, was much more than human. Though I found this hard to believe, shyness won me over, and I never questioned Alastair. This was information he intended for Mate, anyway.

Still sitting on the edge of the bed, Mate lifted his other leg, knee under the chin, heel wedged into the bedframe. He unlaced the second boot almost all the way down, taking this one off himself. It fell to the floor with a thud. He dropped his leg to the floor too, and I gently placed my head in his lap, still kneeling in front of him, cheek against his thigh. The warmth of touch burned from underneath his clothes. I felt his hand softly, hesitantly, brush against my hair. This was as much closeness as he allowed.

As rises dawned and dusked, and the Authority weakened its grip over Loon's City, they began to practise duels again. No games, just practice. Though vivid excitement wasn't Mate's strong point, I could tell he welcomed that: being outside again, being excused from class – especially now, when suspicious stares made classrooms claustrophobic. He never as much as uttered a word of complaint. But I could sense the anxiety spawning inside him when he was cooped up, penned in. He had lived through too much of that as a child. Alastair could sense it too, being protective of his brother. In duel combat, Mate was unleashed, free, at one with Fate. Alastair prioritised practice with his brother now, though he'd grown to trust me enough to take care of Mate too.

My sister had never bothered us again, and I presumed that Alastair had ensured of that as well. Fate knows how, but the Purger Society never as much as mentioned Mate. The lack of enraged letters from my father indicated that my parents were similarly unaware. This was reassuring; the tingling sense of guilt and sorrow brought up by the sheer thought of Mate getting into trouble because of *me* was enough.

I lay with my head in Mate's lap, until the stroking stopped, and I turned to find Alastair leaning against the door frame. Mate and I both straightened out; I shuffled a little distance away. A smirk spread across Alastair's face, amused by the intrusion.

"Nin stopped by," he said casually to his brother.

Mate's brows furrowed in response, his cheeks sucked in slightly as he thought. "Is it another...?" Mate's voice trailed off.

Whoever Nin was – the Grims' adopted sister of sorts, as far as I could tell – she had warned them of the last horrific events, the ensuing presence of the Authority in the city, and the need to stay low.

"No, the demon was spooked. It will stay underground for a long time now – a few decades at least, a century, perhaps," Alastair assured.

"Let's hope it doesn't return while we're still alive – you especially, if it indeed hides for a century." Mate's tone lightened, his lips turning into a vague smile.

Alastair frowned and crossed his arms. "I see your sense of humour is back." He looked at me then, rarely as he did, acknowledging my presence. "You're clearly a positive influence on my brother."

I felt my cheeks flare up with a blush, and out of the corner of my eye, I thought I saw a rare hint of healthy colour on Mate's face too.

"What did Nin want?" Mate steered the conversation back.

"There is going to be a judgement here, in Sapphire Dragon's. Lots of officers and justicemen. Nothing to concern us, but we should avoid conspicuousness for the time."

"Just as you had dreamed," Mate mused.

"Yes," Alastair confirmed. "I still can't work out what these dreams are about. They're irrational, far-fetched. Perhaps I dreamt of the judgement because Nin was coming to tell me about it, who knows."

"Do you want to talk about it?"

"No, these dreams don't really mean much," Alastair dismissed, already turning to leave the dorm. "There's one person I might need to talk to, but I'll see to that with time."

"Tell Nin I'm upset she never sees me, next time she visits," Mate teased as a goodbye.

"Bet you are," we heard just before the parlour door slammed shut.

I nestled my head back into Mate's lap. It occurred to me then. "Your brother must be exceptionally intuitive, if Fate lets him know about such minor things as surprise family visits." Foretelling dreams typically carried great weight, some drama, a big revelation – a kindness on Fate's part.

Mate stroked my hair again, but the touch was absentminded. "I doubt that Nin's visit is the real reason behind him dreaming of this judgement. He's had several strange dreams lately. Not troubling – just strange because they are nothing to do with *him*. Neither of us understands why Fate would show him things that are about to happen to a stranger, and it is always the same person she is showing him."

"Perhaps he should see a dream doctor?" I offered, reflexively. My mother always made appointments to follow up strange dreams, to ensure she was interpreting them correctly – at the expense of a dozen heads a session.

Mate's breath stammered with an inaudible laugh. "I guess that's what he discusses with Nin in private," he finally said.

"Is she good at interpreting dreams?"

"You could say that she's at one with Fate, yes."

I concentrated on the repetition of his gentle touch, melting further each time his hand passed down my hair. We fell into silence, and I replayed the conversation in my head, remembering each velvety note of his voice.

"What did you mean, when you said 'let's hope Alastair isn't still alive if the *thing* returns after a century'?" I wondered aloud.

"Alastair has a particular… condition, meaning he may – or may not, depending on how sensible he is – outlive all of us."

Mate's words surprised me, not because they were strange and cryptic – I'd learned to take that much for granted with the Grims – but because I didn't expect an answer; for the same reasons, Mate was never too forthcoming about the details of his family.

"Do you have this condition, too?" I whispered, unsure if I wanted to catch his gaze. Whatever *the condition* was, I suspected it impacted his state of blood. In an unarticulated contract, this was a topic we agreed not to discuss.

"No," the answer was quick.

I turned my head to meet his depthless eyes.

"That's a curse he took on my behalf."

CHAPTER 35
LILLY-ANNE SKYROSE

The star around my neck seemed to weigh a ton, and I kind of wished it really did, so that it could snap it.

"Put your formal cloak on," Ruby instructed.

"Why? What difference will it make?"

She had spent the morning ensuring that I looked my best. If it was up to me, my final outfit would have been my favourite pyjamas.

"Just put it on, for stars' sake."

The heavy folds of my formal cloak fell over my shoulders as she wrapped me up. As soon as Ruby let go of her embrace, Sephy immediately took her place, squeezing my torso tightly. Flip circled around my legs underneath the cloak, tail brushing against my calf. Kin patted me on the shoulder.

"It will be all right. I've dreamt that it will be, honest," he said, trying to reassure me.

"I have, too," Ruby added.

I bet they hadn't really, but it was nice of them to say. The words were nothing but meaningless reassurances of a positive outcome to today's events.

I sucked in another deep breath. No matter how many deep breaths I took, none seemed to hold in my empty lungs. My mind and body detached in preparation for the inescapable pain. I felt hollow, numb with fright, no longer attempting to stay afloat because the waves of pain – a different kind of pain than the loss I felt after Uncle Bill – had already brought me under.

Today, I was already mourning the loss of my own life.

I would burn.

At first, Kin had tried to teach me how to protect myself from scalding if the judgement was detrimental, hopeful that justicemen could be reasoned with should Fate not find me favourable herself. He showed me how to deflect the burn in the same way duellers did when fielding: a thin sheath of flames encasing the body part that would come into contact with another's blaze. Fighting fire with fire. But this was hopeless, not only because I was unable to command Force, but because we all knew that the fire of Fate would have the final say. If Fate wanted me to burn, her power could not protect me at the same time.

"See you in a bit, then," Vince said. "Dad will be there, to vouch for you if needed."

I nodded a thanks. Like the formal cloak, Jacob Globesglory would make no difference to my demise.

"You got these numbing spells I taught you?" Bertie asked, more pragmatic about the outcome. "Do you want me to put them on you now, or will you spell yourself when it's needed?"

"She's *not going to burn*, Bertie – cut it out," Vince scolded.

If only. But I'd made my peace with it. I would burn.

They walked with me from the bastion to the main school building, through the corridors now lined with inquisitive eyes of students whose curiosity had been captured by the sudden presence of patrol officers in school grounds. I insisted that my friends don't come with me. They came anyway. We said final goodbyes outside of the great chantry door. Then they filed into a little side entrance, leading up to the pews in overhead balconies.

Damsel, too, headed towards the side door. "Going to see the spectacle, Kindegory?" she asked. "I heard that the last judgement by Fate was a *real* show. Anyway, I hope you can make it to the next Purgers' meeting, we'll be discussing our success in fighting for the lawful cause."

Kin paused at the threshold, the last of my friends to head upstairs. His shoulders rolled back as he raised his chest and adjusted his glasses with a little too much strength.

"Piss off, Damsel," Kin said.

An officer came to collect and disarm me then.

"Your wand," he demanded.

I handed over the tapered stick; as if that could somehow save me anyhow.

With all the spectators in their place, it was my cue to go in. The great, wooden chantry door was framed in arches, radiating keystones above its top, the centre keystone a bright red. Hinges clicked as if commanded, releasing both wings inwards into darkness. The officer nudged me in.

The chantry was spacious, grand. Pitted beams of light struggled to break through tall stained-glass windows at the far end, intruding on the darkness. A cold, damp smell hung in the air, like rotting earth. Organic: a natural end. My footsteps echoed through the hall, heavy on the ancient paving. Rows of statues draped in red lined my pathway towards the hearth. Living statues, the still and silent justicemen and justicedames.

I sensed a shifting in the darkness above – my audience, gathered in the balconies either side.

One red-hooded statue turned its head in faint acknowledgement as I moved past: Jacob Globesglory.

I moved further down the hall, no need for the officer's escort. I couldn't run now. More figures emerged into the light, closest to the hearth. Dressed in navy paisley, Professor Fellblue stood with his hat folded between his hands. By his side were Professor Artsback and Chancellor Arden. Nearest to the hearth was the young justiceman I recognised as Krebbles.

I stopped some yards in front of him, unsure of the stage directions for my part in this tragedy. Someone orchestrated that I ought to move into the hearth and turn around. That I did, overstepping the stone kerb lining the edges of the shallow pit, slowly spinning to face my audience.

I breathed slowly, anticipation rising with each shallow breath. No fire yet. My gaze met their faces, the solemn justicemen convicted in their purpose, the avid students in the balconies blurring into an indistinguishable crowd.

Krebbles cleared his throat. "Justicemen and justicedames. We have gathered here today to bear witness to a judgement, sanctioned by our mother Fate, our creator and our master." He lifted his arms up to the darkness of the heights. "Oh, Fate," acting on his words as cue, rows of the red statues joined their hands and lifted them up too, "the all-knowing," Krebbles prayed towards the heights.

"The all-knowing," the statues chanted in return.

"The all-present," he continued.

"The all-present," they repeated.

"The all-mighty, everlasting," echoed lastly.

"With no beginning and no end. By your will we continue to exist; existing we continue to enforce your will."

Krebbles's voice sprung with ecstasy, arms outstretched as far as the confines of skin would allow, an absent look in his eye; absent, yet climactic, as if he himself was up there in the darkness of the heights, some power commanding his voice on his behalf.

"Oh, Fate, our protector, we your loyal servants who strive to understand your ways, humbly ask for revelation of your wishes on this day."

Pulse pushed adrenaline through my veins. It was coming – the fire, the burn. I forgot all the parts of the numbing spell.

"The accused presented to you, though none escapes your reach, is a Lilly-Anne Skyrose, seventeen years of age, suspected of breaching unknowing rules binding the Earth Islands, on account of no previous permanent address anywhere in the knowing worlds and absence from the register of those who have been introduced to you," Krebbles spoke to the heights. "You have chosen to leave the Islanders unintuitive and unaware, oh Fate, and the accused stands trial for disobeying your will in this regard."

"We welcome your judgement," echoed through the hall.

I closed my eyes.

Here comes my end. Regardless of whether everything is fated, an end is always inevitable. Whether it's predetermined and planned, or unforeseen and impending, whether it's on Earth or somewhere else – somewhere beyond the fringes of imagination – bodies are mortal just the same.

Through my eyelids, my vision registered a glow.

Funny thing – living. Making memories, breathing; here or elsewhere, just the same. It's hard to know you're *really* living, especially when everything you've ever known and taken for granted gets turned upside down. What if I was dreaming still? Or is it only in death, that we are truly convinced of having been alive? I guess that's something each finds out for themselves – the dead don't live to tell the tale.

The glow grew blinding even through closed eyes, a white light that I diminished in. Suddenly I felt an icy prickling, like submerging into too hot bath water before the scalding temperature registers on the skin. Only that now, it was underneath the skin. If you ever felt an electric shock, you'd know what I mean. I once got a slight shock from turning on a desk light. It wasn't even plugged in.

My muscles tensed and tendons pulled on their own accord. Each neuron fired simultaneously. My spine arched, and head flew back. A surge of cramps ripped through my core, through each tiny cell that blood could reach. Something alien was flowing through my veins.

My eyes were pried open by the force commanding me. It registered then: the white flames engulfing me. Just as I'd predicted. I burned.

There was an awful commotion, and I wondered what was going on. I'd lost track of time. I'd lost track of everything that was going on, in fact. I was exhausted and scrunched up, lying on a cold, hard surface – the floor, I think – with no intention of getting up.

"Fate has departed, it means she's satisfied – consider that the verdict."

I recognised the voice, though I couldn't put a name to it. It came from somewhere nearby, and soon enough something started prodding me in the side.

"Perhaps we should give it more time, justiceman. I mean, how can we *truly* be sure that the judgement is finished?"

This voice was familiar too, though it wasn't one I liked very much.

"Why, doesn't your intuition confer to you that a decision has already been reached? You wanted your judgement, Krebbles, so there you have it. Now, if you don't stop acting like you're doubting Fate's own decisions, we'll be happy to hang around and watch you step into the hearth too."

Someone turned me over and tried to stand me up: Jacob Globesglory.

"By our intuition and as decided by Fate herself," Jacob Globesglory said louder.

I wobbled to my feet between his red cloak and Professor Fellblue's steadying arm, opening my eyes in the precise moment to see him proclaim down the stretch of the chantry:

"The accused is hereby pronounced innocent. This concludes the judgement."

*

Outside was a pleasant night, the verge of summer. The streets of Loon's City once again began to crawl, teeming with all sorts of life that amalgamated to cast the city's patchwork character. Tourists, vendors, and artists climbed the summit rising from the shoal, pouring into this cup of life and conducing to its overspill. It was several weeks too early, however, for the crowds to swell and their confines to burst beyond the lower levels of the citadel. Aside from its usual residents, the summit remained undisturbed.

The Nest was packed, stuffy with excitement and the spicy smell of drinks, peppered with warm candle glow. We managed to secure a little table in a corner, much too small to fit all the glasses belonging to our group that bulged around its edges. Chatter rose and blurred beneath the low ceiling, saturating the air with an audible asphyxiation. A warm breeze filtered through the window cracks, hardly helping to disperse the heat from rosy cheeks.

"Darn, it's gone out again." Dean blew out the candle sitting in the middle of our table. "Can you do the honours, Lilly?"

"Oh, for the love of—" I began to protest, but he started patting his hand across the table, nearly spilling a few drinks.

"Quick, light the candle, I can't see anything." Dean's hand wreaked havoc across the table-top. It wasn't even dark inside, and it was the third time he blew it out this evening.

Dean was having too much fun. I leaned in and snapped my fingers over the wick.

"Waahey," he sung, satisfied, as a warm glow lit up our faces once again.

Ever since the judgement, I discovered a new talent, much to the excitement of my friends, especially Dean and Kin – not to mention the twins. Or rather, I discovered it a few days later, when Professor Fellblue had us lighting candles in Force control. Otherwise, it wouldn't have occurred to me to even try. It was a strange feeling, one I couldn't think too much about to bring into existence; a tingling in the blood, a flash flood of warmth across the fingertips.

Dean leaned across the table again.

"Don't you dare," I warned. "I'm not your circus monkey."

"Not my *what*? Don't give me none of that Earthen lingo," he grinned. "You're one of us now."

"What's more, that judgement is going to go down in the history of the Continent," Ruby said.

She still had the newspaper clipping tucked among her books. I'd bargained with Dianne to keep it more or less anonymised, but it made the *Seer*'s front page anyway.

"And you know who's going to go down with it?" Francesca added, putting down her drink. "Piutrach Krebbles. Apparently, the whole trial was his idea entirely. He insisted that he found a serious security breach, and that he should carry out the judgement himself – he's lining up to take over High Judge Potts's chair, you see. Not that he stands a chance. But they wouldn't let him anyway, said he wasn't intuitive enough to judge. So they decided to call on Fate to carry out the judgement – Krebbles couldn't exactly object to that. Besides, he thought he'd take the credit regardless, seeing how the last judgement by Fate went down. And now that Fate has declared you innocent – well, let's just say that trust in Krebbles's intuition has gone down the drain."

"How do you know that?" Ruby interrogated.

"Damsel said," Francesca defended her source.

"Oh, friends with Damsel now, are you?"

"You bet I am. She's invited me to the Purgers' meeting tonight and everything." Fran took a nervous sip, reminding us of something that we'd happily forgotten about.

"I thought The Purger Society just died a natural death," Dean said. "I haven't heard from Damsel in a while."

"Not quite. I think Damsel is looking to restart the meetings in a new light," Fran announced. "She said I should come tonight, especially if I can bring a *certain someone* along with me."

We all followed Fran's hopeful gaze, which she fixed like a neon sign above the *certain someone*. Kin pushed his glasses up and gulped.

"Do you think you can help me with the magic homework tonight, Rubes?" he quickly asked.

"What magic homework?" Ruby wrinkled her brows. "We don't have any magic homework due—"

Kin retorted with a kick underneath the table.

"Oh, *that* magic homework," she realised. "The one that... uhh..." Ruby rambled, looking around for help in forming a convincing lie.

"The one that Flashmight only set for me," Kin clarified.

"Yes, that one," Ruby blushed. "Of course I can help."

"Looks like your certain someone is busy tonight." Rupert finished off a cream beer, his fifth tonight, nodding to Fran. "Want to bring along a certain someone else? I haven't got any plans tonight."

"Sure," Fran muttered with a terrible lack of excitement.

We sat in comfortable silence for a while, soaking in the atmosphere. Summer was just around the corner. We'd made it through first year. I thought about the last ten months. To say that my life had turned upside down would be an understatement. The worlds – world, as I knew it then – had changed beyond recognisable shape. Was I confident in knowing their true colours? Not quite. In the overlaps of stories, I found myself bordering each point of view, each different understanding, as the otherworlds gradually revealed themselves.

"I think this candle is broken, Lilly," Dean interrupted my reverie. "Do you reckon you can fix it?"

I snapped my fingers and lit the damn thing again. Dean was certainly pushing his luck with my patience tonight.

"You're really quite a natural – you know that?" I heard Vince say, and realised he was watching from across the room. "I've seen you spark four times in a row this evening, each at first time. You should really join the team for training next year, Lills," he said.

"I hope you're joking," I called back to him.

"Nah, Vince never jokes – never learned the meaning of the word." Bertie suddenly appeared, helping himself to the last drops inside our pitcher.

"I think Vince just has an eye for talent," Melanie defended him. "He knows one when he sees one – and can smell cheating from a mile away."

"Yeah? Perhaps your definition of talent is quite narrow, then – anyone with a passion for long words might struggle to be included in it," Bertie circled back, having drained our table dry.

"Perhaps if your personalities didn't take up so much space, Bertie, you wouldn't struggle to fit in the talent hoop," Mel retorted.

Bertie walked right up to her, too close for comfort to Mel's face, checking first behind her left ear, then the right.

"Uh, what *are* you doing, Bertie?" Mel swatted his hand away.

"Looking for the horns, 'cos it sounds like you're a cow," he said.

"All right you two, cut it out," Vince stepped in.

"Snip, snip," Bertie echoed in what I assumed was an agreement to the peace treaty. "I was on my way, anyway. Got some words to put together, things to conclude."

"Going to see Rebecca?" someone prompted.

The relationship didn't seem to be aging well. Apparently, Rebecca wasn't enjoying Bertie's sense of humour after all. Last I heard, he fell asleep when she took him to have their portrait painted and shrunk his arms – temporarily – when she signed them up for a ball dancing class.

"Nah, she's stuck in botany, quite confined," Bertie piped up.

"How come?"

"Meyer's got the whole orchestra, and now the choral group too. Got them all playing and singing to this tiny music tree, but it just won't grow.

They've got no idea why."

A few people laughed, though Sephy seemed to find this most hilarious.

"So, what are everyone's plans for summer?" Rupert asked, when the energy subsided.

"The Royal Show, of course," Dean returned with a new round of drinks.

"Is everyone going to be there?" Rupert helped himself to Ruby's share when she declined.

We all nodded.

"What about you, Fabian, you going as well?"

"Hopefully, I've got a ticket and all." Fabian fiddled with a coaster. "Don't think Dad will be too keen to hear I'm going, but I'll try to make it anyway."

"Thought your old man wasn't one of *those* Empyreans," Dean's words washed down the glass as he tipped it to his mouth, but we all heard anyway.

"Well," Fabian cleared his throat. "La'dore-ono is an open-minded place, we've got two members in the Senate. And there's the alymthium mine – I guess that's why we've got two justicedames in the first place, though."

"I was under the impression your father quite liked the climate on the Continent," Ruby offered, trying to soothe the divide that suddenly seemed to hang in the air.

"I guess he does," Fabian mused. "I do, my mum and little brother, Quincy, do. But you know what they say: you can leave the Empyrean, but the Empyrean never quite leaves you."

"So where did you get the ticket from, if your old man didn't give it to you?" Rupert pressed.

Everyone's eyes wandered to random stains on the walls, and soon enough, Kin's generosity with the tickets was all too apparent. Rupert's ability to read the room was selective at best, but he managed to pick this one up.

"What, so everyone's got a ticket already, then?" He sat back and crossed his arms. "Even you, Ruby?"

"Y-yes," she huffed. "Why wouldn't I?"

"Where from?" Rupert demanded, then noticed one too many of us glance at Kin. "Got any more of those tickets, Kin, by any chance?"

Kin pushed his glasses up and slumped, as if to hide. Ruby shot him a pleading glance. Although she was no longer hiding from Rupert, his failed attempts to ask her to the ball had left a sour taste in her mouth.

"Terribly sorry, Rupes— Rupert, I'm all out," Kin finally said.

"Dang," Rupert sighed. "I've dreamt of myself going, you know. But I haven't got enough silvers for a ticket. Someone's got to give Fate a helping hand because I swear she wants me at the show."

"I got you, Rupes." Dean started patting around his pockets. "Got a spare somewhere in my wallet. Parents get a whole bunch every year. I keep them for the ladies normally, but reckon I can spare one for you," he winked.

Ruby rolled her eyes.

"Thanks, Dean. See, everyone, that's a real king right there, you can tell he's got Rachthawnian blood in him," Rupert said, but his enthusiasm dwindled when Dean took a little too long searching through his pockets.

"Sorry, buddy, looks like someone's swiped my wallet," Dean apologised.

"How convenient for you." Rupert crossed his arms again.

"Maybe you lost it at the bar," Sephy suggested, "when you bought the last round."

"I must have." Dean got up to look for it, but for the remainder of the night, his wallet was nowhere to be found.

*

I had a hard time getting to sleep that night. Savouring the verge of summer, my mind couldn't be put to rest. Schoolwork was scant by now, the teachers busy preparing second-years for interims and seniors for final exams. I couldn't help imagining what the Royal Fonsland Show might be like; Dean promised a plethora of magical oddity. Ruby wasn't helping with the sleeping either.

"What do you think the lawkeeper's house is like?" she wondered.

The plan was to go to Kin's house at the end of the semester, from where we'd travel to the show together.

"So big, Arabella probably hands out maps," Sephy said from across the room.

"I heard the guild are going to have a stall at the show," Ruby whispered, "where you can register interest in spellsmithery."

"There's going to be a slug pageant and aurochs racing too," Sephy added.

"The new *Auto-correct 5* wand model is meant to be revealed, with predictive casting – not that I would need it."

"And there'll be a demonstration of Dr Conspicuous's new invisibility boots."

After the Royal Show, I looked forward to spending time in the Empyrean until school restarted. Having learned about my judgement – after the events, of course, because I wasn't going to admit to it beforehand – Gabriel invited me over right away.

We're not giving them another pretext for a ~~jajm~~ judgement. You're not going back to Earth, he wrote.

I invited them both to the show too, Gabe and Billie. As it turned out, Kin still had a spare bundle of tickets at hand.

If only I could convince Dad that it was fated I go to the Royal Show, came the reply. *But he says the whole thing is a target on a plate. Won't let us go – sorry, Lilly. Will see you after. Dad overreacting, as always. You have a great time. P.S. if you see anyone selling this thing called 'clutch', can you bring me one? Not sure what it looks like. You probabebly know – for the carrs. Will pay back. Nobody selling clutch in the Emp.*

Once I finally drifted off to sleep, I fell in such deep slumber that their continued conversation didn't bother me. Limbs numbed so profoundly, I don't think I could have moved them even if I willed them to try. In this borderland of consciousness, my mind conjured familiar images. The dream took me to the domed cave again. I'd been here quite a few times since the judgement, watching dust flicker in the light beam across the empty room and settle on the altar. A different kind of light – static, almost sparking – still pulsed through the strange text of the ancient book. This dreamy space was by now familiar enough that I even knew the precise layout of the chisel marks that honed the walls. Nothing ever changed in this timeless room.

Nothing, except this time, I was not alone. I edged towards the hooded figure stood behind the altar. It wasn't Uncle Bill, however, nor the woman.

"Professor Fellblue?" I asked in my dream.

He smiled, saying something, but of course my dreams always lacked sound.

"I can't hear you," I tried explaining, but he continued to deliver inaudible words, while I pointlessly tried to lip-read behind the bushy beard.

He wasn't wearing a hooded cloak, I realised, but rather what looked like a nightgown and cap. I'm sure I'll feel embarrassed about this after waking up. He pointed things out around the room, in the book, but it was a while before sound – as it always did – returned.

"I'm afraid my time is up. This is goodbye, Lilly-Anne," Professor Fellblue said.

I jerked awake, heart pounding so hard I felt its thudding between my ears. Moonlight snuck into the darkened room, wrapping around Sephy's frame where she slept tangled in her duvet. Ruby snored lightly across the room.

Fully awake, I wasn't embarrassed – I was *terrified.* A deluge of déjà vu crashed down on me, releasing floodgates of panic and setting off an awful memory. The last time someone entered my dreams to deliver a message, terrible things followed in reality.

The last time I had dreamt of someone, I was too oblivious to act.

The last time, the consequences were deadly, and that someone was Uncle Bill.

*

Jumping out of bed, I threw on my dressing gown at the same time as my feet shuffled around the floor, searching for some shoes. Not a minute later, I was heading down the staircase, across the common room, and out of the bastion. The gremlin porter snored by the front entrance, positive his duties would be uncalled for at this hour.

I didn't stop to think. If I did, I would have certainly questioned what the hell I was doing. That would have only wasted time.

And there was no time to waste. I practically ran across the school grounds, which wasn't easy because the only footwear I managed to find were Sephy's fur-lined slippers. They kept sliding off my feet. No wonder she was always losing her damn shoes. Muffled slipper footsteps echoed faintly through the empty corridors as I hurried through the main school building. There was something eerie about the stillness of the night. Stars shone exceptionally bright.

I didn't allow myself time to think until I reached the door. What the hell was I doing? I stared at the planks of wood bolted together to fashion the entrance to Force control. It was way past midnight, so Professor Fellblue wasn't even going to be in his office, tucked away behind the classroom. I had no idea where he lived either. Yet *something* told me this is exactly where I needed to be; the same strange feeling that ripped me from my dream.

"Come in, Lilly-Anne," I heard through the door.

Pushing it gently, I stepped inside. I hadn't knocked.

Professor Fellblue sat behind the heavy desk in his classroom, leaning back in his chair and looking out into the starry night behind the windowpanes. Dressed in nightgown and cap with a blanket draped over his shoulders, he straightened up as much as his old frame allowed, interrupted in his musing.

"Can't sleep, professor?" I asked, completely unable to explain the reason why I'd come.

"I could say the same to you, Lilly-Anne," he smiled. "Have you seen the celestials? It's a tremendously clear sky tonight."

"Actually, professor…" *What the hell are you doing, Lilly-Anne? How are you going to explain yourself? Hello professor, I've come to warn you because you were in my dream, and the last time I dreamt of my uncle – well, I hate to say it, but he kind of died.* "I was asleep. It's only that I had a dream."

Fellblue raised a brow, so I continued.

"You were in it, in fact. Saying goodbye and all," I mumbled, hoping he was a bit deaf.

"Ah, yes – we'll get to that part," Professor Fellblue simply said.

I stared at him, wide-eyed. "What do you mean, professor?"

"Well, Lilly, bodies are transient things, and I am quite old," he half laughed. "I've been expecting it for a while, frankly. You do, once you get to my age. And Fate has been letting it be made known for some time now – each time more vividly. I hate to brag, but I always considered myself to be a loyal servant. And now – well, now I have confirmation that she considers me so. For you see, Lilly, Fate has kindly alerted me to the fact that, once I go to sleep tonight, I shan't be waking up."

He *knew*. Professor Fellblue knew he was going to die.

"Thus, I'm putting sleep off for a little while yet. There remain a couple of things I need to wrap up before I drift away. And since you're here, Lilly-Anne, one of those can get done now," he continued.

"But *professor*," I almost shouted because he was so goddamn calm. "How can you just *sit* here and *wait* for it to happen? Why don't you do something – I don't know, head down to the infirmary! I'll wake Nurse Poppy, I'm sure she has some spell, some… some… *something*… to make you right!"

"As brilliant as she is, unfortunately there's naught that Nurse Poppy can do when Fate decides to claim back what's rightfully hers," Fellblue smiled again.

"But there must be *something*, I don't know – some way to keep you alive." I refused to give up. I refused to understand how he could *know* about being at death's door and not at least *try* to keep alive. Or be frightened about it.

Instead, Professor Fellblue began fiddling with some wooden puzzle, the kind you'd buy as a stocking filler at Christmas time. The pieces didn't fit together right.

"Are you any good at these, Lilly-Anne?" he asked. "I can't quite figure these two pieces out."

"Professor!" I cried. "Is there *nothing* that can be done? Surely there are kinds of… magic… that may help?"

"Everything is fated, Lilly-Anne," Professor Fellblue sighed. "There are various kinds of potent magic, unlawful magic, which have the ability to prolong life, resurrect, multiply the number of lives one holds, even."

"Well, if everything is fated – if Fate has created these kinds of magic –

why can't you try it?" I spat back, no restraint to my tone.

I felt as though I was having this conversation not with Professor Fellblue, but with Uncle Bill. Uncle Bill, who most likely knew he was going to die too – by natural or forced means, I still didn't know. Uncle Bill, who did nothing but accept death either.

Something wet plopped down onto my toe, which stuck out from beneath the slipper's strap. I slipped my foot out to wipe it on my pyjama trouser leg and realised that Sephy had drawn clouds on the inner sole. A few more tears rained down on them.

"Everything is fated," Professor Fellblue agreed. "However, I am not fated to use dark magic, Lilly-Anne. There are others, who are, of course, but I am not one of them. Fate has predetermined everything, and we can only hope to understand her plans and accept them. She has decided that tomorrow I shan't wake up, and she has decided this long before I was born, at the beginning of time."

"But—"

"But before I fall asleep, there is something I would like you to have," Professor Fellblue said.

"This puzzle?" I asked because he was still fiddling with it.

Professor Fellblue laughed. "You can have it, if you wish," he said, then leaned across the desk to push the glass paperweight towards me. "But I would like you to have this."

I moved closer to the desk and reached for the familiar paperweight that Uncle Bill had given him. A token of death, I thought bleakly, passed from one consciously dying man to another. Was I next?

"I think you're old enough to look after your own prophecy." Professor Fellblue picked up the glass ball, placing it in my outstretched hands.

"My what?"

"Your prophecy." He sat back, more at ease, as if freeing himself of some burden. "This is a prophecy stone, Lilly-Anne."

The familiar glass ball morphed in meaning right there in my hands. No longer useless clutter, it was a *prophecy,* hiding in plain sight all my life.

"A prophecy is similar to a…" Professor Fellblue picked up a book lying unfolded at the spine on his desk. *Island Dictionary* was its title. "… an insurance policy," he read out, then looked back to me to explain. "Parents sometimes make these for their children. A prophecy contains details about heritage, claims to assets, any information that Fate may have revealed to parents about their children before birth."

"I… I have a prophecy?" *Parents, heritage, birth.* I felt my knees buckle.

"Yes, made by your parents. Now, I understand this may sound like a lot, however, please don't be alarmed," he added because my mind swirled so much that I thought it safest to sit down. "Prophecies don't have to be *fulfilled,* as such, they're simply vectors of information, made for no other reason than lest this information be questioned by anyone. Their function is to prove. Sceptics would say it's all one, big fairy hoax – and mind you, the fairies have made a fortune selling these…"

Professor Fellblue persevered in his explanation, though I must have stopped listening at that point. A *prophecy. My* prophecy. Made by *my* parents.

"What does it say?" I interrupted him.

"I'm afraid you need an oracle to tell you that."

"What's an oracle? How do I get one?"

"Rather, *who* is an oracle. Prophecy holders are typically acquainted with their oracles. Oracles are individuals with whom the prophetic information is also entrusted – again, for proof purposes. An oracle is familiar with a prophecy's encryption and can vouch for it."

"Who is my oracle, then?" I mumbled, stroking the smooth glass, trying to comprehend this revelation. The familiar arrangement of crystals sunken inside the glass – a stellar constellation, I always thought – stared back with disapproving cynicism. Distracted, I almost let go of the reasons why I came here tonight.

"I'm sure Fate will reveal that in due time," Professor Fellblue said, and I must have frowned because he added, "We cannot hurry Fate's plans, Lilly-Anne. You are intuitive, so will know when the time has come. Do be watching out for signs."

"What signs?"

"Well, dear William, when he came to visit me last year, he only mentioned that you shall need a key."

"A *key?* To open what – this?" I held up the glass ball. "There's nowhere to insert a key here."

"I am positive that you will figure it out. Fate will guide you when she deems it time. Now," he rose slowly, struggling to push up from the arm rests, "if you'll excuse me, I believe I have another visitor on the way."

Professor Fellblue shuffled around the desk, headed for the door. "It was an honest pleasure to teach and know you, Lilly-Anne. I hope to have served you well. Fate will have you in her favours, I'm sure of that."

He held the door open, and reluctantly, I got up to leave.

"But I'm afraid my time is up. This is goodbye, Lilly-Anne."

I had achieved nothing. Professor Fellblue was knowingly, compliantly (and I hoped at least peacefully) going to die.

"Goodbye, professor," I whispered on the way out.

Burying the paperweight – the prophecy – in a deep pocket of my dressing gown, I didn't want to look back. Keeping my gaze to the floor and trying to shut out the news we would all wake up to tomorrow, I watched Sephy's fluffy slippers slide along the cold, stone tiles stretching down the corridor.

It was only when I looked up to check if the library wing was still open – thinking I may be able to cut across there on my way back to the bastion – that I saw *him*.

Stood at the top of the stairs, right where I needed to go down, he leaned on the balustrade and waited. The school building was deserted, not a sound to indicate anything else going on – what was he doing? His bold, resolute eyes locked with mine, refusing to drop at my approach.

With arms crossed and still fully dressed despite the hour, he delved the stare right into my soul as I hedged closer in my dressing gown, trying fruitlessly to repel the scrutiny.

Yet the closer I got, the clearer it became that this was no coincidental meeting between two strangers who happen to be awake in the small hours.

No.

He waited for me to pass by, it seemed. His seizing stare persisted, furrowed underneath thick brows. I gulped, suddenly terrified. A potent energy emanated from his mien – demanding, furious, struggling to rein himself in.

I stopped short several yards away.

Yes, furious. Most certainly and unapologetically furious. Almost berserk, as if trying to regain his bearings in a situation that was most potently outside of his control. As if he'd been tasked with something so awful, so inconvenient, so incomprehensible, and had no choice but to comply. And in his unrelenting stare, I felt at once the cause of this fury: me.

In that instant, he pushed off the balustrade and headed down the corridor towards me.

My muscles froze, rooting me in place. I braced myself for the senseless wrath that loomed closer with each stride.

Was this still about the stupid match?

I thought I saw his lips ebb with silent words, but at that moment, something whirred inside my mind, dislodged it temporarily, as if someone had reached inside with grubby hands and churned it rudimentarily.

He passed me, by the time I came to realise.

Spinning on my heel, I watched as he domineered down the corridor, stopping only when he reached the Force control classroom door.

"Come in, Alastair," invited a faint voice from within.

"That's her, the child?" was his reply.

His head slowly panned back, and with one last, strained sideways glance to meet my eyes, Alastair Grim went inside. And in that gaze was not only fury, but a promise too. Some kind of a tie, an unbreakable covenant, an assurance, a conviction. A deadly one, I'm sure, for Alastair Grim was the last person to ever see Professor Fellblue alive.

ORLE GIGGLY LOBBSTER

"She doesn't really know me," said a whiny voice. "I mean, she thinks she does, but she doesn't. She has this phoney *idea* of me, and this idea-me apparently likes to hold hands, get take-outs, and just sit there staring into her eyes. And she's got a terrible sense of humour."

"You ought to tell her that, before it's too late and you break her heart."

"I've already put together a healing spell, if she wants that for her heart. I doubt she will, but anyhow. Besides, I haven't got the guts to do that," the voice rambled on.

I realised it was me – my voice – who didn't have the guts to tell Rebecca Charlie that she was boring the stars out of me. I didn't have the guts because I spilled them to Panacea that night.

"Rebecca's wise. Her aura tells me she senses it's not working out." Panacea swung her legs.

We sat on the cloisters wall. Stars, I loved how she could just swing her legs so free. Rebecca never swung her legs. She crossed them, in fact. My legs didn't swing either, but that's because I was too tall. I'd need a taller wall – the rampart, perhaps. Off there, I could swing my legs into the clouds above Loon's City. Fly into the night.

Fly into the smoke clouds, from the pyre. We'd said goodbye to Professor Fellblue tonight. Now his life, his Force, was rising into the starry sky.

"May Fate welcome him into the heights," Chancellor Arden said, and the funeral pyre was set alight.

The cloisters were filled with students, teachers, and the like – I was too busy feeling rotten at that point to recognise them all. The cloisters were crammed – that's a more accurate description – because there wasn't enough space to comfortably fit everyone.

I bawled my eyes out tonight. My eyes and mouth, actually, because bawling is a bit more than emotion pouring from the eyes. I wasn't bawling because of Fellblue as such, though it did make me sad. Perhaps that's what got me started, really. Perhaps I imagined he was my uncle, to whom we never really said goodbye. Haunt was nearly crying too, but that's on account of the grass we trampled crowding here.

I fully started bawling when I realised about the grass. Stars, I was in hysterics. If Fate was in everything all around, then surely she existed in each blade of grass. And we stomped all over it. Perhaps Haunt knew that all along, and that's why he told us to keep off the grass. Perhaps Haunt was really a decent guy. That pushed me off the edge. I nearly fell off the wall. Then everyone – everyone who could – reached up to the celestials and waved their flame to honour Fellblue; wave him goodbye. Now that Fate had claimed him, he burned in each and every one of those little flames that everyone waved for him.

By that point, it was too much. I started bawling for them all: for Fellblue, for my uncle, for that guy who got killed earlier in the year, and all those who disappeared too; for those who died in the Murders, just before, and since; for those whom Fate had claimed hundreds of years ago and for those whom she kept alive too.

By the time the pyre smouldered and everyone cleared out, I was still wailing. I was bawling, whining, *and* spilling my guts. Only Panacea stayed behind, to be alone and to pick them up. But she didn't just hand them back to me – my guts, that is – she must have rearranged them too because if she had just put me back together the way I was, I would still be feeling rotten. And I wasn't feeling quite so rotten anymore.

I told her about everything. Words started pouring out: about Orle, about the dirt, about me, my treacherous eyes; about not liking take-outs, about all these things I'd messed up, about pretending not to care because it was easier just to laugh; about my spells – my only asset; about wanting to see myself like she saw me, only that my eyes crossed paths then, and I couldn't quite make that point clearly enough.

Panacea listened most intently, offering a few words here and there, never obstructing my verbal avalanche.

The words made sense, I hope, in the order they were placed. She never said, but with her – and your – patience I was graced.

Yet I couldn't ignore the feeling that seeped out from within her silence. There were troubling times ahead, I reckoned, of chaos, plight, and violence.

I'd love to tell you more about it, but now is not the time. For you see, here the story pauses by design.

And anyway, it's hard to tell sometimes which words are true. Keep patient, however, for you may find the answers in Book Two.

Acknowledgements

A Reverie Tale as it stands before you could not have come to be without the people who have shaped me and given me a chance. Therefore a special thanks goes to: the editorial and design team at Cranthorpe Millner, for giving this story a chance and for your patience with me; my friends, near and far, for keeping me busy and for your honest opinions; George, my A-level literature teacher at Paston Sixth Form College, who was the first to instil confidence in me about my writing; and of course, my parents, for always having unsolicited faith in me. *Dziękuję Wam najbardziej.*

ABOUT THE AUTHOR

Anna M. Tusk is a debut author in her mid-twenties. Having moved to Norfolk as a child and recently completed her degrees at the University of Cambridge and University of East Anglia, she currently works as an archaeologist in the Midlands. Her First Class BA (Hons) was recognised with three academic awards. With a background in archaeology and anthropology, her interests include perceptions and understandings of reality, the nature of truth, symbolism, and epistemology.

Above all, she is a dreamer, and her imagination refuses to cease dwelling on these questions within imagined worlds, their conflicts, and conundrums. Being bilingual and binational, she explores what it means to straddle two worlds, attempting to make sense of both while calling one a permanent home.

Find out more at annamtusk.com